TRIAL BY WATER

GEORGE CUOMO

TRIAL BY WATER

A NOVEL

RANDOM HOUSE 🏠 NEW YORK

Copyright © 1993 by George Cuomo

All rights reserved under International
and Pan-American Copyright Conventions.
Published in the United States by Random House, Inc.,
New York, and simultaneously in Canada by
Random House of Canada Limited, Toronto.

Library of Congress Cataloging-in-Publication Data
Cuomo, George.
Trial by water : a novel / by George Cuomo
      p.   cm.
ISBN 0-679-41230-1
I. Title.
PS3553.U6T75   1992
813'.54—dc20   92-53645

Manufactured in the United States of America
2   3   4   5   6   7   8   9
First Edition

Book design by Oksana Kushnir

for
Osa
Doug
Erin
Stephen

All night the image recurred: he could see the car dangling from a chain, spotlighted above the black lake, water cascading as if from some jagged rupture. Bulbous weeds clung everywhere, draped over bumpers and grilles, over mirrors and tires, incredibly entangled outside and in, glossy and slithering over the kids' bodies, the kids' faces.

Earlier, as surely as if he'd been trapped himself, he could feel the car settling down through slime-smooth tentacles into soft silt, the incoming rush of brackish water—through vents, windows, floorboards. He recoiled from the shock of that first cold drenching, water roaring in from every direction with such force that it flung your head about like a rattle.

Would you watch, eyes widening, as the water engulfed you, or clench your eyes shut, convinced that if you *didn't see it,* it would turn out to be nothing but a summer nightmare when you looked again?

You were only a few feet, a few inches, from moonlight, air, horse-play with your friends, a drive around the park. And being trapped in a car seemed altogether wrong. You had a feeling for cars. They'd done all right by you. They got you away from things, got you to things, and if you made out anywhere, you made out in the back seat of a car. Maybe with another couple up front, each wondering how far the other was getting. You'd never forget the sweat, the smell of upholstery, the wet mouths.

The guys in the crowd, even some of the girls, knew the name and price of every car on the market, horsepower and torque, engine displacement, dual carbs and mag wheels, rack-and-pinion steering, anti-locks, zero to sixty, knew the exact model of the muscle machine they dreamed of one day showing off to the world as their very own, moonlight flashing off its perfect finish.

Maybe you would not struggle at first, staying cool, shrewd, alert, saving your breath to give your friends time to pull you out and let you glide up to that first gasping gulp of honey-sweet air. How easy it would be! You'd drift up those few short feet and explode out of the water with a buoyancy dazzling to your friends. You'd wave, laughing, as you soared up into the air in a great froth of bubbles. Your friends would laugh along with you—and cheer. You'd made it! Everyone was clapping! You were safe, free, a couple of sweet, good-natured kids on the loose again, having the time of your lives.

So you kept your feet flat on the floor, hands on knees pointing straight ahead, like a kid outside the principal's office, scared maybe but confident things would work out. It'd only been a lark, after all, a new way to show the gang you could handle anything, something to brag about at the lockers: *Hey, you should've seen it—the car sank like a god-damn rock and everybody figured we were goners. You should've seen it.*

All you want at this moment is to get on with the rest of your life. You'd appreciate it now, this life, this breath. You'd take advantage of every miraculous minute God gave you.

Only the water forces you higher. You're standing on the seat, your body curved like an insect's trying to wriggle free from some impossibly gummy surface.

Your eyes are stretched open, your head and shoulders pressed up against the roof. The water engulfs your thighs, splashes your stomach and chest. You twist and jam one cheek as high as you can. The water laps at your other cheek. You twist harder to keep your nose up, the two of you clawing and scratching now in a ferocious embrace of love and terror and hopelessness on that last, fading sill of time, thinking, *Where is everybody? Where's the rest of the world, the sky, the moon, the air? Can't people see what's happening?* You try to scream, clutching each other as water fills your mouth, your nose, your lungs. . . .

I

MORP NIGHT

Florian Rubio, at forty-seven, still thought of himself as the young kid hot off the streets of the Bronx. He remembered double-dating in high school when the other guy turned out to be an obnoxious rich kid from Scarsdale or someplace. Not only did this Joe Westchester actually zip around in his own powerhouse Buick, but he gloated when he drove up the curved driveway to his house. "Look!" the guy cried, touching a button on his dash. "Magic!"

By God, it did seem magical, having that kind of control at your fingertips, although at the time Florian kidded the ass off him. This was late forties, right after the war, and Florian had never even *heard* of a garage door opener.

He still remembered the feeling. It wasn't just that he wanted the money, the cars, the girls, the houses. He wanted the magic. He longed for the world to astonish and delight him.

Well, he'd done all right in getting the world to do pretty much what he wanted it to. He'd just never gotten over the feeling that he should've been laying roadbeds somewhere, shirtless in the blistering sun, hunching over a whirring lathe in a factory loft, standing on his feet cutting hair ten hours a day. Not that he hadn't worked hard. He had, but he still realized how much worse life could have worked out for him and was thankful for every right move, every decent turn along the way.

The one big setback took place ten years ago, after he'd made his way in real estate and construction back in New York, when Elly swept up their three kids and left the big house overlooking Long Island Sound for Walnut Creek, California, with some landscape designer they'd hired to put in shrubs.

After he crashed, Florian knew he needed to start over somewhere else, somewhere different, and picked Mt. Early County in western Massachusetts, the Village of Trent. There he built another big but more modern house on a couple of acres of wooded shoreline on Bottleneck Lake's South Corner. The new place, the new house, put a seal on the divorce, and the day after a picture and story appeared in the Home section of the *Mt. Early Express,* Florian picked up a used Jeep and some topographical maps and set about generating some cash.

He loved the county's rough landscape, the mountains and back roads, the apple orchards, the meandering hand-built stone walls separating the abandoned farms, the nineteenth-century mansions and land-holdings. He used whatever financing he could piece together to buy up some properties that struck his eye. The timing was perfect. The Trent Theater Festival had just begun to flourish, soon to be followed by all manner of other summertime groups and shows and music, attracting those thousands of annual visitors who, by driving up for the weekend or the month, drove straight up the prices of all those pieces of good land Florian had bought sooner, and cheaper, than almost anyone else.

On this lovely June afternoon Florian left the small house on Nailing Hill that served as his office to take care of a couple of items on his calendar, both of which promised to be fun. For the first, he drove north fifteen miles into Medway, where the handball court was located on a block of warehouses and storage units, between an electrical appliance outlet and Soda and Pet Food City, down the block from the Pick and Pay discount supermarket. Medway was the only place in Mt. Early County where you found blocks like that, where there were still bars like Mio's and the Polecat, still bakeries and candy stores, good and bad neighborhoods, fish markets and grocery stores and VFW halls and Polish-American clubs. There you encountered kids, good and otherwise, being screamed at by mothers, saw kids hanging around storefronts, sidling around corners at night, slashing tires or pulling ignition wires for the fun of it, laying rubber to beat red lights, sneaking into mall movies, razzing girls in stretch tops and clunky ankle bracelets, hassling store owners, Frisbee-ing garbage can covers.

None of this was strange to Florian; he'd grown up with it, and worse. He'd just been surprised, when he moved up, to find streets like this in any part of Mt. Early County.

For the handball crowd, telegraphic conversation was the specialty of the narrow steamy dressing room off the shower stalls, since you had only the few minutes it took everybody to get into and out of his clothes before and after. It was also the home of the snappy punch line.

"No, I didn't say who the girl was," the kid told his friends when he finally got out of the confessional, *"but the priest gave me three more good leads."*

Some of the older players were in their fifties, one pushing sixty, so you checked out each other's excuses. How's the shoulder, Tom? Any better? The back, Sam? The knee? The ankle? Hey, a new elbow brace? Do any good? What'd the doctor say? "If you constructed an athlete from the best functioning part of each of us," Florian had once pointed out to the others, "you'd end up with a minor league second baseman batting .213."

"No," Grant told Dave, the trivia specialist, "I didn't know the eye was the only human organ that doesn't grow after birth. From seeing you guys naked around here all the time, I would've figured it was the dingdong."

"The moose, lady, is an intractable beast."

When Tony begged off one day because of a pulled groin, Steve said he must've gotten it from sex. Which, Squire added, became more dangerous as you got older. Maybe, Joe said, he oughta give it up. Or at least, George suggested, try it with a partner.

Afterward they always went down the block to Mio's for a lunch of midget franks and a pitcher, or maybe a couple of longnecks each, before heading into the rest of their day.

Today, for Florian, it meant heading back into Trent for the closing at the bank. With the onslaught of July tourists still a few weeks off, traffic was light as Florian swung onto Elderberry Street in his meticulously tuned and tooled and cared-for cream-colored Corvette, a classic now, a mint condition antique, twenty-two years old and smoother than ever. He'd never followed automobiles much, and when he bought it ten years ago, as part of his move to Trent, he'd just wanted something American and top line that didn't look like it belonged to a retired accountant from Jersey. Only what did it do now, after all these years of sweetly purring perfection, but conk out on him in the middle of the goddamn street, in full view of a bunch of gawking teenagers downing Slurpees on the sidewalk.

Florian slapped the steering wheel in disbelief. Not a bang, a rattle, not even a cough. It'd been whispering along, 283 horses coasting, a picnic, a snap, and the next second it died. Where was the logic in that?

A couple of drivers trapped behind him waited a few minutes before politely dinking on their horns. This was Trent, after all, not New York. But the sidewalk slurpers got a real kick out of seeing him as helplessly abandoned by his shiny supersmooth model as they or any of their friends had ever been in their own lopsided heaps.

Rob's Mobil was just a couple of blocks away, and in a few minutes Rob swung his throbbing red wrecker behind the Corvette. Silent in his oil-smeared coveralls and a soft black cap, like something Greek fishermen wore, Rob yanked up the hood and after a quick look slammed it shut and climbed back into the truck. Florian figured he'd swing in front and clamp on the dangling hook and pull him to the station, but Rob just waited, drumming his fingers on the wheel, engine idling with its throaty rumble. Apparently he'd decided to skip the hassle with the hook and just push him to the station with the two-by-eight bolted to his front bumper.

Why not? Florian figured. It might even be fun. He shifted into neutral, but before he could wave Rob on, he felt and heard the crash and his head snapped back as the car lurched forward.

Normally Florian loved driving the Corvette, his own foot juicing the accelerator, easing off for curves, intersections, pedestrians. But once Rob sent him hurtling forward, the guy never let up, slamming into him from behind, goosing him faster and faster until Florian felt trapped in some weird steeplechase free fall. Clutching the wheel like death, afraid even to touch the brake with all that roaring propulsion behind him, Florian helplessly envisioned some car swerving in front, some gray-haired granny stepping off the curb.

This had to be Rob's idea of a joke, and as much as the guy had to be enjoying the hell out of himself, Florian was sure he wouldn't be laughing. Rob never laughed, and rarely spoke. But he had his own way of putting a few kicks into his life. Did he realize how unnerving it was to have someone take you so totally out of the picture, to seize your moment so completely, even in fun, that you were left with no options, no voice, no control whatsoever in what was happening to you?

Although the steering was still in your hands: you could hit a telephone pole if you wanted, or run over a fire hydrant.

As they sped toward the first intersection, Florian hit the horn, then hit it again, like a fire truck honking warnings. Everybody in town had to be watching by now, which was fine, exactly what he wanted, everyone else as terrified as himself. His dead-ahead eyes narrowed the street to a sunlit tunnel. Horn blaring, he felt himself flung forward along the second block and into that intersection, cars on the cross street braking and dipping as they flew backward out of sight at the edges of his vision.

Rob didn't ease off until the last instant, sending Florian zooming across the sidewalk and up the station incline, horn screaming, pedestrians scattering. Florian braked with all his might, stopping with the Corvette's grille inches from the rollaway glass doors of the repair bay.

He knew damn well Rob had enjoyed the hell out of himself, a pleasant break in the monotony of a day at the gas pumps, and knew too that Rob would never violate the mechanic's lifelong vow of stony impassivity by letting on how much fun it was. Well, Florian sure as hell wasn't going to show what a tingle it gave him either.

"Next time," Florian suggested through the open window as Rob came up, "just bring a big rubber slingshot and shoot me here."

In silence, Rob touched his black cap. It wasn't clear what he was acknowledging—Florian's skill, his courage, his survival?

Florian pushed open the door and got out. "I don't know what's wrong, but I have to have it today."

Unimpressed, Rob responded with a small nod.

"I'll take that for a definite yes," Florian said, tossing Rob the keys. "If you got time, wash it down, give it a quick polish. We want it looking real nice tonight."

Walking away, Florian noticed high above Elderberry Street a white banner flapping between two Victorian lampposts, proclaiming in garish multicolored letters:

MORP NIGHT!!!
Trent High—Friday, June 20

They were the Courtiers, Trent High, and in one corner of the banner an elegantly dressed and plumed swordsman brandished a rapier.

Florian smiled at the thought of those high school kids, including Brian, thumbing their noses at draggy old-fashioned senior proms by staging their very own assbackwards MORP.

He saw, too late, Harry Diggs descending upon him.

"They say there's no trouble like car trouble," Diggs informed him.

Was that all Harry Diggs had to do—slouch around Elderberry Street like an ambulance chaser? "I take good care of it," Florian said, "and this is the thanks I get."

Diggs's smile took on a wisdom-of-the-ages look, as if reminding Florian how deeply he, Harry Diggs, was aware of life's terrific ironies. "We can stroll down to the bank together."

In the early afternoon Diggs's inevitable white carnation still looked fresh—fresher by far than the voluminous pin-striped suit. Diggs wore the tailored eight-hundred-dollar three-piece jobs you'd expect from your typical old-money, old-line Trent lawyer, but they always looked as if he'd been wearing them for days. Maybe that explained the bright flower every morning—to let people know he *did* care about appearances, that the disheveled suits represented, in some kinky way, a matter of choice.

Florian didn't wear suits. Or, for that matter, ties. "We've still got time," he said, checking the big round sidewalk clock in front of Mt. Early Savings.

"And it's quite déclassé appearing anxious," Diggs said with a jowly nod, his thin and feathery hair seeming weightless for a moment, "especially when you're the one scooping up all the chips."

Those suits were probably 56 portlies, with tented vests and great flapping trousers. Although Florian had never seen Diggs drunk, the man generally ordered his first manhattan when the Mountaineer opened at eleven A.M. Nor was he ever known to deprive himself when a thirst overtook him at any other time of day or night. That and young men were his two passions, neither of which he made any attempt to curb or hide. One of the guys at the handball court who'd dealt with Diggs said he looked epicene. Florian checked the dictionary and agreed.

That part didn't bother Florian. All he really had against Diggs was that Elly had hired him from California ten years ago as her local representative to negotiate her divorce settlement. Otherwise Florian might even have gotten to like the guy, although he'd never been altogether sure of that.

"If we walk slowly," Diggs suggested, "we can arrive precisely one minute late."

"Perfect."

They met with Bob Crawford and signed the papers around the oak table in the bank's conference room, beneath the scrolled mahogany lintels and the Victorian wallpaper, greenish with flowers, near the eight-foot-wide never-used fireplace that would have been perfect for the manor house of a duke. No matter where you sat at the table, you faced two or three grim and blackening oil portraits, with beards and boiled collars, of former bank presidents, the gilt frames thick with curlicues and cupid's bows. Florian could not enter this room, which he did maybe a few times a year, without feeling like an impostor. Even though what was taking place here was every bit as enjoyable as the hour he'd spent on the handball court, and a lot more profitable, there was no way he'd ever feel as comfortable here as he did in sweaty gloves and T-shirt or lounging through lunch with the guys at Mio's.

Diggs earned his goodly fee checking out clauses for the bank; Ira Wachtel did the same checking them out for Florian. As for Crawford, the bank's cut was substantial enough to move him to fetch a bottle of sherry and four tiny glasses from the sideboard. Florian generally avoided combinations of sugar and alcohol but went along, wondering how many chips you had to scoop up to rate a decent scotch.

It wasn't that Florian didn't like or appreciate bankers, even lawyers.

He just regretted their penchant for reducing even the most joyful occasions—the buying of your first car, your first house, waving your kids off
to college, the enthusiastic discovery of a piece of land you'd absolutely
fallen in love with—into something about as exciting as a bunch of rusty
lug nuts.

"A beautiful estate, Greenhills, a lovely property," Crawford said,
toasting Florian, "and although I'm sure you're sad to let it go, I can
guess how pleased you are at having nailed our hides to the wall.
Cheers."

"Cheers," Florian said. "I always had a special place in my heart for
Greenhills."

"But of course, for the right price, it's for sale."

Florian dismissed this with an easy laugh. "I've got my eye on some
new pieces that are even nicer."

"Would you mind telling us exactly where?"

Florian laughed out loud at this. "If you tell me what the prime
rate's going to be next year, I'll give you a sure-thing tip on a piece of
land."

Outside Diggs spoke to Florian on the sidewalk. "Someday you
really must reveal the secret of your horse trader's eye. A city boy like
yourself."

Florian caught the hint of disapproval. He had friends, got along
well around town, up at the handball courts, but to a deep-rooted New
Englander like Diggs, Florian had some obvious shortcomings. Not only
was he, as a native New Yorker, still an outsider after ten years, but he'd
also made a lot of money buying up land under the very noses of the
natives.

"Maybe that's the secret," he told Diggs pleasantly enough. "You
have to grow up on pavement to really appreciate open land."

Diggs accepted this readily enough. Whenever you were good at
something, people liked to believe it was all luck. Otherwise how could
you possibly outshine them? That was okay by Florian, because early on
he'd learned that it never hurt to let people convince themselves you
were just a dummy on a hot streak.

"It's nice to see a man enjoy his work so much."

"It's more fun than I've ever had in my life," Florian said, and
Diggs, studying him with his small lawyerly eyes, surely realized it was
the truth. Who wouldn't enjoy himself—barreling an old Jeep over a few
thousand square miles of beautiful countryside, with all the time in the
world to appreciate it? Time, of course, was the *real* secret. Patience. As

long as you didn't get greedy and start pushing things, the cash eventually took care of itself.

"If your car's not ready," Diggs offered, "I can give you a ride."

"I got all the faith in the world in that car," Florian said, and he wasn't even angry as they split up. Sometimes Diggs got on his nerves, but today he felt right on top of everything. He even had to admit to taking some pleasure in watching the last son and heir of all those generations of New England Diggses being grateful for whatever scraps he could pick up by elbowing in on the deal of this upstart nobody from the Bronx.

Florian gaped up at a kid on an incredibly tall ladder, steadied at bottom by four friends, attaching a red-slashed addition to the MORP banner:

TONIGHT!!!

The boy's daring awed Florian, even scared him a little, making him glad it wasn't Brian tottering up there in the gusty June breeze.

Rob showed him the old fuel pump, tossed it into the metal trash can with a grunt. They could go at any time, but everything was hunky-dory now, good as new, guaranteed. Rob didn't say this, of course. It was all in the meaningful nod, the master mechanic's professional shrug.

When Brian came east last summer, Florian had been delighted. So had Lucille and Salvatore. In their seventies now, they couldn't get over their good luck. A family again, three generations under one roof, someone to be responsible for. Lucille especially, although she'd never admit it, loved having a lively, funny, sometimes mystifying grandson to fuss over all year long, to get off to school, to fix snacks and meals for, to shoo out of her kitchen along with the friends he'd bring home from school. Florian himself was so happy to grab the chance of getting to know his son that he never pressed Elly for the real reason she'd let Brian go. All he had was the letter last August, the first he'd received from Elly since the divorce:

I don't expect sympathy but it's too much for me to handle a teenage boy all by myself anymore. I'd like you to pitch in, at least for a while, when school starts in a couple of weeks. Brian says he has no serious objections. This will be his senior year, in case you've lost track.

In his excitement over Brian's arrival, Florian had to fight to keep from spoiling him. One rule, though, was no car. He was willing to lend him the Corvette for special occasions, but he wanted the kid to understand that having money didn't mean seventeen-year-olds got handed everything on a platter.

"I wasn't expecting a car," Brian had said. "I've got my bike." All year long he'd biked to school and back, except during the worst winter snows when he'd tramp out to the bus stop.

Dusk now, Florian drove down the unmarked dirt road leading to Bottleneck Lake's only public beach, unmarked because the locals had no interest in helping summer visitors find the place. He parked in the almost deserted paved area, walked past the wooden concession stand, already shuttered for the evening, and down to the sandy strip. If they were going to jazz up the place for tonight's big fling, they hadn't got to it yet, although Brian had already hung the sign on the big chair:

NO LIFEGUARD ON DUTY
SWIM AT YOUR OWN RISK

Using his hand to shade his eyes from the sun lowering toward Mt. Early, Florian saw three guys still splashing in the water, a few people scattered around on blankets, but no Brian. A couple of girls in bikinis stood chatting on the sand near the lifeguard stand, and he wondered if one might be Brian's date for tonight. He trudged over. Nice-looking girls. A guy as tall and blond and good-looking as Brian (all, except for the height, from his mother's side), with that swimmer's body, too, could figure on hanging around with girls like this.

Oh, yes, they knew Brian. One sort of giggled and glanced mischievously at the other, who seemed more serious. "Maybe," the serious one said, wetting her upper lip, "if you're really looking for him, you could try over at the boatyard."

He was about to when Brian, his lifeguard binoculars dangling around his neck, emerged from the wooded area separating the public beach from Hammond's Boatyard a few hundred yards up toward the neck of the lake. Florian thanked the girls and met Brian halfway. "Tough life," he said, motioning back toward the girls. Then something tightened in his throat, and he felt his smile dissolve. Brian, a young kid in great shape, the best long-distance swimmer on the team this year, was puffing away like some old geezer on his fourth flight of stairs. "Hey," Florian said softly. "Hey."

"It's nothing," Brian said, chest heaving.

Florian reached up to remove Brian's wraparound sunglasses and stared, putting two fingers on the side of his son's chin to keep him from turning away. A large raw scrape ran from his forehead almost to his jawbone, just missing his nose but extending over his left eye, although the eye itself looked all right. "You diving into empty pools or something?"

"Look, Dad, no big deal." Brian paused, steadying his breath. "Some guy in one of Hammond's rentals kept buzzing everybody, coming in full throttle at the ropes and practically knocking kids over with his backwash. So I went over before and, you know, had a few words with the kid who works there."

Florian waited for more.

"I just checked now to see if he was still there, but he wasn't. That's it, Dad, the whole exciting story. I got a little steamed and kind of bumped into a stack of canoes. It was my own damn fault."

"Everything's our own damn fault," Florian said.

"It's just a little scrape. On to the MORP, I say."

Florian handed back the sunglasses, and Brian put them on, all that tinted acreage practically a mask, although not completely hiding the scrape. "One of those girls your big date tonight?"

"Oh, no, not them."

"Whoever, you're gonna look terrific for her."

"Hey, it'll give me a little flair. Along with the Corvette."

Florian tossed him the keys. "Drive back, okay? For the practice."

Back home, Brian headed upstairs to get ready, and Florian found his mother at the kitchen sink, washing vegetables and tossing them into her wooden cutting bowl.

"How we doing?" Florian put his arm around her narrow shoulders and bent down to kiss her on the cheek.

She twisted away, working a potato under the faucet like a pitcher massaging a baseball. "You know how late they're gonna be?"

Florian broke off a piece of clean carrot and sat at the kitchen table, tuning the tiny radio next to the napkin dispenser to the Sox pregame. "It's a big deal for them, staying out all night. Let them have their fun."

She whipped around to face him. "On a beach! First they got parties everywhere, and then what are they gonna do all night on a beach? They're gonna wanna go *zif-zif,* that's what."

"There'll be teachers all over the place." Florian popped the end of the carrot in his mouth. "Hey, didn't we have this conversation thirty years ago, when all you had to do was worry about me?" But his mother wasn't one easily diverted from her preoccupations, so he added, "The principal's gonna put on a funny apron and make pancakes for breakfast. How wholesome can you get?"

"And you—where you gonna be?"

He laughed. "I got something on, Mom. Why not let Brian off the hook and just worry about me, like in the good old days, even though I was just an old stick-in-the-mud?"

"Sure, a big stick-in-the-mud." At the knock, Lucille frowned. Some time ago Florian had snipped the wire of the ding-ding-DONG bell because he couldn't stand the cutesy sound. Padgett was probably off somewhere with Salvatore since the arrival hadn't set him barking. Padgett was hopeless as a serious watchdog. Even when he was around, he'd just WHOUFF! away happily at anyone who came by.

Florian pushed back the curtain and peeked out: a tall, sleek, tanned girl with jet black hair down past her shoulders stood on the stone footing, a ten-speed leaning jauntily against her long bare leg. She wore a white polo shirt with something across the front, torn-off jeans, sneakers. "Must be his date," Florian said.

"His girlfriend? Here?" Lucille turned off the faucet and dried her hands on the apron. "The boy doesn't pick up the girl anymore?" She tore off her apron and flung it under the sink. She touched her gray hair at the sides and back. She was still attractive, still carried herself well, and wouldn't walk to the store for a loaf of bread without changing clothes, putting on makeup, making sure her shoes and pocketbook matched. She cast an eye down at her faded flowered housedress. "Why didn't he *tell* me! Ooh, I'll fix him!"

"It's okay, Mom," Florian said on his way to the door. "She's not expecting the Queen of England." Actually, it seemed a little peculiar to him, too, but what could you do? They were kids and went their own way. They had their own games, their own rules, and didn't even *want* you trying to understand.

"Hi," the girl said, in a lively, almost frisky voice. "I'm Veronique, but everyone calls me Nique." She pronounced it with a lilt: *Knee-key*. Her polo shirt read:

ETARBELEC!
PROM A SI EFIL!

Florian spelled it out letter by letter, then realized he probably shouldn't be staring that hard at her nicely pointed breasts. He looked out through the open door to see if she had an overnight bag on the back of her bike, for her party clothes. She didn't, and the bike itself was pretty banged up.

"Come on in. This is Brian's grandmother." Florian stepped aside to admire his mother's expression: Lucille could be as extravagantly theatrical as a silent movie star.

"Is—is something wrong?" Nique asked.

"Oh, no," Florian said quickly. "It's nice meeting you." He debated *Brian says nice things about you,* but Brian had never mentioned her. She had a lovely face framed by that long, straight, glistening black hair, clear blue eyes, skin as smooth and glowing as a baby's. Sometimes Florian suspected that, compared to the lumpen crowd he'd grown up with, the boys and girls these days all looked like they'd stepped out of a TV commercial. Not true, of course, but even if it were, Nique had to be something special, and he felt a little glow at the thought of his son showing up for the festivities with a knockout like this on his arm.

Nique nodded at the radio, maybe to get away from Lucille's round-eyed stare. "How are we doing?"

"Just starting. You a fan?"

"I die agonizing deaths with them every year," she said with that same lively cadence.

"Brian is bored to death with anything that bounces or that you kick or hit with a stick."

"I'm working on him," she confided.

Lucille still seemed stunned by this exuberant long-legged girl—a good head taller—in jeans torn off as high as jeans *could* be torn off. Inside, Brian barreled down the stairs, two or three steps at a time, an avalanche, and burst into the kitchen in his oldest, dirtiest pair of jeans and a polo shirt reading TSAL TA EERF! Over the polo shirt, as maybe his ultimate put-down of high school prommery, he'd loosely knotted a formal black silk tie.

Florian couldn't help laughing, and Lucille, who'd always disapproved of his lack of seriousness about important matters, gave him a sharp look. Brian still wore his wraparound shades and had done his best to powder over the scrape, but Lucille seemed too taken up with their outfits to notice.

"You made it," Brian said to Nique, and she, picking up some private meaning, gave him the A-okay sign. Brian glowed, flushed, laughed, full of that spontaneous energy and enthusiasm that he always generated with his friends. "We're taking the canoe out, okay?" he said to Florian. "Nique's never been on the lake, so we'll paddle around a bit."

"Aha!" Lucille said, rousing. "And *then* you get all dressed up for the party!"

They looked at her quizzically, and Brian reached out to chuck her teasingly under the chin, clearly showing no more seriousness than his old man. "We are dressed. Like it?" He put an arm around Nique's waist and pulled her close, hip to hip, like a couple grinning for an amusement park camera. "Pretty dashing, eh?"

"Ooh," Lucille sighed, her sideways glance pleading with Florian to *do* something.

"Maybe," he offered, putting his arm around her shoulders and giving her a squeeze, "he'll give a phony name if anyone asks."

Joyce's husband, Bennett Johnway, consulted to businesses engaged in the manufacture of women's clothing, and it wasn't unusual for him to drive down to New York or fly to the Coast for a few days of very profitable advice giving. "That's my job," Benn would tell people with a shrug. "I save desperate men."

This afternoon, when he got off the phone and told her he had to leave right away for California, she'd felt again that puff of excitement, flaring like a trumpet-shaped flower in her chest. The elation, the anticipation were so real she was afraid she couldn't hide them, and when Benn went upstairs to pack, she took the cordless extension onto the flagstone patio by the pool and got Florian at his office. "Terrific," he'd said. "That is, if you're sure, if you're ready."

"Yes," she'd said under her cupped hand. "As soon as I get back from the airport."

The airport was an hour from the house—give or take, as Benn would say, and on the ride out this evening Joyce tried to control her impatience as Bennett talked about the company in L.A. The owner died from a coronary last year, and his son had taken over. It wasn't that the kid didn't know the garment business; he'd worked there for years. He just didn't have the knack.

The twenty years Benn had spent putting out fires for various cloak-and-suiters around the country accounted for the way he sometimes talked, more big-city tough than you'd expect from an Episcopalian out of Westport and Williams and Wharton. "What I have to do is kick-start the kid—who is no kid, he's pushing forty—into learning more in five days than his father taught him in a lifetime."

Bennett was no doubt looking forward to the challenge, the game of it, although a dryness in his voice suggested that maybe, this time, it wouldn't be all fun. "I knew the old man, of course. His idea of impressing a client was taking him around the corner to the kosher deli. Cabbage soup and kreplach, with sawdust on the floor, don't spare the horseradish. He took me, and all afternoon I smelled like the bottom of a pickle barrel.

"Fifty-six minutes," Bennett announced at the curb of the airport departure area. He shifted into park but made no move to get out. A jet screeched overhead as he stared across the seat at her, his face splotchy in the greenish artificial light from the glass walls. Hardly a flattering pose, but in general Benn looked all right these days. Maybe he'd put on a few pounds over the years, and his hair was thinning fast, but he dressed well, took care of himself, made a good appearance. "I guess you'll manage to keep yourself entertained," he said.

Joyce couldn't remember his ever before mentioning what *she* might do while he was away. After all, she had her lesson plans, her bluebooks, her classes and meetings and conferences. Waiting for him to get out, she realized how odd it was that he'd be arriving in L.A. late on a Friday night. To spend Saturday and Sunday with a forty-year-old kid who didn't have the touch? None of that sounded like Bennett.

"Sure," she said, anxious for him to leave. "I'll be fine."

He leaned over for a quick kiss and was gone.

As she drove back to Trent, all that kept Joyce from flattening the pedal was her lack of confidence with Bennett's Lincoln. She was wearing her wraparound teal skirt and white linen blouse. Bennett hadn't been the least surprised to see her dressed up. Accompanying your husband to the airport was a social occasion, calling for appropriate clothes.

She steered the huge, shouldery Lincoln up Nailing Hill Road and onto the drive that led to the one-story house Florian used as his office. He'd bought it furnished when he arrived in Trent, he'd told her and Benn when he had them over one afternoon. He'd left everything as it was except for putting a desk and a bookshelf in the living room. Typical of Florian, she'd come to realize: working alone in the house without secretaries or file cabinets, without even an answering machine. Three walls were covered with detailed maps of Mt. Early County, a panorama encircling Florian's desk. On the fourth wall a huge cork bulletin board displayed a haphazard arrangement of maybe a hundred thumbtacked photographs of his family, not just recent shots but old dog-eared sepias and grays from the thirties and maybe before, parents and kids and aunts and uncles and cousins and friends.

As she pulled into the paved turnaround, she was startled to discover that the car parked there wasn't Florian's flashy white sports job but something old and yellow and battered. Were those *Medway* decals? Could some of her students have found her out?

Then she heard Florian call, waving as he skipped down the steps. He pulled open the car door for her and sensed her confusion. "Brian's got the Corvette for his big night. I'm using my father's Duster."

She clutched his hand, pulled him down to kiss him. "If I had any practice at this," she said, "I guess I could play it more coolly."

She saw him smiling down to reassure her, but looking pleased, too, maybe simply at the fact that she hadn't chickened out. At the same time she couldn't help wondering if her admission—which she hadn't really planned on making—of her prior faithfulness hadn't, in his mind, conferred on her a kind of virginal status.

He led her onto the porch. The house sat high and alone on the edge of Nailing Hill, and on this warm, clear night she could see all of Bottleneck Lake sparkling in the moonlight, the distinctive shape that gave it its name outlined by house lights along the shore, except for the huge black expanse of Fischel State Park.

"Isn't that something?" he said, taking in the view that he must have seen hundreds of times before but that clearly still moved him.

"The Indians called it Lake Shaped Like a Pear," she said. "It was the white settlers who changed it to Bottleneck Lake."

"All those grizzled trappers and freebooters probably had a lot more contact with bottles than pears."

"Local legend also has it that some long-ago governor built a lovely house on the lake for his mistress, on the theory that it was so far from Boston no one cared what happened out here. At the moment at least six local owners insist their house is the very one."

"How do you know all this?"

"It's part of what I teach."

"Governor's mistresses?"

"Local history. Sometimes the two overlap." She straightened up to look at Florian. "Can we stay here tonight? Wouldn't it be nice, all that time together?" She was surprised when he laughed. "What's so funny?"

"My mother's already shook up over Brian partying all night with his luscious girlfriend. Wait till she hears about my luscious girlfriend."

"Oh—is that what I am?" She put a finger on his lips to keep him from answering. "Is your mother really worried about Brian?"

"You should have seen her eyeing the girl's cutoffs. She'll be up pacing all night."

"I didn't realize the Trent kids were putting on their MORP just to end up doing something as old-fashioned as cozying up under beach blankets."

"You sound like my mother. There'll be teachers all over, and you know what they're like."

"Of course I do; they're wonderful. Is Brian really into the MORP thing?"

"It's not always easy knowing what he's into. Hang on." He went inside and returned with a bottle and two glasses. "If you like red wine," he said in that offhand manner of his, "this is red wine."

They sat on the porch swing, talking quietly. He had his arm around her and buried his head in her hair, kissed her on the forehead, on the lips, squeezed her shoulder softly, moved his hand lightly over her back. She shivered at the touch of his fingertips through her light blouse but was glad he wasn't impatient, that he seemed happy just to be with her. Back when *dating* was still the term, she couldn't recall many boys who ever showed anything resembling patience, who cared about anything resembling companionship.

He reached down and picked up a bag from beneath the swing and handed her a flat gift-wrapped box.

She hesitated. "I'm not sure."

"You don't even know what it is."

She realized how silly it was to be willing—eager—to make love with someone but too fastidious to accept a present. She opened it, drawing in her breath when she saw the interwoven strands of fine gold chain. "It's beautiful."

He motioned her around on the swing and fumbled with the clasp. "I could never figure out how women got these things hooked without even looking."

"That's the trick," she said. "Not looking."

He finally managed and bent to kiss her, to pull her close against her.

"Will you take me out in the boat?" she asked.

"*My* boat?"

"Of course, yours." She'd seen Florian and his father fishing out on the lake from their little fifteen-foot inboard, whereas Bennett's Sierra Sunbridge was a lot closer to a yacht. She loved being on the water but couldn't remember the last time she and Benn had gone out together. "Wouldn't that be nice?" she said, ignoring his dubious look. She got up from the swing and pulled him after her. "C'mon—out on the lake with the moon and stars all doing their bit. And if your dear mother frets, tell her a tiny fib. It won't, I bet, be the first time."

"Fishing by flashlight?"

"Charting the moon's gravitational pull."

"That's it," he said. "We want the moon in on this. Island paradises. Continental hotels. Endless sandy beaches. Nights of hot rum and torrid music."

"All on little old Bottleneck Lake?"

"You can do it. Turn on the magic."

She laughed easily and slipped her hand inside his shirt, pressing up against him, spreading her hand wide on his chest.

"You're not making it easy for this old man's gravitational pull," he whispered into her ear.

"See," she said. "The moon doesn't just work on women."

Separately they drove down Nailing Hill and past the absurd guard booth that stood vacant at the entrance to South Corner Estates, Florian leading in his father's rattling Duster, checking the mirror to make sure she was still behind him. He watched her swing into her driveway as he continued, full of excitement, along Mark's Lane to his own, six houses down.

Padgett bounded up floppily to thump and slobber over Florian as he stepped out of the car. The dog would do the same for a maniac with a knife between his teeth. "Down, Fang!" Florian muttered good-naturedly, edging it away with his foot. He realized how high he was riding when he even felt kindly toward an animal featuring this level of clumsiness and ineptitude. "Go chase your tail," he suggested. "Attack a windmill."

His mother rushed to the door as soon as he opened it. Her face fell.

"It's only ten-thirty, Mom. Give the kid a break."

Salvatore emerged from the TV room but only out of curiosity. Lucille was the worrier.

"I came for the boat," Florian said, getting a laugh out of Lucille's pained expression. (How old was he when he first discovered the irrelevance of his parents' wisdom, his parents' concerns, to his life?)

"What, are you crazy? This time of night?"

"You got it," Florian called over his shoulder with a wave as he went out the sliding door onto the patio. At the end of the dock he hopped down into the Runabout and hit the ignition, wincing at the explosive roar, then shrugging. Who cared? He steered at low throttle down the quarter mile or so—all the South Corner houses had a few hundred feet of lake frontage—and helped Joyce aboard from the end of her dock. He skirted Benn's Sunbridge and switched on his running lights, heading for the middle of the lake.

Joyce nestled within his arm as the boat slapped easily through the water. He burrowed through her hair and kissed the side of her throat. The moonlight seemed to encircle them, the glittering reflection making the lake look like the dull side of aluminum foil. He could feel her tension, though, and when he squeezed her, she gave a little puff of surprise.

"Sorry," she said.

"You know the old saying: the lady would like to, but is afraid."

"Not afraid," she said. "I just hate messes."

"Is Bennett the problem?"

"He's my husband. He's got to be at least part of the problem."

Bennett was also the one they could thank for bringing them together. Bennett was not a man Florian had known well or been particularly drawn to, a pasty, round-faced guy who always looked worried, and maybe always was, although the word was that he did pretty well in some kind of one-man consulting business. When he first approached Florian a couple of months back, looking for free advice on some development deal, Florian could only think of reasons to say no. Over the years he'd grown wary of giving advice to people, even when they asked for it. Honest advice usually annoyed the hell out of them. What they wanted was praise and reassurance, along with some neat trick for making money without knowing anything or working hard.

But the gods must have been with Florian on that day because for no reason he could figure out, he said yes. While they were sitting out on Bennett's patio, talking over this Blackberry Hollow deal that looked fishy to Florian from the beginning, Joyce showed up from school, leaning out the sliding glass door to wave hello, loaded down with a big pocketbook and a file drawer's worth of papers and folders clutched to her chest and looking pretty bedraggled. But Florian got the impression she nonetheless felt pretty good about having slogged her way through the day, and after changing into jeans and a loose blouse, she brought out a cheese tray and a bowl of nuts and joined them for a while, lithe and alert, slim, lively brown eyes, brown hair brushed now, cheeks freshly scrubbed.

All Florian had known was that she was the second wife, a lot younger than Bennett, maybe thirty-five. Some casual acquaintance's other half, that was all, but once she showed up, everything seemed more important and exciting—for Florian. Bennett looked annoyed at the interruption, bored by her presence. Florian liked the way she

moved, and talked, and listened. He liked her smile, the slight tilt of her chin. He ended up feeling so good just looking at her, just talking to her, that he probably went easier on Bennett's dumb-ass idea than he should have.

"We could go back and think all this over," Florian offered as the boat moved steadily toward the center of the lake. He'd taken her silence for indecision, for some real misgivings, and he already liked her too much, the first woman in years he'd wanted to get close to, to feel a need to force anything tonight. "There's no point going ahead unless it's going to feel good and comfortable and be full of nice things for both of us."

"Oh, no, let's not go back," she said, shaking her head for emphasis, her hair softly aloft for a moment.

Florian cut the motor to let them drift and held her, sitting together on the bench, swaying gently with the rising and dipping of the boat. "I kept reminding myself that you were married," he said evenly. "I tried very hard to ignore you, to stay clear of you. It just didn't work. And then when I saw maybe you were interested . . ."

"I guess I'm just not totally free and easy yet—like you, right? You've had time to work it out, to learn how to enjoy being on your own."

"As a kid I always assumed sex was the most elusive thing in the world. There were years when I really never believed it would happen to me."

"But now you've been single all these years . . ."

"Single isn't always sensational, but it does give you options. You can always sit home and watch the Sox."

"As opposed, say, to making love to a beautiful and exciting woman."

"A tough choice. I'd really have to think that over."

She kissed him hard, her mouth opening under his, and he could feel her clutching at his back as if to say, *No more talking. No more discussing.* She twisted her head one way and then another, pressing up against him, not letting up, and he slipped one hand under her blouse, slid it up to her bare breast, and with his other hand started unbuttoning the blouse. "One of the first exciting things about a beautiful woman is touching," he murmured. When he spread the blankets, she knelt on them, and he helped her out of her blouse. Her breasts reflected the moonlight as he carefully unwrapped her skirt. Her face, her whole body, shone in the moonlight: a statue with warm shadowing, soft shapes.

"You look wonderful in that necklace," he said.

She touched it, then took his head and brought it down to her breast, stroking his cheeks as he went to first one nipple, then the other, then kissed her on the mouth, circling his hand in wider and wider circles around her navel. She broke free and scrambled under the top blanket. "Come and get me. It's too chilly out there."

In a minute he had his clothes off and was under, too, stretched tight against her. Her mouth was warm, her hands, her whole body. Still, he didn't want to rush her. He kept kissing her, his tongue to her breasts, touching her between the legs, where it was first dry and rough, then softer, damper, then wet and swollen and spreading, until she rolled over onto him and guided him in. He moved deeply but slowly inside her, letting her build with him, but suddenly she'd gone past him and he had to pump wildly to catch up, with the boat slapping faster and faster, louder and louder, against the water.

In the silence, afterward, still under the blankets, holding her against him, he luxuriated in the heat and faint aromas of her body.

Sometime after midnight they heard the shout. It carried—rang, reverberated—over the smooth lake, but Florian couldn't make out the words.

Both of them sat up, Joyce wrapping a blanket around her. Florian leaned forward, trying to see across the lake. The moon had drifted behind a cloud, but a small boat materialized out of the haze.

"What is it?" Joyce asked.

He heard the rhythmic chunk and squeal of oars as the heavy rowing became louder. A faint gray rowboat sharpened until he could make out a hunched form rocking back and forth. The rowing stopped maybe twenty yards away, oars dripping into the glistening water. Only when he heard the thick, urgent voice did Florian realize who it was.

"Florry," his father called. "You better come back right now."

2

He remained oddly composed. He could see the lights of his house. He was steering, he knew the way, everything was under control. Then, like a seawall caving in, he imagined the screams, the long looping skid, the smash of crunched metal and exploding glass, the broken bodies flung across pavement.

He reversed throttle as the dock loomed up. Still, the boat thudded against the tires hanging from the piles. He was barely aware of Joyce behind him as he hurried up the lawn to the redwood deck with Padgett romping at their heels. The Corvette next to the Jeep in the parking area startled Florian: a cottony nighttime glow. It looked fine, perfectly okay. Maybe everything was perfectly okay.

He slid back the screen door and stepped into the living room. He heard Joyce follow, pulling the door shut. Brian sat at one end of the big tan couch, still in his crummy jeans and TSAL TA EERF! T-shirt but without the black silk tie. Was that, was every detail, ominous? What else should he be noticing?

Brian wet his lips, staring without reaction at his father and this woman he'd never seen before. The scrape on his face seemed rawer now —the powder or cream had worn off. He sat quite still, expressionless, not calm but dazed.

And the leggy girl with the shiny black hair? Had he dropped her off —*Knee-key!*—with nothing more than a good-night kiss or was her absence another omen, another revelation?

Lucille stood in front of the couch in her flowered housedress. She must have been sitting next to Brian—comforting him? scolding?—must have gotten up when she heard them outside. Her shoulders square, her long fingers entwined at her waist, she took a breath and gestured toward Brian, as if to say she knew nothing; only he knew. Brian's eyes didn't flicker.

Florian walked slowly across the carpet, went down on one knee, and put his hand on top of Brian's. He spoke quietly. "Is everybody all right?"

Brian looked past him, maybe at Joyce, maybe out toward the lake. "Not exactly."

Florian squeezed Brian's hand to get his attention. "*Who* is not exactly all right?"

Brian seemed unable to speak.

Florian stood up, light-headed. He searched for a place to stand, a position, a vantage point. He walked over to the big window and saw in the moonlight his father climbing out of the rowboat.

"I think a couple of kids drowned," Brian said without emphasis.

Florian whipped around. "Drowned? You mean, dead? Two people dead?"

"I think so. The police had divers, oxygen tanks, but the kids must've been in the lake over an hour." He shook his head and actually seemed to be trying to smile. "I don't even know who they were. I left before they got the car up."

"Left where?"

"The boat ramp. That's where it happened."

"And your girlfriend?"

"She went home earlier. She's not involved in any of this."

"Did the police arrest anyone?"

"They were too busy trying to fish up the other car."

"What other car?" Florian demanded.

"Their car. Jesus Christ, what do you want me to tell you?"

"I want you to tell me what happened!" Florian yelled back. "How can there be an *other* car unless there's a first car? I want you to tell me in what possible way you are possibly involved in what happened!"

Brian jumped up from the couch, and when Florian tried to grab his arm, Brian flung his hand off and lurched away. He paused for just an instant to glare back at Florian, angrily, breathing so hard the breath seemed to rattle in his throat. He stomped out, up the stairs, along the second-floor hall. Lucille lowered her eyes at the slam of his door.

For a moment, in the reverberating silence in the big room, the three of them could have been statues. Then they turned as the screen door slid open and Salvatore stepped in from the deck. The rowboat was always soppy and the bottom of his red leather slippers were stained black. He studied his son, his wife, and then, dubiously, the woman too dressed up to be out in a boat in the middle of the night. *And Brian?* his eyes said. *Where's Brian?*

Florian had all but forgotten Joyce. "I'd better go upstairs," he told her.

"Of course."

Salvatore moved closer, his slippers squishing on the carpet. "Trouble, eh?"

"Maybe not too bad," Florian said. Unaccountably he laughed. It was almost a cackle, a sound he'd never heard himself make before. "We just have to straighten things out, that's all. Would you drive Mrs. Johnway home? Just down the road. Take the Duster," he added quickly.

What the hell, none of this had anything to do with Joyce. All she needed was a bunch of righteous cops wondering what she was doing here. *It's not, ma'am, that we, as officers of the law, are interested in the peccadilloes of your private life, but we understand that you, a married woman, and your paramour, after being discovered in the middle of the night in the middle of the Lake Shaped Like a Pear, were the first to confront young Brian Rubio after the aforementioned events on the aforementioned evening.*

"Really, I can walk," Joyce said.

"Let my father take you."

Gingerly Joyce touched his arm. "If there's any way I can help . . ."

"Thanks," he said, and she left, followed by Salvatore. "I'll go up alone," Florian said to his mother. "We don't want to be ganging up on him."

Florian knocked, pushed the door open when he heard a grunt from inside. Brian was sitting at the built-in desk next to the big window that looked over the lake, his stereo so low Florian could hardly hear it. He usually played it loud enough to shake the house. He was cutting small shapes out of colored papers with an X-Acto knife. His newest hobby: montages out of snippets, his room smelling of rubber cement. Some were just designs, others trains, outdoor scenes, faces, figures. He never kept them; as soon as he was satisfied with something, he'd tear it up and throw it away. But Lucille had come across a farmyard scene while cleaning his room and had taken it for the kitchen wall: hundreds of tiny colored pieces, like a delicate mosaic. Brian didn't complain or take it down or, for that matter, even mention it.

He turned his attention to a purple piece of cardboard, using a ruler to guide the X-Acto knife, but the knife was shaking in his hand.

"Better watch it," Florian said.

The boy took a breath, reached up to turn off the stereo.

"What did you mean, Brian," Florian said evenly, "by the *other* car?"

"Their car. It was banging back against the Corvette, and the next thing I knew it was in the lake."

Florian closed his eyes for a breath. "What'd you do, let some god-damn drunk take the wheel?"

"I was at the wheel."

Florian wavered, clenching his teeth so hard they hurt. "Will you please just tell me what happened?"

"I'm trying to, if you'll let me," Brian said angrily. "Meanwhile, maybe you could at least give me the benefit of the doubt."

"Believe me, I'm giving you every benefit of every doubt in the world. Okay, no more questions. Tell it your way."

Brian glanced down to the desk and began, aimlessly, moving a green sheet around with one finger. A lefty: Florian used to think he'd make a great pitcher, but the kid never got interested.

"Anyhow, it was ramming back against the Corvette because the Corvette was blocking it, and I was trying to tell the guy, 'Okay, stop a minute, for Christ's sake, give me a second to finish your way,' but maybe he couldn't hear me in all the noise and excitement. There were kids yelling and screaming and running around, beating up on each other, everything going on all at once, and it all happened in a second, in the middle of all this craziness. It wasn't actually until afterward and I left and had a minute to pull my head together that I figured it out. I mean, I saw it at the time, but it didn't register. Only the driver in the other car must have been confused in all the chaos, too, because after he looked back and saw I was ready to let him go, he turned around to the wheel again and yanked down on the gearshift and practically flew off the ramp."

"Why?"

"Maybe he forgot he was already in reverse, so when he pulled down, he put himself in drive, or maybe low, and when he gave it the gas . . ."

Florian had listened as if cracking a code, afraid to miss a single clue. When Brian stopped, though, he blinked in astonishment at the magnitude of his relief. "That's it?" he said, his voice rising. He almost laughed. "That's what happened?"

His elation seemed to stun Brian. "Jesus, Dad, there's two kids dead."

"C'mon, that's terrible, that's awful. But look, if the guy got into the wrong gear, they can't blame you for it. If he's dumb enough or drunk enough or whatever to drive into the lake, it can't possibly be your fault. Did you mention any of this to the cops?"

"They never even talked to me. I told you, it was really a madhouse." Brian paused, and they both listened to Padgett outside welcoming Salvatore's return in the Duster. Brian cleared his throat. "I didn't want to say too much when Mrs. Johnway was here."

"Oh—you know her?"

"I know who she is. She teaches at Medway High, right?" Brian steeled himself briefly. "I'm pretty sure the kids that drowned were from there."

"I thought you didn't know who they were."

"I don't, but there was this whole gang from Medway, including the guy and the girl in the car."

"A girl? A girl drowned?"

"Yeah. I didn't even know until afterward. I figured it'd get Mrs. Johnway all upset, especially if she knew the kids. Besides, I wasn't sure how much I should say in front of other people."

"Nothing," Florian said sharply. "Absolutely nothing." He blew out his breath in a quiet, steady stream. "Is there anything else?"

"Not really. I'm pretty bushed actually."

"Right on." Florian grasped Brian's shoulder, easily slapped the outside of his arm, feeling the hard, smooth muscle.

"It just *happened*," Brian said. "These Medway kids were trying to wreck the hell out of the Corvette and—"

"Christ, you should have just let them! I don't give a damn about the Corvette!"

"Then suddenly they were into the drink . . . just like that . . . and it was all over." Brian squinted against the tears.

"Look, it's okay. It's a real shame about those kids, but it wasn't your fault. Right now that's the main thing."

"I'm beat, Dad."

"That's it, get some rest. You want anything from downstairs?"

"Thanks, I'm okay."

Lucille accosted Florian at the foot of the stairs, Salvatore right behind her. "I told you not to let him out like that. He's a little boy. How does he know to be careful?"

"It's all right, it wasn't his fault," Florian said. "He's gonna be okay."

"Only how terrible. Two little boys dead."

"One was a girl," Florian said.

"Jesus, Mary, and Joseph."

"Let's all get some rest," Florian said quietly, a casual suggestion. "We can talk in the morning."

As soon as the others were upstairs, Florian dialed, standing up, looking out at the faint shimmer of moonlight on the lake. He let it ring and ring.

"Put on some clothes, will you," he said when Ira Wachtel finally picked up, "and get over here."

"Now?" Wachtel asked after a pause.

"Now," Florian said. He must have sounded convincing because Wachtel hung up without another word.

Canada was only hours away. From there they could fly to Europe, the Caribbean, let things settle while they figured out their next move. Give the kid the Grand Tour. Hell, he'd take it himself along with him. He'd never seen those museums or churches, those canals and bullfights and native markets. They'd have themselves a ball and let Ira Wachtel take care of all the crappy crap back here.

"You mean, take Brian and run?" Wachtel wanted to know.

"Look, he didn't do anything. But two kids are dead and Christ only knows who they'll try to blame, what kind of scapegoat they're looking for."

"With all due respect, Flo, this is the wrong time for you to be making decisions. And since your son, unlike me, was allowed to get his normal night's sleep, there's not much to do until we're both awake at the same time."

"I want you to understand I'm just worried about him getting blamed for something he didn't do. That's why I wanted you here, to protect his rights and not let anyone pull a fast one."

"I'd like to know how you were able to tell me what happened."

"What do you mean?"

"Were you on the boat ramp? Did you see those cars bumping into each other? Did you hear those kids yelling at each other?"

Florian could barely control himself. "What are you handing me?"

"Sure, you just want to help your beloved son and heir. Look, you know some real estate agents. Who's the last person in the world a real estate agent wants underfoot when he's showing a house?"

"Don't play with me. I'm in no mood."

"So we agree, it's the owner, pointing out the wrong feature at the wrong time in the wrong tone of voice. Let us in our common wisdom consider the plight of your average everyday dime-a-dozen lawyer drug out of his bed in the middle of the night by some father whose kid is maybe in some kind of trouble. What's the last thing I need? The heart-felt daddy, grilling the kid for an hour or so beforehand, conspiring over this beautifully crafted story that's sure to fool the pants off everybody from the local flatfoot to the judge and jury and the stringer from CBS news."

"What the hell are you talking about?"

"The worst thing you could've done was force Brian to come up with a story to satisfy you. You're a vaguely intelligent man, Flo: any kid's going to want to get his father off his neck, and sometimes he'll tell him whatever it takes to do that. And then along comes me, the local legal hired hand, and the kid has to decide what to tell me, which sure as hell better be the truth, but he's already stuck with the half-assed fairy tale he made up to satisfy his old man, or that his old man helped him make up to fool the cops. All of which means I have to break through his story to find out what I need to know to keep from making an ass of myself defending him. I'll be back in the morning and see what we got here."

"No, stay. There's sheets in the front guest room. You want a drink?"

"I had my nightcap four hours ago. I'll just hit the sack unless you want me to call Red Penneman at headquarters and see—"

"No. Don't start anything. Maybe everything's all right."

"Let's all hope so."

"It is, I'm sure it is," Florian said. "I just want you here in case."

Florian waited until he figured Wachtel—everyone—was asleep be-fore slipping quietly outside. He put Salvatore's Duster into neutral and let it roll down the incline away from the house before turning the ignition. It started with a series of hiccups, springs groaning, handling like your run-of-the-mill coal barge. Still, it was quieter than the Jeep, and he sure as hell wasn't going to take the Corvette.

From some distance away he saw the white glow in the sky, then slowed as he came upon the Medway police cars angled across the ramp entrance, emergency blinkers flashing. This part of the lake, the neck, belonged to Medway. Two wreckers illuminated the area with their floodlights: loads of cops, a fire truck, a single car that didn't seem particularly banged up, or even wet.

Two cops stared impassively as Florian drove slowly past. Behind the patrol cars, a strip of yellow phosphorescent ribbon, sagging and puffing in the breeze, stretched across the entrance. Driving back, he felt as if he'd been spinning woozily for hours through some weightless atmo-sphere, arms outstretched, head thrown back.

He coasted into the parking area with the engine cut and walked out on the deck to check Brian's window: dark. He let himself in quietly and stayed downstairs long enough to pour some scotch, skipping the ice for fear of waking someone. He drank it sitting in bed, wondering what it must be like in that final freeze frame of your life—at what? Seventeen? Eighteen? He wondered, too, what you'd feel knowing that somehow, no matter how accidentally, no matter how innocently, you had a part in closing the book on those two kids. Was it something you'd ever be able to shrug off?

Hardly two hours later, at six A.M., he woke with a start when a Medway cruiser pulled into the parking area, followed by another, identical except for the designation on the side: Chief of Police. The sun was barely up over the lake, the morning still cool, the trees alive with starlings. It was the kind of morning you'd love on a vacation, getting up early, warming your hands over a fire while the bacon sizzled, heading off for a hike through the woods. Maybe Canada would've been the right idea. Only how—in the Jeep with its canvas and plastic doors? His father's chugging Duster? A cream Corvette that every cop in New England would be looking for? He wavered for a minute, afraid he'd lose his balance completely. The whole thing seemed as crazily unreal as cowboys and Indians, hooves thundering over hardscrabble desert landscapes as you pulled your kid closer, trying to protect him from the shots echoing through the canyon.

Three policemen emerged from the first car, briskly, their eyes darting. Still, they moved with a kind of stately reserve, a steadiness of purpose.

Another cop climbed out of the chief's car, and then, without hurry, Red Penneman himself. Penneman wore his usual gray double-breasted suit (which in winter he topped with a long black overcoat). His eyes did not dart as he headed for the front door, still in no hurry. Florian had always liked him, a tall, lean man with blunt hands and a straightforward but friendly way of dealing with people. Penneman had slowed a bit but was in good shape for a man in his sixties.

Florian remembered Nique's bicycle out there. Was it something they'd study, dust for fingerprints, somberly tag, and wrap in Saran for the lab? Did Medway have a lab?

Hurrying downstairs, wondering if anyone else was awake, Florian was startled—it was six o'clock in the morning, barely light—to see his father at the kitchen table, hands surrounding a mug of coffee. Wachtel

sat across from him, rumpled in last night's suit and shirt. Lucille, standing, said, "I saw at the window. All those policemen."

Florian walked to the door, aware of his steps on the polished wood
floor, and pulled it open.

Red Penneman touched his fedora. He always maintained a kind of
folksy, down-home politeness. "Morning, Flo."

"Morning, Red." Penneman wasn't really a friend, but he'd been
Medway chief for more years than people could remember and they'd
traded a few jokes and stories at fund-raisers and Little League dinners.

"Looks like we're all up bright and early," Penneman said.

"Looks like it."

"Can we have a word with Brian?"

"All of you?"

At Penneman's nod, the patrolmen stepped back a few feet. None
paid any attention to Nique's banged-up bicycle leaning against the wall.
Florian led the chief into the kitchen, where his parents and Wachtel
were standing now. Penneman nodded with his hat in his hands. "Morning, Mrs. Rubio, Mr. Rubio." His dome was framed by fringes of sandy
hair. "You got here pretty fast," he said to Wachtel, who shrugged.
Penneman looked around, studied the farm scene montage of colored
bits and pieces on the wall. "And Brian?"

"Fast asleep," Wachtel said before Florian could respond.

"I'm afraid he'll have to come downtown for some questions."

"Not until he talks to me first," Wachtel said.

"Five minutes."

"I'll go up with you," Florian said to Wachtel, annoyed at the two
of them casually working everything out themselves.

Wachtel shook his head. "It'd be best if he and I could talk alone."

"He's my son."

"That's why you want to do what's best for him." Wachtel turned
to Penneman. "I'd appreciate fifteen."

"Ten."

Feeling like a goddamn fifth wheel, Florian listened to Wachtel
climbing the stairs, the knock, Brian's voice. At least the kid hadn't slid
down the drainpipe to hightail it off into the woods with a knapsack full
of chocolate bars and baloney sandwiches. Maybe that was a good sign,
that Brian was clear enough of conscience to face the music.

"Enough for everyone," Lucille said, offering the porcelain coffeepot, gesturing toward the plate of toast, the bowl of scrambled eggs.

"Thanks, no, Mrs. Rubio," Penneman said, patting his hard stomach. "All that caffeine."

Lucille was disappointed. That was always her first move, offering food and drink to anyone who walked in. Back in Italy, you protected yourself from strangers by showering them with hospitality.

She returned the pot to the stove, but Florian decided on a cup himself. He started pouring, then quickly pivoted away from the others; his hand was shaking as bad as Brian's last night with the X-Acto knife. He returned the pot to the burner, still with his back to them, and took a sip even though it burned his tongue. He faced Penneman, who'd been watching the whole time. The guy hadn't been a cop for forty years for nothing. "How bad, Red?"

"Don't clearly know. We're picking up at least three others, but you know how it is. Brian was the one tooling around in the 'Vette."

"It's right outside. We're not hiding anything."

"We noticed. That bike, though—Brian using a girl's these days?"

"His date left it last night."

With an amiable smile, Penneman added this to whatever else he'd already picked up or figured out. "Just so you won't have to wait for the afternoon paper . . . Something like eleven kids, including Brian, were on the ramp when a '74 Plymouth Valiant went into your lake out there. We sent everybody we could, along with the troopers from the state barracks, the fire people, the ambulance people, divers from the scuba club at the Y, the crane from Riverton Construction. Unfortunately it was too late, and we ended up with that poor boy and girl drowned, although the medical examiner and the people from the county crime lab are, of course, checking other possible causes."

"And for alcohol, I hope. Drugs."

"Sure thing. Meanwhile, Father Carrolton from St. Ignatius came and administered last rites." Penneman paused. "I know how you feel, Flo, your boy possibly connected in any way to something like this. We'll just have to do our best to get to the bottom of it."

"Who drowned?"

"Willa Hufnagle and Paul Dunn, who apparently everybody called Polly. Neither one, from what I hear tell, ever been in trouble before."

"Neither has Brian."

"We know that, Flo."

Lucille had been standing with her arms folded across her house-dress, her eyes like slits. "What are you trying to say, that it's his fault? How do you know? Who says it's whose fault?"

Salvatore got up to put a hand on Lucille's arm and stand next to her, as if to show his support, while at the same time trying to keep her from losing her temper altogether.

Still calm, still polite, Penneman fingered his hat in his hands. "It's not for us to say whose fault anything is or isn't, Mrs. Rubio. I only wish it never happened, just like everybody else. The girl there, you know, was only thirteen years old."

"Jesus," Florian said. He felt it like an ice pick.

"Oh, no," Lucille cried out. "A little girl like that? Out at that time of night?"

"'Fraid so, Mrs. Rubio. And between us and the four walls, Brian shouldn't have left the ramp afterward. It don't just make my people look bad for not grabbing him—although of course, they had other things on their mind—but it don't do him much good either, leaving the scene. It took a while, as you can see, to find out he was involved, and now the blood tests will be six hours after the fact, and not nearly as conclusive as we'd like."

"He wasn't drunk," Florian said, maybe too insistently. "We talked last night, right afterward." Could the shock have been enough to clear Brian's head? Most of all, the boy had seemed stunned, his eyes blank.

Red Penneman pulled back one side of his mouth. "It's no picnic having kids. They keep you laughing and they keep you crying. You gotta bear with it."

"Brian's a good boy," Lucille said, as if disputing an accusation. "Always he's been a good boy."

"I never doubted that for one minute," Penneman said.

Wachtel came down first, then Brian, dressed in clean cords and a neatly tucked-in shirt. Was that what Wachtel had been doing, making sure Brian looked like a real polite, clean-cut kid? As for Wachtel himself —well, he'd freshened up a bit, buttoned his shirt, tied his tie. In truth, Wachtel was hardly anybody's idea of an imposing guy. People didn't fall silent when he walked into a room or gape at him across a restaurant. Some years back, he'd run for county prosecutor and come in fourth out of four. He was a lousy public speaker and looked like a medium everything, except for the eyeglasses, which were thicker than most.

Brian kept his eyes down. It was hard to tell whether he'd slept.

"We'll follow you in," Wachtel told Penneman.

"Me, too," Florian said quickly, ready to fight this time, although no one seemed to object.

"We'll have to impound the 'Vette," Penneman said. "Maybe Mr. Wachtel can give you and Brian a lift."

As they walked out the door, Brian slipped on his wraparound life-guard sunglasses. Florian tensed. What the hell was the kid supposed to be—the neighborhood sharpie?

* * *

As familiar as he was with the fifteen-mile drive into downtown Medway, Florian felt disoriented viewing it all from the passenger seat, following his own car being driven by a uniformed cop.

Wachtel was no help, not saying a word. Maybe Ira Wachtel was a mistake, instead of grabbing a big-name hotshot from out of town. Florian wasn't much for lawyers anyhow, for anything. It was your business, your family, your life. What'd you need outsiders butting in for?

He turned to face Brian in back. Behind the dark glasses, the kid looked even tighter than before, although he could have passed for some classroom cutup, embarrassed at being caught but hoping to tough it out behind his shades. For the first time Florian thought of Elly, of having to tell her. *Sure, Flo. Only would you please inform me how come the kid can live with me for sixteen years without any trouble whatsoever, and in less than a year with you* . . .

"How're we doing?" Florian asked Brian, immediately realizing how dumb the words sounded.

"Okay, I guess."

"Last night—were you drunk?"

"I'm no drinker, Dad. You know that."

"Lay off," Wachtel said from behind the wheel. "Don't make him go through it a million times."

"This is the first time."

"The second. And sure, he's gotta tell you because you're his father and have a vested interest. Then he's gotta tell his mother. Then his grandparents. And what about that wagonload of paisanos you're always bragging about down in New York? When they get on the phone tomorrow, maybe he can answer all their questions, too. Then there's his buddies down at the ice-cream parlor, sipping soda through a straw. I thought we settled this last night, Flo. You'll have him so frazzled he won't know if he's coming or going."

"What is it, he can talk to the cops but not me?"

Without taking his eyes off the road, Wachtel answered in that bland, all-knowing professional lawyer's tone: "All things considered, we might as well toss Brian to the sharks as have him talk to the cops right now."

Frowning, Florian glanced back at Brian, who hardly seemed to be listening, before turning on Wachtel. "What sharks, for Christ's sake? Don't exaggerate."

"I'm not exaggerating. Both of you had better understand that."

* * *

While Brian and Wachtel were upstairs refusing to talk to the cops or the DA or whoever (how did that prove your innocence?), Florian got antsy waiting on the bench in the reception room, opposite the desk sergeant and the glassed-in dispatcher, with Wanted posters tacked at odd angles on the walls. He went out for some air to the cobblestone parking area sandwiched between police headquarters and city hall. It was almost eight, a brisk Saturday morning, the parking spaces mostly empty.

Slowly he circled the Corvette, a chunky Denver boot clamped to a rear wheel. He hunkered down for a closer look at the front bumper and fenders. If it'd rammed another car, it hadn't been hard enough to leave signs, although the fiberglass body was practically impossible to scratch, let alone dent. Still, it couldn't have been more than a tap. (Where was the car they'd hauled out of the lake?)

He straightened up to discover a man—his age, maybe a few years older—watching darkly from just outside the station house door. Hawk-nosed, kind of sallow and cadaverous, scowling, he wore a light sport coat and narrow tie and seemed grimly pleased to have been noticed. A plainclothesman keeping an eye on the state's most expensive piece of evidence? Or maybe—*oh, Christ!*—the father of one of the drowned kids. Florian wasn't ready for that. He couldn't face it.

Then, from the same station house door emerged Harry Diggs, more or less escorting another man and three women. It was the earliest Florian had ever seen Harry awake and abroad, so early that his florist or gardener or whoever hadn't yet snipped a white flower for him: the lapel of his wrinkled suit jacket looked positively bereft.

Harry put a heavy arm around the cadaverous guy's shoulder, gave him a kind of reassuring squeeze, and led him forward along with the others, a goddamn entourage. "Dr. Zack Arkins," Harry announced as the guy, at his urging, held out his hand with as sour a look as you'd ever run across, although God knows the others hardly looked like world-beaters either. "I'm representing his son, and the sons of my other clients here. They're all friends of Brian, all in this together, so you might as well get to know each other in a comradely fashion."

3

Joyce had hardly slept, and after getting up shaken and drained, she received a call Saturday from a secretary in the PE department. "This is an ASAP message," the secretary said, sounding both awed and excited although she was probably reading directly from the red ASAP card they'd all received. "Please write down and confirm the time, date, and place. Ready? One P.M. tomorrow afternoon, Sunday, June twenty-second, in the school auditorium."

(The *school* auditorium? Was Brownie afraid people would end up at some other auditorium?)

Brownie had returned with the All School Alert Program from a principals' conference in Texas, but they'd never used it. In theory it allowed the eighty or so employees to be reached within minutes. The principal phoned his four assistants, who each phoned four more people, who each phoned four more, assuming everyone was home.

Saturday afternoon's *Mt. Early Express* gave the drownings a banner headline:

LAKE ACCIDENT CLAIMS TWO LIVES
Medway Youths Drown
In Midnight Tragedy
At Bottleneck Lake

Joyce shook her head over the huge grainy photo of the car being hoisted from the water, dangling on a chain. The police were looking into "the nature of an altercation that reportedly preceded the accident." Except for the two Medway students who'd drowned, the police didn't name anyone involved, nor was Florian identified as the owner of the "luxury-model sports car that may have caused the death vehicle to plunge into the murky waters of the lake."

The shocker, of course, was that one of the drowned kids was Willa Hufnagle, a thirteen-year-old girl, an eighth grader. It shocked Joyce, certainly. Still, she felt torn over the idea that the death of a thirteen-year-old girl would seem more terrible than that of a seventeen-year-old boy. Was everyone, Joyce included, simply assuming the girl had to be more passive and innocent than all those hell-raising boys? Maybe they also wondered, with a little shudder of disapproval, what this kid still in junior high was doing running around past midnight with a bunch of guys four years older.

The Boston Globe used the drownings as its lead story in the State section, accompanied by the photo of the dangling automobile. The New York Times ran it inside, small headline, no picture:

2 Mass. Youths
Drown in Auto
On Prom Night

The Express carried obituaries of Polly Dunn and Willa Hufnagle, along with their portraits, his stiff and wall-eyed from the Annual, hers frowning, almost suspicious-looking, with stringy hair in a snapshot that made her seem rather unattractive. Polly Dunn played football and American Legion baseball. Willa helped build sets for the drama club. Both were scheduled to graduate next week, Polly out of high school on the industrial-commercial track, Willa out of junior high.

The story explained how the MORP had been dreamed up by Trent seniors, with everyone wearing their rattiest clothes and contests for a Court of Uglies and the election of a Gnik and Neeuq.

Unfortunately, fate intervened, and those lighthearted activities were cut short just after midnight by the horror that unfolded in the waters off the public boat ramp of Bottleneck Lake.

News of the deaths of the young boy and girl from rival Medway schools spread quickly among the partygoing Trent students. In pairs and small groups, in carloads, they gravitated toward the death site.

Laughing teenagers became mourners, until the hand-holding couples drifted away. Their night of celebration was over. They comforted each other as best they could and then, crestfallen, went home to tell their disbelieving parents the shocking news.

Even though this year's prom had become a MORP, Princi Harold Martinson had promised to cook the traditional breakfast for graduating seniors. He'd been given an

MORP committee, with STNEDUTS EHT FO EVALS! ("Slave of the Students!") printed across the front.

On the public beach, planned site of the nightlong festivities, coffee urns and milk containers, gallons of maple syrup and orange juice, sheet metal griddles and barbecue pits, stood unused.

Medway police declined to release the names of the students of either school who were being questioned.

Some officers spoke off the record. "What you have on a night like this," one of them said, "is a tremendous amount of intoxication going on." He confirmed earlier reports of rowdiness and "cruising around" but said it appeared to be no worse than usual for a night of high school partying.

Authorities declined to categorize the drownings as accidental or otherwise but said their investigation was continuing.

Joyce knew nothing at all of Willa Hufnagle. Polly Dunn had been in one of her freshman history classes three years back; she barely remembered him, although she'd seen him around a few times since, large and clumsy-looking, wearing his football jersey or whatever, hanging around with the other jocks. She could hardly claim a closeness with him, or the girl she'd never seen, but still felt unnerved at the thought of the two of them drowning horribly, trapped in a car.

And Florian's son: she didn't know him either but had heard him trying to make sense of what had happened, then running from the room—in rage? Frustration? Tears?

The one name Joyce knew all too well she heard over the phone from Katarina Scanlon, her best friend at school, who called early Sunday to say that one of the Medway students on the boat ramp was Jamie Pitt. "Big surprise, eh?" Katarina said. "One wonders, doesn't one, what the dear boy was doing there."

Who else but Jamie Pitt would you expect to be smack-dab in the middle of everything that could possibly go wrong? In some ways, ghoulish as it might sound, the miracle was that he'd survived.

She remembered during the year glancing down from her homeroom window at noon recess and seeing Jamie and a few other boys playing shirtless basketball in the schoolyard, and some other kid crashing into Jamie while trying to score, sending Jamie ignominiously flying and tumbling. Jamie leaped up, got the ball, and threw it, smashed it, int-blank into the other kid's face.

knuckle pressed to her lips, drawing a raspy intake of air beth. Joyce had watched from the window, wanting to believe they were still having fun, that Jamie's anger was all show, all teenage bravado, that he'd suddenly laugh at the joke he'd pulled.

Only what else could you expect from teenage boys with more muscle and energy, more gnawing tension than they knew what to do with? They gloried in that explosive physicality. Perhaps, she'd thought at the time, they'd all end up going off with arms around each other's shoulders, looking for—what? A root beer float? A joint and a couple of beers? A girl in a gauzy blouse and swirling micromini, sweating from the same lubricious itch?

The next day she learned that Jamie had been given a week's detention, not for the flare-up on the court but because he'd come back into the building so infuriated that he'd flung the door monitor's chair through a huge pane of safety glass. She hadn't inquired further, feeling no special responsibility.

Just last week she'd seen Jamie Pitt after school with his thumb out, seemingly heading in the wrong direction, out toward Bottleneck Lake. He lived with his parents and an assortment of brothers and sisters back near the giant smokestacks of IE Plastics. Motionless near a parked car, Jamie maintained the typical hitchhiker's glowering mask. She'd have thought the more intimidating you looked, the less likely anyone would stop. But with a little laugh she was willing to concede that somewhere beneath her leathery teachery hide there still lurked a belief that being decent to kids was part of the deal. She waited stiffly as he ran up and yanked open the door, turning wary as soon as he recognized her: "Oh —hello."

Although she'd heard that Jamie starred on the swimming team, he was built more like a wrestler, squat, with heavy shoulders, thick chest and neck, short, bulging arms which his stretched-tight polo shirt did nothing to hide. His features were rough, a large, bent nose and what seemed, in class, a loose perpetual smile. She'd had him all year in local history, where he'd distinguished himself mainly through that smile. It was almost a mask, to keep other kids, teachers too, from knocking him down one more time, handing him one more humiliation that he'd have no choice but to avenge.

He was heading for Hammond's Boatyard, he informed her. He'd started working there a few weeks ago, getting things ready for summer, swabbing, caulking, painting, cleaning up. Afternoons till school ended, then full-time.

Right on her way, she said, but he shook her off, as pleasant and polite as always. "You gotta cut down James Road for South Corner. I can walk from the intersection."

"It'll take me two minutes," she said, wondering how he knew where she lived. Students found your personal life more fascinating than anything you presented in class. "At least you'll be able to keep in practice there," she added, trying to match his cheerfulness.

"Practice?"

"Don't you swim for—?" She stopped, embarrassed. He'd be graduating, not on the team anymore. Was he good enough for a college scholarship? Like most Medway kids, Jamie had gone through on the industrial-commercial track, which maybe at one time made sense, back when the flourishing local plants of International Electric snapped up anyone who could tell one end of a wrench from the other. "Are you thinking of college somewhere?"

He gave her a quick sideways look. "No, I ain't thinking about that right now." He seemed to imply more promising options.

She drove past James Road and up toward Hammond's, the glistening lake now on their left. The neck was maybe a quarter mile across, with the public beach and ramp and Hammond's Boatyard all located there. The more expansive southern end of the lake, in Trent, offered no public access. The shoreline homes became larger and more luxurious as you moved toward South Corner, where the properties, including theirs and Florian's, six houses apart, used the unspoiled acres of Fischel State Park as a buffer against the rest of the world.

Joyce let Jamie off in front of Hammond's, with its stacks of brightly painted upside-down canoes. Angled sailboats and rental outboards lay on the bare dirt around the bait shack, while the big flashy inboards perched on trailers. Most lakesiders, including Benn, serviced their boats at Hammond's and stored them there over the winter.

"Will you have to hitch out here all summer?" she asked.

"Someone always stops," Jamie assured her with serene good cheer. He could have been the world's premier optimist, so radiant seemed his faith that if Jamie Pitt needed to get from one place to another, some generous soul would come forth eagerly to help him do so. "Thanks," he'd said, and strolled off toward the bait shack, those wrestler's shoulders and arms rolling in his squat, bulldog walk.

Perfect: some grungy Medway kid eager to pick up whatever he could—minimum wage?—swabbing down boats so South County year-rounders and summer folk could cavort around their favorite body of water. The irony, of course, was that despite its picture postcard setting Bottleneck Lake was incredibly polluted. By midsummer every year the rampaging proliferation of algae and milfoil took over. Joyce had her classes do projects on it: eutrophication. Acid rain wasn't the only problem. Septic tanks, erosion, detergents, the flush of nitrogen fertilizer from surrounding farms and lawns and gardens, each doing its part to turn a once-crystalline body of water into a peat bog.

About ten years ago Benn got the other lakeside homeowners to join in a "lake restoration" project. First they tried to kill the milfoil with herbicides, but discovered that you needed bigger doses every year and that the thousands of gallons of silvex you poured into the lake didn't simply do its job and disappear. It steadily leached dioxin to be absorbed by the native pike and perch and trout.

They also learned that whatever you did to destroy the weeds immediately encouraged more weeds to grow in their place. The newly cleared water let sunlight penetrate down to the muck, bringing on new and healthier crops of surging, light-seeking growths. And the bulbous tops chopped off by boat propellers provided thousands of cuttings to take root wherever they settled.

Next, Bennett and the others rented a weed harvester, an ungainly, noisily stammering scow featuring a giant paddle wheel, chugging along the shoreline to cut off, scoop up, and bind the weeds like a combine. It was slow going. The boat had to pull ashore regularly to unload the slimy, dripping bundles, which were then carted off to the county dump. Again, the cleaner the water got, the more luxuriant the new weeds became.

Finally they tried drawing down the lake every fall, to let the winter freezes kill off the exposed weeds. But come spring, they grew back in great riotous profusion.

A state university scientist said it took eight pounds of fertilizer per acre to grow lake weeds. Each acre of Bottleneck Lake contained three hundred pounds.

"You can't fight Mother Nature," Bennett had said finally. "If the fucking lake wants to die, it's gonna die. The good news is it'll probably take another fifty years, so right now we'll just shut up about it and leave the fish for the tourists to pull in."

Joyce remembered how lovely Greenhills had been back then, in April, with the trees and the grass richly green from spring rains, the hills in the distance green too, wildflowers rioting underfoot as they walked across the fields and Florian took her hand to help her up the rickety stairs of the old buildings. He told her about the lavish parties at the turn of the century, the horse-drawn sleigh rides in winter, the summer galas under lawn tents, back when the servants outnumbered the family on estates like Greenhills. He showed her the huge kitchen with its bank of ovens and slate sinks, its dumbwaiters and cutting blocks, all of which later proved quite adequate for the feeding of sixty boys and twelve brothers when it became St. Paul's School.

"Some Fall River shipping tycoon built it in the 1870s," Florian explained as they walked through the main mansion, with its broad portico under which carriages delivered their passengers out of the weather. "It was one of the first great Estates."

Florian wasn't even aware then that she taught local history, that it was her favorite subject.

"There were some heavy misgivings among the brothers when they found out that the pious seadog made his millions from the slave trade. But they accepted the estate anyhow. Maybe they figured the prayers of the schoolboys would save him a few centuries in purgatory."

Florian had bought the estate from the Catholic order some years back—for a song, according to Benn—when some sort of economic pinch forced them to close the school. ("You always hear about these guys," Benn had explained, "who could've made a fortune twenty years ago, ten years ago, if they'd just been smart enough to buy up acreage outside Tucson, or in Florida, North Carolina, wherever, when it was going for peanuts. Well, ten years ago Flo showed up and turned into that rare guy that actually manages to buy at the right time, because he did it just when the county was starting to boom with all these summer properties and everything, except for Medway, of course, but Flo wasn't buying in Medway, he was buying out in the boondocks, waiting for the next wave of people to arrive, and it always did arrive for him, and he ended up pulling in a lot more dough than us working stiffs.")

Florian's personal tour had come about because they'd been seated at the same table at Abby Allen Oliver's spring gala for the Trent Theater Festival. Benn had kidded Florian about the killing he was about to make on Greenhills, and Joyce, thinking of a field day for her class, said she'd really be interested in seeing the place.

"I'd love to show you around, hon," Benn had said. "Only, Jesus, you know how busy I am these days, and we got the world's leading expert standing right here with a glass of scotch in his hand. Flo, you planning on any more strolling around out there?"

He was, Florian said. He needed to check out some secondary structures.

"There you are," Bennett said with a tip of his glass. "Your tour guide."

"Are you sure that'd be all right?" she'd asked Florian.

"My pleasure."

It'd been as simple, as innocent, as that.

Looking into a dark corner of one of the old barns a few days later, she'd jumped back and grabbed Florian's arm. An eerie dot of fluorescent greenish light flickered on and off against the wall. "What's that? A broken wire?"

He too seemed puzzled. They leaned forward, cautiously, her hand still on his arm. "A firefly," he said.

She bent even closer. The firefly was trapped in a spider web, unable to move, maybe even paralyzed, but with its greenish light still pulsing. She shivered and pressed close to Florian. "Let's go. It's chilly in here."

"We could head over where the golf course will be. It's got the best views."

"Let's not talk about golf courses. Let's just enjoy it the way it still is."

He laughed at what he must have seen as her squeamishness. "Hey, golf courses can be kind of beautiful."

She'd asked if he played, and he said no, he couldn't stand the people, and she, without thinking, said that Benn loved the game. After eyeing each other warily, they both laughed.

High above Bottleneck Lake, they wandered across the grounds and through wild bushes and brambles. A forsythia blossom caught in his hair, blazing yellow in the sun, and they laughed at this too. When she removed it, she placed it in his hand and told him to make a wish on it. He did, closing his eyes.

They sat and talked for hours on a grassy knoll in front of the estate house, she leaning forward to look at him with her cheek on her knees, her arms wrapped around her legs.

"How old are you?" she asked, shading her eyes from the sun.

"Forty-seven."

"Don't make a face. What's wrong with forty-seven?"

"What you're supposed to say is *No! You! Forty-seven! I don't believe it!*"

"How old do you think I am?" She was teasing, of course, making a joke of it, but still realized she hadn't asked this question of anyone, let alone a man, in as long as she could remember.

"As Uncle Gennario used to say, *I may be dumb, but I'm not stupid.*"

"I'm thirty-eight."

"A great age. A vintage year. My God, when I was thirty-eight, there was no stopping me. I could leap tall buildings."

"How old did you think I was?"

"Thirty-one and a half. Pushing thirty-two."

She got up and pulled him to his feet. "Let's go have a drink while this madness is still upon you."

They had cocktails at the Red Wagon—late afternoon now—and talked for hours more. They weren't worried about anyone seeing them. After all, Benn knew they were together, and it was all—still—innocent enough. But she could tell, maybe anyone could, that he was as caught up as she was. They were nonetheless almost comically cautious. The question was everywhere, in his eyes, his voice, his hesitations: *Are you married to Bennett Johnway or aren't you? What's going on here?*

At that moment she wasn't altogether sure herself. It took Florian to make her face the question. Not that he pushed her. He just wanted her to straighten things out in her own mind, and she agreed, and before long that was exactly what she did. And then called Florian to see if he might perhaps be interested in another walk.

When she didn't hear from Florian all through Saturday, Joyce kept reminding herself how hectic it had to be for him. Sunday turned out to be a lovely warm day, and since the faculty meeting wasn't until one o'clock, she walked up to his place around eleven. Why not? His whole family had seen them together Friday night. It spoke volumes about South Corner, with each house surrounded by acres of woods, that she and Florian had hardly spoken through all the years they'd been neighbors.

Florian's door did not seem to have a bell; she knocked, and his son —Brian—answered, seeming even taller than in the living room Friday night, with straight blond hair and a wonderful youthful smoothness, a fair complexion that obviously didn't come from Florian.

"Hello," he said, flustered.

"Hi, Brian." She wanted to get the tone right. "I'm really sorry about the accident. It must be terribly hard for you right now, but I'm sure it'll work out."

"Thanks. It's nice of you to come." He wrinkled his eyes in thought. "Did you know them?"

"Not really. I had the boy years ago in a large class."

Brian nodded. "Everybody must feel pretty bad up there."

"Of course, a terrible accident like that . . ." God, she was doing worse and worse, so she braved a smile and said, "I was just out walking and thought I'd say hello—if your father's in."

Brian faltered only briefly. "Sure. Come on."

The house seemed different in daylight, coming in this way rather than from the patio. The entryway was airy and bright, with a lovely Herez on the hardwood floor, with the big white kitchen off to the left, the huge living room on the right, its windows and glass doors overlooking the sunlit lake.

When Brian stepped aside, she walked in on Florian standing in front of a living room couch. Clinging ferociously to him, a woman wept loudly enough not to have heard Joyce enter.

Florian held up one hand, as if to stop Joyce from bolting, then patted the woman on the back, politely, and said, "You're worn out. You need some rest."

He eased her away, and the woman turned, slowly, to stare at this stranger, this intruder. She dabbed her eyes with the rose-dotted handkerchief already in her hand. Almost immediately, remarkably, a coolness replaced the tears.

"Joyce Johnway," Florian said. "A neighbor. Elly, Brian's mother."

Of course: the frantic mother flying in from California the minute she heard the news. "I'm terribly sorry for barging in on you," Joyce said.

Elly was quite attractive, a little older than Joyce but younger than Florian, her blondish hair perhaps subtly touched up, nice figure accented by pleated cotton skirt, soft-shouldered silk blouse. Dry-eyed now, cool, very cool, she spoke to Florian. "I'll be back this evening and we can talk some more."

"Please don't leave," Joyce said. "I'm going anyhow. I just—"

"We've talked enough for one afternoon." Decisively, Elly moved out of the room, Brian hurrying behind.

"She feels the strain," Florian said when they were gone. "She just got here—jet lag, the whole bit."

"Of course." The few times Florian had mentioned her he'd used the same term: Brian's mother. Only now she'd become a *presence* Joyce hadn't been prepared for. Possibly the woman had heard from the others that Florian had been out dallying with this very neighbor just when a responsible father would be making sure their son wasn't messing up his whole life.

"How've you been?" Florian asked.

Joyce couldn't help smiling; *she* wasn't the one with problems. "Thinking about you, about Brian." She paused. "Is his mother staying?"

"We'll have to see what we're up against, how long it'll take."

"I've got a meeting at school but I'll be home tonight."

"I'd love to come over," he said, apparently not finding anything strange in a Sunday meeting, maybe so wrapped up that he hadn't even heard.

"Please do." She glanced over her shoulder, toward the last they'd seen of Brian. "Is he in real trouble?"

Florian ran his tongue, quickly, over his lips, something she'd never seen him do. "Christ only knows. Thanks for coming by. I appreciate it."

She waited, but he seemed frozen to the spot. Then he took her hand, both hands, drew her close, her head on his shoulder, and hugged her without a word.

Florian found Elly and the others chatting in the big TV room. Lucille and Salvatore had always liked her, and Florian often suspected he was the one—even though it'd been Elly's idea—they'd never forgiven for the breakup.

"She seemed nice enough, your neighbor," Elly said. "It was sweet of her to drop by."

Lucille stood up, then Salvatore, then Brian. "You two want to talk," Lucille said, herding the others out.

"It's nicer outside," Florian said, "if you like water."

Elly had arrived on the red-eye this morning, without telling anyone, and had taken the airport limo to the Hollisworth, where she'd been able to get a room because the season hadn't begun. After discovering that the only taxi driver in Trent disconnected his phone on Sundays, she'd called Florian to come for her.

Florian had picked her up in the Fairlane he'd leased from Howland Ford. The Corvette was a lost cause. "We have to run tests, then stash it away as material evidence," Red Penneman had said. "Generally all we get is wrecks, so this gives the garage a little class. I read somewhere about these 'Vette clubs, where they meet every year and look over each other's rigs. You don't do that, do you, Flo?"

"It's a car, Red. It gets you from here to there. If they had a decent trolley system in these parts, I'd use that."

"I used a trolley once in New York. They hand you little paper transfers."

Florian wanted to lease something decent, but Wachtel gave him the word. "We're not asking you to plead poverty, but a little modesty would go a long way. You know, the common touch."

"Sure, some lawyer in a fifty-dollar haircut lecturing me on the common touch."

Wachtel gave him an odd look. He probably didn't spend fifty dollars a year for haircuts. "I don't see what anybody needs a bullet-shaped car for anyway. The main thing, right now, is not to have people dumping on Brian because his old man's loaded."

Was that the thinking you paid lawyers for? "Hell, I'm not going to drive around in a Rent-A-Wreck. A Buick maybe, an Olds?"

"No."

"Some Japanese sardine can?"

"Stay American."

"A Ford, for Christ's sake?"

"Mid-line," Wachtel said.

So he leased an ugly purplish Fairlane, a big soupy job smelling of plastic and fake leather. "I bet you like it so much you end up keeping it," Buddy Howland, ever the salesman, said.

"You're on," Florian had told him.

Out on the deck, Florian gestured at the view. "June's still spring up here," he said, "and nights stay cool all summer. It's what attracts the sweltering city folk." Looking at the sunlit lake, at the hills on the other side and Mt. Early in the distance, Florian remembered his own first sighting from here. It had, he'd always felt, changed his life.

"Everything's brown now in the Bay Area," Elly said. "It's only after the fall rains that the hills turn green."

Florian had last seen her six years ago, on a trip west to visit the kids, when he'd taken Brian and Joe camping in the Sierras. Annamarie was already married by then, off in Seattle. Usually Elly wasn't around when Florian showed up for the kids, but that time she'd answered the door.

She hadn't changed much since, hadn't gained a pound, although her eyes seemed a little harsher, less trusting, maybe heavier eye makeup, maybe just the way things had worked out. She was forty-four now and had been nineteen when they met, with tawny hair and long eyelashes and a lively swiveling walk that sent her skirts flying, with an eagerness about discovering and experiencing things of the world. Now the enthusiasm seemed dulled, as if nothing had turned out to be that big a deal. What came through was a kind of dry impatience.

(What was she noticing? He hadn't fattened up either, but his skin was a bit rougher between shaves, his hair thinner up front, and if you looked real hard—Elly was someone who looked hard—you could spot some gray coming through. His eyes? His expression? His sense of ease with himself?)

She spoke with an edge. "Somehow I figured you for the kidney-shaped swimming pool."

"You're looking at a three-mile lake to swim in—as long as we dredge the shore a couple of times a year."

"Where are you hiding your yacht?"

"We've got a canoe and rowboat and the little Runabout there. That's three more boats than I ever figured on." Where on the scale between absolute strangers and onetime lovers and husband and wife were they supposed to establish a connection, find some way of dealing with each other again?

"When you put him in that public school," she said, "I should have stopped you right then. He'd been doing fine at Courtney. It was small and they paid attention and he got along with everyone."

Courtney was an expensive commuting prep school just outside Walnut Creek. Florian had paid for it even though he hadn't wanted Brian to go. He'd wanted him, like Annamarie and Joe, in public school, but from the beginning Brian had been Elly's favorite, and she'd wanted the best for him, which she couldn't afford by herself. Elly did newspaper and magazine layouts for an ad agency, but the gardener who'd swept her off to California had long since disappeared into the western land-scape. Florian got some inkling of his successors through offhand refer-ences by the kids. He'd never met any of them although once he'd spoken to a guy on the phone who sounded reasonable and didn't react to Florian's name. Maybe he'd never heard it before.

"Trent's a good school," Florian said. "The other one, Medway, you wouldn't like."

"What's going to happen to him, Florian?"

"We don't know. Wachtel's trying to find out what—"

"Wachtel?"

"Ira Wachtel. Our lawyer."

"I don't know any Ira Wachtel." She watched a powerboat whip a water-skier through a huge circling turn, spray flying. The only lawyer Elly knew in all of Mt. Early County—the only person, outside the family —was Harry Diggs, and she'd of course been delighted with the divorce settlement he'd gotten her back then, when her only contact with him had been over the phone. She'd picked his name off a list provided by the state bar—closing her eyes probably, poking with a hairpin.

"Ira Wachtel's a first-class first-rate lawyer."

Elly ignored this with a shrug he recognized: she would save her arguments for a better time. He was determined not to let it bother him. He could do without that clenching of his teeth, that sour burning at the back of his throat. She'd probably hoped for the same, but it was slipping away now for both of them. He saw the annoyance in her eyes, the straight, grim line of her mouth. Just what they needed, to drive each other crazy again.

"You seemed uncomfortable when the woman showed up," she said. "That's far too flattering to yourself, and insulting to me, to think I'd care."

"I felt uncomfortable for her. She wasn't expecting to find you here."

"I'm sure it'll be nice having someone right next door during all this fuss." She made an abrupt gesture that included the house, the patio, the lake, maybe even the birdfeeder. "The good life, eh? It's funny, but two things that never occurred to me were that you'd leave New York or end up living with your parents."

"What never occurred to me was that you'd ever send Brian off to anyone, let alone me."

She tightened. "Don't lay that on me, okay. I certainly didn't expect you to let him get into a mess like this."

"Let him? Should I have tied him to the bedpost at night? Is that what you did out there?" Florian stopped, shook off his anger. "Look, we split back then for a whole bunch of reasons, but at least one was we couldn't get along, so we figured, okay, we'll go our own ways and won't *have* to get along. Only right now we do, and damn well better. The one thing we both want is to help Brian, and maybe the best way to do that is to forget all our own little bitches and quibbles for a while and pull together for a change."

She listened somberly, nodded, added nothing. "Do you talk to him much? Do you have any idea what's going on in his head, or even the vaguest idea what he feels, what he does?"

Florian waited a moment. "We had a lot of catching up to do. For nine years he was on the other side of the country. How was I supposed to know what he was like?"

"Would you know any better if he'd been right under your nose?"

Elly always expected stardom for Brian—although his teachers didn't share her enthusiasm. Smart but inattentive, smart but bored, smart but something. Of the three kids, Brian was the one who talked earliest, who loved books and wrote stories and figured out puzzles and always asked the sharpest questions. Florian remembered him in first or second grade helping his brother, two years ahead of him, with his arithmetic. He just never seemed to care enough to put himself out for anything. He got along with people, though. He always had lots of friends.

"This fellow," Elly said, turning away from the lake, "what's his name again?"

"Ira Wachtel."

"What does he expect to happen? What does he think we should do?"

"Everybody's still trying to figure things out. They may just write it off as an accident."

"Is that what your friend thinks?"

He spoke as calmly as he could. "Wachtel's not my friend. He's our lawyer."

"*Why* is Wachtel our lawyer?"

Florian took a breath. "Because he's the best guy we could possibly get and has been working his ass off for us."

"You're really angry with me, aren't you? After sixteen years of my taking care of him, you let him screw up and somehow it's all my fault. Only what you and I think doesn't matter right now. The lawyer, the right lawyer, is going to have to call the shots."

"That's why I picked Wachtel," Florian said, trying to look every inch the man who'd shrewdly and confidently made his decision and hadn't doubted it for one minute since—although he'd doubted it for every minute since. He'd doubted everything. But there were only two absolutely top-notch lawyers in Mt. Early County. No one argued that. You got Harry Diggs or you got Ira Wachtel, end of discussion. And over the years Wachtel had done well by Florian, in all kinds of situations. The guy was sharp, he worked like a dog, and somehow he always managed to come out on top. Besides, everyone agreed you'd be crazy bringing in someone from outside. If they ever went to trial, a local guy would be a big advantage, especially a guy like Wachtel who'd grown up in Medway before working his way through law school, who'd always practiced in Medway, who had good contacts up there and could undercut some of the antagonism against this rich kid from Trent.

"What we've got to deal with," Florian said, "is a boy from one high school behind the wheel of one car—"

"Your car. Your goddamn Corvette."

"That's right. My goddamn fucking Corvette. Does that make you feel better? So Brian's behind the wheel of my goddamn fucking Corvette right on the ass of this other car as it goes into the drink. That's what Wachtel has to deal with. That's why I'm glad we got somebody as good as Wachtel to do it."

"Harry Diggs thinks it's important," Elly said, more quietly, trying the reasonable approach, "that all the parents stick together and—"

"You saw Harry? You got off the plane this morning and the first thing you did was go running to Harry Diggs?"

"I called to say hello, and he came right over. He showed me the local papers, brought me up-to-date. Why should that bother you?"

"C'mon," he said, getting up from the deck chair. "We'll grab some lunch and then add Harry to the tour."

Soon after moving to Trent following the divorce, Florian had been urged by his new friends at the handball court to fight back. "You got rights," they'd tell him in the changing room after a game. "They're your kids too." But these were younger guys who practically considered divorce the natural result of marriage. Florian could never get over the sense of *failure*, his failure, when things between him and Elly got so bad that she packed up the kids and left.

After he'd built the house on South Corner, Florian had driven his parents up to give them a feel for Bottleneck Lake. At the time they still lived in the four-room apartment on Decatur Avenue where Florian had been born, and he wasn't sure how tempted they'd be to leave all the relatives behind for Mt. Early County.

Salvatore, though, at sixty-three, had just lost his job in the patio furniture factory, where he'd run the machine that strung rubberized wires back and forth across outdoor lounges. He couldn't find anything else around New York, and at the time IE was hiring in Medway.

"But I don't know nobody here," Salvatore had said, gesturing from the deck out to the deserted lake on that chilly March morning. It was as if, instead of all that snow-covered ice, he expected horns and whistles, lights flashing, buses stammering black smoke. "It's so quiet you go crazy. What do you hear at night? Animals, that's what you hear."

In the daytime, Florian promised, he'd hear snowmobiles in winter, powerboats in summer. Fishermen. They'd get a boat and Salvatore could fish.

"Worms," he'd responded.

Lucille, though, argued that they weren't getting any younger, that the fresh air and open space would be good for their lungs, their digestion and bowels. Besides, the house was too big for Florian alone, whereas she enjoyed keeping a place neat and was tired of cleaning the same four rooms all these years, cooking for the same two people.

She'd pointed out to Salvatore that he could work as long as he wanted at the big factory and in his spare time could plant flowers or tomatoes or whatever in the yard. He could work on his car, like always, only here he'd have the big space behind the house, instead of his piece of the curb on Decatur Avenue, where the cars were parked bumper to bumper and everybody on the block butted in all the time.

Eventually, as always, Lucille prevailed, but Salvatore had been right about Trent: there was no one for him there, no friends like those he'd known in the neighborhood bars on Decatur Avenue. Trent didn't have bars. It had the overpriced Mountaineer and the tinkly, tuxedoed piano player at the Broadhurst. It had the hundred-year-old Hollisworth Inn, where on chilly evenings you could sink into overstuffed chairs and watch the logs glow and crackle behind the fireplace screen. It had self-proclaimed intimate cocktail parlors featuring acoustical ceilings and low wattage, along with glitzy lounges whose waitresses wore black mesh and served awful fruity drinks with rice paper parasols sticking up jauntily.

Salvatore, of course, soon discovered the Polecat, but none of this, Florian figured, would be of much interest to Elly; he'd just give her a quick look at Trent High before swinging up to Medway, where he hoped she'd get a sense of the range and extent of Mt. Early County.

Trent High was just north of town (twenty minutes from South Corner for Brian on his bike), a half-dozen cellular brick units connected by covered glass passageways. Tennis courts, oval track, solar heat collectors. "Good teachers," Florian said, driving by. "Four years of math and science, six foreign languages. Even Russian. Isn't that something, kids studying Russian? Nice gym, new pool. I'm chairing the pool committee. We raise the dough to maintain it."

"The pool committee? You?"

"We went to all the meets to cheer Brian on—Lucille and Salvatore too. First they give you a stopwatch and next thing you know you're on a committee."

"You sound as chipper as ever. Your regular old lively self."

"Sure," he said. "Why not?"

"I can't believe people are after Brian. My God, the crimes you hear about that no one ever gets caught for. You read about a typical night in New York or Washington and you've got a half-dozen murders no one even notices."

He let Elly take in the spring leaves and wildflowers and mountain views along Route 15 up to Medway, slowing down the Fairlane when they hit Crestwick Avenue, just inside the Medway line. Elly gazed without comment at the gas stations and narrow run-down stores selling secondhand furniture and dry goods, liquor and hardware, television sets and refrigerators, at the pizza parlors and sub shops and check-cashing establishments, at grubby real estate agencies and every World-Famous hamburger house in existence, plus *Ray's Chicken and Ribs* and *Toppers Family Style*. And bars. Lots of bars. *Tires New and Retread—Hub Cap City—Rebuilt Carbs—Deb's School of Dance*. And a second-floor window with a hand-lettered cardboard sign: *Pearl's Cut and Curl*.

"Just giving you the lay of the land," Florian said as he drove.

Downtown was still okay. Medway had never been a slum, just hard-luck working class, and the small common was well kept, neatly picked up, nicely grassed, lined with maples and elms and firs. Young mothers pushing baby carriages, a couple of kids toddling alongside, something you never saw in Trent.

He parked behind Lagerfield's, the city's venerable department store, struggling to survive against the new Mountain Mall on the outskirts of town. Nothing was open on Sunday, so the sidewalks were deserted. He showed Elly the vaulted three-story façade of Medway First National, then led her into the tiled vestibule of the office building next to it. "Nice, eh? Old but a good address, with classy touches, right here in the busy hub of the only city in Mt. Early County." He gestured toward the chandelier, gilt mirror, leaded glass light fixtures. He led her up the marble steps, worn into smooth depressions in the center, to the first floor, the banister a little sticky to the touch.

She made a face when they got off the elevator in front of the clouded glass door:

IRA G. WACHTEL
Attorney at Law

"Great," she muttered sourly.

"Can't tell the players without a scorecard."

"It's Sunday afternoon."

"I told you he was working hard for us."

"For you," she said.

Florian guided Elly into the empty reception room, bringing out a quizzical Wachtel from the inner office. "I thought I heard something. What's up, Flo?"

Florian tried to see Wachtel through Elly's eyes: a good age, early forties, but his middling size probably a drawback. Elly appreciated *presence* in a man, shoulders, height, impressiveness of brow. Still, Ira Wachtel was no candy ass. No John Wayne either, but steady, steady, with no-nonsense wire-frame glasses and the eyes of a man not used to making a fool of himself. Florian also counted heavily on the button-down shirt, the quiet tie, the walnut brown suit with red flecks and, as he was sure Elly would guess, the right label inside—all this on a Sunday after-noon, working alone in his office.

"This is Elly, Brian's mother."

Wachtel carried it off without a flutter. "I'm pleased to meet you."

"We have to run," Florian said, which did throw Wachtel. "I just wanted you two to say hello." He hustled Elly out the door and past the elevator and down the single flight of metal-tipped stairs, not wanting to give her or Wachtel the chance to start jawing at each other.

When they'd started going together, Florian couldn't figure out why someone as blond and suburban as Eleanor Lund wanted anything to do with a *swarthy* (her parents' term) curly-haired wop from a part of the Bronx no better than Medway was now. He was twenty-one and four years out of school; he'd held three jobs and had just set up his first business, selling sandwiches and Danish at construction sites in Queens. He was making good money and even began drawing coffee-break cus-tomers from nearby offices, including this blond suburban coed studying art at Queens College and working part-time for a local ad agency. Only later did he figure out that where he came from, how he looked and talked, even how he earned his living, were not problems for Elly but attractions.

"Why were you afraid to let me talk to him?" Elly said as he drove back along Crestwick Avenue, out into the countryside again.

"I figured you were tired and would go for a simple hello. One more brief stop, okay?"

"You're treating me like a goddamn baby," she said. "Yanking me around by the hand and showing me where the potty is. This from the guy who a half hour ago tells me how hard we should try to get along."

Stung, knowing she was right, Florian said, "I'm sorry. I just wanted to give you a feel of the place. Those dead kids were from Medway, and the kids being investigated are from Trent. I wasn't sure you understood that, flying in from Walnut Creek."

"Harry Diggs explained it all to me quite well."

Driving into Trent, Florian headed for the Mountaineer Lounge. It was one of the local hot spots during the season, but Harry Diggs had his own table year-round, favoring the establishment first of all for its location, a few doors down from his home and office in the big colonial on Elderberry Street.

Years ago the Diggs house had been one of the premier showcases in town, but these days it needed work: the dead lawn, the lopsided porch steps, the streaked and whitish blue siding. Harry's widowed mother, Mrs. Wilhelmina Diggs, pushing ninety, lived on the second floor, steered around in a wheelchair and dosed with medicines and semisolid foods by a trusted old black woman in a white uniform. The rest of the house provided Harry with offices on the first floor, lodgings on the third, and a connection between them via a back stairway that avoided his mother's suite. Florian didn't know if the two were in touch these days. Word around town was that the woman looked upon her elephantine sixty-year-old son, upon whom she and the world had lavished such fond hopes, with the rheumy, saddened eyes of lifelong disappointment. True, he was maybe the second-best lawyer in the westernmost and least populated county in the state, but the family had expected more.

The Mountaineer's other attraction for Harry was its reputation as a meeting place for young men, many of whom, despite Harry's age and size and generally dog-eared appearance, seemed to enjoy his company. The group was fairly small off-season but grew appreciably when the regulars from New York and Boston showed up in July.

Harry's mother had never seen him holding court among his admiring dandies at the Mountaineer. When she was still able to get about, Harry had been more discreet. Everyone assumed it was to protect his public reputation. But as soon as his aged mother took to her rooms, Harry moved openly and cheerfully into the Mountaineer set, making it clear—to his credit, Florian had to admit—that he had never given a damn what anyone else thought; it was only his mother's sensibilities that concerned him. Around that time Diggs seemed to stop buying new clothes or sending his old things to the cleaners.

Elly stared at the canopied entry as Florian maneuvered the big Fairlane up to the curb. "He's not there," she said.

"What?"

"You want to surprise Harry Diggs boozing it up with his cohorts, in contrast with your straight-arrow Boy Scout plugging away in his office. Only Harry's not here. And just let me say something. So Harry's gay. So what?"

"He'd probably have more fun if he was gay, or at least something. Do you know what *epicene* means?"

"I'm not interested in Harry's spare-time activities."

"Neither am I. But he's gotten every goddamn break anybody could possibly want, all the money and brains and schooling, all those generations of family connections and deals and payoffs, and he ends up like a fish tossed into a pail. You can hear him flopping around, but he's not getting the oxygen."

"Would you actually refuse to let him help Brian?"

"Brian doesn't need his help."

"He's my son too. Why should you make that decision? My God, Flo, what if they put him on trial? What if they send him to prison?" She gave herself a moment, then said, almost businesslike now, "Harry's in his office, waiting for us. I said we'd come by."

Florian let his eyes close for a moment, reminding himself how much he wanted to keep things pleasant, rational, low-key. He tried to sound very low key. "Please feel free to see whoever you want, but Harry Diggs is not my lawyer, and I am not going to that crazy old house to see him."

"Not even for Brian?"

"Wachtel and I are already doing everything we can for Brian."

"Do you want Harry to come out to the house?"

"No. You fly in from three thousand miles away and haven't even reset your watch and know only one person in the whole county and you're ready to run the show."

"We could meet at the Hollisworth—not my room, in the lounge there, neutral ground. Give him ten minutes, okay? For Brian. At least hear what the man has to say."

At their first ever Sunday meeting, their first ever ASAP meeting, almost everyone arrived early, gathering beforehand to console one another, exchange stunned looks, offer theories. Even Katarina, always the liveliest of the bunch, looked grim.

Speaking from the stage, Brownie didn't mention Trent High or MORP night. He talked about "Medway's son and daughter, one about to leave our school, one about to enter," and all around her Joyce heard people crying amid the faded art deco scrolls and curlicues, the tattered burgundy curtain, the peeling lamination on the collapsible armrests gouged with inked-in initials and hearts and *PUKE* and *Chas* and *Uggily*.

"The only thing they asked of the world was a chance, a future . . . and a future, of course, is the one thing they'll never have." Brownie's voice broke for a moment. A team of "skilled grief counselors," he went on, would join them when everyone returned for the last two days of school. The students would remain in their homerooms to voice their emotions and memorialize both Polly Dunn, their fallen classmate, and Willa Hufnagle, their fallen neighbor, and each room would be visited by circulating grief counselors.

(Was the junior high having its own meeting, its own memorial?)

School would not be dismissed for the funerals, Brownie announced. He didn't want hundreds of students descending upon the ceremonies. At all costs, they would avoid even the *potential* of further trouble. But the traditional funeral cortege, weaving through the neighborhood to St. Luke's Cemetery, would pass the schoolyard so that the students could offer a final salute as the hearses, the flower cars, the caravan of mourners moved slowly past.

Medway's senior prom, scheduled for Friday, would be canceled.

Joyce had agreed, once again, to act as chaperone. Each time they asked her she tried to beg off, since she'd served the previous year, but no one else ever volunteered so she'd end up going again. Medway parents still wanted grown-ups guaranteeing the purity of their children, and Medway kids still believed in proms. They took over the Monarch restaurant, decorated it with streamers and balloons and Mountain Lion banners, hired a DJ and danced not only to rock hits but also to "Stardust" and "Deep Purple" and Marty Robbins singing "A White Sport Coat and a Pink Carnation," the boys in their dinner jackets, the girls in strapless gowns with corsages at the wrist. The prom queen made the first cut in the layered graduation cake, and all night long they envisioned themselves as connoisseurs of restaurants and hairstyles and sophisticated banter.

They wanted to do what everyone else had always done, so they wouldn't look dumb.

The prom was heady stuff for boys who might well end up wiping windshields at the Sunoco station or sweating over a grill at Taco Bell, for girls with a better chance of sewing gowns than wearing them. A lot of girls came back afterward to visit Joyce. They brought toilet water, a handkerchief, cupcakes. Oh, yes, they were doing fine: their own checkout counter at Price Chopper, an apprentice chair at Cut and Curl. The brighter ones said they were secretaries, although in Medway any woman within sight of a typewriter called herself a secretary. Most came back to show off their first or second or third baby. But they all had their glittery celebration to look back on, their one starry night of glamour and pretense before that dim gray world settled over them.

And whatever you might say about a formal prom, it was at least better than a MORP. Drollery and condescension came easily to Trent kids, who loved being bored by the very things Medway students found elegant and exciting. Trent produced the sophisticated liberals, the freethinking individualists, whereas with rare exceptions Medway children turned out as straitlaced and conservative as their parents, who were mostly white, mostly Catholic, mostly working-class. God knows Medway High had its share of drinking and drugs, of fifteen-year-old girls walking around in roomy overcoats before dropping out to have their babies. But Medway kids, like their parents, took life seriously. They were serious about teams and television and holidays. They were serious about church and work and would eventually become serious parents, patriots, moralists, Red Sox and Celtic fans. They spoke out earnestly in class against abortion and drunk driving and, when forced to put pen to paper, would demand the death penalty for pushers and "drug attics." What was so strange, then, about taking their senior prom seriously?

She wondered if Jamie Pitt had planned on going. She had trouble picturing him in a white dinner jacket, dancing dreamily with a girl's head on his shoulder.

After finishing her master's at NYU, after meeting and marrying the recently widowed Bennett Johnway, with two teenage daughters, Joyce tried to find something at Spenser Academy and Trent High, but only Medway was hiring. They needed someone to handle the state and local history requirement. How was she on all those Adamses and Bradfords, Bradstreets, Lodges, Kennedys? Could she develop units on Mt. Early's Indian tribes, the Mohawk Trail, the Gilded Age mansions, the Medway paper mills, the 1936 IE strike? What about the resident painters and potters and poets, the first summer symphony at the Music Barn, the year Katharine Hepburn did *As You Like It* at the Trent Theater Festival?

She enjoyed teaching at Medway, liked the kids, and didn't even apply a few years later when an opening developed at Trent. Benn stayed angry for weeks and maybe, in some rumbling subterranean way, was still angry, although he knew full well that Medway was no inner-city jungle of a school. Benn actually disparaged the place because it *wasn't* overflowing with all that turmoil and explosive energy. At least the black kids in New York and Boston, he'd say, sang and danced and excelled in violent leaping sports, both on and off the pavement. What the hell did Medway kids have going for them?

A year or so after she started, the students voted Joyce best teacher. She was touched, but a few years later, when the girls named her "The Teacher Who'd Most Changed Their Lives," she broke into tears at the ceremony. She could think only of how little she'd done to change their lives, of how little, it seemed, anyone could do.

At the end of the meeting, Brownie had everyone in the crowded, sour-smelling auditorium stand for two minutes of silence, one minute for Polly Dunn, one minute for Willa Hufnagle.

* * *

Back home, Joyce changed into shorts and a T-shirt. The sun shone high and strong on the lake, and from the patio extending out over the water she could see the Sunday sails and motorboats and canoes, the water-skiers and fishermen. With the sound of boats only a distant hum, she hurried inside at the jangle of the phone, hoping it might be Florian.

It was the Medway police, who wanted to come by to talk to her.

She looked down at her bare legs, at the old short shorts with the shredded blue piping, the white T-shirt that made it obvious she wasn't wearing a bra, and went upstairs to put on her unspectacular black slacks, an everyday bra, a perfectly prim striped blouse.

She took out the gold necklace and held it up against the blouse. It wasn't quite right, but she put it on anyhow. It excited her to see it against her throat. She could still feel the touch of Florian's fingers as he clasped it, feel his warm breath from behind.

What did the police expect? She ached at the thought of those two drowned kids. She'd studied their pictures in the paper, read about their clubs and activities and nicknames and friends, looking for hints, clues. Was there a gleam about either of them that indicated some wonderful potential forever snuffed out? Having thought about him so much, she now recalled Polly Dunn's too-tight clothes, maybe hand-me-downs from an older, thinner brother. His shirt buttons stretched the material into elongated loops, exposing his undershirt. And if the girl had lived long enough to show up at Medway High, maybe to get into one of Joyce's classes, what would there be to remember about Willa Hufnagle?

The doorbell startled her. You could always hear the popcorn crunch and crackle of automobile tires on the white stone of the parking area. You could even hear people walking unless they deliberately kept to the lawn. She'd never worried about intruders, but certainly the cops wouldn't hike in from Mark's Lane—burly uniformed spacemen with dangling guns and nightsticks to scare her out of her wits.

Pressing her cheek against the window, she saw him at the door, Jamie Pitt, chin up, arms folded. He was dripping wet and wore only satiny black swim trunks. She recoiled from the glass with an intake of air, almost a gasp. He *did* know where she lived. Did he also know she was alone, even though Bennett's Continental was sitting next to her VW?

She shook her head sharply and walked to the door. He was a student, a kid, and might be in real trouble. She wasn't going to refuse even to open the door for him.

* * *

So the three of them had a drink on the glassed-in veranda of the Hollis-worth Inn, among the authentic rough-hewn interiors that the summer people loved. But the tourists hadn't arrived yet, or the summer waiters, the college kid assistant cooks stirring the fish chowder in the kitchen, and the Sunday afternoon crowd was sparse.

"Let's start," Elly said to Harry Diggs, "by telling us what you think of this thing of Wachtel's, telling Brian not even to speak to us about what happened."

"My dear Elly, it would be quite unethical for me to comment on another attorney's procedures."

"Are you letting those other kids talk about it?"

Diggs seemed mildly amused. "I warned my boys that I would personally cut out the tongue of the first one who said anything to anybody, including their parents."

My boys! "Exactly which kids are you representing?" Florian asked.

"The three very good friends of your son, who were with him on the ramp during that unfortunate incident. Zack Arkins, a longtime cli-ent, immediately asked me to represent his son Tiny, and then, at Dr. Arkins's suggestion, the other parents followed suit, agreeing that it might be best if all three boys had a single counsel." He paused briefly, maybe expecting a reaction from Florian, before going on. "I'm of course very aware of your concern for your son, but in every instance an attorney's responsibility is exactly the same: first to discover the truth, then to use it in every responsible way to protect and defend his client. This is Sunday, and the unfortunate accident occurred very early Satur-day morning. Please don't expect overnight miracles."

"Harry's worried," Elly said when Florian remained silent, "that other people won't be as quick as us to believe Brian. A car zooming off into the water of its own accord? Can't you see the police having prob-lems with that? A prosecutor, a jury?"

Florian was already sorry he'd come, but this really got him. Jesus, Brian was her son. She sounded ready to play judge, jury, and hangman.

Maybe Diggs saw how annoyed Florian was, because he gave Elly a calming nod. "Allow me a friendly amendment. I did not say I was worried. I am not in the least worried because I know Brian to be in competent hands, and I know how deeply you both believe in his inno-cence. I merely offered my opinion, at your request, as to the matters Mr. Wachtel has to deal with."

"Tell Flo what they are," Elly said.

She sounded both resigned and depressed—did she believe in the kid's innocence or didn't she?—and Florian's first instinct was to tell

Diggs, *Skip it, forget the whole thing, I was just leaving.* Instead he waited.

"The first and most major consideration," Diggs intoned, "is that Brian was alone in the Corvette at the time of the regrettable accident. Second, the movements of the other car remain in great doubt. Third, there was obviously bad blood between the students of the two schools, culminating in some kind of hectic confrontation on the ramp, which perhaps led to, or perhaps simply preceded, the other car's plunge into the lake. Fourth, although the facts remain clouded, Brian apparently had some kind of ax to grind with the Medway boys, in other words a strong motive for wanting to get back at them. Last of all, the age of the girl, although having no bearing on Brian's guilt or innocence, unfortunately serves as an aggravating factor."

"You know what I think?" Florian said to Elly, ignoring Diggs. "I think he sounds like a lawyer working very hard to save his kids by screwing the hell out of someone else's kid."

"Please, Flo—" Diggs said, stretching an arm in some kind of harrumphing gentlemanly protest at the unfairness of the accusation. He was so agitated he struggled to get up, inching his captain's chair back and heaving to his feet, his large sloping chest curving outward beneath his wrinkled jacket and gray striped vest to that barrel-staved stomach. Two seventy? Three hundred? Yet his eyes were as small and depthless as the button eyes on a toy seal. "Believe me, it will be all to your benefit to understand the difficulty of the situation Mr. Wachtel is facing."

"You can talk to my ex-wife as long and as often as you want," Florian said. "She can even be your client all over again if she wants, for the rest of her natural-born days, along with Zack Arkins's kid and anyone else's kid you can round up. But I don't think me or my son want your help, or your advice, or even your good wishes, okay?"

He must have been yelling pretty good, because the people were looking up from the other tables, and one couple, being led to a spot by the hostess, stopped in their tracks to stare before hurrying past with their eyes down.

"I'll leave you to discuss this by yourselves," Diggs said with a nod to Florian, a small bow to Elly.

Elly watched Harry leave, then got up herself and lurched past his chair, almost stumbling over the leg, and threw her arms around Florian, her face pressed alongside his so he could feel her tears. "Flo, I'm frightened to death. . . ."

*   *   *

Jamie Pitt still had his arms folded when Joyce opened the door. He'd been staring up at the house; slowly he lowered his eyes to meet hers. His black swim team trunks, a glistening skintight sheath, had a small Mountain Lion patch on one hip, *Medway* scripted across the other. He wasn't winded, but his face and hair were wet, his chest and arms, his hard stomach. His near-naked body was square and powerful, his legs even thicker than she would have thought.

"I didn't mean to surprise you." He smiled, disingenuously, with an easy toss of his head. A pose, maybe, that high school girls found winning: the shy, toe-in-the-dust innocent, the barefoot Huck chewing on a blade of grass and telling charming complicated lies to Aunt Polly. (That got you about teaching: every year they remained the same age, and before you knew it, you *were* Aunt Polly.)

"You swam here, didn't you?"

It bothered her, as she'd never dreamed of anyone sneaking up that way. And of course this was the time of year for it, when the lake was still relatively clean, before the fibrous tentacled weeds had fingered their way up to the surface.

"From the boatyard," Jamie explained. "My afternoon break."

"On Sunday?"

"Our busiest day."

"It must be miles." When he didn't respond, she said, without emphasis, "The police are coming."

He seemed to reflect on this. "You mean they wanna talk to you too?"

"Too?"

"They already talked to me. Maybe they're just talking to everybody. I guess that's how the cops operate. Suspicious of everybody, right? Checking all the angles. But I came because I thought maybe *I* could talk to you."

The living room hardly seemed right for someone dripping puddles, so she led him around to the patio.

"A real nice place," he said, gesturing toward the house as he sprawled back on a webbed chair with his knees spread, his hands clamped to his knees.

She wondered how long he'd been hiding in the bushes, casing the house, peering in windows. Had he been watching her outside before in her shorts and clinging T-shirt? "I heard you were on the boat ramp Friday night," she said.

He raised an eyebrow. "I didn't think you'd be so up-to-date on everything."

"That's what people at school are saying. Isn't the boatyard right next to the ramp?"

"Near it, but I wasn't working that night, if that's what you mean."

"It's hard to believe you were on the ramp and have no idea at all what happened."

"Oh, I got an idea. I got a lot of ideas. But that don't mean I was doing anything."

"Do you know Brian Rubio?"

He seemed to be considering the implications of this. "He had the car there, the fancy sports job."

"Is he the one you talked to the police about?"

Again he let some time pass. "I mean, Mrs. Johnway, it ain't for me to decide any of this. The cops say they want me to tell the truth, so I'm telling the truth. And maybe for this Brian Rubio guy, that's gonna present some kind of problem when it all comes out, but what am I supposed to do, lie? Make up stories? I mean, they were my friends, Polly and Willa, that are both dead now. I owe it to them, don't you think, to tell the truth about how they died?"

An uncomfortable silence—for her, at least—lasted until she asked, "Do you have a lawyer? If you were involved in any way, it might be a good idea. The public defender's office would—"

He laughed her off. "What would I want any kind of defender for? I got nothing to defend. I just happened to be there on the ramp, like you said, and saw what went on. What I guess it makes me, like they say, is a witness. So the cops just wanted, you know, my version of things." He hopped up from the deck chair, clearly happy to be moving again, and boosted himself backward onto the redwood rail, leaning forward with his elbows on his bare thighs, his bare feet on the lower rung. He studied their gleaming custom-made L'Oasis "patio cooking island" (as the salesman had insisted on calling it), eight thousand dollars' worth of polished redwood and stainless steel grills and dangling tools, wet bar, icemaker, ceramic tile workspace, that Benn used maybe three times a year. Wrinkling his eyes in the sun, beneath thick black brows, Jamie checked out the Sunbridge anchored about thirty feet offshore. "I was just wondering, Mrs. Johnway, what you figured on telling the cops? Besides," he said with a sideways look, almost a wink, "what a good kid Jamie always been in class."

"Why would I tell them anything else?"

Jamie was almost dry, his mahogany tan taking on a burnished glow. He probably worked with his shirt off at the boatyard. Was that the most he'd ever get out of a job, a nice tan? Still, caulking canoes at the lake was better than inhaling acid in IE's plating department or stooping over a lathe for the next thirty years. Sometimes she felt the real downer for most Medway kids was that they found themselves more or less on the sidelines, confused and threatened, angry and hurt, as the incoming Koreans and Thais and Vietnamese and Chinese showed the world again what could be accomplished when threat and deprivation and prejudice somehow got transformed into yearning, into ambition, into drive.

Was Jamie, though, an exception? That was what you always hoped, for each one you got to know. Maybe, despite his contradictions, Jamie truly believed he'd discovered a way of shaping the world to his peculiar needs, convinced he'd end up with more than a sweet nut-brown tan for all the girls to admire.

"I really haven't any idea of exactly what happened Friday night," she said. "Unless, of course, you tell me."

"Sure, like you was a priest in the movies, and the cops can't make you talk about a confession. Only I don't think that goes for teachers, does it?"

"Did you know those boys from Trent? Was there some kind of grudge?"

"You never seen me hold any grudge against anybody, did you?"

"It's not the sort of thing I'd necessarily see," she said.

God knows that was the truth: kids showed their real selves only in their own world, as part of that teenage culture that you only occasionally glimpsed, by accident, in bits and pieces. And it wasn't only their own language and music and dress codes and hairstyles that they gloried in, their own food; more important, they had their own attitudes and ambitions and morality, precious little of which resulted from what parents and teachers tried to instill in them. The language, she had to admit, could still shock her when she'd catch them unawares in full scatological bloom. As children, she and her friends would hide behind banisters or crouch in hallways to snoop on the grown-ups, wondering what the words meant. Now it was practically the other way around.

"You know, Mrs. Johnway, sometimes, even when it's not really your fault, you just find yourself stuck somewhere with all kinds of bad stuff going down around you."

"I guess the smart thing would be to move on."

"Hey, everybody knows that, but it ain't always that easy."

They both looked up at the sound of a car crunching, popping, onto the white stones on the other side of the house. "It may be a neighbor I'm expecting," she said, wondering if Flo would have bothered driving such a short distance. "Or the police."

"It's okay if it's just your neighbor lady. But I wouldn't want the cops seeing me sneaking away like I had something to hide. I could just keep out of the way while you talk to them."

"Why'd you come in the first place?"

"To keep the cops from surprising you, that's all. I didn't know you already knew about them."

"Aren't you afraid of being found here?"

"I already told them you were my adviser. So I'm here getting advice."

The doorbell rang twice.

Cheerfully, Jamie slid down from the railing. "You want me to hide somewheres?"

"You shouldn't have come." It offended her, being dragged in like this. Why should she help anyone dodge the police? But she really didn't want them—or, even worse, Florian—finding Jamie here. "Come," she said, and led him in through the sliding glass door and down the hall to Bennett's small downstairs den. "Don't come out until I tell you."

He nodded approvingly toward the couch, the television. "I can watch the Sox," he said, adding, at her frown, "with the sound off."

She hurried through the house, not sure who she was less prepared to deal with, Florian or the cops.

A lone Medway policeman, crisply uniformed, touched his cap when she opened the door. "We just have a few questions about one of your students, ma'am," he began, and proceeded to ask them in the most perfunctory way imaginable. (Maybe he resented being left to deal with the schoolteachers; surely some of his fellow officers had more exciting assignments.) He never moved beyond the entryway, standing with his cap under his arm and writing briefly in a small spiral pad. The questions were all about Jamie Pitt. No, she told him, Jamie had never caused trouble in her class. No—she hesitated just a second—he'd never seemed any more aggressive than the next high school kid.

"A tough age for everyone concerned," the policeman said. "I got one myself."

"At Medway?"

"Started this year. You don't know him. I asked."

"I hope he likes it."

"Oh, sure, it's a good school. Did all right by me."

No, she wouldn't characterize Jamie as a *good* student. Average. His attendance was fairly regular; he generally turned in his work. No, she'd never heard him say anything about Trent High or Trent students.

"Have you ever noticed any physical threats toward the girls at school, any abusive attitudes?"

"Of course not. I'd have reported anything like that."

"Thank you for your help, ma'am."

As soon as the cruiser swung out of sight, she hurried to the TV room, calling ahead, "It's okay now." The silent ballpark on TV glowed in the empty den. "Jamie?" She backed into the hall, looking both ways. "Jamie?" she kept calling as she checked the guest bathroom, the rear bathroom, every room on the second floor.

After circling the house outside, she shielded her eyes from the late-afternoon sun and stared out over the lake. If he was swimming back, he was already too far for her to spot. No matter how strong a swimmer Jamie might be, it had to be dangerous swimming that distance alone. For an instant she debated going after him, not in Benn's big ungainly Sunbridge but in their canoe. Sure, there he'd be, chunking through the water with powerful, tireless strokes as she glided alongside, lifting her dripping paddle to lean over politely and say—what?

Back in the TV room she stared for a moment at the sunlit image of a batter practicing swings. Had Jamie left the set on because something caused him to bolt? Maybe he came from a family where you turned the TV on in the morning and left it on until the last person went to bed at night. People could be off in other rooms, doing other things, but the images would still be flashing and flickering.

She noticed a business envelope on top of the TV set, a still-unopened bill from the utility company. Benn usually went over the mail while watching the evening news, leaving behind a pile of bills and ads for her to take care of. Jamie had written carefully on the back of the envelope, using the pen from the gold monogrammed set Benn had gotten years ago from a grateful client:

It was nice talking to you.

4

Well, Jesus, he was scared to death too. It wasn't a matter of believing in your son. You just never knew what kind of hand life would deal the poor kid with everything on the line, and you wished the hell he'd never gotten its attention in the first place.

Living three thousand miles away from your kids for almost ten years, seeing them maybe a half-dozen times a year for lunch or an A's game or an afternoon at the Oakland Zoo, you didn't develop much sense of what they were like. But once Brian settled in last August, Florian was delighted to see how quickly he made friends. He went out with girls, went out with guys, had girls over and guys over, went to parties, spent hours on the phone. Sometimes Florian would overhear him out on the patio with friends, laughing and joking, telling stories, trading gossip, tossing Frisbees, all with a teenage boisterousness that had to make you smile.

Of course, you couldn't expect that right now. It wasn't even that Brian seemed worried or depressed. He was just quieter. Well, so was Florian, who had a woman down the road who he liked more than anyone he'd met since the divorce, and he could hardly pull himself together to say hello, to give her a kiss, to take advantage of Bennett's remaining days on the Coast. Only months before, just after meeting Joyce, he found himself standing next to her at a Theater Festival fund-raiser, with maybe five other people in the same little circle, wishing the others would quietly disappear so he could talk to this woman, listen to her, and maybe even, when the orchestra started up again, in spite of his hopelessness on a dance floor, take her hand, touch her, move closely with her. He didn't, that night, but thanks to her husband he'd soon afterward gotten the opportunity to take her hand, not on a dance floor but out on the Greenhills estate. For him, at least, things had not been the same since.

Yet here he was, sitting on his patio, giving the Sunday *Times* a few halfhearted passes, when Lucille and Salvatore emerged from the house, probably wondering what he was doing out here. Neither of them much used the patio, Lucille preferring to stay inside, Salvatore spending his open-air time in the garden or the rowboat. They probably wondered why he was hanging around, since Brian had taken Elly on an afternoon tour of the local galleries and studios.

Elly knew a lot about art. Brian probably did too. That was something kids probably got taught in Walnut Creek, maybe in Trent too. Did Florian get any of that back in the Bronx? He vaguely remembered music appreciation, but mostly it seemed like spelling and multiplication tables. All his life, Florian realized, he'd had to learn things, sometimes uncomfortably, sometimes too late, that other people seemed to be born knowing. After Abby Allen Oliver lured him onto the Theater Festival Board, she told him their annual gala would again be black tie. Florian hadn't the foggiest idea what that meant. Elly would have known; Joyce too. All the women he'd gone with over the years (including Abby Allen herself, a few summers back) knew more about more things than he did, and he sometimes wondered what they thought about his deficiencies of dress, of pronunciation, of cultural chitchat. At least when Brian got invited to a black-tie affair, he'd damn well know what it was and how to behave once he got there.

"So," Salvatore said. "Elly, she looks good. Things must be all right for her out there."

"I'm sure they are."

"I don't understand," Lucille said after a moment, with the kind of sigh—she had a number in her repertoire, all meaningful—meant to signal a change of subject. "What are they doing? What's gonna happen to him?"

"Nothing maybe," Florian said.

"Let's hope," Salvatore said.

"Sure, maybe nothing," Lucille said, flaring one hand. "Only maybe something, right? I mean, it was his fault, is that what they're saying? Then what? They gonna put him in jail? They gonna do things to him?"

"What do you want me to say?" Florian demanded. "I don't know, all right? I don't know the first goddamn thing." He lurched for the glass door, then stopped, stayed there for a while before walking back. Salvatore kept his eyes down, but Lucille greeted his return with a fierce level gaze. "Sorry," he said.

His mother relented a bit. "All of us, we're . . ." She shrugged, unable to come up with the word she wanted. "Anyhow, it does no good to yell."

"Does he ever take communion?" Florian asked. The idea had been gnawing at him, as if this modern up-to-date kid might have inherited such a deep medieval sense of guilt as to feel driven toward, or away from, the awe of a formal confession. "Did he today? Does he ever?"

"If you came sometime, you would know." Lucille believed in forgiveness for all except the most mortal transgressions and therefore considered Florian's drift away from the church a failing he could atone for at some later date. As always, Florian's casualness irked her, and she never missed a chance to strike for atonement.

"Does he receive or doesn't he? Did he today?"

"He doesn't. You feel better now? He doesn't today, he doesn't anytime. Why suddenly you're so interested in church—you gonna start coming with us?"

Florian shook his head; that's all Lucille needed to *really* upset her: seeing him so worried that he'd start praying in church again.

Brian returned alone and joined Florian on the patio. Lucille had gone inside to make dinner, Salvatore was fishing. He leaned back against the railing, one leg bent, one long leg stretched forward.

"How's the art scene out there?"

"Fine. Mom's napping at the hotel and'll be here for dinner."

"What with one thing and another, we haven't even mentioned school being over. Congratulations. You're graduating, you made it."

"I guess we'll find out when the slides come out. I'm really not sure about trig."

"If they gave you grades, for Christ's sake, you *would* be sure." Florian thought he was saying it jokingly, ribbing the system, and hadn't expected to sound so vehement. He'd have to be careful; everything was close to the surface. He didn't give a damn about the slides—those long-winded fuzzy-wuzzy "evaluations" teachers wrote instead of handing out grades. He didn't even know why they were *called* slides or what exactly you were supposed to get from them. Back at Blessed Sacrament, when the nuns gave you an F, you knew exactly what that meant, and so did your parents: you were effed.

Brian hadn't knocked himself out on the books this year, but apparently hadn't in California either, so you couldn't blame it on the move, or Trent High, or his mother's absence, his father's bad influence. Brian was such a tall, springy, athletic kid that he looked out of place at a desk. Knifing down a pool lane, generating all that showering spray, that was Brian's natural element—or on his ten-speed, pumping away as effortlessly as a kid who might decide one morning to pedal to Boston and then proceed to cover the hundred-plus miles by evening (although Brian, always a stickler for the truth, would probably say, *No, fifty or seventy-five maybe but not a hundred, not in one day*).

Whenever Florian looked at Brian, he saw Elly's blond hair and Nordic skin, Nordic cheekbones. What did Elly see of Florian in the boy? Not much probably, maybe only that combination of shrug and smile when something struck the kid as odd, or pointless, or beyond any sort of reasonable discussion. Brian was not just better-looking than Florian; he looked more American, more suburban. Florian sometimes thought that maybe, except for the coloring, that's how he himself would have looked a generation later, what with all the vitamins these days, the prenatal care and nutrition and exercise. When Florian was a kid, his mother would give him a penny and he'd run to the candy store on Webster Avenue for licorice sticks or glossy sugar drops that you bit off strips of white paper. Back then even the *dentist* handed out lollipops, whereas Elly's idea of a snack for the kids, to her great credit, had been a swipe of almond butter on a celery stalk.

"Your girlfriend—Nique, Veronique, whatever. Are you going steady?"

"Those aren't exactly the terms anymore, Dad. You don't call Mrs. Johnway your *girlfriend*, do you?"

"You know what I mean," Florian said. It was the first time Brian had mentioned Joyce since they'd come off the boat together Friday night. Florian hadn't thought it'd bother the kid, considering all the men Elly had brought home over the years. Maybe he was having trouble with Joyce being married, but Florian wasn't about to get into that now. "I was just wondering whether Nique feels any commitment to you or was just someone you took to the prom."

"The MORP."

"All right, the MORP, the goddamn MORP. Look, okay, I don't know the right words for what seventeen-year-olds do anymore. But I'm a real expert in the way fathers feel about their kids. They believe in them and want to help them. They'd cut off their goddamn left arm for them if they had to."

Brian had listened with his eyes down. He looked up with a smile, a quiet acknowledgment. "Sometimes Grandpa goes on about that—families sticking together, how you could always count on that."

"You sure can, no matter what," Florian said, with a rush of something like gratitude. Yet it hurt too, a pang, because it'd been Salvatore instead of himself who'd made the point. That's how it happened maybe:

things were supposed to skip a generation. And if it was easier for Brian
to learn from his grandfather, at least he was learning.

"That's why I'm asking about Nique. I'm wondering how close you
were, how she'd feel about helping."

"I told you, she never got near the ramp. There's no way she could
help."

Florian let this go, not wanting to push the kid.

"I don't know if your mother mentioned it, but she—well, she had
some questions about Wachtel."

"Oh, yeah. She mentioned it."

"I don't want to put you in the middle on all this." Brian's laugh
stopped Florian. "Okay, okay," he said, laughing himself, figuring that
for a good sign, both enjoying the joke. "I take it back. You're *right* in
the middle. So what about Wachtel? Is he all right? Do you feel comfortable?"

"Oh, yeah, he's fine," Brian said with about as much passion as a
guy picking out his cereal for breakfast.

"How do you feel about his idea of not talking about it to anybody?
Are you comfortable being forced to clam up like that?"

"It's okay. Mr. Wachtel says it almost has to be one extreme or the
other. If you start talking at all, there's no end to it. It's like a dog
worrying a bone, he says. People can drive you crazy making you go over
the same thing again and again. Look, would it be all right if I take a
little spin in the canoe?"

"Sure, get all that museum air out of your lungs."

Brian was already down on the grass, almost to the dock, when
Florian called, leaning over the railing: "Hey—you never even told me
her last name."

Although Sargasso River Highlands sounded like a checkerboard of tacky
pink houses with cellar rec rooms, the square mile or so of Mt. Early
foothills contained the priciest real estate in the county. You couldn't
estimate how much the five properties were worth—a few million each,
probably—because none had changed hands since they'd been built a
hundred years ago, huge turreted mansions of brick and masonry surrounded by gardens and pools and fountains and woods, by outbuildings
and hothouses and stables and servants' quarters, high over the conjunc-
tion of the Sargasso and Penitent rivers with a view, in the other direction, of the whole of Bottleneck Lake.

The Five Families lived there, the current residents now far removed
from the flamboyant nineteenth-century originals who'd stomped over

everyone in sight to make their fortunes in shipping or railroads or textiles or, in the case of the Thranes, shoe production machinery. They didn't mix with the rest of Trent, ignored Mt. Early's politics and problems as well as its summer attractions, left shopping to their maids, spent a good part of the year occupying other equally splendid homes in equally splendid locations throughout the country, Europe, the islands. If they worked, they did so elsewhere, in brokerage houses or boardrooms or international law offices. When their kids married after Princeton or Smith or Vanderbilt, it was always to someone from somewhere else. People in Trent wouldn't even know about the wedding until they spotted the chauffeured out-of-state Bentleys and Cads and Jaguars streaming toward the Highlands. If any locals did get invited, they'd maintain the expected silence, which mightily annoyed the society editor of the *Express:* the most extravagant bash of the year taking place right under her nose, and her first clue would be the big spread the next day in *The New York Times.*

With families that rich for that long—by comparison, Harry Diggs and Bennett Johnway were strictly middle-class, Florian a working-class stiff—the peasants in town loved trading rumors about the tragedies, the scandals, the humiliations of their betters. All those millions squandered by some dissolute heir off in Paris studying art, or on a Wyoming ranch trying to become a man, or in the hills of Kentucky drying out at a fancy drunk tank. Kids pumping poison into their veins, being ravaged by gruesome diseases picked up in the brothels of Marrakesh. Wives numbing themselves on vodka and cranberry juice watching afternoon game shows while their hubbies dallied with models or starlets in white-carpeted condos high over Central Park. Florian's favorite story had a whole family—anybody's choice as to which—sitting in darkness day after day behind drawn brocade drapes, doomed to live with the memory of the aunt's mysterious death, the wordless, staring son committed for life to some gray cinder-block institution, the suicide of everyone's beloved teenage niece.

"I'm Nique" was all she'd said when she arrived at the house Friday night in her cutoffs and emblazoned polo shirt

ETARBELEC!
PROM A SI EFIL!

and Florian hadn't given her family name a second thought.

Maybe it wasn't surprising that Brian hadn't mentioned it. As a kid Florian generally avoiding talking to his parents about anything more personal than dinnertime and homework and playing ball in Crotona Park. As for girls, his parents were always the last to know. If he went long enough with someone, Lucille might eventually pick up her name, maybe see her once or twice. But there were girls his parents never knew existed that he counted the late days with, discussing options in low, desperate voices.

Elly as a kid had been altogether different. Always open with her parents, she'd been like that as a mother too. She'd drag Florian into heart-baring sessions and interminable democratic debates over garbage assignments and haircuts and permissible TV shows. Florian didn't know how Brian had eventually taken to all that, since he'd been too young to participate when Elly took them off to California. Whatever Elly's influence, Brian had arrived in Trent at sixteen and a half as a perfectly amiable and polite kid—but also one private enough not to get around to telling his father until an hour ago the last name of the tall and beautiful girl with the china doll face who'd ridden to the house MORP night on a banged-up bicycle.

Which bicycle, its rear wheel sticking out, spinning, was angled into the trunk of the Fairlane as he pulled up to the Thrane layout late Sunday afternoon. The Thranes resided behind a spiked eight-foot iron fence that must have run for a half mile circling the estate, the only entrance a locked gate between two stone pillars, each with a brass heraldic plaque at top, maybe commemorating shoe manufacturing machinery. You couldn't see the house itself from the gate. Florian pushed the button on the left pillar, and eventually, along the curving road inside the property, a balding, round-faced man limped up gamely. He wore blue serge trousers and a brown vest, looking like the frayed survivors of a couple of once-fine suits, his or his master's. With the scuffed shoes and smudges on his face and clothes, he was obviously an outside man, gardener maybe, potting shed attendant. (Mrs. Thrane was supposedly into greenhouses and flower shows, while Mr. Thrane occupied himself running Thrane Industries, still headquartered in Brockton although their factories were down South, producing machinery for the shoemaking sweatshops of Korea and Taiwan and Hong Kong.)

"What is it?" the man inquired brusquely through the iron gate. An Irish accent? Welsh?

Florian had come in summer slacks and an open-necked shirt, which he now realized was a mistake in these parts. He tried to redeem himself by passing his business card between the bars. "I'd like to see Mr. Thrane."

The man held the card at arm's length, wrinkling his nose, then handed it back. "No one here, sir."

"Can you tell me where I might find Mr. Thrane? It's important we talk."

"Sorry, sir. Not here. Gone for the summer."

"Maybe I can see Nique. I've brought her bike." He motioned toward the open trunk, and when that brought no reaction, he walked back, lifted out the bike, and rolled it to the gate for the fellow's inspection. "She was visiting my son and left it behind."

The man stared hard. "Leave it right there if you would. We appreciate your returning it. Please use the turnaround to swing about." When Florian hesitated, the man dug into his pocket. "A reward, eh? Very well. Will this do?" He offered a fluttering ten-dollar bill through the gate, holding it by one corner, and seemed mildly taken back when Florian swung about for the car.

It was the goddamn Fairlane. No one would have dared tip him in the Corvette.

He would've scaled the goddamn fence and dealt with the gimpy gardener and anyone else who tried to stop him if he thought he had any chance of finding the girl there. She'd spent the whole evening with Brian, and even if she'd gone home before the car went into the lake, she had to have some idea what went on beforehand, why he'd ditched her for some stupid free-for-all. It was even conceivable she could help Brian, and wanted to. After all, she'd been his date and must've have seen something to like in him. It was worth a shot; anything was worth a shot. Even if she couldn't give Wachtel something to use, she might at least provide Florian with additional reassurance that Brian wasn't to blame for what happened to those kids. Not that Florian doubted his son, but God knows he would have welcomed a little more understanding, a little more satisfaction and peace than he'd been able to claim these last couple of days.

Only considering the kind of people the Thranes were, with their connections and resources, the gardener had probably told the truth: they were gone for as long as they'd have to be gone to keep their kid from getting mixed up in anything.

Worst of all, for Florian, he simply didn't know what the hell had happened, and no one seemed the least bit inclined to give him that information, not Brian, not Wachtel, not anybody. On the drive home he decided on another tack.

After dinner he left the family at the table and took his coffee up to his room, where he methodically dialed Red Penneman's home number. He hated nothing more than asking favors. Even as a kid he always wanted to handle things on his own, wanted to be in control of himself and whatever was going to happen. If anything got screwed up then, he'd know it was his own fault and wouldn't be tempted to find excuses or blame anyone else. Besides, he didn't like advertising his troubles, his uncertainties. When you begged a favor, you owed in return, and Florian didn't like being obligated. Right now, though, he wasn't thinking in those terms. He'd sign an IOU to anybody, for anything, if he could just know once and for all that Brian was free and clear, that it'd been nothing but a mistake or oversight or exaggeration.

"You don't know how hard this is for me," he told Red.

"Sure I do, Flo. Only there's not much I can—"

"I don't want you to *do* anything." He'd taken on a low, conspiratorial tone, as if they were hunched together on a street corner, in a doorway. He tried to lighten up. "I just want to *know,* that's all. You could do that much, couldn't you—as a favor?"

"Not in any detail, Flo. We've still got an investigation going on."

"Skip the details. Just tell me if they're going to file charges."

The silence lasted so long he wondered if the line was still alive. Finally Red said, "We've got a lot of unanswered questions, Flo, but it looks to me like Delehanty's planning to go to the grand jury with what we do have."

"On Brian?"

"Looks like it."

"What about the other Trent kids? What about the guys from Medway?"

"I can't talk about anyone else, Flo. I shouldn't even be talking about Brian."

"Do they usually indict when the DA wants them to?"

"Look, Flo, you got a good lawyer working for you. Go with him. Don't get all frazzled over things you can't control."

"Maybe you could just give me your personal opinion. Nothing official, just an opinion. Do you think things might improve when the grand jury meets?"

Only after another silence did Penneman respond. "I wouldn't rightly expect a whole lot of improvement, Flo."

"Thanks," Florian said quietly.

* * *

On the way down the hall he noticed that Brian had left his door open, for the first time he could remember. The closed door had never bothered him. A kid had rights too, and after having grown up sharing rooms in a Bronx apartment, Florian didn't begrudge his son a little privacy. Yet he hesitated only long enough to make sure the others were still talking downstairs. Had Brian left it open purposely, as some kind of signal? Florian stood in the center, hands on hips, looking around to see what, if anything, might have been designed to tempt him.

On Brian's desk, amid stamp albums and loose stamps and cellophane envelopes stuffed with more stamps, and the inevitable scraps of colored paper, his eye caught a large flat book with a red vellum cover: *The Round Table*. It was subtitled *A Verily True Account of the Life and Adventures of the Noble COURTIERS of Trent High*. Florian flipped through the mug shots, group pictures of teams and clubs, photos of Winter Carnival, Spring Picnic, basketball games, swim meets, victory dinner for the lacrosse team, school plays and concerts, along with maybe a hundred signed greetings. He was impressed, a newcomer like Brian making that many friends in a school where most kids had been buddies since kindergarten.

> *For BR who's OK from JJP, with Best W's!*
> *Don't ever forget the Love Apple a day—you guys were great, Betty-Ann*
> *Fellow Aviator in the skies above Mediocreville—Soar and Soar, good budd, and don't swallow pool water or you know what!—Tony A.*
> *Is their life after THS? Let's connect up a few years hence and decide. Meanwhile don't cha-cha with anybody I wouldn't cha-cha with. Ol' Benny the Noodel.*

Beyond the written greetings, some illegible, some beautifully scripted, Florian was surprised by how often Brian's picture appeared—with the swim team, at dances, at the Spring Picnic, with the MORP committee, the OXFAM club, the Math Team, the Radio Club, the Debating Team. Maybe the kid was cut out to be an undercover agent. He could have been chief Kremlin mole for all Florian knew. But he was pleased.

The *Senior Superlatives* section pictured students in humorous poses as Class Artist, Moodiest, Nicest Eyes, Class Gossip. And there was Brian as Class (Boy) Bod, in his skimpy swimsuit on the diving board, arms overhead, chest puffed out, smiling at the silliness of it all.

Florian picked up a spiral notebook. Brian had created a fancy title page with large multicolored calligraphy and background swirls and curlicues:

MINE

The entries were written in what looked like a hurried scrawl, most a paragraph or two long. They didn't seem to be school assignments, although a lot dealt with stuff he'd read: *The Autobiography of Malcolm X, The Good Earth, The Grapes of Wrath,* Jean-Paul Sartre, Mark Twain, Chekhov, Dostoyevsky, on and on, writers and books Florian didn't even recognize. *Fear and Loathing in Las Vegas? Naked Lunch?* None of the entries were dated.

Florian paused at one titled "For Now":

We say we'll do something, or put up with something, for now, usually things we'd rather NOT do, or shouldn't do, so try to make them seem temporary. What's interesting is that for now implies the inevitability of something happening AFTERWARD, as if no point in life could ever be the last point.

But isn't life itself just for now?

An untitled entry began, *It's important to distinguish between the ICONS of American culture (wealth, success, power) and the IDEALS of American culture (freedom, democracy, humanity). Universal good only results when people are willing to sacrifice some part of themselves KNOWING that nobody will ever discover their true—* It broke off at that point.

Some were short and funny:

Eternity

By mistake a housewife brought home two jars of Tabasco sauce. She put one in the refrigerator and one in the pantry and announced to the family, "Now I know there's something in life that will outlast us all."

The one that stunned Florian was set up like a poem:

What My Father Taught Me

The difference between
My name is Brian Rubio
and
I am Brian Rubio.

When Elly called upstairs about a ride back to the hotel, Florian quickly replaced the books and headed downstairs, trying to get his expression back to normal.

Pulling to the curb in front of the Hollisworth, he turned to Elly on the front seat. "Why, after all these years, did you send him here?"

Elly seemed about to bolt. Then she shook her head, harshly. "Don't lay all that guilt on me, okay? I don't need that right now."

"No guilt," he said. "I love having him. We all do. It's been great."

"Until you learned he couldn't keep his dick in his pants long enough to finish high school, right?"

Florian shook his head, mystified, trying to deal with the idea of a mother stomping all over her own kid.

"What's so funny?"

He hadn't realized he'd been smiling. He wasn't sure what *kind* of smile it was and just said: "You gotta be cheerful, right? The whole thing's a regular barrel of laughs, especially people who figure they got everything all figured out. I'm still working on my own version."

"It's perfectly clear what happened, Flo. Someone zeroed in on Brian's big date and from there on everybody was out to get everybody else. Thank God, is all I have to say, that it wasn't the thirteen-year-old in her training bra that he was trying to score with that night."

"Jesus."

"Sure, you see everything from his angle. After all, what were you doing when all this was going on besides getting laid or whatever out on the lake yourself? Don't look at me like that. Of course they told me you were out with your ladylove next door. There's nothing to hide. You got every right."

"If I hadn't been out with her, do you think it'd have made any difference? What'd you expect me to be doing? Tailing Brian all night in Salvatore's Duster?"

"It's not worth our breath even talking about that. You want to know why I finally gave up on Brian back there in California? Because I just couldn't deal with this kid on the make. Okay, I thought, maybe Florian understands, maybe he can sympathize, because I just can't handle him by myself, can't get on the same wavelength with a seventeen-year-old stud who doesn't even have to chase the hot numbers because they're all chasing him. Maybe, I figured, Florian can deal with it. I've spent a lot of my life bringing this kid up right and I really don't need him around twenty-four hours a day reminding me how I screwed up."

"Wow," Florian said, slapping the steering wheel.

"I actually thought he'd be better off with you. Good old Florian, for all his faults, could at least teach the kid a few tricks about staying out of trouble. Wasn't that some bull's-eye?"

"Yeah," Florian said. "Right on target."

After dropping off Elly, Florian swung out a few miles on Quahog Lane. Sure, it was eight o'clock on a Sunday night and no time to be bugging your lawyer, but Florian wasn't feeling too good about Red Penneman's talk of grand juries and wanted at least to bounce it off Wachtel. The guy was probably home watching opera singers on public TV and wouldn't mind a little break. Besides, Florian wouldn't stay long; he really hoped to see Joyce tonight.

Wachtel and his wife and kids lived in a big white colonial, with a rose trellis arching grandly over the swinging gate in the picket fence, all those white pales glowing luminescently now in the deepening darkness. Maybe the guy didn't look—or sound, or act—like anyone's idea of a slam-bang legal wizard, but he'd obviously satisfied enough clients to manage this rambling showcase with twenty acres of woodsy backyard just outside Trent. Actually, it wasn't all that far from his office in Medway, either, but when you looked at this place, Medway was the last thing in the world you'd think of.

Wachtel himself came to the door, which was just as well because Florian had met his wife only a couple of times over the years and couldn't remember her name. Wachtel stared at Florian for a while, then inquired, mildly, "Are you lost?" He was holding a book in one hand, a finger stuck in to keep his page.

"I've been running around most of the day and figured since you've probably been trying to get in touch with me, I'd just drop by on my way home to let you fill me in."

"Why didn't you ask to be filled in when you dropped by my office this afternoon?"

"I was with Elly then."

"I noticed. How are you getting along?"

"No stab wounds so far." He nodded toward the book. "Some big legal tome, right?"

"A novel."

"Hey, that's what everybody wants: a lawyer who spends his time reading novels." He wasn't angry, not with Wachtel. He just wanted to keep the guy on his toes. "Anyhow, maybe you could fill me in now."

Without much enthusiasm, Wachtel motioned him in and led him down a hallway, pausing to yell up the staircase, "It's nothing, just a client." He ushered Florian into what must have been Wachtel's den or library or sitting room, big desk and walls of bookcases and a few comfy-looking chairs. The lights were already on, so Wachtel was probably sitting in here reading his novel when the bell rang.

Florian took a chair. "Sure, nothing but a client. Attention-level zero."

"Look, Flo, you got kids, I got kids. Two kids are dead, and yours might be in trouble. Don't ever accuse me of taking this lightly."

"I was joking. Lightening things up. Anyhow, that's what I'd like you to fill me in on—just how much trouble you think Brian's in."

Wachtel sat and crossed his legs; he was wearing suit trousers, a matching vest, but no jacket, no tie, his white shirt open at the neck. Maybe he'd dressed earlier for a visit from his in-laws or someone and had come in here for a little peace and quiet.

"We haven't made any great leaps forward," Wachtel began, "but I'll give you what I got. One Medway High kid, Jamie Pitt, keeps turning up all over the place. He was on the ramp when the car went under. He spent most of that night with Polly Dunn, the boy that drowned. He knew Willa Hufnagle, the girl that drowned. Earlier that day he and Brian had a run-in at Hammond's Boatyard."

"Brian mentioned some kind of shoving match, although not the kid's name. He said someone from the boatyard was buzzing the swimmers with a boat." Florian paused, unable to tell if Wachtel was pondering this or dismissing it. Florian went on. "Brian said it wasn't a real fight, that it wasn't important."

"Maybe it didn't seem so at the moment. But through most of the night a bunch of Medway kids, including Jamie, and a bunch of Trent kids, including your son, were running around spoiling for a showdown. A lot depends on who you listen to, but at some point Jamie and his buddies apparently grabbed Brian's date and dragged her into the woods."

"Dragged her into the woods? Did he have a fat club? Was he wearing his *Alley Oop* caveman outfit?"

"We're still checking things out. Maybe he raped her; maybe he tried; maybe he slapped her around."

"Her last name is Thrane, you know. Nique Thrane."

Wachtel gave him a quizzical look. "I know her last name, Flo. What kind of lawyer do you think you got here? I ask questions. I write things down. I own a file cabinet."

Florian laughed. He actually laughed. "Good Christ," he said, "if this guy raped Nique Thrane, why isn't the DA talking about putting *him* before the grand jury?"

Wachtel raised an eyelid. "Who said anything about a grand jury?"

Florian hadn't expected to bring it up this way. Then he realized he didn't care how he brought it up, didn't care about a lot of things. It surprised him, this expansive, liberating feeling. He had only one thing on his mind and truly didn't give a damn about anything else. "Red Penneman mentioned it," he said. "We were chatting and he let it slip."

Wachtel's expression made it clear how unhappy he was about Florian actually learning something on his own. Finally he said, "The reason no one's bringing Jamie Pitt up on charges is that no one's accused him of anything. As far as the drownings are concerned, he was just standing there watching."

"Maybe if people really wanted to find out what happened to the girl in the woods, they could ask her."

"She's not saying."

"But look, if this Jamie Pitt really raped her, you could just point that out and—"

"Get Brian in a lot of trouble," Wachtel said.

"Brian? How could Brian get in trouble when another guy rapes his girl?"

"Can you think of a better reason, Flo, for your son to want to get even with those guys any way he could?"

When he got back to the house, Florian called a quick hello to Lucille and Salvatore and Brian in the TV room on his way upstairs. He dialed Wally Brown, another lawyer he knew from handball who always seemed okay although they'd never had any business dealings.

"Jesus, Flo, it's Sunday night."

"That's right. I'm sorry. I guess you heard about the drownings and everything and—"

"Sure, Flo. No problem. What's up?"

The response stunned Florian. Sure, everybody knew about the drownings, but why would that make Wally Brown so goddamned understanding? Did everybody in the county, or at least every lawyer, know that Brian was involved? How much did they think he was involved? Were they already feeling sorry for him, for Florian?

"Flo—are you there?"

"Yeah, just thinking. I'd like you to help me out a bit, regular fees of course, no favors. Could you find me the names of a couple of reputable detectives?"

"A *couple* of detectives? Flo, all these years I've been whipping your ass on the handball court, never in my wildest dreams would I imagine you'd someday want the services of not one but two detectives."

"I could've asked for two shrinks."

"In which case I'd simply assume you were pulling my leg. Anyhow, the word I hear is Wachtel's handling things for you."

"In case they try to drag my son into the drownings somehow, and of course I want him to concentrate on that. This is a different thing entirely, and I'd as soon you didn't mention it to him. But I'm looking for someone out in California, and someone back here, and figured it'd be cheaper than having one guy fly three thousand miles back and forth. Anyhow, let's move on that, okay? It'll probably take them a couple of days anyhow to dig up what I want."

"Which is?"

"Personal stuff."

"Unless you're looking for something in the phone book, I'd guess weeks, not days."

"All the more reason to start. As soon as possible, okay? Tomorrow if you can manage."

When Florian still hadn't called by seven, Joyce watched the local news on Medway's Channel 6. They were playing the story as energetically as the *Express* and once more opened—how many times had they *already* used it?—with the shadowy, waterlogged car slowly being raised out of the water like some shrouded nighttime monster. They interviewed Willa Hufnagle's parents from the living room of what the announcer called their "modest home a few blocks from Medway High." The mother held the framed certificate her daughter had gotten for regular attendance throughout the eighth grade and pointed out earnestly, straight into the camera, that the girl was "almost fourteen." Joyce never understood how people could expose every raw nerve of their being—this woman's daughter had just drowned!—for the seven o'clock news.

Even worse, they then presented Ursula Dunn as "perhaps the person most affected by the tragedy." Not only was Polly Dunn her older brother, but Willa Hufnagle was her best friend. She looked pitifully younger than thirteen as they showed her standing alone in a schoolgirl-ish white blouse in front of the three-decker where her family lived, a tear rolling down each cheek as she nodded agreement to the reporter's asinine question as to whether she expected to miss her brother and her best friend. What did he expect her to say, no?

Pat Delehanty, county district attorney with briefcase under his arm, a real bear of a man, spoke from the courthouse steps. The investigation was ongoing. They were looking at all aspects. They would get the facts and proceed from there.

She was about to flick off the sports news when the local softball scores came on but stopped when she saw Bob Manatee, Medway's football coach, rigidly formal in his PE office, blinking rapidly. "It's off-season of course," he said, backed up against the peeling wall, "so of course the squad isn't together right now. Of course I can tell you it hit all of them, everybody, tremendously hard. They're a close-knit team, of course. We take real pride in that. And of course it's sad news, terrible news. Polly Dunn made a real contribution last year."

They ran clips from last season, stopping the action to superimpose a white circle around one helmeted, padded figure, number 55. In the voice-over Bob Manatee said, "That's Polly there now, on defense, covering his man coming out of the backfield. . . ."

Following a bouncy ad for a rinse to protect your hair from styling stress, the redheaded weatherwoman reported sixty-eight degrees and partial clouds.

A little after nine Florian showed up at the door, looking like he hadn't slept in a week. "I walked," he said, almost apologetically. "I figured the air would be good for me."

"I was going to offer you a drink, but maybe we could both walk."

"Let's go."

They held hands, and that was nice, she thought; it had the right feeling. They turned left on Mark's Lane, away from his house, toward the empty guard booth. The moon was almost full, their only light.

"I wanted to come earlier," he said, "but I'm just not on top of things at the moment. It seems like there's a million people to see and talk to, including Brian. Including everybody."

They walked in silence, and she could see he was pulling himself together, this guy who'd always seemed absolutely on top of everything.

"I've just never faced a deal like this before," he said, sounding as if he were talking through clenched teeth. "Can you believe it—your own son maybe ending up in prison? I can't figure out if it's my fault because I wasn't around all those other years, or because I was around this year. And Jesus, I oughta be *doing* something, *helping* the kid somehow. I feel as useful as a kite in a hurricane."

Joyce could understand his frustration: she'd been struggling with the seeming impossibility of helping *Florian*.

After the briefest, angriest of pauses, he said: "Do you know a kid at school named Jamie Pitt?"

"Yes."

"Well, on MORP night Wachtel says he dragged the girl into the woods and probably raped her, or at least tried to."

Joyce stopped, pulling her hand free. "Raped who?" All she could think of was the thirteen-year-old who'd ended up drowned.

"Brian's date," Florian said, as if the whole thing should be perfectly clear. "Veronique—Nique—Thrane. Her parents—well, let's not get into them."

"I know who the Thranes are. Doesn't everybody? Anyhow, is that what the girl says, that Jamie raped her?"

"She hasn't said anything. I don't think they even know where she is."

"I'm not sure exactly what you're saying. Is Jamie going to be charged—with rape, with anything?"

"I hope so, although there's nothing like lawyers to mush up your brain. Great, I tell Wachtel. The other kid started everything so Brian'll look better, right? Wrong, he says. What can you do with that kind of thinking?"

"I didn't mention it before," Joyce said after a pause, holding his hand more tightly now, "because I didn't think it was important, but Jamie Pitt came to the house today."

Florian almost whirled on her. "Your house? Why? Did he threaten you?"

"He's a high school kid. I deal with a couple of hundred a day. He gave my name to the cops as a reference, and I guess—"

"Were you alone?"

"Of course I was alone. Why are you so angry?"

"I told you, he probably raped this girl."

"Is probably raping the same as being almost pregnant?"

"I didn't think women joked about rape."

"I'm not joking. How can your lawyer be so sure what happened if the girl hasn't said anything? Has she mentioned Jamie at all? Has she filed a complaint? What's all this *based* on?"

"Maybe your student just dragged her into the bushes for a friendly chat."

"He's not *my* student. He just happens to be in my class."

"Is he a guy you could see doing something like that?"

"Please, Florian—what would that prove?" But even as a possibility, the idea unnerved her. When Jamie said he'd given her name as a reference, she'd felt curiously flattered, never expecting him to single her out like that. At the same time she realized how thickly Jamie could lay it on, had seen how much he liked *handling* people, other students particu-

larly, but teachers too. She also knew how misguided even his best intentions could be. A couple of years ago Jamie's teacher sent him outside to
help get a ground-floor window unstuck; Jamie ended up putting his
hand through the pane. He took a dozen or so stitches without a mur-
mur, and Brownie sent an icy memo reminding everyone of the existence
of janitors and maintenance men. Joyce wondered now if Jamie hadn't
volunteered for the job, seeking and then strolling into his bloody-
handed fiasco as blissfully as a toddler chasing butterflies.

They turned around to head back at the Market Spot, closed and
without lights at this time on a Sunday night.

"My mother walks here to shop almost every day," Florian said.
"She says it keeps her young."

"How's it doing for us?"

"Okay," he said. He put his arm around her shoulders, then her
waist. Only a few cars passed them on the road, headlights blinding for a
moment as they moved off the shoulder and out of the way. "I feel
better, I really do," he said, and pulled her close as they walked, hip to
hip, thigh to thigh.

"I'm really sorry for Brian," she said as they passed the guard booth
and moved onto Mark's Lane. "And I guess for us too. Everything
seemed so wonderful Friday night. And then . . . well, it was probably
the worst possible time, with everything suddenly coming down on
you."

He let out a sharp puff, almost a laugh. "It's the Italian concept of a
balanced universe, of God's ultimate evenhandedness. So when things go
well, really well, you naturally assume you can't *deserve* all that good luck
and that sooner or later you'll be made to pay for it. Friday night was this
great thing for us, and now—" His voice broke; he tightened his arm
around her shoulders as they kept walking, staggering for a couple of
steps. "What really worries me is that even though I don't understand
the stuff that passes for thinking among lawyers, I have a fair idea how
the world in general operates. Being innocent has never been any guarantee against getting screwed."

"I feel strange," she said. "I don't know how to behave."

"Join the club."

"I could still offer you that drink," she said as they approached her
private road. "But I'm not sure . . . entertaining you in Benn's
house."

"Let's stay out of there. Maybe," he went on, shaking his head and
laughing again, as if suddenly everything was funny, outrageous, a weird
joke on all their sobriety and earnestness, "if we get all scratched up and

fall into a thorny bush or something, God will accept that as sufficient payback for any other fun we have along the way."

"Do you really believe that?"

"Not at all. I just ain't gonna mess with it."

They reached her road and stopped. She could feel the pressure, softly, of his hand on one side as he turned her into him and kissed her—not passionately, though, steadily, deeply. When she broke away, still pressing her body against him, she said, "It really is funny but I *don't* know what to say, to do. I know how terrible you feel about Brian and—"

"I know. The only thing I've thought of for days now is Brian. Even the possibility, the faintest, most distant and unlikely possibility, that he might be in trouble scares me to death." He hesitated, not looking at her, trying to control his voice. "At the same time I want more than anything to dump all the guilt and worry and uncertainty out the window and just be with you."

"If I can dump my guilt, maybe you can dump yours, and maybe, maybe, if we feel really good about each other, we can *be* good for each other."

She could feel his head shaking against her, as if he were saying, hopelessly, *I don't know, I don't know.* Then he said, "Let's just lie down together. Just for a while."

"I'd like that," she said, taking his hand and leading him into the trees. "That's what I want right now; that's all I want right now." She tugged on his hand, forcing him to keep up as she moved faster into the thickness of the undergrowth, avoiding the trees and spinning off the bushes, pulling her clothing free of the nettles and stickers with a sharp, ripping sound. At a small clearing she twisted free and rolled onto the ground, rolled onto her back, her skirts flaring, her hands up. Again, the thrill of uncertainty made her gasp, but he was down on her in a moment, his mouth on hers, his tongue working furiously, his hands fumbling with her blouse, her skirt, touching her everywhere, his tongue on her everywhere.

"Oh, that's nice," he panted. "I want you so much. . . ."

She was panting too, moving with him, wanting everything, wanting it all at once, wanting it again and again.

She found a single message on the answering machine: Bennett, from Chicago, infuriated at her for not being home, was coming back early, and his flight out of O'Hare would get in just after midnight. Would she please be good enough to meet him at the airport?

She sank into the small Louis Quinze chair that once belonged to Bennett's grandmother, listening to the machine beep and click and rewind. Every nerve in her body seemed deadened. She thought of Benn up at thirty thousand feet, with his tiny bottles of bourbon and his wide first-class seat, maybe over Lake Erie now, going through the airline magazine, doing a crossword, while some corpulent banker dozed next to him with his headset on *The Inner Game of Golf* spinning in his lap. At precisely that moment she decided to tell Bennett, not about Florian, which was a different thing entirely, but that she no longer had any desire to live with him.

Driving out to the airport, Joyce realized that she no longer even resented his coming back early. After all the turmoil and bickering and uncertainty, everything suddenly seemed breathtakingly simple. Did the really important decisions always come this way, as if of their own volition, settling down over you like a soundless calm?

Although at one point, driving through the nighttime mountains, she became quite annoyed—not at Benn but at Florian, for being so caught up in his own worries that he hardly seemed to notice what was happening to her. The mood passed: what else could you expect from the poor guy?

No matter what Bennett might think, or how it looked, she wasn't leaving because of Florian. For years now the marriage had simply taken a lot more out of her than she got back from it. Even without Florian, she'd still have reached the end with Benn, at least for now, at least until she could get some things straight in her mind.

They met when she'd barely turned twenty-four, coming out of the sixties with a head full of curdled dreams and confused ideas and a nagging sense of personal responsibility for universal wrongs. Benn was forty and miraculously untouched by all the verities that had shaped her life. He was also attractive and lively and bright and successful, and not bitter then, or so quick to announce how wrong everyone else was about everything. That came afterward, gradually, as he became more and more accustomed to telling other people how to run their businesses, and then their lives.

Benn's first wife had died two years before. A good marriage, he said, and he had two beautiful daughters, twelve and fourteen. She'd felt a warm rush at the thought of being part of the rest of their growing up.

She was waiting at the security gate as Benn walked through, carrying his leather underseat satchel with its multitude of pockets and compartments. Benn could cram unbelievable quantities of clothing into those tiny spaces, and yet, ten minutes after arriving at his hotel, he'd emerge looking as if everything had just been pressed by his valet.

He kissed her on the cheek. Maybe he'd come back early because it had not gone well with the prodigal son in California, or with the whores of Babylon; he seemed annoyed in that pinched, inward way he had. "Let's get going."

Taking the wheel, driving out of the airport, Benn said: "It even made the L.A. papers, and I could see in one minute what the score was. Those goddamn delinquents you're supposed to be teaching up there have been itching all their lives to stick it to Trent. I'll give you odds those sons of bitches started everything in the first place."

Joyce stared across the seat at him, his face glossy and pinkish from the dashboard lights. "You mean that's why you came back? Because of the drownings?"

"I'm just tired of those deadbeats tearing things up whenever the mood seizes them. Hell, we neuter cats and dogs and it really cuts down on the scratching and clawing, to say nothing of the mutts getting born that nobody wants or needs."

"What are you so angry about? How in the world does it affect you?"

"We'll see who it affects," he said, driving furiously, dropping the subject.

Worst of all, she truly believed that Benn felt so grievously offended by the idea of a bunch of scummy, mutty kids from Medway blaming anything on decent upstanding Trent kids that he would not only cut short his California junket but return to take over the crusade that would forever make it clear how sick and tired he was of being pushed around by whining, shiftless, mewling malcontents.

And yet she had all the sympathy in the world for Brian Rubio. That was perfect for Benn, forcing her into all kinds of wrenching and contradictory emotions. Never, in all their years together, had she felt so angry toward him or so clear in her mind what she wanted to do.

When they got home she packed some things—nowhere near as efficiently as Bennett, she was sure—and went downstairs to talk to him. He was on his second bourbon, to say nothing of whatever they'd served on the plane, and was pretty hot under the collar with someone on the phone, yelling about investments and capital resources and long-range pullbacks. Patiently she waited till he got off the phone to tell him she was leaving, she didn't know for how long, and meanwhile would be staying in a motel.

At first he truly seemed amazed, but he finally realized that she was serious. "Get out!" he screamed. "Get out! You're not leaving—I'm throwing you the fuck out!"

She spent the night at the Log Cabins, on Route 15, Room 9, and after a few hours, and a couple of glasses of white wine, slept somewhat better than she'd expected.

II

FIREWORKS

5

Elly talked about staying on at the Hollisworth until the grand jury convened, but Wachtel said that was probably a couple of weeks off. Seeing how slowly things moved, how little good she, or anyone, could do along the way, she decided to go back to California. After all, she had a job out there, her own life. Florian had promised to keep her informed. So had Wachtel. So, probably, had Harry Diggs. And Brian, who'd called regularly throughout the year, vowed to do so even more often now. And of course she could always return if by some chance things took a turn for the worse. When Florian drove her to the airport, with Brian and Lucille in the back seat, they all reassured each other how little chance there was of that happening.

On the ride back they agreed to call off the annual Fourth of July reunion. Sure, everyone always enjoyed the weekend, the barbecue, the swimming and boat rides, the sunsets and starry nights, the fireworks over the lake, and Florian had especially been looking forward to it this year because Brian had never attended before. Even when he became old enough to fly alone, Elly insisted that he had no interest in traveling without her. Besides, she pointed out, even if all those old aunts and uncles and cousins from the Bronx meant something to Florian, they certainly didn't to this boy who'd grown up three thousand miles away.

Anything you did eight straight years was a tradition, a family ritual that you didn't drop lightly. It hadn't been easy, spending the rest of the day and all that evening calling relatives, saying the same things over and over, listening to the same sympathetic sighs, the same fervent good wishes, the same promise of prayers, the same small whistling intake of air—did everyone in the family do this, a kind of Rubio signature? Florian could see the pursed lips, the rolled eyes, the shaking of the head. What was wrong with Brian, anyhow, getting mixed up with the police like that? Why hadn't Florian taken better care? Why hadn't Brian's mother? Poor Lucille and Salvatore must feel terrible.

Florian remembered the two prime virtues expected of an Italian boy growing up. On the one hand, you were to show *furberia,* the quickness and cunning needed to get by on the streets of an unfriendly city full of strange customs. But at home you'd get cracked across the head if you didn't display *osservanza,* the proper obedience and respect and family loyalty.

They'd always given Florian high marks on the first but worried about his commitment to the second. Sure, he'd ended up making more money than the rest, but he'd also been the only one to get divorced, to separate from his children, to move away from the others. They looked up to him, bragged about him and his big success, but at the same time, among themselves, surely wondered about those simple commonsense ideas that you'd think he'd have figured out by this time. (Was it that hard, if he was supposed to be so smart?) Just because you build a great big house on a lake doesn't mean everything will always fall in your lap. You still could have wives who'd walk out on you, children who could in a blink of the eye end up in all kinds of trouble. God was in no rush. Sooner or later everything evened out.

And now, as Florian explained again and again that they were waiting for the grand jury to meet to see whether or not Brian would be charged with anything, at least a few relatives must have taken some understandable satisfaction from seeing Florian brought down a peg, with his oh so blond and faraway California son finally having to face the dirty everyday world lurking outside even the fanciest doors.

Still, they took Brian's troubles onto themselves, and almost all asked, *What can we do? How can we help?* Florian knew that if he offered even the subtlest encouragement, they'd pile into their cars or the next bus or train and head up into what they surely thought of as the wilderness of western Massachusetts, a procession, an entourage, a chattering caravan of Rubios of every age and size: Uncle Mario with his glass left eye; Aunt Gloria, the oldest of all at eighty-nine, and Aunt Stella with her arthritis and metal walker; Uncle Gennario with his smudgy socialist newspapers and latest library book that, if only everybody else read it as carefully as he did, would surely solve the world's problems. And Cousin Vinny, the CPA, and Willy, the fireman; Johnny and Sal, both owning stores on Long Island; Gracie, still single, who worked as a secretary for the phone company; Bella, who married a Jewish purchasing agent and moved to New Jersey and had four kids who wanted to go to college and become artists or professors or whatever; Mary, who had two kids before her first husband died and two more by John Verano and then decided that she'd have to support her children if God took yet another husband from her, so started a catering business from her kitchen and had since taken over an old bakery on Arthur Avenue. To say nothing of Rita and Joe and George and Ida and Jean and John and Winnie and Jeannette, Jo and Johnny and the two Als and Murray and Frank and everybody's wives and husbands and children and in-laws. Sure, exactly what he needed, the whole horde of them descending upon Mt. Early County, upon him and his house and lawn and Runabout, driving Padgett crazy with kids romping and playing everywhere.

It'd be even worse for Brian, that onslaught, that invading army with a thousand questions. And yet, as tedious and painful as it'd been explaining Brian's troubles so many times to so many people, at least they cared and wanted to help, to make things better, to save this long-lost child who no one had even seen in ten years, who could have been no more real and substantial to them than a ghost. (Through it all, Florian couldn't help wondering how they would rate Brian for *furberia*, for *osservanza*.)

On one of his rare breaks from the phone, it rang. Some relative he hadn't reached yet, he figured, who'd already heard the news from some-one else. Instead it was Joyce. She asked how they were doing, and he told her about calling off the reunion, about talking to the relatives.

"Your voice does sound scratchy. How long have you been at it?"

"Hours."

"I'll spare you then. I just wanted to say how nice it was the other night, and that I've left Benn and am staying at the Log Cabins."

"Jesus—all that in one sentence!"

"Which is about how fast it happened."

On the surface, at least, she sounded calm enough. Florian was impressed, because the news rocked him. Finally, despairing of coming up with anything really sensible or helpful, he said, "Did something suddenly trigger it?"

"If you keep waiting for the big final explosion to justify it, it might never come. I guess I was feeling pretty down at the time, the kids drowning and Brian in all that trouble, and out of nowhere Benn's com-ing back early from California. When I realized he was probably the last person in the world I wanted to see at that moment, I took it as a revelation. A sign."

"I'm just surprised—that it happened so suddenly." He wondered if he should reassure her that she'd done the right thing, but she'd already run out on Bennett and probably didn't need anyone else knock-ing him. During his own split he remembered people trying to buck him up by telling him how little they ever thought of Elly, which always came out meaning what a jerk he'd been for marrying her in the first place.

"I've got a lot of odds and ends to finish up at the school the next few days," Joyce said, sounding not so smooth now and eager to get this chore over with, "and you've got that whole army of a family to deal with. We'll be in touch, all right? Maybe we can get together once the dust settles. Let's see how it works out."

They did keep in touch, calling each other almost every day.

She was doing okay, she'd tell him, but still felt a little shaky. "You don't walk out on your husband without a little emotional fallout. I've been keeping busy at school, which helps, although I've about run out of file cabinets and supply closets to reorganize."

They were warm on the phone, interested in each other, glad to talk, sometimes going on almost an hour. Neither, however, seemed eager to get together yet.

"Maybe I'm going about this all wrong," she said, "but right now being alone seems the right thing."

"Sure, I understand," Florian said, and he did. He also knew that right now he was no more ready than she for further complications.

As the grand jury session grew closer, Florian pushed Wachtel about the case the DA would be making.

"It's hard to say, because Delehanty's really playing this close to the vest. But obviously he'll try to convince them that one way or another Brian and his friends caused that car to go into the lake. Remember, though, he doesn't have to prove anything at this stage. He just has to convince them it's a reasonable possibility. The proof has to come at the trial."

"If there is a trial."

"Right," Wachtel said.

The point, Wachtel went on to explain, was that you never could tell with a grand jury, which could only be counted on to make up its own sweet collective mind. Brian and his three buddies, represented by Diggs, could walk out with big grins and handshakes and that'd be the end of it, no more two A.M. phone calls to lawyers who could use the sleep instead. No more nightmares about people trying to pull something on your kid.

After two days of closed hearings, the grand jury rushed to finish before the long holiday weekend, handing down its sealed findings in time for Judge Ingersoll to schedule the arraignment Thursday, July 3.

"It looks like they may be coming up with something," Wachtel said.

Florian's hope—beyond his *real* hope of Brian going free—was some rinky-dink charge, a fine, a few months' probation.

The worst of it that morning was the spectacle. They really hadn't been prepared for that; something that had been private and personal, an inward hurt, had become as public and gaudy as a circus. Reporters and cameramen clambered all over the steps of the Hall of Justice, and Florian was sure that for once in their lives the whole family would make the newscasts, tomorrow's *Express,* God knows what else. Maybe the Donahue show, a guest shot on Johnny Carson. Was all this really such unadulterated *fun* for everybody?

Ever since the rumors got around that Brian was one of the Trent kids involved, Florian had refused to talk to reporters. He slammed the door on those who came around, hung up on those who called. This morning he'd ignored them on the courthouse steps, and Wachtel did the same, the two of them—with Brian right behind, Salvatore and Lucille behind him—bulling their way through the yelling and the shoving, waving aside the microphones stuck in their faces.

The sour-faced Dr. Zack Arkins and his wife came with their son Tiny, a small, flat-faced, unattractive kid who Florian had seen around the house a few times. It was odd; the kid was actually thin but still gave the impression of being soft, almost flabby. The two other Trent families showed up with their kids, Harry Diggs shepherding the whole gang. They sat on the other side of the room, everybody pretty much ignoring everybody else. Harry's kids hadn't talked to the police or the grand jury either, although other Trent and Medway kids had, especially Jamie Pitt. Jamie Pitt, according to Wachtel, had talked reams.

The grand jury, Judge Ingersoll announced, had indicted Brian and three other Trent seniors on two counts each (one for Willa Hufnagle, one for Polly Dunn) of assault and battery, and two counts of manslaughter. He released all four kids to the custody of their parents and set trial for September 2, two months away.

Sitting on the hard courtroom bench, Florian felt himself go numb. He did not see anything. He did not hear or feel anything. He could envision himself turning into wax, into wood, into stone.

Back at the house, Brian went upstairs to phone his mother with the news. Florian led Wachtel away from the others—with Padgett romping along behind—down the sloping lawn to the lake, just beyond the big maple with the hanging birdfeeder. They talked looking out at the water, occasionally turning when a goldfinch or jay or cardinal swooped onto the feeder.

"It could've been worse," Wachtel said.

"I was hoping you'd get us out of this," Florian said, maybe sounding more wistful—helpless?—than he intended. "I figured there'd be something you could *do.*"

"The grand jury belongs to the prosecutor, Flo. It's his ball game, and he does all the talking. We don't get our swings until the trial."

"What about the gearshift thing? Brian swears he saw the kid yank it into drive."

"Maybe he did. Only the lab report says it was in neutral. So right now it doesn't help, it doesn't hurt."

"And the other lab reports?"

"Nothing spectacular. Willa, the thirteen-year-old, had been drinking some. So had Polly Dunn, but so what? The DA says someone killed them, and even killing blind-drunk teens is a crime."

Florian pretended to be staring over the lake, checking the power-boats and skiers, the fishermen and canoers. With Wachtel now, in all his lawyerly casualness, dropping the idea of *killing* into the conversation, Florian tried to absorb the possibility that Brian could actually be convicted even if committing a crime had been the farthest thing from his mind. Once the prosecutors zeroed in on you, anything could happen. Florian fought off the idea, incapable of dealing with it. Yet he didn't want Wachtel thinking he was too wrought up to be of any use and so, just looking for information, just checking all the angles, he asked with a shrug, "What about Brian's blood tests? He said he hadn't been drinking."

"Like Red P. said, it'd have been better getting a reading sooner. He tested okay, but six hours too late to mean much."

"Why weren't any Medway kids indicted?"

"None of their sworn enemies drowned. Anyhow, manslaughter is what Delehanty's going for. A and B's the backup. The big surprise is that Tiny Arkins and Brian's other buddies were charged the same as Brian, even though they weren't in the Corvette. That probably means Delehanty will push for continuous action, claiming that the fighting on the ramp—or who knows, even some earlier run-in between the Trent and Medway kids—initiated a series of inexorable developments that culminated in two deaths, and therefore anyone involved during that sequence shares responsibility for the final action."

Florian puzzled over this for a moment. "Good or bad for Brian?"

"Hard to say, though I'm willing to bet Diggs is unhappy over it."

"I couldn't care less about Harry Diggs."

"Just passing the thought along." Wachtel bent to pick up a stone, looked at it, tossed it into the lake. He seemed surprised when Padgett plunged hugely into the water, swam out past the end of the narrow slatted dock and paddled in frantic circles, looking for the stone.

"Manslaughter scares the hell out of me, Ira. What's it even mean? What can you get for it?"

"Delehanty's going for involuntary, causing death unintentionally while involved in an unlawful act. If you punch a guy in the nose and accidentally end up killing him, you're talking involuntary manslaughter." Wachtel eyed Florian steadily. "You can get twenty years." Almost immediately he added: "But that'd be unusual. Serious charge, though. Nothing to play around with."

Padgett had finally given up and paddled back and was now emerging from the water. *"No!"* Florian shouted, stepping back. As Wachtel looked on, the animal shook itself furiously, ears and jowls flapping. Florian had taken himself out of range; Wachtel caught it full flush.

"He's not much on obedience," Florian explained. "Followed my mother home one day from her walk to the Market Stop, and I think he's confused because she loves and feeds him but leaves him out here with my father, who can't stand the sight of him."

"Who named it Padgett?"

"It's some actor on a TV show my mother watches."

Still wet, Padgett romped playfully up to Wachtel again. "WHOUFF!" he barked companionably.

Florian grabbed the dog by the collar and cupped his other hand under its wet rump and potato-sacked it away. *"Get! Scram!"* The animal seemed to enjoy the byplay but under Florian's commanding gaze dimly lumbered off a few feet and collapsed with a huge sigh onto the grass beneath the birdfeeder.

"The mental effort wears him out," Florian said.

"Brian will have to give up his job," Wachtel said. "It's a public beach, after all, crawling with Medway kids, and he'd be a sitting duck on his big wooden chair. And we could do without that headline: RICH KID CHARGED IN DROWNINGS STILL WORKS AS LIFEGUARD AT DEATH LAKE."

"Death Lake?"

"Headline writers are known to poeticize. But Brian can go to a movie, see his friends," Wachtel went on, as if merely passing along instructions from some Higher Authority. *(Just do what we tell you when you buy a house, get married, go into business, file your taxes, get divorced, sue your doctor, die. We'll take care of everything.)* "We just don't want him working at the same place every day."

"He's not a goddamn fugitive," Florian said, and then, when Wachtel didn't respond, he let his frustration out. "Everybody tells me what a knockout lawyer you are. What have you done? The kid's indicted."

"So are his friends, and they've got Harry Diggs."

"What have either of you done then?"

"If you wanted me to buy off Delehanty, or the grand jury, or Judge Ingersoll, you should've given me the shoebox full of unmarked twenties."

"Where'd you go to school? I never even knew."

"Because you didn't care. Columbia as an undergrad, NYU Law. I played football at Columbia."

"A Jewish football player?"

"A small Jewish football player. A twinkle-toed defensive back known affectionately to all the big wop linebackers as the Little Hebe. I think I still hold the Columbia record for interceptions, although who's counting? Maybe by now some young—"

"Columbia hasn't had a decent team since the thirties. My aunt could've played for them. It hardly counts."

"It counted for me," Wachtel said.

"What are we going to do at the trial?"

"Anything that'll help Brian without getting me disbarred. If you come up with a better strategy, give me a buzz."

"Have you given up on him? Do you think he did it?"

"Did what, Flo? Commit manslaughter? Commit assault and battery? Not by my reckoning, although the old law school joke is that trials don't reflect real life; life's more logical. Delehanty's going to beat the jury over the head trying to connect certain actions of the Trent kids, especially Brian, with the drownings. If he can make it stick, make it cause and effect, it's manslaughter. We'll do our damnedest to break down that connection and toss it out the window. Our biggest problem is that Brian, rightly or wrongly, had plenty of reasons for going after Jamie Pitt and his buddies, and juries, unfortunately, love motivation." Wachtel had been talking in his standard lifeless voice, without gestures or emphasis, while intensely studying the far side of the lake. Now he faced Florian. "Meanwhile, he's your kid, Flo, a nice kid, a great kid. You love him and'll do anything for him, and I think he's pretty neat too. He's also my client, and I got a lot of pride. So let's not shoot each other in the foot. I need you behind me, Flo, whether I'm stalling or hurrying or farting Annie Laurie through the keyhole. That's your canoe there, right? Use it much lately?"

"Hardly at all. Why?"

Wachtel was already walking toward the canoe, upside down on the grass, and by the time Florian caught up, Wachtel had flipped it over. "Who does use it?"

"Brian, pretty much."

Wachtel pointed to a dried purple stain, maybe a foot across, splotchy and irregular, inside the canoe. "A hit," he said. "A palpable hit."

"What are you talking about?"

"War games. Brian tells me that before the MORP him and his girl and some other couples met in the middle of the lake with balloons full of colored water and kept score while bombarding each other."

"I'm stunned," Florian said.

"Why? Youthful high jinks. Innocent teenage fun."

"Not that—this is the first thing you've ever mentioned that Brian told you."

"Because it's of no significance whatsoever. Your dog's asleep."

"Padgett!" Florian yelled. *"Wake up, for Christ's sake!"*

The animal leaped up with a quavering howl, sending the finches wildly fluttering from the feeder.

"He obeyed you that time."

"It's more than my lawyer does," Florian pointed out.

One night, alone in his bedroom at two or three in the morning, trying to read and drink himself to sleep, Florian had without any particular forethought methodically rolled up the Sunday *Times* magazine as tight as he could. He then twisted it with one hand at each end, like wringing out a wet towel, until he ripped the hard paper tube apart. He looked at the shredded piece in each hand, then flung first one and then the other as hard as he could against the wall.

That was before the grand jury had even convened.

After Brian's arrival last summer, with three generations together under the same roof, it was as if they'd proved that even away from the rest of the family in the Bronx, even out here in the middle of nowhere, amid the trees and animals and insects and birds and fancy houses, you could still keep important things alive.

Brian had barely begun school when the divorce came through, so there were all those lost years to make up for with this great-looking, almost grown kid who Florian remembered reading to at bedtime, playing blocks with, pushing on a swing, a little kid who had been full of enthusiasm and scampering curiosity and gurgling good humor, making pleasant chattery sounds even before he learned words. Maybe being the youngest had something to do with that beaming disposition. Rather than fight for attention from his bigger sister and brother, Brian developed a good-natured knack of doing whatever was needed to survive. When they were out camping, Brian would wake up earliest and crawl out of the tent to get first crack at the little box of sugar snacks from the six-pack, rather than be stuck with corn flakes.

In Brian's first-grade Thanksgiving pageant, the kids all wove chaotically around the stage in their Pilgrim and Indian getups until Brian as Squanto gave his long speech—God knows, it seemed long to Florian— about brotherhood and freedom and planting fish heads with your corn. He'd gotten the role because he was the tallest boy in class and had, the teacher said, the posture you expected in an Indian. Elly had designed and sewed Brian's buckskin costume. Florian had lashed a sharp stone to a stick for a tomahawk that, as Elly pointed out, both he and his son pronounced "tommyhawk." They loved the way he stood up before the whole school and breezed through his speech, as if for the first time ready to reveal that he possessed potentials that not even his own parents suspected.

Over the years Florian had stayed in touch with the two older kids by phone and trips to Seattle and Denver, and every Fourth he'd fly them in for the annual weekend on the lake. Florian hoped it would eventually work out as well with Brian as it had with his brother and sister. With each year, though, he grew more fearful that this youngest child might be lost forever, until Brian arrived last summer, suitcase in one hand and duffel bag in the other, sunglasses pushed up on his forehead, and Florian learned how little you knew about a sixteen-year-old son after nine years apart, and how exciting it could be to find the whole of him again.

Florian poured himself some coffee while his mother, an apron protecting the nice dress she'd worn for the indictment, chopped onions and peppers in her scarred wooden bowl. She'd brought it from the Bronx along with the curved hand chopper, her *mezzaluna*, which she sharpened and oiled every time she used it, and the blackened flop-sided toaster and battered porcelain coffeepot from the Year One—all this in a kitchen with a top-of-the-line microwave and powerhouse dishwasher and frost-free fridge and butcher-block work station. For lunch, she was frying sausages, a favorite of Brian's, who would smother the fat sweet links with peppers and onions on a hunk of Italian bread. Lucille had been making his favorite meals a lot during the last couple of weeks, while they'd waited for the grand jury to meet.

"At least his appetite's still good," Florian said.

"What, he doesn't sit around and mope enough? He can't have something good when he comes to eat?"

"That's not what I meant," Florian protested. "What are you jumping at me for?"

His mother gave him a sharp look, then angrily dumped the peppers and onions into the sizzling olive oil. "Sure, that's what we need, everybody yelling and screeching, like a bunch of monkeys in the zoo."

Salvatore came into the kitchen and poured himself the dregs from the coffeepot. He'd changed from his court suit into stained tan trousers, plaid shirt, old shoes broken down at the heels. He sat heavily, looked at Florian across the table and shook his head slowly a few times. "What the hell," he muttered. "Brian still on the phone?"

Florian nodded.

"After we eat, maybe we'll go fishing."

"Sounds good," Florian said.

It was hard to tell how much Brian had changed in the two weeks since the drownings, but with school over, he'd seemed to have nothing to do, nowhere to go, which of course would get even worse without the lifeguarding. Whether he was the one who'd pulled back, or the others, he saw fewer friends now, talked less on the phone. He spent a lot of time with his grandfather, though, and even though he'd never shown much interest in cars, he helped Salvatore work on the old yellow Duster, pulling plugs and tinkering with the timing and whatever else they could do to keep the thing from collapsing into a pile of old fenders and exhaust pipes.

"What are they going to say up there?" Florian asked.

Salvatore of course knew what he was referring to. Neither of them, nor Lucille, ever called the place by name. It was always "up there." But the Polecat Bar and Grill, smack in the middle of all those Medway factories and lofts and used-clothing stores and patronized mostly by IE retirees, had been Salvatore's spiritual home ever since he'd discovered it soon after moving up from the Bronx. Even Lucille, who'd never liked him wandering off afternoons for a few beers, seemed relieved that Salvatore had found friends up here. The place had become even more important to him when things turned slow at IE a few years later and Salvatore, laid off, finally admitted that his always troublesome legs had gotten too bad for him to hold down a job anymore.

"They don't say much up there," Salvatore said. "They know how it goes. Things happen."

"But they're all from Medway. They're not crazy about Trent kids."

"That's no change," Salvatore said.

Lucille turned from the stove to stand over them, arms crossed. "How can anything change up there? You sit and you drink. What's supposed to change?"

"We talk too. We watch the television. At five-thirty we watch the news." They'd had this conversation before, with Salvatore pointing out to Lucille the Polecat's social and humanitarian values, its warm camaraderie and, the clincher, its civic-minded presentation of the local news every afternoon. Only right now all three of them must have had the same vision of the regulars up there listening grimly to the names of the indicted Trent kids.

"Maybe," Salvatore said thickly, "by the time we catch some fish and do a little weeding, there won't be time to get up there today."

"We don't want to change everything," Florian said. "We want everything absolutely normal, like always." His parents frowned, wondering what the hell had come over him. "Okay," he said, "so some things are a little off. So he can't work and'll be seeing himself on TV, and people'll start staring at him. That's the point. There's so much loony stuff going on we gotta at least keep everything else on an even keel."

After a silence Salvatore said, "Where's the big even keel for you? You look like you don't even think of anything else anymore."

It was true; he'd hardly set foot in his office the last two weeks. Of course, he'd never felt the need to go there every day. The work was simple enough: he put miles on the Jeep looking at land when there was land to look at. He talked to people, considered possibilities. He flipped through registries of deeds studied maps and surveys, reports, perc tests. If he got serious, he scouted out financing. Maybe a few times a year he bought, a few times a year he sold. But there was no daily grind, no secretary to keep busy, no co-workers, no appointments he hadn't made himself. (At handball the IE engineers bragged about their new computer network; no matter where you were in the world, you could punch a couple of keys and connect with the home office, pick up your messages and printouts, exchange notes with other IE globe-trotters. Their eyes lit up when they talked about it. "That's pretty impressive, but IE hasn't turned a profit here in years," Florian had pointed out, "and I'm making a bundle.")

"I'm working tomorrow," Florian announced, and meant it. He'd go in even if it meant reading *Time* and *Newsweek* from cover to cover. He'd get back to handball too, three times a week starting tomorrow. "And you," he told Salvatore, "you should keep going up there, have a beer, spend some time with your friends. We don't want the kid thinking we're all sitting around teary-eyed just because of him. How the hell is that going to make him feel?''

During the winter, Florian and Brian had become real cross-country skiers. "Can't do this in Walnut Creek," Florian would call ahead, the icy air smarting in his nostrils. They saw movies, watched TV together, played Scrabble or sometimes pinochle with Salvatore, who'd taught the game to Brian as he'd taught it to Florian forty years earlier. Now, determined not to have the kid twiddling his thumbs all summer waiting for the trial, Florian figured he could pick up enough theater and concert and even ballet tickets to keep both of them busier than they'd probably want. But what the hell, that was the local industry, a lot more profitable than IE. It was what Mt. Early was famous for, all that goddamn culture. They might as well get in on it.

When Brian finally came down for lunch after phoning his mother, he looked pretty shaken, maybe from the indictments, maybe from having to tell Elly about them. "She said hello to everyone. She sends her love."

Florian doubted that, at least in his own case, but no matter what Elly might have said, Brian was someone who'd put a good face on it.

Over lunch, in the hopes of convincing the kid how perfectly normal life was these days, Florian chatted away about the Fitzwilliam property, a few hundred acres on the western edge of the county that had just come on the market and might be worth looking at.

Surprisingly, Brian perked up. "Hey—you usually fly over them, don't you?"

"Sure, with big pieces like that," Florian said with an easy toss of his head. "I just haven't set it up yet."

"I've never been up in one of those little tinny jobs."

"All rubber bands and Elmer's glue. Hardly the California jet set but lots of fun." Florian tried to measure Brian's interest—never easy— before going on. "We could do it together, maybe sometime next week, first thing in the morning. I'll want to hike around too, so afterwards we could backpack lunch in and make a day of it."

Brian, using his fingers to keep the peppers and onions from sliding out from his sausage sandwich, said he thought that sounded great, and Florian had to look down at his own plate to keep the flush of pleasure from giving him away.

But a few minutes later it hit him again: they were out to get this kid for manslaughter, and they weren't fooling around about it.

*　*　*

A few hours after the indictment, Florian got a call from Zack Arkins, the sunken-cheeked doctor who'd come up to him outside the police station the morning after the drownings, with Harry Diggs at his side, followed by the parents of the other Trent kids. Could Florian attend a meeting of the parents of the indicted kids tomorrow afternoon, the Fourth? No sons, no lawyers, just parents, so they could speak their pieces without pulling punches.

"*Where?*" Florian had said, sure he'd heard wrong.

"The Johnways," Arkins repeated, annoyed at Florian's denseness. "You know—Bennett Johnway—right down from you on the lake there."

"Why his place?"

"Because he offered it. He's been real nice all along and just wants us to know that even with the indictments and everything, he's still behind us."

Maybe, Florian figured, Bennett simply had plenty of time on his hands these days, with Joyce still at the motel.

"Anyhow, can we count on you?"

With a real reluctance, Florian said yes, mainly because he was afraid if he wasn't there they'd spend the whole time thinking up ways to screw Brian.

He'd taken the call in the living room, and when he hung up and glanced out the sliding glass doors, he saw his father standing on the patio in his floppy hat, talking to Joyce.

His father backed off as soon as he could, tipping his old hat. "Things to do," he said, offering his grease-stained hands, palms up, as proof of how deeply involved he'd been—fixing the Duster maybe, or working on their aged Toro, which also needed some coaxing to get moving. "I just say hello, that's all, until you come out."

Joyce's expression darkened when she turned to Florian. She'd heard the news on the radio and had come right over; she'd hoped Brian would be let off and was really sorry about the indictments. She hesitated and then stepped forward and pressed close against him.

"I'm glad you came," Florian said, and when she leaned back, tentatively, to gaze up at him, he tried his best to give her a smile. She looked as good as ever, those steady brown eyes and nice cheekbones, the easy movements of her head.

He took her hand, and they talked as they walked down the grass to the water, back to the patio to sit in the soft light of the setting sun on the wooden bench at the edge. She wore a thin green cardigan against the oncoming chill, and the color really looked good on her although he wasn't sure exactly why.

"I just found out," Florian told her, "that Bennett's invited the parents of the indicted kids over for some kind of meeting tomorrow."

"I didn't know; we've hardly talked. But that's why he said he came back early from the Coast, to keep the Medway people from blaming everyone in Trent for the drownings."

"Unfortunately they're not blaming everyone."

"Oh—I'm sorry. I didn't mean it that way. Was it really bad at court today?"

"Maybe the best thing was that Brian seemed to take it okay, better than the rest of us. But it's scary as hell, and on top of everything else all the goddamn prying and publicity makes you want to crawl under a rock."

For a moment she seemed to be considering what she wanted to say next. "Did Jamie Pitt talk to the grand jury?"

"According to Wachtel, he's their case. He was on the ramp when whatever happened happened, and evidently he's been talking ever since."

"The last time I saw him," she said, "was the following Monday at school, when he came up and asked me if I'd speak to his parents."

Florian couldn't believe it. "What'd he want you to tell them—what a real sweetheart their son was?"

"Please—I know how hard this is for you, but you've never even seen Jamie Pitt. Don't assume the only way you can help Brian is to blame Jamie."

Florian dropped it, realizing how close to the edge he was, how easily he could screw everything up. He thought of telling Joyce that he'd been haunted by the idea of visiting the parents, not Jamie's, but those of the two dead kids. Willa Hufnagle. Polly Dunn. The names burned. Only what could he possibly say to their mothers and fathers? How could he reach beyond that unimaginable pain and loss? How could he ask them not to hate Brian?

"I don't mean to stomp all over you," he said.

She seemed willing to let it go. "When I went, I didn't even see his father—Jamie's. He's never around, it seems. The mother does odd jobs, cleans, baby-sits, fills in at Woolworth's. She seemed okay except she automatically assumed that since the cops had been talking to Jamie, he must have done something terrible. Hardly what people these days would call supportive. And the father, when he's around, must be even worse, because the mother kept saying, *If James Pitt*—that's the way she referred to her husband—*if James Pitt hears about this, he'll cut Jamie's heart right out*. I told the mother that Jamie wasn't a problem in class. He did his work, he was passing, a perfectly okay kid. She simply wouldn't believe me. *Just wait*, she kept saying, *until James Pitt gets his hands on him."*

Then she added, after another pause, as if each time she spoke about Jamie she had to think ahead to make sure she got it right: "One time, at school, I mentioned to him that *Pitt* was the name of one England's famous prime ministers. The Great Commoner. He even had a son who also became prime minister. Jamie just gave me this really weird look. He'd never heard of them. Maybe he thought I was pulling his leg."

"I never heard of them either," Florian said after a couple of seconds.

"You would have if they'd been Rubios."

Florian wasn't sure about being congratulated for being less dumb than Jamie Pitt.

"What would you think," he began, careful of his tone, "if I tried to see Jamie? No funny business," he added quickly when he saw her look. "Just talk to him, see what he has to say."

"Please, Flo—suppose he says something to the prosecutors and they charge you with intimidating a witness or whatever. Think what that'd do to Brian." She leaned close on the bench and reached over to touch his hand. It surprised him, and he almost broke. She was only being sympathetic, understanding, but even the suggestion of condolence unnerved him. Had she already written Brian off? Had everyone, including Wachtel?

"Even though the holiday's not till tomorrow," she said softly, "maybe you could take a day off from worrying and we could start on it now." She stretched up and kissed him on the lips, then smiled. "Maybe if I head back to the Log Cabins, you can follow me in your car in ten or fifteen minutes. That way I'll have time to pick up the laundry and wash my face."

After letting herself into faithful old No. 9 with the big key dangling from the even bigger plastic medallion, she scrubbed her face with the threadbare washcloth, brushed her teeth, brushed her hair, freshened her lipstick and eye shadow.

When she opened the door for Florian, he came in with gratifying enthusiasm. "I'd about given up," she said, sliding the bolt. "I said ten and it's been almost fifteen."

"I wanted to give you enough time to get *really* beautiful." He kissed her long and hard, his back against the door, and then said, "Can I hang around, or do you have some pressing social engagement on tonight?"

"I've canceled all my engagements for the evening. The next thing on my schedule is a bon voyage lunch Monday with a friend from school. She spends her summers in Europe."

"You teachers sure have it rough. Go, go, go, around the clock, twelve months a year." Slowly he began unbuttoning her blouse. "All those books. Those complicated seating plans. Those inky initials gouged into desks."

She didn't laugh, didn't even smile. She stood perfectly still, staring at him, and after a moment his expression disintegrated.

In bed she pulled him close, could feel his breath on her breasts, could feel the knotted tension in his shoulders, his back. "Let me hold you," she said.

He gulped for breath, unable to speak.

They'd left a small light on, and she studied his face as she brought up his head to put her cheek against his. "It's all right," she said as he remained motionless. "We don't have to do anything. I'm just glad to be with you." He made a little shrugging movement that she could feel against her. "Look," she whispered, "that's not why we're here—for a romp with the lady in Number Nine."

"It'd be more fun if we were."

She could feel his hand, surprisingly cold, on her back. Slowly, lightly, he moved it in circles.

"That's nice," she whispered. "It's nice having you here." She wished she could discover some marvelous thing to do, some way of holding him so tight, so long and breathlessly, that it would make everything else go away. For both of them.

"I feel like I'm letting you down," he said.

"That makes it sound like I'm putting demands on you. I'm not. We're together. Let's not worry about anything else."

"Okay," he said. His voice had thickened, as if he were about to drop off any second, and she realized how exhausted he must be. It was still early evening.

"I don't know where the hell I am," he went on. "I'm scared to death for Brian and feel absolutely helpless, which is no combination at all. I wish I could just start all over again and somehow save those poor kids that drowned, save Brian, and then we could all go on with our lives. Something like this just jams a bootheel onto your neck and says,

This is my show. I call the shots. You don't do anything or take one single goddamn breath without thinking of me.

She sat up, wriggling free of the sheet to lean back against the pillow and the bedboard, so that she could look down at him. He was turned toward her, his elbow digging into the mattress, and she could see the hurt in his eyes. She pulled his head gently against her. Eventually, after a long silence, she fell asleep too.

In the morning she wakened with the sun, but even the blaze of yellow window shades depressed her, and she could feel it, the world she'd made for herself, descending once again.

They both got up, showered, dressed. She sat on the bed, Florian in the chair.

"Some pair," she said, trying for lightness, giving them a chance to ease up. "A coupla real trendsetters."

But this only made him apologetic. "I'm sorry the way I went on. You've got enough problems of your own."

"I'm going to have to see Bennett," she said after a moment. "I need more clothes than the few things I grabbed on the way out back then." She could have added, but didn't: *Don't you see what's happening? Benn's done with. Gone. The past. And maybe, maybe, real maybe, you might be the future. But right now the present is a dreary room in a dreary motel—how's that for sitting pretty?*

Florian kissed her and kept his arms around her until she could feel the tears welling in her eyes. She leaned back and wiped them away before looking up at him.

"Let's make it easy for each other, all right?" she said. "We'll get together if it feels right and not if it feels wrong or just makes things harder for either of us. This meeting with Bennett tonight—are you all invited then to stay for the fireworks?"

"Oh, no. It's for five."

"I'll call first to make sure you're gone before I come for my stuff. I hope it goes well, for all of you."

As part of his determined effort to get things looking normal again, Florian drove up to handball courts in Medway for a noon game of cutthroat with two engineers from IE who had the day off for the Fourth. He played okay, but more important, he saw how much he needed the running and banging, the sweat, the concentration on something else for an hour. It was good seeing the guys again too, especially since they were as willing as he was to leave Brian's troubles behind after a few sympathetic comments while they were dressing to play.

"Tough luck, Flo. Sure hope it works out."

The dressing room consisted of four bare white walls and a couple of wood chairs and a small bench, a row of hooks, a mirror, an upright scale next to the open door to the two showers.

"I guess Trent's got four pretty famous high school students," Florian said, trying to make it a throwaway line, "although they're not students anymore. They all graduated, even Brian."

"Even?"

"He's always saying how lousy he's doing, then makes the honor roll."

"Well, hey, Flo, that's all right. You all go to the graduation?"

Florian still felt bad about that, but Brian had insisted he wasn't getting involved in that kind of celebration. "We haven't gone to much of anything lately," Florian explained.

All three of them felt more comfortable moving on to politics and work, the Sox, the latest jokes, the NFL training camps, both while they were dressing and afterward at Mio's, where they went for their standard midget franks and pitcher of beer.

He got back home around three, with maybe an hour to kill before getting to Bennett's, but Lucille told him he'd gotten a call from someone whose name she carefully wrote down but who wouldn't tell her why he was calling. She handed him the scrap of paper.

It was the East Coast detective that Wally Brown had dug up for him.

Florian showed up right on time, driving the Fairlane to Bennett's even though it was only down the road; he wanted to get moving as soon as the damn thing was over but was in such a rush to leave that he was the first to arrive. Everything about the meeting seemed wrong. Florian had never been a joiner and wasn't eager to become part of some kind of grieved parents club. He appreciated that they all were as determined to help their kids as he was to help his, but that wasn't necessarily reassuring, especially since the others were comfortably under the wing of Harry Diggs. Nor did he like Bennett Johnway anointing himself gracious host and honorary father.

Bennett came to the door and grabbed Florian's hand, put his other hand on Florian's shoulder, spoke hoarsely, as grim and determined as Florian had ever seen him. An act? A real, although surprising, show of sympathy? "I guess all we can do, Flo, is hope the hell things work out.

Isn't that for the birds, though? You do your kid a favor, toss him the car keys for his big night out, and what the hell happens?"

Florian pulled free of Bennett's hand. "I only came," he said without a second's hesitation, "to say I can't stay. Something's come up." He felt better already. If the first thing out of Bennett's mouth was Brian behind the wheel of the Corvette, there was no way this afternoon would improve. He should have followed his instincts—always follow your instincts—and stayed away.

"Ah, that's too bad," Bennett said, not seeming all that disappointed. "The truth is I invited you early so we'd have a chance to talk about something else first. You at least got a few minutes, haven't you?"

Oh, shit, here it comes. He's found out.

"Scotch, right? C'mon, we'll sit outside."

Outside was obviously where the meeting would be, by the wet bar, with platters of goodies around, plenty of glasses, ice buckets, sun umbrellas on the only patio on South Corner built on stilts over the water. The lake was crowded with holiday boaters and skiers, and Florian could hear the swells rolling and flapping beneath the redwood planks, like waves surging into a cave. Maybe fifty feet away Bennett's Sierra Sunbridge gently rose and dipped.

And this was the weekend the whole family should have been here, the weekend for feeding and putting up everyone, for renting canopies and tents and catamarans, for seeing the old dodderers for what could always be the last time, for meeting the new husbands and wives, the new nieces and nephews, for kidding one another and fanning the charcoal and trying to entice the goddamn beer out of the keg as something other than pure 100 percent foam. Only what the hell was he doing? He was killing time with someone he didn't like, confident that whatever the guy had in store for him, it was nothing good, and could be something really bad.

"I love getting out on it," Bennett said when he noticed Florian giving his yacht the once-over.

It was a piece of work, all right, the Sierra, with a horseshoe of cushioned seats and a glassed-in cabin, probably teak-lined interiors, custom fabrics, brass instrument panel. But it belonged on Cape Cod, Upper Michigan, Long Island Sound. On South Corner, with three miles of lake, a boat this big and fast and expensive really didn't say the sort of thing about you that Bennett clearly thought it did.

Bennett busied himself fixing their drinks, and Florian watched closely, trying to read his mood, getting ready with the snappy answers if Bennett put the cards on the table about Joyce.

Bennett was shorter than Florian and thick through the body and arms, although with small pinkish hands. Normally a three-piece-suit man, with silk shirts and handmade ties, Bennett was at home today in European-tailored slacks and sport shirt. From his straw-colored hair and roundish face, from those shrewd but somehow *untested* eyes, Bennett Johnway looked like a man who'd surely made himself richer on his own but had just as surely been at least a little bit rich the moment he was born.

"I know what a blow those indictments must be, and just want you to know we're behind you one hundred percent. What gets me is the way people think we can buy our way out of anything, when God knows the grand jury proved just the opposite. And do you really think we'll ever get twelve trial jurors that'll be any fairer? Who gets on juries? Bankers and businessmen? People who can at least read and write and have some stake in the community? No. Shoemakers get on. Cleaning ladies. Laid-off machinists and retired garbage collectors, jazzbo car washers, that's who gets on. Five-and-dime clerks and bus drivers and tiddly little gray-haired biddies from checkout counters. You think those people are ever, ever, going to give you and me or our kids a break? Don't make me laugh."

Bennett sounded awfully angry, and Florian wondered if maybe Joyce had left behind a husband so bitter he was flailing out in all directions.

"You said you wanted to talk about something else."

"Sure, I can see you're anxious to leave."

"Very anxious," Florian said, and then decided to get right to the only point that concerned him: "I thought maybe your wife would be here, since it's sort of a family get-together."

Bennett shook off the idea. "She's visiting her sister on Long Island." He paused, as if to see how Florian was taking this. "Between you and me, things aren't all that rosy between us these days. You know how it goes."

Florian waited for him to go on. He and Bennett had never discussed anything even remotely personal.

"It was one real surprise, let me tell you. There I was, busting ass to get back, because those dead kids could've come right from her own classroom for all I knew, and no matter what you or I may think of that crowd up there, Joyce can get soppy over anything from a lost puppy on up."

A lost puppy? Two kids dead?

"So I fly back to make it easier for her, and what does she do? She packs a few bags, grabs her curlers, and takes off. Ta-ta. Bye-bye. Sayonara, old pal." Bennett shook his head, once, mouth pulled back, as if still trying to figure out the perverse logic of it all, the awful dynamics. "Anyhow, this is between us, okay? It'll probably blow over once she gets her head back on straight."

"Was this what you wanted to talk about?"

"No," Bennett said, finishing his drink and repairing to the wet bar for another.

Relieved, Florian nursed his drink, thinking of the drive ahead.

"I know how stressed out you must be and feel funny even bringing this up," Bennett said when he returned to his chair, "but remember that little venture I mentioned a while back?"

"I remember. Blackberry Hollow." At the time Florian was sure Bennett was trying to trying to save his own ass by carving one very large chunk out of Florian's.

"I just wanted to take advantage of your expertise in the real estate world."

"Only raw land," Florian said. "Acreage. Virgin forest."

"Anyhow, we're in a bit of a temporary bind."

"Sorry to hear that."

"The only reason I got involved was I figured I'm pushing sixty soon, and a one-man dog-and-pony show out of a briefcase isn't something you can leave behind."

"I always figured you did real well."

"I always have. But if you think of your wife, your daughters, there's nothing in it for them. So Blackberry Hollow looked tempting, promising, and when I couldn't swing what was needed on my own, I got a few others to come in. We're not talking the national debt, but for some people it was pretty big money. Still, we're short on capital and have to stem the outgo to give it a chance to catch on, and then with the right mix we could still clean up."

"I don't know," Florian said, and added, "I hope so."

"More than anything we need the right person taking charge. I mean, all of us, this isn't our field. We just wanted to set something up for our families."

"We should've talked more back then," Florian said. He wanted to leave, to start driving.

"I thought maybe we could get together after the trial and everything," Bennett said, "because we all thought that with your touch you might be the answer."

"I only handle raw land," Florian said. "Acreage."

"Virgin forests," Bennett said, looking pretty downcast. "I get it. Anyhow, if at some point you'd take another look at Blackberry Hollow, I'd certainly appreciate it."

"I'll get back to you. No promises, though."

The doorbell rang inside, and they both got up. Bennett put a hand on Florian's arm. "You know," he said, his brow furrowed in the sunlight, "maybe it's my imagination, but I got a hunch Joyce somehow got a whiff of money trouble and figured it might be a good time to look for greener pastures."

"You really think that?"

"Just a hunch," Bennett said, heading inside now, Florian following. "You never know with women, do you?"

Zack Arkins and his wife stood outside the door; Florian hurried past them to his car, leaving Bennett to make the excuses.

6

Joyce usually looked forward to July Fourth and the official beginning of the season, when she would be free of school and could savor her own choices from all the offerings that turned Mt. Early County into such a hotbed of unabashed culture. The Memorial Shell presented outdoor concerts, both Trent and Darby had professional ballet companies, and the county as a whole became temporary home to scores of painters, sculptors, potters, macramé artists, glassblowers, wood-carvers, all ready to throw open their studios to anyone willing to tromp through the wood chips and paint splatters and clay dust while displaying at least a feigned interest in buying. And then, in addition to the summer stock companies, there was the Trent Theater Festival, Joyce's favorite and the granddaddy of Mt. Early's summer attractions.

At the moment, though, the prospects looked flat and unappealing.

Shortly after Florian left, she picked up an *Express* from the vending machine in front of the attached café. Standing on the sidewalk, she shook her head over the banner headline and front-page pictures of Brian and his three friends. Did anybody, even the prosecutor, believe that they were actually *trying* to kill that boy and girl?

The maximum penalty for manslaughter, the paper said, was twenty years.

When she called, Benn suggested eight o'clock as a good time to come. He didn't seem angry, or even surprised, although they'd barely talked since she'd left. "Sure, take whatever you want. That's fine."

Dusk was deepening as she drove past the vacant guard booth onto Mark's Lane, then down their twisting driveway, parking next to Benn's Lincoln on the crunching white stones. Wearing slacks and a sport shirt, Benn stood silhouetted by the vestibule lights in the open doorway, watching her approach. She was astounded by the *objectivity* she felt, as if seeing some acquaintance after years apart. She was almost coolly aware of the glistening crescent of scalp exposed by his receding hair, of the thickness of his jowls, the thin straight line of his mouth. *This is Benn,* she had to tell herself. *This man is my husband.*

"Hello," he said, his voice hard, his look hard. "Come in."

In a way he almost sounded as if he'd been expecting someone else, although surely not another woman. Despite his flings on the road, she'd never suspected him at home. It was as if she'd conceded him his freedom everywhere else for first dibs in Mt. Early County.

She walked into the living room incredibly conscious of her steps; how disorienting, being politely ushered into a house you'd decorated and furnished and taken care of for years. Turning away from the small tufted chair, *her* chair, she faced Benn coming in behind her. She kept her shoulders straight, her head up. She could have been a visiting nurse, an Avon lady, a neighbor collecting to cure cancer, protect the environment, support liberal candidates. Never having imagined this sensation, she realized how truly unprepared she was to deal with Benn right now. She'd counted on being competent and focused, not overwhelmed by a rush of unexpected images.

"How're you doing?" he asked.

"Fine. And you?"

"Terrific. No complaints at all."

"I'm just here, as I mentioned, to pick up some things." She wanted that clear from the beginning, so he wouldn't for an instant misinterpret her motives.

"Sure, go ahead." He sounded, naturally, as if it were all her fault, bringing this sadness upon them, whereas he, the innocent bystander, had no choice but to grit his teeth and suffer. She'd expected more: sarcasm, fury, accusations.

"How's everything else going?" she asked.

"Just fine. Everything else is just hunky-dory."

Upstairs, alone in their bedroom, not even glancing at the king-size bed, she quickly filled three small valises with blouses and skirts and sweaters and summer dresses. She dropped some unboxed shoes into a plastic bag and underwear and odds and ends into her Mt. Early Music Barn tote bag and was ready, anxious, to get out. Then she heard a car crunching, stones popping, in the parking area, the front bell, the door opening and shutting. She couldn't hear voices.

She thought of Jamie Pitt hiding from the police before running off. She wasn't about to hide but was ready to sneak out the side door with her valises.

Benn called up the stairway. "Joyce—got a minute?"

She walked down slowly, again eerily uncertain as to how to play her entrance—a guest, a hostess greeting a guest?

Harry Diggs got up heavily, an effort, from the couch and offered her a small bow. "Happy Nation's Birthday." He enunciated fastidiously, as always, and wore the usual rumpled suit, the inevitable white carnation.

"Have you come for the fireworks?" she asked, knowing they couldn't be seen from his house in the center of Trent. She also knew that Harry Diggs was practically the Typhoid Mary of the divorce courts. Wherever he appeared, you could expect a contentious breakup soon after. Was that why Benn wanted her to come at this time, to let her know he had options too, with his ever-willing lawyer ready to handle the sticky details?

"Harry's here to talk about the drownings."

She wasn't wholly convinced, although she knew that Harry was defending some of the Trent boys and that he and Benn had been close for a long time. Years ago, when Harry's drinking had gotten out of hand, Benn was the one friend who didn't give up, who worked with him, got him to pay attention, who saved not only his career but probably his life too. Not that Harry qualified as an AA success story. He still drank far more than he should, ate far more than he should, had the blood pressure of a steam boiler. But at least he was no longer falling down on the street or embarrassing himself in court.

"The parents got together here this afternoon," Benn said. "No big news or anything, just mainly closing ranks for the long haul."

She nodded but said nothing, wondering how Florian had fared.

"Joyce here," Benn said to Harry, "had Jamie Pitt in class."

"So I understand," Diggs said. "How would you characterize him, Mrs. Johnway?"

"Like the rest of the kids. Nothing special."

"He's the heart and soul of the prosecution's case, you know."

Again she remained silent.

"Do you know him well enough to have some idea how . . . trustworthy . . . he would be as a witness?"

"You mean, do I think he'd lie under oath?"

"She's very defensive about those kids," Benn said, as if excusing her for some incurable disease. "She thinks they're the salt of the earth."

"It's not simply a question of lying," Diggs explained. "We wonder about his dependability, his conviction, even his verbal facility. Twelve good and fair jurors will be listening very closely to what he says, and we wonder how quick they will be to give him credence."

Did he really think she'd formed an opinion about Jamie Pitt's dependability and conviction, about his *credence,* for God's sake? "Benn's right," she said, "you can't trust me about those kids up there."

Diggs glanced at Benn, as if for some sign as to how he should continue, and maybe saw something helpful in Benn's look. "Right now we're preparing for all eventualities," Diggs said. "And each defendant, of course, will have his own story to tell."

"Do they have honest faces?" Joyce asked. "The kind of verbal facility that'll sweep the jury off its feet?"

"One would certainly hope so," Harry said, pleasantly enough. "And having gotten to know those boys quite well these past two weeks, I can certainly vouch for their character and integrity."

She was aware of Harry's heavy-lidded eyes on her and without thinking she raised a hand to her throat, as if to see what had attracted his attention. With the tip of one finger she felt the thin gold strands of the necklace. She'd forgotten to remove it before coming here, although a new piece of jewelry was hardly the sort of thing Benn noticed.

She waited for Harry Diggs to make a comment, but he went on instead: "We simply want to make sure all the Trent boys are treated with *scrupulous* fairness." Harry Diggs had a reputation as a somewhat ponderous courtroom orator, and he seemed now to be warming to his task. "Bennett can vouch for my lifelong abhorrence of the Soviet system, yet they have a useful charge—hooliganism. How can a grand jury characterize those unfortunate drownings as manslaughter, or even assault and battery? After all, young men have always shown a tendency to raise a little more cain than they ought, merely to advertise their manly virtue."

The broad inseams of Harry's trousers flapped as he crossed his legs. He placed his hands on his stomach and smiled. "Without putting too fine a point on it, surely a successful teacher like yourself looks upon the children in her care with an almost parental concern, defending and protecting them as a mother would. *In loco parentis.* After all, you invest a great deal of yourself in their development, their progress, so it's a sad and disturbing moment when—"

A resounding explosion startled them; they turned and watched the brilliant flashes of color beyond the big glass window.

"The view's better from the patio," Joyce said, standing up. "If you'll excuse me now, I have an appointment." She looked to Benn, who nodded, as if in confirmation.

She hurried upstairs, finished packing, and moved the three valises and two bags into the hallway outside the bedroom door, realizing now she had far too much to take down in one trip. Benn appeared, his face set, to block the hallway.

"You're deserting your company," she said.

"Harry's gone. It was business; he didn't come for the fireworks."

"I hope he can help those Trent boys." One of the loudest explosions so far seemed to rock the house.

Benn made a little movement with his mouth. "You really feel that way?"

"Of course. What good will it do those two dead kids to ruin four other lives?" She glanced down at her suitcases, letting Benn know she was ready to leave.

"Maybe we can talk," Benn said, with no more animation than he'd shown all along. "We can wait until the fireworks are over."

For the first time she understood that Benn felt offended, grievously wronged, by her desertion.

"Although of course," he said, "I don't have much to say. After all, I'm not the one with the new ideas all of a sudden." He paused to let another echoing explosion fade off. "It wasn't me that kept smiling and smiling and then ran off one fine night. I'm the same old son of a bitch I've always been."

"I'm sorry it had to happen that way. But I had to get out. I'm not blaming you . . ." She shook off the thought.

"You hardly say a word when you leave. Now you come back and you still won't say anything."

"I don't find it easy to talk about."

"Have you seen a lawyer?"

"No," she said. Each new burst of fireworks startled her. "Have you told Diggs?"

"Harry's shrewd enough to suspect. That's why he left, not to be in the middle of anything. He'll keep quiet, though. I don't know who *you're* talking to, but all in all I'd just as soon not have everybody and his aunt Hattie spreading this around."

"Why would I spread it around? You think this is fun for me?"

"You tell me. Are you having fun?"

"Benn—let's not make it worse for each other." She watched him glaring at her, his mouth open just slightly, as the fireworks continued exploding. She became conscious of the lemony wallpaper with its pattern of tiny fleur-de-lis that she had picked out just last year when they'd redone the second floor. She remembered not enjoying it at all, being bored by those huge sample books; maybe even back then she'd already had a sense that it was all coming to an end, that she was spending hours and hours redecorating a house that she'd soon be walking out of for the last time.

Benn stepped closer in the hallway, trapping her against the wall, his face only inches from hers. "I know I'm having a few problems now," he said, "but I never figured you for someone who'd run out at the first sign of something like that."

She felt her eyes widening. "What are you talking about?"

"I just want you to understand, no matter what happens, you'll be taken care of. It seems to me that maybe after all these years I deserved a little more consideration, a little more leeway, but that's okay. That's my worry, not yours."

"I'm not understanding you at all. Maybe we should set a time when we can talk."

"We're talking right now. And what you should do, if we want to keep talking, is just put all this stuff back where it came from and put yourself right back in the bedroom where you belong."

"I don't think I'm ready for that right now. I've got to sort things out, Benn. I can't pretend my feelings don't exist."

"Your feelings? Is that the big thing, then—your feelings?"

She'd never in her life felt this way with Benn, with his face so close, his body hemming her in, the sweet smell of bourbon like a bell ringing in the air. It left her almost dizzy with apprehension. She ducked quickly to step around him and grab two of the suitcases. "We'll be in touch," she said. "I'll call. We'll arrange something."

"I'll take these," he said, picking up the third suitcase, the plastic sack of shoes, the Music Barn tote bag.

He followed her down the back stairs and out the side door. She turned toward the parking area, then realized he'd gone the other way. "Benn!"

Still carrying her things, he climbed the wooden steps onto the patio and out of her sight.

It was as if she were unable to move, weighed down by the two suitcases. She heard the first splash, a second, a third, before another fiery burst exploded overhead.

She ran to her car and threw the suitcases inside and spun her wheels on the white stones, certain that in seconds, for whatever reason, in whatever insane state of mind, Benn would be roaring after her.

At the end of their long twisting driveway she took a right onto Mark's Lane, farther into South Corner. She saw no lights behind her and hoped that Benn would assume she'd gone the other way, out. She drove as fast as she dared past five driveways on Mark's Lane and then careened sharply into the sixth, Florian's, and pulled up tight against the trees, still out of sight of the house. She cut the engine and lights and waited in the silence, her pulse fluttering.

Maybe he was still at home, storming out again and again to the end of the deck, hurling bags and bundles into the water, everything she owned, like some crazed captain throwing ballast overboard to save his sinking ship. Was that it—fear—that had driven him to such an inconceivable display? If he wasn't racing after her, skidding around curves, perhaps he was staring numbly at the fireworks. Perhaps he'd flung himself onto the king-size bed, giving way to tears as unthinkable as what he'd just done with her suitcases.

Why had she chosen Florian's driveway? Maybe she'd instinctively believed that if Benn did follow her, she could run to Florian for protection. Maybe she simply no longer wanted to wait until tomorrow to see him.

She got out, feeling the knots in her calves, the tension in her neck, and walked down the long driveway, the dense overhanging branches screening out the rockets. The Fourth had always been a company day for Bennett and her, as for most lakeside residents. Florian really splurged, with all his relatives coming up from New York, but most people merely invited their viewless friends for drinks and barbecue, after which they'd settle back for the fireworks. It was like having a Manhattan apartment overlooking the Macy's parade. How better to pay back all those unreturned dinners? This year, though, she'd left before they'd sent invitations, and Bennett had obviously decided not to go it alone.

Even though Florian had called off his reunion this year, Joyce thought he might nonetheless have company, and so she slipped into the woods as she neared the house, picking her way through to a secluded sandy spot at lakeside. She could see the Rubios' narrow dock from there, the lawn sloping down to the water. Florian's mother and father, looking up, sat on chairs on the grass as their huge dog romped about them, howling and baying at the explosions overhead. Perhaps Florian and Brian were out of sight somewhere, but at least there didn't seem to be any company around.

Between the dog and the fireworks, she didn't hear the splash of the oars and was taken by surprise to see Brian alone in a rowboat no more than twenty feet away, moving parallel to the shore. It looked like the same boat Salvatore had come out in that night, searching for Florian in the middle of the lake. When Bryan caught sight of her, he abruptly hit the water with his oars to stop the boat. He nosed in with a single strong pull, skidding onto the shore and tilting to one side—all this illuminated only in flashes, in stop action, like those pulsing multicolored light shows she'd gone to as a kid.

He climbed out of the boat, barefoot in cutoffs and open shirt. "Are you all right, Mrs. Johnway?" He seemed genuinely concerned, even frightened.

"Of course," she said, embarrassed at being discovered.

He put his hands on his hips, but with none of that arrogant teen-age bravado you sometimes saw in the classroom, the schoolyard. He seemed to be trying for a pose that'd be comfortable for both of them. "I was just paddling around," he said, "watching from different angles."

She nodded: lots of people went out on the lake for the fireworks. Benn would sometimes take out their guests on the Sierra Sunbridge. Those were the only times he used the boat, when he had people over, business friends. "The show seems to be going on longer than usual this year," she said, although that hadn't occurred to her until just then.

He checked his wrist. "A little, maybe. My father's away, you know."

"Oh," she said, sure that he heard her letdown. "No, I didn't know."

"He'll be sorry he missed you." Brian gave no indication how he felt about his father having a woman friend, a married woman friend, fond of midnight trysts out on the lake.

They both looked up at the spectacular grand finale—one rocket after another screaming up in rapid-fire trajectories, until her ears and eyes ached for relief.

After the last drifting ashes faded, she faced him in the darkness. "I want you to know how terribly sorry I am about what's happening." She spoke with such intensity that it almost brought tears to her eyes. She couldn't get over how *nice* this kid seemed, how innocent and polite and sweet. Even worse, she couldn't separate it from what she'd just gone through with Bennett. She wished she had the courage to cradle him in her arms and say, *I can see how decent and fine you are, I can feel it in my bones. Please, please, don't let the world, don't let anything or anybody, rob you of that!*

Brian spoke quietly, and surprised her by saying, "You must feel pretty bad about the kids that drowned."

"Of course, everyone does. People feel sorry for everyone concerned. Has the summer become really unbearable for you—all this waiting?"

"At least I'm still alive," he said. "I see friends, go places, do things." He moved one shoulder, a little offhanded shrug. "It's like being stuck in an elevator between floors." He seemed to be wondering how much further he should go in talking to the Medway schoolmarm from down the road.

Joyce tried to encourage him with a smile. She wanted him to understand that it was all right, kids talked to her a lot, about all kinds of things.

"The worst," he said, looking down at his bare feet before raising his eyes to her, "is knowing everybody feels you let them down. No one *says* it, of course, but they're hurt and angry and really disappointed . . . somehow you're the one making this big mess for everybody."

"Brian, I'm sure your whole family thinks the *world* of you."

"All the more reason they're disappointed, having to go through all this trial and publicity and everything."

"The last thing your father would care about is publicity, what other people think. All he cares about is you, and he's certainly not blaming you for something he knows deep in his heart can't be your fault."

The boy nodded a couple of times, slowly, not so much in agreement, it seemed, as in acknowledgment of her willingness to say those things. "Dad says you had Jamie Pitt in class."

"Yes." Good God, was that her claim to fame now? But the boy seemed so downcast there was no way she could fault him for that. "Did you two know each other—before all this happened?"

"More or less," Brian said. "You could hardly call us friends, though."

"I've lived and taught here for a long time now and honestly can't recall a single instance of Trent kids and Medway kids being friends."

"That's kind of funny. My grandfather, you know, Salvatore, he hangs out in the Polecat up there. Those are all his friends, Medway guys that used to work with him at IE."

"Your grandfather could probably make friends anywhere."

"Except he wouldn't *want* friends from Trent." Brian laughed, and she did too. "Even my father," he went on, "isn't really a Trent type when you come right down to it. I'm the only one in the family who is. I mean, I've always had it easy; none of them ever did."

She could see he was on the verge, right at that moment, of going on. Then he pulled back, maybe not trusting a woman who might well pass everything on to either his father or Jamie Pitt or both. "It was nice talking to you, Mrs. Johnway," he said, sounding for the first time like what he was, a teenager talking to an older woman, a teacher, a member in good standing of that universal grown-up conspiracy that made all the rules that they then made sure the kids obeyed. "Would you like to say hello to my grandparents? I'll row you over."

"No—really," she said quickly. There hardly seemed much point to it, with Florian away, and she didn't want to loom up before them once more, as she had that other terrible night, like some apparitional Lady of the Lake. And what had Florian given them as an excuse that night for going out in the boat with her? Maybe lying to your parents was so instinctive for boys on the make that the impulse stayed with them forever. Girls too, she had to admit, remembering the lulus she'd handed her parents in high school and beyond.

"Would you like to wave to my grandfather?"

She turned to look; Salvatore had moved from his chair to the end of their dock. "Halloo!" he called between cupped hands. "That you? You all right?"

"C'mon," Brian said. "I'll row you over and you can say hello. It's real brambly through the woods."

She took the hand he offered to help her into the boat. Then she noticed her small suitcase.

"You'd better sit." He pushed off and hopped in, stretching his long arms out to the oars. "I don't think anything inside got too wet. I saw a plastic bag floating around too but couldn't find whatever was in it."

"Shoes," she said weakly.

Salvatore waited for them on the dock, the dog waiting, too, highly agitated, as Brian nosed the boat alongside. He tossed a rope to Salvatore who, not seeming that surprised, not making a big thing about it, helped Joyce onto the dock.

"Hello, Mr. Rubio," Joyce said. "I was just taking a walk . . . watching the fireworks."

Salvatore touched his floppy hat and bent forward. He was not nearly as tall as Florian, let alone Brian, and seemed a little hobbled. "It's a nice night for that."

Brian climbed out of the boat with the dripping suitcase, gangly weeds still clinging to it. By this late in summer, beneath the surface, the lake was as overgrown as a jungle. The boy carried the suitcase casually, part of his normal gear, needing no more explanation than his cutoffs, his bare feet. Salvatore glanced at it before returning his gaze to Joyce but said nothing. It was as if his lifelong code, already inbred in his young grandson, kept both from even considering a question that might embarrass a lady.

"Come," Salvatore said, touching her elbow. "Lucille, she'll want to say hello."

They walked across the grass, Salvatore leading Joyce with Brian behind, carrying the suitcase, to where Lucille sat in the webbed folding chair, cooling herself with a round woven fan and steadily watching their approach.

"Oh," Lucille said. "It's you." Her tone was direct but not unfriendly. "You still around, eh?"

Joyce wondered if she knew that she'd left Benn and gone off somewhere, but then Lucille added with a shrug: "We thought maybe you were with Florian up there. He never says, that one."

"She was taking a walk," Salvatore said.

"To watch the fireworks," Joyce added. "Since I was so close, I thought I'd say hello." After a pause she asked, "Up where?"

"Who knows?" Lucille said. "Maine, somewhere like that. He didn't even say how long. He said he'd phone when he got there to say where he was, but so far he hasn't."

He certainly wasn't up in Maine for a vacation weekend. It must have had something to do with his son, although Joyce couldn't imagine in what way. For perhaps the first time she felt the need to acknowledge the fact that Florian would simply not surface as himself again until the troubles swirling about his son were resolved. What had she expected under the circumstances, some lively and easygoing guy, full of fun around the clock?

"Maybe you have some coffee, ice tea?" Lucille said. "We got nice cinnamon buns."

"Really, I'm fine," Joyce said, not wanting to appear brusque but anxious now to get back to the motel.

"You walking all by yourself, this time of night?"

"Actually my car's right up the road. And I really should go."

"I'll walk you there," Brian said. He'd been hovering in the background, and as he stepped forward, Lucille narrowed her eyes. The suitcase. She glared at Salvatore, expecting some kind of explanation for all this craziness.

"I'll be right back," Brian said, moving away, and Joyce followed. Their movements energized the big, somewhat formless dog, who'd been hovering in the backyard, and Brian shouted, *"Stay!"* It tagged along anyhow up the driveway. "Grandpa says it's named Padgett," the boy said offhandedly, "so no one will think it's Italian." His bare feet made a whispery sound under the arched overhanging branches, her own flats a sharper noise.

"Your grandmother's dying to grill you about the suitcase."

"What suitcase?" he said, sounding more like his father than perhaps he realized. He pulled off the clinging weeds and tossed them into
the trees, causing the dog to bound furiously after them, although it
skidded to a stop at the edge of the woods. She unlocked the trunk, and
Brian put the suitcase in and slammed the lid shut.

"Did you see how it got in the water?" she asked.

"Sort of, from a ways out." It took him a moment to go on. "I
guess maybe you're having trouble at home. I mean, it happens. It happened to Dad and Mom when I was just a kid."

They stood awkwardly alongside the car, the driver's door open,
and for the first time she felt as if maybe, maybe she had some idea of
what this boy must feel, having his father disappear for all those years
and, then, last year, for whatever reason, being sent away by his mother.
It chilled her, shook her, the sense of estrangement, desertion.

Perhaps he sensed some emotion in her that he couldn't handle; he
nodded, backing away, and hurried toward his house with the floppy dog
switching back and forth behind him, as if playing out its own role in
some vastly enjoyable game.

She eased the car away from the bushes and branches and headed
out along Mark's Lane, swerving lightly when she saw a car parked not
far from Florian's drive. Her headlights showed no one inside, and she
envisioned a couple of teenagers ducking quickly from the sudden glare,
in whatever state of passion and undress. She sped up to the outlet onto
James Road, then slammed on her brakes, skidding to a stop. Floodlit
police cruisers and fire trucks blocked the road, lights flashing. The
quaintly rustic guard booth that had decades ago been designed to protect residents from the rampaging Huns and Goths of Mt. Early County
but had never even been occupied by a single guard, vigilant or otherwise, that had degenerated over the years into a local joke, was now a
jumble of smoldering black timbers. A single fireman straddled a thick
hose, spraying the wreckage as cops and other firemen stood by in glistening, bulky uniforms.

A policeman flagged her onto the shoulder, around the trucks and
cruisers. "A little fire, ma'am. Nothing. You live in here?"

"Yes," she said after a hesitation. "Heading out at the moment."

She drove slowly past, wrinkling her nose at the acrid smell of wet
charred wood. She couldn't understand how it could have caught fire, or
why the firemen would even bother trying to save it.

As soon as she got to the motel, she called Benn. "I don't know

what's going on with you, but I'm not about to let you throw my be-
longings—"

"Going on? With me? You're the one upsetting the goddamn apple
cart. Anyhow, the moving people are coming Monday to pack everything. Where do you want it delivered?"

"Medway storage," she said, and hung up.

She was amazed to have gone so far so quickly. You counted on the
luxury of some long, quiet, unhurried interlude, during which everything would remain exactly as it was, but then in a flash all that leisurely
thinking-it-over time shrinks to seconds, to a telephone call in a motel
cubicle, and it's over, flying past, out of control. You might as well stand
at the foot of Mt. Early in May trying to hold back the melting snow.

Besides the shoes, she'd just lost underwear in the tote bag. The
suitcase Brian had fished out had been in the lake just long enough to let
the water seep through and leave everything—including her favorite skirt
and sweater outfit—smelling like a swamp. After hanging the wet clothes
from the shower rod, she unplugged the phone and went to bed.

It'd taken a long time, with Florian itchier by the minute, for Wally
Brown's East Coast detective to ferret out the address. Florian didn't
mention the find to Wachtel, who truly believed that someone trying to
help his own son was *meddling*.

The California detective, Wally Brown said, still had his nose to the
ground, sniffing out leads, and was sure to come up with something out
there before too long.

When Florian told his mother and father he might be gone a few
days, they obviously assumed he was heading north for a weekend fling
with his girlfriend down the road.

Maybe he should have been more patient with Bennett and the
other parents, spent a few hours seeing what they were like, what was on
their minds. Only then he'd be fighting to stay awake as he drove
through the night to get to Isle de Pierre, a few hours past Portland and
Casco Bay. This way he'd arrive before midnight.

Maybe Bennett had decided to host the gathering because it gave
him an excuse to lure Florian out to his place and put the squeeze on
him to bail out Blackberry Hollow. *See, Flo, how I'm really knocking
myself out supporting your kid in all his trouble, so maybe, in return . . .*

At nine o'clock Florian saw the fireworks light up the sky from small
towns on both sides of I-95.

The Fourth gave most Mt. Early people a funny feeling. A few years
back the mayor of Medway decided to begin the fireworks from the

public beach—where this year's Trent seniors had planned their MORP breakfast—by tugging on a rope slung over a tree branch, thereby raising a blazing lantern to signal the volunteer firemen from Trent, on a barge in the middle of the lake, to set off the first rockets. All the local dignitaries attended, and Abby Allen Oliver, never one to miss some local exposure, had her young theatrical charges prancing around in colonial costumes. The lantern had barely reached full height when the mayor let go of the rope and dropped to his knees in the sand. He wavered briefly, like an awed supplicant, before toppling onto his back with arms flung out. The lantern smashed onto the beach and spread a small flaming oil slick.

The mayor died instantly from the heart attack, but there was no way to get word to the fireman out on the barge. While Abby Allen's patriotically costumed actors and everyone else on the crowded beach screamed for a doctor, an ambulance, while some intrepid souls frantically tried to revive him, the fireworks continued, with the explosions echoing across the lake as the spectacular greens and reds and whites blossomed overhead, illuminating the mayor's body on the sand.

He got to Isle de Pierre at eleven-thirty. The detective had suggested reservations at the Grande Colonial, but Florian never liked expensive hotels. Cars were one thing; you got what you paid for with an automobile. Houses too, but hotels were something else. A bed was a bed. You didn't need a dozen towels and a basket of tiny plastic bottles of French lotions and shampoos, or closets you could roller-skate in, lobbies the size of football fields. The Grande Colonial would have set him back two, three hundred a night, maybe more. He found a U-shaped two-story stucco deal a few miles inland for sixty-nine fifty and free ice from the machine down the hall, which was easy to find by just following the clanking. But the room was fine, hardly Maine's version of Tobacco Road, with an orgy-size bed and two full walls of mirrors in the bathroom (so you could watch yourself spraying into the swirling blue water?) and three in the living room. They either wanted to make the room look bigger or were aiming for the muscle beach crowd.

He called home to let them know where he was, watching his foot jiggling in two mirrors at once. Brian was upstairs, Lucille said. Sure, he seemed fine, the same. "What'd you expect? Why shouldn't he be the same? Anyhow, what are you doing way up there? The lady next door is still around."

"What?"

"She was out watching the fireworks and came to say hello. You're there all by yourself, then, or is there someone else?"

"Of course I'm by myself. How were the fireworks?"

"It's more fun with the whole family. It's too bad, no? This would've been Brian's first year here with everybody, and something like this has to happen."

He kept trying Joyce at the Log Cabins until giving up at eleven.

He couldn't find anything on late-night TV from Bangor (why did you *watch* TV but *see* a movie?) and drank his scotch in silence, trying not to give in to the depressing motel thoughts of those thousands of other people who'd sat in the same chair, slept in the same bed.

What really got him about Jamie Pitt was the way this goddamn high school kid, without a lawyer or anything else going for him, seemed to be calling the shots—not only with Joyce but with the police and the DA and even the grand jury. No doubt he was getting all set to play big shot at the trial too, with the whole county hanging on his every word.

Florian relished the idea of shaking the kid by the throat until his eyes bugged. *Okay, what the hell's going on? You better explain a few things to me or I'm gonna leave you in little pieces.*

Only who was he kidding? He'd never in his life done that to anyone, let alone some high school kid. He'd never before even thought of doing it. He was someone who went about his own business and never felt much need to go after anyone else.

And now for the defense I would like to ask if Mr. James Ding-a-ling Pitt dares to deny that it was his own threats upon Mr. Brian Rubio and his female partner for the evening that set in motion the events that left Mr. Brian Rubio with no choice but to . . .

To what? Jesus, whatever Jamie did, couldn't Brian have had the sense—the luck—to forget all that idiocy and go off snuggling with his long-legged date?

Florian finished his scotch and stood up in the clean artificial silence of the motel room, steadying himself, and held the plastic glass directly over the wastebasket, sighting with one eye like a bombardier. He let it go, dead center, watched it bounce around, and went to bed.

Joyce enjoyed getting together with Katarina Scanlon away from school, and her spirits rose for the first time in days when they met for their Day-Before-Her-European-Blast lunch at the Apple and Crocus. Katarina, who had never married and delighted in spending her summers in Europe, was leaving in the morning for Lisbon. Considering the festive nature of the moment, they ordered a bottle of Soave at a small table near a bay window. On her first glass, Joyce told Katarina about leaving Bennett.

"Wow," Katarina said. "What did it, all those times Bennett was on the road screwing the local bagatelles?"

"Not really. I'm not sure exactly why, but I've been putting up with his roadside encounters for years. I guess finally it wasn't any single thing, not even the way he seems to have changed over the years. Somehow, he's harder now, angrier, more gnarled and inward, less open toward me or anyone else. Of course, maybe I've changed too."

"But only for the better, as all your friends will attest. There must have been some climactic moment, no? Some astounding revelation that this marriage, alas, had not been made in heaven?"

Joyce laughed. "If there was, I guess it skittered by before I noticed. Maybe being together simply stopped meaning anything, or bringing anything, promising anything, to either of us. Isn't that how it works?"

"Thanks to God I wouldn't know."

On their second glass, Joyce mentioned Florian.

"Tell me all about him. Only his kid just got indicted, right?"

"It's been awful hard on him, the whole family. But he's really very nice," she added, maybe more soupily than she intended because Katarina rolled her eyes. "I like him a lot."

"The only way to fly," Katarina said.

"Of course last night I found out he'd gone roaring off to Maine, probably in connection with his son's trouble. He's got so much tearing him apart he can't pay attention to anything else."

"Including you?"

"I'm beginning to think so. It might be doing him a favor to stay out of his way for a while. If we'd had the chance to set ourselves up a little better, it'd be different. But the timing was unfortunate all around, and we never got the momentum going."

They fell silent while the waiter cleared their dishes. Joyce noticed Katarina staring at her the whole time, with a little twist to one corner of her mouth, and as soon as the waiter left, she said, "Joyce, will you tell me exactly what you plan to *do* with yourself all summer? You've got a husband who's taken to tossing your undies into the lake and a handsome boyfriend so racked up over his kid that right now he's not worth the paper he's printed on. You want a kindly, friendly suggestion?"

"Sure."

"Lisbon's great. Guaranteed. Let's zip over to your grungy motel to grab your things and check you out. Anything you lost in the water you can replace; they got stores over there too. We'll spend the night at my place so we can get an early start for the airport."

"I'll have to get my passport from the bank box. And it takes me days to get—"

"Why? I'll take care of the tickets and reservations: as a long-standing bull-in-the-china-shop world traveler, I've learned how to give it to, or take it away from, any ticket agent or concierge who ever lived. You don't need to find a house-sitter or someone to feed the cat. And let's face it, right now you don't even have anybody to say good-bye to."

"I'd want to say good-bye to Florian."

"If you could find him. Write him a sweet, glowy letter that'll make him really look forward to your coming back."

"I'll drop it off at his house on the way to the airport. I want to make sure it's there when he gets back."

"I myself prefer to let men squirm a bit when the opportunity arises. Thanks dearly for the lunch; now dig out your plastic and let's be on our way."

When the alarm went off at six, he put on his sneakers and swimming trunks, checking himself out, a little sheepishly, in the mirrors. He buttoned up a beach shirt, put on his Sox cap, looped the strap of his binoculars over his head, slid his wallet into his shirt pocket, picked up his briefcase, and left.

According to the detective's hand-drawn map, there were two approaches. Either you got through the gate guard on the private road or you hiked along the shoreline, scrambling like a goat over a couple of miles of jagged, slippery rocks. Florian set out over the rocks. Thirty feet below, the secluded beaches were separated from one another by outcroppings that fingered into the ocean. Perfect for a private doze in a beach chair, but this far north the water was cold enough to turn your toes blue. The summer "cottages," though, were spectacular, built by people who must have *wanted* an area without attractions or activities, without decent restaurants or theaters or music to speak of, without even an ocean warm enough for any creature to survive except the cod and lobster and migrating whale. All that, and the hefty drive north from Boston, kept the hordes away, which obviously was the way the Isle de Pierre people liked it.

Yesterday morning, before handball, he'd called ahead from Trent and gotten a woman with a trilling Spanish accent. "Yes? Who is it? Hello there?"

"I'd like to speak to Mr. Thrane."

"What? Who is this calling please?"

"A friend from Trent."

"There's nobody named like that around here," the woman said, still with a cheerful lilt. "You must please I think have the incorrect number."

The Thrane place had been in the family for generations, the detective said. It didn't belong to the Trent branch, but to some cousin or uncle, which was why he took so long finding it. Their real name was Thraneau, and they'd come over from France hinting about court connections back to some Louis or other in a powdered wig, but of course the New Englanders wrote them off as another gang of renegade Canucks, one more family of roughneck woodsmen and fishermen and shiftless drinkers scooting down from Quebec. The Thraneaus therefore went Anglo by turning themselves into Thranes, and by now had moved well beyond mere social acceptance into big money and corporate boards and exotic gardening on their landscaped acres back in Sargasso River Highlands.

The detective also told Florian over the phone that Nique was practically at the top of her class, although her teachers considered her something of a hellion. A hellion? Florian hadn't heard the word in years. Who'd recommended this detective to Wally Brown, Agatha Christie?

He also informed Florian that Nique was one of the few locals attending the Spenser Academy which, despite its half century of existence in the heart of Mt. Early County, had a student body consisting mainly of rich girls from elsewhere. "It was named, you know," the fellow confided, "after some famous poet."

"What did he write?"

"*The Faerie Queene,*" the guy said, and then spelled it out.

"Good enough," Florian told him.

Florian worked up a sweat even in the sharp, cool wind coming off the ocean as he crouched, jumped, clung, grabbed, crawled, slid, skidded, and scuttled over the brambled rocks, every move made clumsier by the briefcase and dangling binoculars. The houses were set back fifty yards or so on his left, the small beaches and coves below him on the right. The older houses were hotel-size nineteenth-century gingerbreads with eaves and cupolas and wraparound porches. The newer ones looked like imitation Frank Lloyd Wright, all glass and stained wood and clean, lean, jutting angles—although God knows some might have been real Frank Lloyd Wright. Every house had its own access to its own beach, a path or wooden staircase over the rocks and down to the water, and every beach was deserted.

He couldn't even spot a footprint in the wet sand and began to feel like Robinson Crusoe, wondering where the natives were. The ultimate

Isle de Pierre privilege, possessing a beautiful private beach that you never bothered to use. Maybe they spent all summer in their houses, yawning, with their backs to the view that Grandpa, running his paper mills or shoe factories, had worked a lifetime to afford.

It took two hours to cover the two miles. His handball sneakers had gotten too scuffed ever to function on a court again, but what he really missed were gloves. By now his fingers were scraped raw and he'd gotten a real cut on his palm from a broken clamshell. He made himself as comfortable as he could in the wind and glare on top of a level stretch of rock, hidden by a larger rock formation from the Thranes' three-story beauty with its bay windows and mansard roof and elegantly railed widow's walk. It didn't take long to realize that sitting on an exposed rock face like an Indian mystic could get you a class A burn. He should have worn a big white fisherman's hat instead of the baseball cap, summer trousers instead of trunks. He should have hauled along a gallon of lotion. His ears and legs were in for it.

He passed the time going over stuff from his briefcase. Right now he wasn't much interested in zoning board hearings and wetland regulations, in water tables and perc tests, or in *Barron's* or the *Mt. Early Business Monthly,* but made himself stay with it, make plans, take notes. He wanted to save for last, as a kind of reward, the folder on the Fitzwilliam property—almost three hundred relatively inaccessible acres of possibly no earthly use or value whatsoever. But if Brian was interested in flying over it, and tramping through it, Florian was ready to fly, to tramp, and maybe even to buy.

Every so often he inched forward on the rock to check the empty beach below, the sand glaring in the sun, and used the binoculars to look for some sign of life about the house. What the hell were they doing up here in God's country—playing Scrabble? *The water's warming up by the minute,* he felt like yelling. *Give it a goddamn try!*

Just after noon Nique emerged from the house, tall and slim with her long black hair flowing over the collar of her blue beach robe. She carried a blanket and beach bag, and she was alone. Florian kept panning the binoculars back to the house to make sure no one was tearing out after her. When she started down the whitewashed wooden steps to the crescent of glistening white sand below, Florian crawled to the edge of the rocks and refocused the binoculars.

She spread out a blue blanket that matched both her beach robe and beach bag, fished a tape deck from the bag, and switched on the music, loud and coarse and driving. After placing the deck on the blanket, she took out a can of soda, which seemed to be already open, tilted her head back, and drank. Then she flared open her robe and let it drop.

It took Florian a moment to react to the swell of her breasts, the sharply defined nipples, the black patch of hair between the creamy thighs. Slowly he lowered the binoculars but still gaped. She stretched out on the blanket, on her back, her arms straight at her sides, her legs together, her toes pointing toward the surf. Florian glanced down at the binoculars, as if it was their fault, making him feel like some creep ogling his son's girlfriend. He scuttled back from the edge to put her out of sight.

The main thing was not to give her the wrong idea. Only it might be hours before she'd put the robe back on, with maybe the mother or father or downstairs maid showing up along the way.

Still flat on the rock, Florian cupped his hands around his mouth and shouted: "Toro—come back! Here, Toro!" It was the lawn mower his father had out in the garage. Too late he realized he could have called *"Padgett!"* but it hadn't occurred to him.

He counted to six, the ridges of rock cutting into his ribs. "Toro! Where are you?" He counted to twelve, to fifteen, then stood up, binoculars dangling, briefcase in hand, and walked to the top of the white-washed stairs and struck a lackadaisical pose. Below him on the beach Nique was also standing, tying her robe, looking up.

"Hi there!" he called down. "Did my dog come running by?"

She spread her hands, palms up, and shrugged. Then, apparently as an afterthought, she bent quickly to turn off the tape deck.

"I thought he might be romping in the waves." Florian moved down the first few steps, then a few more, not sure if Nique recognized him yet.

She stood motionless, arms folded, bare feet set wide.

He paused at the bottom, offering her a final chance to shake him off. As he walked over to her, he felt the sand lumping up inside his sneakers. It was much hotter here, the rocky slope cutting off the wind, concentrating the sunshine. Once more he was struck by her height, the black china doll hair and face, the perfect teeth, the large, clear eyes. Yet she seemed more inward, more suspicious, as if affected by some vast teenage weariness, than when she'd biked over in her cutoffs and MORP T-shirt.

Gazing steadily, maybe she noticed some differences in him. "You came all the way up here just to find us, didn't you?" she said as quietly as the waves allowed. She seemed briefly impressed, then tossed her head as if to say, *What does it matter now, after everything else?* Her expression changed once more. "If my parents catch you . . ."

"Oh?"

"Mother sunbathes. She'd throw a fit if she found strange men peeking around."

Florian nodded, the sober citizen commending her mother's prudence. "I tried to find you before the grand jury, but the trial's even more important. Brian's in a lot of trouble. What do they say up here? A peck? A passel?"

Her dark eyes, which seemed somehow *older* than you expected, wavered for an instant. "I wasn't even near the boat ramp when it happened, Mr. Rubio."

She said *Mr. Rubio* as if he was a hundred and sixteen years old. "What did Jamie Pitt do to you earlier?"

She grabbed her Diet Sprite and swung around but only headed for the rocks. She sat on one, angrily, her robe swirling. She patted the edges over her legs, covering herself down to the ankles. Emptying the soda can, she tossed it back toward the blanket. "I sure hope you're not trying to make everything my fault."

"Of course not." He walked over and softened his voice. "But I can't help wondering why your parents felt they had to hide you away up here."

"It won't help talking about my parents, okay?"

Not sure exactly how to take that, he plunged ahead. "Do you have any idea what manslaughter entails?"

"I read, you know. I'm going to be an attorney."

Florian tilted his head; he'd never heard Brian publicly admit to reading anything, let alone becoming anything. He wondered, in a flash, what *her* private notebook might look like. "I'd think a future lawyer wouldn't hide from a grand jury investigation."

"I'm not the only one who hid, Mr. Rubio."

Florian's mouth tightened. "Clamming Brian up was the lawyer's decision. That's—"

"Different. Sure."

"Maybe the trial jury ought to know what Jamie Pitt did to you. Did he rape you? Did he try? Did he slap you around? What happened?"

"What makes you so sure anything I said would help Brian? Suppose I started blabbing away and all it did was make things worse for him? How do you think I'd feel then?"

"If you just helped us learn exactly what happened, maybe then—"

"Brian can tell you exactly what happened, can't he? If he wants to,

I mean. Of course the guy and the little girl there, the pudgy one—what's her name again?"

"Willa Hufnagle. The guy was Polly Dunn."

"They're the ones you really feel sorry for, ending up at the bottom of the lake. Although like I said, I wasn't there when it happened. I never got within miles of the ramp. So the only thing I could tell anybody was what happened before the ramp, long before, and who knows, right, whether you'd even want me talking about any of that."

She stood up from the rock to face him, her gaze level, both the same height. (God, as a kid he played *center* on the schoolyard basketball teams.) She was clenching her jaw so tight a muscle twitched. For the first time her voice faltered. "If when the trial comes, Mr. Rubio . . . and it seems right . . . I mean, if his lawyer thinks I could do him some good . . . would you help me get there?"

"Who'd try to stop you?"

"You're not answering."

"Of course I'd help." He envisioned himself hustling her away from her screaming parents while the family bodyguards filled the night air with shotgun blasts. With her stuffed into a laundry basket? Scrunched into the Fairlane's trunk? He'd do it. He'd do a lot more if it'd help.

"I'll let you know if that's what I decide," Nique said. "Only don't try to get in touch or I'll end up in Rio or Dubrovnik and no one'll ever find me."

"Can we count on you coming?"

This threw her; she seemed to be struggling with five, ten, twenty possibilities. "How do I know what you can count on? I don't even know what *I* can count on. Only don't think," she added after a pause, "I don't care about Brian." She fetched another Sprite can—already popped, lifting it carefully so as not to spill any—from her tote bag and drank.

"Why did Jamie Pitt go after you? Did he know you? Was he trying to get back at Brian for something?"

Frowning at him, maybe annoyed at him for even *asking* these questions, she turned to look at the waves coming in. She'd been trying to show how grown-up and worldly she was and doing a decent job of it. Brian had said she was *going on* seventeen and would graduate next year as the youngest kid in her class at Spenser. What, sixteen and a half? A kid with a future and in a hurry to get there, to college, to law school—moving right on through life with those great looks, those long strides, that tall, beautifully postured sense of herself. But you had to put all that aside and remind yourself that she was a kid who'd gotten into a bigger mess than she ever bargained for, maybe even raped in the process. What did that do to you, for Christ's sake? On top of that, whatever her involvement, she must have felt some responsibility for those two kids, pudgy or otherwise, trapped at the bottom of the lake.

What frustrated Florian was his certainty that if he could just hit the right button she *would* talk to him, everything spilling out in one non-stop rush, but that she didn't feel easy enough with this old guy to let her guard down. What the hell, it was only a six-hour drive each way, once you got the slug of a Fairlane up to speed.

He made a final stab: "The reason I came up here is that I'm sure if we could learn everything, put everything on the table, it'd be clear how innocent Brian is."

"Well, gee, Mr. Rubio, I'm sure he's innocent too. But the question, right, is whether or not I can help him prove it, and I'm not really sure I can."

The loud electronic ring seemed to startle Nique, although not nearly as much as Florian. She hurried over to the blanket and removed a small black handset from her tote bag, pulled out the silvery red-tipped aerial, and spoke into the grille. "Yes?"

"VERONIQUE—WILL YOU BE STAYING THERE FOR A WHILE? I'LL JOIN YOU."

"Hang on a sec, Mom." Nique released the button and smiled at Florian. "You really want to meet my parents?"

"Sure, if it might do some good. Except if it'll get you sent off to South America."

"Probably not this first time." She held the button down and spoke into the grille. "There's a Mr. Rubio here dying to say hello. You know, from Trent."

Only after a lot of dead air did the crackling resume. "VERONIQUE—ARE YOU JOKING?"

"Come see for yourself. He's the one with the briefcase and Red Sox cap."

This provoked an even longer silence. "STAY RIGHT THERE!"

Nique dropped the intercom and tape deck into her beach bag, emptied the Sprite can onto the sand. "It gets too warm to drink after a while," she said, and nodded toward the whitewashed stairs. "Maybe if we meet them halfway, they'll invite you for tea."

"Maybe things are going to get too warm in general. Is there anything you want me to pass along to Brian?"

"I can always write. I mean, it's not like I'm in prison, is it?"

By the time they got to the top of the stairs, two guys were pounding toward them across the broad sandy plateau. The mother must have decided, or been told, to stay clear of the loony in the baseball cap. The bald guy, Mr. Thrane, Carl J. Thrane, was huffing and stumbling, arms flailing. He looked like a comic strip parody of a balding tourist in out-size color-splashed walking shorts and flapping shirttails. He'd obviously been caught off guard, and maybe unprepared to meet the world in his accustomed vacation wear. A large man, maybe an athlete gone to seed, he pounded up red-faced and heaving, even the top of his head glowing, and stole time to catch his breath by giving Florian a long hard look, and then his daughter an even longer, harder one, as if she'd arranged all this just to torment him.

The other guy was in his twenties, black, big too, but in better shape, all muscles in shorts and sleeveless sweatshirt.

Florian offered his hand. "Hello."

Thrane ignored him, still puffing. He turned to Nique. "Please go back to the house."

"I wouldn't have said anything to Mother if I thought you wouldn't even let me listen in." She was still working on that cool, perky tone, but the instant her father showed up you could see a shadow of uncertainty fall over her, maybe a mixture of awe and resentment. (Was it true of Brian too, of all kids? No matter how much you tried and cared, their prepared expression was all you ever seemed to get?)

"Please go. Your mother wants to talk to you."

Florian could see how tempted Nique was to confront her father before a stranger and force him to have her lugged off kicking and screaming over the bodyguard's shoulder. Then she turned dutifully (reluctantly? resignedly?) toward the house. She stopped to meet Florian's gaze. "It's almost time for the Sox anyhow. Hope you find your dog—Tojo, right, like the Japanese admiral."

Florian was impressed: a teenager who knew the name of World War II admirals. "Toro," he said. "Like the lawn mower."

He stared as she walked away, head up, one arm swinging while the other clutched her matching blanket and bag, her swirling blue robe doing nice things for her figure, her carriage, her determined stride. Then he realized the two men were watching him watch her.

"This is private property," Thrane said. "I could have you arrested."

Florian didn't argue. He'd never spoken to Thrane before although he'd seen him around a few times. Like the rest of the Sargasso River Highlands crowd, Thrane kept to himself and therefore didn't have much local reputation one way or the other, although rumors had him as either the shrewdest of a long line of moneymaking Thranes or the darling of the Las Vegas gaming tables. Maybe he was both.

Impatiently, Thrane shooed his man away. "Wait for me on the porch." When the fellow was out of earshot, Thrane said, "You're the one whose son is in trouble over the drownings."

"That's it," Florian said. "And of course you've got children too, so you know what it's like. I was hoping you'd understand and maybe help out."

"Of course I understand, but there's no way we could possibly help."

"Your daughter was my son's date that night."

"We were not at the time aware of that fact. If we had been, we would not have allowed her out of the house."

"It'd sure be nice if we had her cooperation. We're not talking after-school detention here. He's facing a manslaughter charge."

"Why do you feel anything she said would be to his advantage?"

"Because I'm assuming she would tell the truth, and I figure the more of that we get, the better off we'll be."

"Let's be honest with each other, Mr. Rubio. Even if she were interested, I wouldn't allow it. I'm not going to let her be hurt in any way, or have her reputation further besmirched."

Further? "I understand that. I'm out for my kid, and you're out for yours. But mine's the one in trouble, so I guess I'm more desperate."

"Whatever your level of desperation, Mr. Rubio, you'd be making a serious mistake by challenging my authority over my daughter in any way." The sun seemed to be getting to Thrane; he wiped his forehead with his hand, then the top of his head, then wiped that palm—almost surreptitiously—on his multicolored shorts. He glanced back at the house to make sure his man was on the porch, keeping an eye.

"Our children insist on going their own way—isn't that so, Mr. Rubio? All our advice to the contrary, they want to make their own choices. I'm sure your son's a fine young man. And we of course love Veronique, but so many of the children these days, they're soft, isn't that so? Sentimental. They carry in their hearts a whole list of beautiful sympathies, for the whales, the forests, the air, the cows and chickens and pigs. They'd rather live off nuts and grapes than see a fish on a hook."

As if catching himself going on more than he intended, Thrane hardened his expression again. "We brought Veronique here for her own good, and we're going to continue protecting her every way we can. I'd particularly like to discourage you from even *thinking* about forcing her to testify. That would be a very grave mistake. And now, since we didn't see a car, I assume you came over the rocks. Did you stay in town last night?"

"Yes, at the—"

"Grande Colonial, of course. My man will drive you. What about your dog?"

"He'll find his way," Florian assured him.

He pulled onto Mark's Lane just as it was getting dark, having decided to say hello at home before trying Joyce at the Log Cabins, but braked at the charred wreckage of the guardhouse. His first reaction was to laugh. They'd never needed the stupid thing in the first place. Then he slammed down the pedal and roared off, spinning pebbles.

His mother hurried into the hall as soon as he stepped inside. "It's all right," she told him quickly. "Brian's okay. Everybody's okay. They're inside, him and Salvatore."

But they were already rushing through the house, coming up behind Lucille.

"What happened?" Florian demanded.

No one seemed eager to answer, as if not wanting to be part of whatever had to be reported. Salvatore finally put his arm around Florian's shoulder and led him into the living room, the others following, everyone silent, a processional. First Florian noticed the breeze coming in off the lake, then the broken windows. But the floor, the carpet had been cleaned, no pieces of glass anywhere.

"Because of the holiday," Lucille said, "they can't come to fix it until tomorrow. If it was the middle of winter, I guess they could come."

"Last night," Salvatore said. "After the fireworks, ten o'clock maybe, suddenly we hear all this breaking glass. Brian and me, we run outside, and Lucille grabs the broom and she runs out too, waving the broom and yelling and screaming bloody murder, and I guess they saw us and thought there was more still inside, still coming, because they took one look and ran. They had their car up on the road somewhere, because we could hear them yelling and cursing at each other, and then zooming off, really loud and skidding and everything."

"Terrible language," Lucille said. "What'd they think, we'd be scared by the words, that we never heard them before?"

"You shouldn't have gone outside," Florian said. "You should have locked the door and called the cops and hidden under the goddamn bed."

"We called the cops in the morning." Salvatore spoke as if this was almost as good.

"I didn't want police tramping all over the house in the middle of the night, driving everyone crazy," Lucille explained. "We didn't call you because what could you do way up there anyway?"

"Brian and me were playing checkers," Salvatore said. "Lucille was listening to the lady that talks all night on the telephone on the radio. So no one was nearby to get hurt."

"They threw rocks," Lucille said. "When we called this morning, the people at the hotel up there said they kept ringing but you weren't in your room."

"I guess you couldn't call it a friendly visit," Brian said, as if shrugging it off.

"That mutt!" Florian yelled. "That goddamn animal! Where the hell was he?"

"He barked," Lucille said defensively. "Real loud."

"We thought a rabbit maybe, a raccoon," Salvatore said. "We kept playing checkers until we heard the glass break."

"They hit him with a brick or something," Lucille said. "The poor little dog, he had blood all over and I thought he was dead, but Salvatore and Brian took him to the dog doctor."

"And what—left you here alone?"

"What you think, I can't take care of myself alone? Anyhow, thank God, the dog doctor says he'll be all right. Poor little doggie. I'll show you after, this great big bump on his head. And what does he know, this little dog, why someone comes along in the middle of the night to whomp him on the head with a brick?"

Brian, Lucille, Salvatore, all seemed okay, under control. Hell, maybe they thought Florian was too. He was sure trying to look it.

"As soon as you got back," Lucille said, "he wanted you to call him. Mr. Wachtel, the lawyer."

No matter what, his mother handled things her own way. Except for relatives and close friends, she never referred to people without identifying them. *Mr. Penneman, the policeman. Mr. Wachtel, the lawyer.* Florian wasn't sure if she did it to keep things straight herself or help others do so.

It took Wachtel a half hour to get to the house. The others were inside and didn't join them in the living room, where Florian handed Wachtel a drink and let him study the windows.

"The Trent police put a cruiser on Mark's Lane this morning," Wachtel said. "That should make everybody feel better."

"I didn't see any cruiser," Florian said, hardly comforted. "All I saw was a burnt-out guard booth."

"It's probably moving back and forth. Cruising."

"Then you didn't see it either?"

"It must've been at the other end. It'll be keeping an eye on the whole area for the next few days, although the cops really don't expect more trouble. How come you weren't around anyhow? Your parents said you were up in Maine."

"I got friends all over."

"This was only a piece of it," Wachtel said, motioning toward the windows. "We're not sure of the sequence, but after everybody went home from the fireworks, somebody chopped up Brian's old lifeguard chair at the beach and made a bonfire out of it, just like your guard booth down the road. They also snipped the cables of the swimmers raft and hauled it into deep water and punched holes in the barrels to sink it."

"How many guys were doing this? Do the police know?"

"They got some leads; we'll get to that in a minute. Then they moved into Hammond's around midnight and tore up a half-dozen boats that must've looked ritzy enough to belong to someone from Trent."

"Medway kids—is that what the cops think?"

"Unless some patriots got turned on by the Fourth." They were standing just inside the big window, looking out at the hazy lake, the breeze coming through soft and cool. Wachtel finished his drink, put the glass down, stuffed his hands into his pockets. "What's really scary is how easy it is. Who's on guarding the fort, for Christ's sake? O'er whose fucking ramparts is anybody watching? With all the certified crazies in the world, it's amazing no one's blown up the Empire State Building yet, or poisoned the Miami Beach drinking water. It'd take twenty minutes in the local library to figure out the mechanics."

"It's not very pleasant," Florian said, "having people hate your son, wanting to hurt him, scare him, break up his house."

"Everybody hates everybody, Flo. You got the blacks and the whites, the Jews and the Arabs, the rich and the poor, on and on until you end up with Trent and Medway."

"Christ, you grew up in Medway. Those are your people."

Wachtel bristled. "Like Zack Arkins is your people? They're just pissed up there because they don't think their kids ever get a break, whereas your kid got off real soft. What the hell's manslaughter? They want something to sink their teeth into, like murder one. Oh, yeah—the salmon hatchery off Tompkins Road. The cops figure it was all the same guys, knocking off one target after another while the cops were going crazy answering emergency calls and trying to figure out what they'd hit next. They broke into the hatchery and pulled the plug on the main tanks. By the time the crew arrived this morning everything was bone dry, and a few thousand dead salmon were stacked on top of each other at the drains, where they must have been fighting for that last drop of water. Oh, yeah, they left signs everywhere except here, where maybe they got scared off too soon."

"What do you mean, signs?"

"You know, little hand-painted signs. What they all said was *Rich Kids Can't Get Away With Murder.*"

"Jesus. What about the other kids—Arkins, those people? What about their houses?"

"Actually, that was the worst of it," Wachtel said. "A gang of kids, probably the same gang, somehow tracked down Tiny Arkins alone in his car and beat the living shit out of him."

"The Arkins kid? Is he okay?"

"He looks pretty splotchy, I can vouch for that—a couple of loose teeth, cuts, and bruises."

"Why him?"

"Good question. Maybe they were out for Brian too, but weren't about to mess with your mother and father. Isn't that something—Salvatore and Lucille wielding bats and brooms and shouting Italian imprecations? And the dog too—the dog alone might've scared them off."

"You said the cops had leads."

"Not exactly leads. Hunches, possibilities. Things they might follow up if they were really interested."

"I'm really interested."

"And so is Red Penneman. You know Red, as straight as they come. Only he's just a cop. He's not the prosecutor."

"Meaning?"

"Meaning Red suspects that one Jamie Pitt and some of his buddies maybe decided to have themselves a real Fourth of July fling."

"Good. Maybe they'll finally nail his ass to the wall."

"I'm trying to make a point, Flo, but you're not paying attention."

"Make it then. Make your fucking point."

"My point, Flo, is that the prosecutor, the district attorney's office, the whole interlocking law enforcement establishment of Mt. Early County, is not the least bit interested in coming down on Jamie Pitt in any way, shape, or form. He's their A number one witness, Flo. He's their case and so enjoys, right now, a charmed life."

Florian could barely contain himself. It even occurred to him that Jamie could be the reason the Thranes scooted Nique off to Maine, to protect her from the guy in case he didn't approve of what she might testify. Was the whole county being bullied by that goddamn kid?

"What you're saying is that it's perfectly all right for Jamie Pitt to beat Tiny Arkins bloody if he feels like it. You're saying he can brain dogs and break windows and kill fish to his heart's content because the goddamn DA, who's out to throw Brian in the slammer, wants Jamie to look sweet and pure when they put him on the stand."

"Now you're paying attention," Wachtel said. "Like we used to say in the days of the Vietnam draft, *It wasn't much of a dance, but it kept me out of the Army.*"

The pause, Florian figured, was designed to give him time to enjoy the joke, but then Wachtel said: "The other news is that Harry Diggs called today in a big rush wanting to see the two of us. Only when your mother said she didn't know when you were coming back from Maine, Diggs said it couldn't wait."

"I don't like the sound of this, Ira."

"When I got to his office, Bennett Johnway was there."

Florian liked that even less.

"I never did figure out what Bennett was doing there," Wachtel said. "Diggs, though, announced a deal with Pat Delehanty giving the other three kids a separate trial. Lesser charges, maybe none at all, depending on what happens with Brian."

"Shit. I knew I should've stayed at that meeting."

"What meeting?"

"Bennett's, for all the parents. The minute I left they must've ganged up on Brian."

"I don't know if that was it," Wachtel said. "You could've done handstands, but they still would've grabbed any out they could find."

"Christ, the indictments are down two days and already Diggs has got his kids off the hook."

"Both Harry and Bennett kept saying this wasn't aimed at Brian."

Florian could feel his eyes widening. "You believed those fuckers!"

Wachtel waited a moment. "Remember, they invited you too. It wouldn't have been easy facing you, but they wanted to keep everything up front, so at least give them credit for that. And you can't blame Diggs for doing what's best for his clients."

"I don't blame anybody for doing anything. I just wonder how come Diggs got a deal and you couldn't?"

Wachtel seemed to be measuring Florian. "Delehanty handed that deal to Diggs, and he's not interested in doing the same with us. But there are ways of managing. It's not the end of the world."

"Are those kids going to testify against Brian?"

"Maybe not. Obviously this gives Delehanty leverage over them, but he may not use it. There'll be only this one kid on trial, polite, pleasant, nice-looking kid, and if his three so-called buddies take the stand to put the knife in his back, a jury might start feeling sorry for him."

"Then what's in this for Delehanty?"

"It's easier prosecuting one guy than four. Better focus, fewer complications, less confusion for the jury."

"Why Brian and not someone else?"

"You know why, Flo. Brian was the one in the Corvette when the other car went in. Delehanty naturally assumes his innocence will therefore be the toughest to demonstrate."

"And just how do we plan on demonstrating it? Believe me, I'm not angry. I'm not even impatient. I'd just like to know what the hell moves you're planning while you're sitting home reading novels."

Wachtel gazed steadily at him, then shook his head: he obviously couldn't understand how a calm, levelheaded guy like Florian could be so upset over something as minor as his son being singled out by the DA as most likely to be convicted of manslaughter.

Ever the soothing diplomat, Wachtel maintained his teacherly tone. "Delehanty's a good prosecutor, bright, thorough, hardworking, rarely makes big mistakes. It'd be a real good idea if we didn't make big mistakes either, or rush decisions about what we are or aren't going to do when the time comes. I've already spent more hours digging around than you probably imagine, although maybe you'll be convinced when I bill you for them. I expect to spend even more hours over the summer."

"Hey—terrific. I appreciate your concern."

"Separating Brian from the others isn't necessarily the worst thing that could happen. I for one am delighted to see Tiny Arkins out of the case."

"Why?"

"Tiny Arkins's MORP date was none other than Willa Hufnagle—you know, the thirteen-year—"

"Christ, man, I know who Willa Hufnagle is. Was he screwing that kid? That's a crime, isn't it? That's statutory rape. And he's getting this great deal from Delehanty. Why doesn't it matter what anybody else does, but only what Brian's supposed to have done? Jamie Pitt tries to wreck our house and Tiny Arkins—" Florian stopped abruptly. "Is that why they beat the shit out of Tiny last night? Because of him and the girl?"

"That'd be my guess, although exactly what offended them still eludes me. Anyhow, don't spread it around, okay? I know you're anxious to prosecute everyone in sight for their assorted crimes, but think a minute. We've got a very poor and not very bright thirteen-year-old Medway girl who's dead dead dead, and people are understandably still feeling very sorry for her. There's no way it'll help Brian to yell from the rooftops that this doctor's son from Trent was screwing her."

Florian took a breath. "Okay," he said finally, his anger, everything else, drained out of him.

"Hey, you've actually been listening to me."

"I always listen. I just don't always like what I hear."

"Fair enough," Wachtel said. He checked his glass, finished off the watery remains of his scotch, and got up to leave. "Maybe you should go tell Brian that come September he'll be sitting in there alone. Except for me, of course. I'll be right next to him with my sleeves rolled up and the usual sparks coming out of my ears."

Before talking to Brian, Florian dialed Elly in Walnut Creek. It was still early evening there, and he wanted to make sure he got her. He told her about the broken windows, and she agreed right away: Brian could stay with her until the trial.

When Florian went back downstairs looking for Brian, Lucille said, "I forgot in all the excitement—here, it's for you. There's no stamp or anything. Somebody must've come by this morning and slipped it under the door."

III

AUGUST HEAT

7

There were times—especially now with Brian in California, with Joyce in Europe—when the waiting through the summer really got to Florian. He played handball five times a week, more than he had in years. All things considered, he was in great shape. He logged a lot of miles on the Jeep, looked at a lot of land, talked to all kinds of people about buying and selling and building. He read reports and prospectuses, studied the local papers and business journals, spent hours down at the registry of deeds diligently taking notes on properties that hadn't turned over in years, that might never turn over, and thought about Brian. At least he had his chores, his ways of giving himself things to do. He also went to all the Theater Festival plays and even got more active on the board with Abby Allen Oliver; he chaired the committee overseeing the mainte-nance of the Saddle House and the other Festival buildings, and thought about Brian.

He kept telling himself to take it easy, slow down, let the days come and go. He remembered one of his first jobs, on a bull gang in a piano factory in the East Bronx, moving not only pianos in various stages of construction but all kinds of heavy loads. One day, unloading steam pipes from a flatbed, Florian almost tore up his back from the enormous sudden downward thrust as he slid the first pipe off. The other guys laughed. *Don't fight the material,* the crew boss told him. *Just guide it. Let it think it's going where it wants to.*

Did that work for trials? For manslaughter charges? For lawyers and judges and all those reporters and photographers who couldn't wait until September, when they'd have a real live juicy court case on their hands?

This day early in August Florian made only a brief stop at Mio's after handball. Mt. Early County was suffering through a rare heat wave, with temperatures breaking ninety, and yesterday his father's yellow Duster had boiled over. So Florian scheduled his handball for three o'clock, using the Fairlane to drop Salvatore off at the Polecat before-hand. He never used the Jeep for anything but business. Partly he wanted to keep the tax books legit. He also never liked to mess with anything that had done well by him, like the Jeep, by calling on it to do anything unexpected. On the way home he'd pick up his father and then stop for his mother at the Market Spot.

The Polecat crowd was so faithful that even Florian, who'd come by for Salvatore any number of times when the Duster was on the fritz, still felt like an outsider. The same guys had been hanging out there for years, starting back during their IE days. They were all retired now—retards, they called themselves. The younger IE people, the ones who still had jobs, went elsewhere.

"What you got there is eighty-five and out," a Polecat regular once explained to Florian. Even people who'd never been inside the IE plants referred to it as *there*. "You take your age, see, and add your years there. Like if you're forty and been there twenty, that adds up to sixty, meaning you're twenty-five short. Once you start, though, every year counts two, one for working and one for living. If you go in like I did at seventeen, you're barely past fifty before you hit your eighty-five, and that's it, just trot down to the personnel, sign the forms, have a nice life."

Florian remembered the guy pausing to down some beer, clear his throat, think of what he wanted to say next. At the Polecat you took your time. You stretched things out. (Salvatore fit right in. This spring, after weeks of talking about an underground sprinkler system, he'd decided against it. "It'd take more time putting in than I'd save using it the rest of my life.")

"The funny thing," the guy had gone on, "is I was shop steward in Plating when we struck for that retirement package. I mean, it wasn't like the '36 strike, but we still practically starved to get it. Even though I was just this kid in my twenties then and didn't believe I'd ever *see* fifty, I already hated the goddamn place and couldn't wait to walk out with that pension check in my pocket. Only when the time came, it sure felt funny. I mean, I never stopped hating the place. But it was what I had, you know, and maybe better than nothing, which is what I got now."

Even Lucille realized it was probably good for Salvatore to get up to the Polecat afternoons. He'd only drink his two or three beers, never got in arguments or fights or had trouble driving. Still, Lucille maintained a kind of official disapproval.

"What do you want me to do all day?" Salvatore would ask. "Run after girlies? Recite the Stations of the Cross?"

The Polecat was narrow and low-ceilinged with a blackened wood bar. Maybe fifteen people could crowd up to the bar, eight on stools whose red plastic seats were patched with red Mystik tape. Another dozen or so might squeeze into the four booths. They could have been the elders, the healers, of some ancient tribe, squatting on the outskirts of the village, nursing their gourds of foaming elixir.

Old man Polcari (the only way Salvatore ever referred to him) kept pretzels and beer nuts and beef jerky sticks on the cluttered counter, pickled eggs in a big metal-lidded jar. The walls were decorated with yellowed curly-edged pictures of Little League teams comprised of uniformed kids now maybe as old as the patrons, a calendar from Casey Auto Parts, an illuminated glass picture from Budweiser of a deer in a mountain stream, the lights making the water seem to rush by. Signs all over the place, some handmade, some from papers and magazines, some on small posters:

This is our Flag—Be PROUD of it!

Fishing Trip May 6—6 AM—$40—Black Fish—See Mel.

MIAs-POWs—You Are Not Forgotten

And on a slate blackboard over the bar Polcari (or someone) had chalked in: *Today's Special—So is Tomorrow.* Near the antique cash register a half-dozen collection canisters picked up odd change for the Dominican Sisters, the Salvation Army, Girl Scouts, leukemia, the Lions Club. Dwarfing everything else on the wall was a large poster map of the Wines of Italy.

You could always count on six, seven, eight people at the bar, maybe a few overflows or strangers in the booths. That meant, Salvatore said, you were never all by yourself, and never packed in like sardines. Today there were seven men when Florian got there.

"Afternoon, Mr. Rubio," Polcari called from behind the bar. Short, with a shining head and a huge white mustache, Polcari kept a pair of old dime-store reading glasses in the big pocket of his white apron, one black earpiece hooked outside so he could grab them when he needed to read a tab. Probably in his eighties, the oldest man there, Polcari was always polite and reserved with Florian.

Salvatore made a face. "Hey, so early?"

"You can drink longer at your age," Florian said, "than I can play handball at mine. One more, okay."

Hell, it wasn't all that different here from the handball courts, and maybe when he got too broken down to play, Florian would relegate the after-game foaming pitcher and midget franks at Mio's to the youngsters and join the retards here watching the afternoon local news, joining them too in their willingness to acknowledge that he'd just moved one step closer to the time when there'd be no more steps.

"This is Max." Salvatore leaned back so Florian could see the man on the next stool. "Maybe you met before."

"How's it going, Max? Make it three, okay," Florian told Polcari.

"Well—thank you, Mr. Rubio," Max said with a formal nod.

No matter how many times Florian tried to stop them, everybody at the Polecat called him Mr. Rubio. He'd say, "Look, *I'm* not Mr. Rubio. My *father* is Mr. Rubio." They'd just shake their heads. "Oh, no," they'd say. "He's Salvatore."

The problem was that Salvatore bragged about him, although never in his presence. "I don't say nothing," his father would insist. "I mean, they see things in the paper, they hear about you, and they say, *Hey, that's your son, right?* What am I supposed to say, I never saw you before?"

Right after the drownings, back in June, it'd been tough on Salvatore, facing all these lifelong Medway guys. Still, he was their old buddy, and they'd treated him decently. They felt bad about the whole thing, they told him, how terrible for everyone, the parents, the kids, everyone. What could you say, it was the kids these days. And the broken windows and dead fish, the Trent boy beaten up on the Fourth, the poor dog that Salvatore said was even dumber now from having his skull cracked with a brick. They shook their heads. Crazy kids, just as bad one place as another.

Polcari brought up something from under the bar: the *Mt. Early Express.* "See this yet, Mr. Rubio?" Polcari held up the front page of the feature section.

Florian gave a sideways look to Salvatore, who gave him a look back, as if to say, *Hey, I can't stop them from reading the paper, can I?*

"You want me to cut it out for you, Mr. Rubio?"

"Thanks, but we'll get a copy at the house."

"Okay," Polcari said. "I'll take it home for the wife."

Florian couldn't deal with the thought of Polcari—the others, too? —bringing items about him home to their unsuspecting wives.

Max then chimed in. "That's nice, giving you a party and everything, Mr. Rubio." Polcari, or Salvatore, had probably already shown the story to everyone.

Florian realized how quiet the place had become since he'd walked in. It wasn't as if they were hesitant to talk in front of him; they were just listening so they wouldn't miss anything *he* might say. Christ, if these guys were his age, back in the Bronx, they'd be ribbing the ass off him. "It's not really a party for me," he told them. "It's for the whole board, Miss Oliver too, all the actors." (Why did he call her Miss Oliver? Was he afraid that Abby Allen, which was what everybody called her, would sound pretentious?)

"Hey, still nice," Polcari said. "Ready for one more?"

Florian checked his watch while his father eyed him hopefully. He'd told Lucille they'd pick her up at six. "A quick one."

Until you crossed the city line and got out onto the green rolling curves of Route 15, just about everything in Medway looked sooty, crowded, dreary. Over to your left, IE's enormous brick and corrugated metal structures dominated blocks of moldering tenements, blighted streets with abandoned, cannibalized cars, sidewalks cluttered with torn plastic bags of garbage. Even the stray dogs looked dirty and forlorn, slinking around with heads drooping beneath scrawny shoulders. The cats looked as tough and wary as fighting cocks.

You could see why people in Medway thought of Trent kids as rich. And sure, Zack Arkins was a doctor, and the Caids owned a couple of hardware stores. Denise Sampson was raising her two sons on child support and a comfortable but hardly opulent divorce settlement from an insurance broker. Although none of them, including Florian, was *rich* in any way the term was used these days, from the streets and rotting triple-deckers of Medway they must have looked like Rockefellers and Astors, as powerful as robber barons, railroad kings, oil tycoons.

And what, after all, did old man Polcari really think of this guy on the festival board attending cocktail parties on the lawns of nineteenth-century estates, with salmon mousse appetizers and artistic arrangements of shrimp, with a gilded fountain recirculating a geyser of pink punch over a block of ice sculpted to resemble a faun, every touch designed to extract money from Boston and New York matrons for the production of lesser-known Shakespearean plays every summer? And it probably wouldn't do the least bit of good to point out that he felt as alien on that board, as out of place at those parties, as anyone in Medway, that he never would have dreamed of getting involved if he hadn't hit it off with Abby Allen a few summers back and let her talk him into it in a weak moment, when she assured him that his mere presence on the board would help break down the old-boy, old-line, old-money network that controlled all of Trent's arty summer exuberance. Of course it hadn't done any such thing. Certain networks were not destined to be broken.

Salvatore sat stiffly in the Fairlane. He could never relax in the Corvette and didn't find this car any more comfortable. (He'd never in his life, he'd once pointed out to Florian, owned a car anyone would ever bother stealing.) He wouldn't touch the power window controls or move his seat back or adjust his air vents. He just stared straight ahead, fingering his hat in his lap, like a bus tourist unfamiliar with the native language.

"Not cooling off much," Florian said.

"I told her. But she wanted to walk, so she's gonna walk. At least she got a ride home."

The Tomkins Road Market Stop had opened ages ago, when Trent hardly had another store to its name. It started as a roadside farm stand and had expanded to include a bakery, a dairy, a meat and fish market. It was a mile from the house, but Lucille, a real New Yorker, was used to walking everywhere. She'd take her puller, as she called it, a wire basket over two large wheels that she tugged at a sharp angle behind her, and shop there almost every day. What else would you do—go to some supermarket once a week and eat stale food the next six days?

Salvatore was silent as Florian drove, and then said, still staring straight ahead, "Somebody else there, he was sitting in a booth, maybe you didn't notice, he got relatives in California too. It was funny, when he went out there he took his father along, maybe eighty, ninety years old, who don't understand modern things. When they got there, the father, he was really angry because he couldn't get the Red Sox on their radio out there. 'Next time,' he says, 'I bring my own radio.' "

Florian looked over to see if Salvatore was laughing too. But his father was still staring ahead, with maybe just a hint of that pleased, satisfied look he'd exhibit when making a point. "Maybe," Florian said, "we'll pass that one along to Brian when he calls."

Brian called two or three times a week, a lot more frequently than during the years before. Maybe he felt closer, after living with them almost a year. He'd spend a half hour chatting with each of them in turn. Florian sometimes felt Brian was more open on the phone than he'd ever been in person, even though nothing much was happening, either here or in California. He'd gotten a job out there pumping gas and seemed to be doing okay.

"I still know a lot of the kids from before," he'd told Florian. "And no one here knows what's happening back there, which is kind of a relief. It's not bad, actually. I'm having a decent summer."

Brian rarely mentioned his mother, but they seemed to be getting along. At first Elly had been less than enthusiastic about Brian's return, but when Florian told her about the Fourth—RICH KIDS CAN'T GET AWAY WITH MURDER!!!—she quickly agreed to take him.

Florian had hardly talked to her since, although she'd get on the line occasionally to ask if anything had developed. When he'd tell her nothing was happening, that he hardly even saw Wachtel these days, she'd hand the phone over to Brian.

As for any information from the California detective Wally Brown had put him on to, Florian had just about given up. And who cared anymore? Brian was back with his mother and seemed to be getting along. Did it really matter why last year she'd sent her youngest, handsomest, most favored child across the continent to live with the husband she'd left ten years earlier? Hell, maybe she'd just had a bad week, a funny inkling, a bad karma. After all, they were into that stuff in California, crystal balls and funny cards and everything you always wanted to know about your life and true feelings.

As for Joyce, after that first really long, really nice letter slipped under the door the day she took off for Europe, making an impressively convincing case for this summer being a good time for them to be going their own ways in dealing with their own very difficult, very different agendas, they'd talked only a couple of times, once when she'd called from Rome, once from Lisbon. She wrote more letters, though, something Brian—ah, the telephone generation!—never even thought of, and Florian wrote back, although she'd usually be off to somewhere else and he'd have to hope to catch her at her next stop. She seemed to be enjoying herself, and he was glad. He didn't blame her for getting away from Benn and all his troubles and from himself and all his troubles, although he really missed her. How nice it would have been, he'd thought more than once, if he and Joyce could have had the luxury of loving each other a while without everything else coming down on their heads. Hey . . . did they love each other? Was that all they'd needed—time and concentration, a little more privacy, a considerably larger chance to focus on each other?

Florian turned into the dirt parking area of the Market Stop and eased up to the front entrance, where Lucille usually waited on the shaded bench. "We're late," he said. "Maybe she went back inside."

"Stay, I'll go find her."

Florian kept the motor idling, the air conditioner humming. He punched on the local AM and caught the lottery at six. He hated the lottery, hated all the lures and lies and deceptions it stood for, most of all hated the state for paying some superslick ad agency to entice all those people who couldn't afford a cup of coffee into believing their number might really come up—their anniversary, their kids' birthdays, their underwear sizes—and wipe out all the immutable and universal rules of the whole crummy world they'd known all their lives. Luck, was that what you elected the government of the state of Massachusetts to sell? What the fuck was luck?

The weather lady said the heat looked as if it would stay forever, pointing out that today was exactly six months from the annual ice fishing derby on Bottleneck Lake.

"Florry!" he heard his father call. "Florry!"

Florian scrambled out of the car and ran around the front. Salvatore hovered over Lucille, grasping her left arm, steadying her. An ashen-faced boy in a Market Stop uniform had her right arm. Between them Lucille staggered formlessly, shrunken, her eyes as dazed and blank as wallpaper.

IV

RETURN IN SEPTEMBER

8

Joyce spent the summer traveling through Denmark and Sweden early on, Italy and Germany at the end. The best, though, was the three weeks in between with Katarina Scanlon in the hills outside Lisbon. "You soon enough learn all about the pits and dregs of being unmanned," Katarina had pointed out on the first night after they'd arrived together: painted raffia rockers and a pitcher of sangria on Katarina's second-floor balcony, overlooking the lights of Lisbon and the dark broad swath of the Ebro flowing past the monument at Belém into the Atlantic. "You might as well get what you can out of the good part."

It certainly had been different, with Katarina introducing you to men friends of her men friends as you tried to reimagine a life for yourself. Joyce had hoped that being away from Trent would bring everything into a cool, crystalline focus. She'd have settled for even the least movement in that direction.

"Given what I'm running away from," she'd told Katarina, "I'm not sure that a plunge into Lisbon's social whirl will make life any easier."

"Not easier, more fun. What better help in deciding between the two major loves of your life than auditioning a few minor ones, for comparison's sake?"

"Is that why you never married—because you keep comparing everyone to everyone else?"

"That'll do it, right? Katarina's Law of Diminishing Expectations. The truth is, you're not in bad shape—two choices back home but no chains. Relax, listen to the fado, trust me to steer you clear of the mustache twirlers."

They had a great time going places together, the beach and casino, train rides into the small towns, picnics in the countryside. She and Florian connected a few times over the crackling transatlantic phone, and she sent postcards from everywhere, even a few letters. It was hard for him to catch her on the run, so she may have missed some of his letters.

Those she got at Katarina's just made her already unreal situation—going out with three or four different men—even more unreal. She wasn't at all guilty thinking of Benn but sometimes got a funny feeling about Florian.

"The Japanese crane is monogamous," Katarina pointed out, "and if I ever fall in love with one, I will be too."

Not that Joyce got seriously entangled with anyone; she wasn't interested, didn't see where it would do her head any good to start catting around Europe.

On one notable stroll to the post office she discovered letters from both of them. Florian said he missed her and wrote about the other parents and lawyers and Brian and his family. Bennett's letter was shorter and more businesslike. He didn't say anything about missing her, although she guessed the letter itself indicated some interest. He sounded calm but formal, reserved, not yet ready to forgive her for whatever sin he was charging her with. He mentioned mutual friends, vague business trips, renovations around the house—he'd discovered rot under the deck. All in all, he didn't sound very upbeat.

What gave the two piggyback letters an even stranger effect was that she'd gone out the evening before with a stylish, slick-haired assistant director of the Museu Calouste Gulbenkian, who'd taken her back to his apartment after dinner and, full of brandy and excitement and high hopes, had edged closer on the couch and whispered to her in his throatiest Portuguese. He translated it for her as *I can envision your nipples like ripe red strawberries,* and she hurt his feelings when she burst out laughing.

As the plane swooped down over the green Connecticut hills for its early-morning landing at Bradley Field, Joyce felt little emotion. She hadn't told either Florian or Bennett when she was returning, so took the airport limo to Trent, picked up her VW from storage, and headed out on Route 15. Only then, with Mt. Early looming up over her *(that natural and stupendous eminence,* as an early settler called it), did she feel she was home, realizing that the new and carefree self she'd been trying to create over the summer had been discarded at the Frankfurt airport. She drove with the windows open; it'd been warm everywhere in Europe and she felt reinvigorated by the crisp breeze. By March you were deathly sick of the Trent winter, and those occasional April snows could break your heart, but early September was sharp and winy with the scent of apples, with oaks and sugar maples and roadside hemlocks exploding into gorgeous bursts of color.

The things you noticed after a summer away: driving into Trent,

Joyce was struck by the bastardized colonial McDonald's at the end of Elderberry Street. The year-rounders and all the boutique owners had fought bitterly against a fast-food outlet in this lovely old historic village. Joyce had voted for it in the referendum because the opponents were the worst kind of Trent snobs, who argued that it would attract the wrong elements, meaning teenagers, especially from Medway, along with those tourists and drifters otherwise too poor to inflict Trent with their presence.

In a rare burst of agreement, Benn also supported it. No town, he figured, had the right to tell any business where it could or couldn't operate. In the five years since, neither of them had ever stepped inside. The place did well, and somehow the Village of Trent had survived: three blocks of Elderberry Street lined with craft shops, art galleries, boutiques, gift stores, ice-cream parlors, even Marylou's Mustards, where Marylou herself thrived by selling to tourists twenty or so home-made varieties in fancy, reribboned jars, along with the Hollisworth Inn and a half-dozen either posh or folksy restaurants and the old limestone fortress that served as both town hall and wintertime community center for the town's year-rounders.

It was still only midmorning, on Labor Day Sunday, when she re-claimed with a sigh, a shrug, good old gingerbready No. 9 at the Log Cabins, with its ersatz twigs on the green door. She'd actually wired ahead from Europe to reserve this cabin, but now she barely glanced around the room, as if not wanting to be too aware of this place she'd incomprehensibly chosen to return to, over a beautiful home on South Corner. She'd be the first to admit there was little to be said for the rosy wallpaper, the plastic water glasses in their cellophane wrapping, the che-nille bedspread, the glossy dresser: all together it looked as fake as a Hollywood set. It was all she could do to keep from exclaiming, *Why? Why, dear God, are you doing this?*

School would begin Tuesday, after the holiday, and for the first time ever she'd skipped the whole week of orientation meetings and curricu-lum conferences. She'd wired Brownie from Düsseldorf that her return flight had been scrubbed; she'd make the start of classes but would miss orientation. She hadn't wanted to come back before she'd have a full day of students and classes to keep her too busy to think about Bennett, and Florian, and the trial.

Kicking off her shoes, removing her panty hose, she settled into the one comfortable chair, under the one good lamp, to take a look at the way the Sunday *Express* was handling the imminent trial. It featured long recaps on the drownings, photos, maps, backup stories about the dead kids and the boys on trial, about Patrick Delehanty, the prosecutor, about Ira Wachtel and Harry Diggs, and even ran a long piece analyzing differences between Trent and Medway under the heading:

TRAGIC DROWNINGS
STIR PASSIONS
IN MT. EARLY COUNTY

The *Express* itself, of course, served as the perfect example of the very split it was talking about. It'd won some state and even national awards and was all in all a pretty good paper, considering that Mt. Early was the least populous county in the state and that Medway, its only city, had in the last decade dropped from fifty thousand people to thirty. Trent, the largest of the small towns, had a year-round population of barely seven thousand, increasing to maybe ten in the summer.

Even this small readership was split down the middle. North County meant Medway and the mills and IE Plastics, bars and pool halls and secondhand shops, row houses with painted Virgins staring out from giant clamshells or tiny bathtubs half buried in corner yards. For its Medway readers (Joyce's students and their parents), the *Express* provided lots of comics, an easy crossword puzzle, a hunting and fishing column by the president of the Rod and Gun Club, endless box scores and stories and statistics about the Celtics and Red Sox and all those school and college and professional football teams.

South County was composed of Trent and the other, even smaller, towns with their nineteenth-century mansions and beautiful contemporary homes around Bottleneck Lake and along the woodsy and hilly country roads, and it boasted a caste system as rigid as colonial India's. The year-rounders, or householders, the people who *lived* there, stood at the top (although some, like the Sargasso River Highlanders, stood at the top of the top). Then, in descending order, came the second-homers, mostly from Boston and New York, whose expensive summer hideaways remained vacant the rest of the year. Then those who also stayed all summer, but in rented houses or condos. Then the monthlies, the weeklies, the weekenders, and finally, heaven help us all, the dailies, those untouchables whom even the weekenders looked down on as plodding cowlike hordes cluttering up the streets and sidewalks and gift shops, tossing their candy wrappers into the gutter.

For the Trent crowd, the *Express* ran a full financial section, literate editorials, a second, more difficult crossword puzzle, excellent criticism of art and drama and music, and a Joy of Nature feature by one of the local bird-watchers. It also covered more national and international news than most small-town papers. Even so, it'd never really won over the South County gentry, at whose doorsteps every morning were dropped fat cellophane-wrapped editions of the *Globe,* the *Times,* the *Wall Street Journal.*

The noon news on Channel 6 also devoted a big chunk of time to the trial, even showing the most ferocious collisions from last year's Trent-Medway football game, spiced up with grunts and shouts and explosions of breath and leather and bodies. It was awful, boys flying through the air with arms and legs flailing, slamming into the frozen ground, butting helmets like enraged animals.

The last image, superimposed over the cheering crowd, the jumping and twirling cheerleaders, showed a Trent player woozily making his way to the sideline and dropping to his knees, pulling off his helmet to reveal a stream of blood rushing from what looked like a smashed nose.

And now, with the trial about to begin, residents recall the healthy rivalry played out every year on the athletic fields of these two fine but very different institutions: the Medway Mountain Lions versus the Trent Courtiers. Yet they're unable to forget how, in the early hours of June twenty-first, youthful bravado went awry, and two lives were tragically cut short in the murky waters of Bottleneck Lake.

She jumped at a knock, then glanced at the telephone, reassuring herself of some link to the outside. She remembered the tiny magnifying peephole—a small man with a ballooning head, like an image in a fun house mirror, in gray fedora and suit jacket.

"Yes?"

"Ira Wachtel," he said. "I'm a lawyer, working for the Rubios. Could we chat a minute?"

She'd heard the name from Florian, and the fellow sounded okay, looked okay through the weird eyehole. She raised her voice. "According to the friendly policewoman who talks to the girls at school every year, you never let strangers into your motel room."

"What about the coffee shop?"

"Give me fifteen minutes," she said.

Had Florian told the lawyer where she was, or had he found her on his own, through the police, the motel people?

Wachtel stood up from a chrome-edged Formica window table

when she entered: few customers, none nearby. His hat lay on the glossy red seat beside him, and his thinning hair and speckled eyeglass frames, his small mouth, made him look like someone Benn would write off as a lost cause who, despite a decent law practice, didn't play golf or tell raunchy jokes or, kiss of death, possess a strong, confident handshake. Still, the man hadn't scared off Florian, and his eyes, at least, seemed intelligent.

"You found me with impressive dispatch," Joyce said. "I just got back."

"Don't blame Florian; he was no help at all." He spoke in a curiously flat but very focused tone.

The gimpy middle-aged waitress brought over a mug of coffee for Joyce and eight—eight?—little plastic containers of half-and-half. The place was a café, a truck stop, boasting of enormous breakfasts and homemade cream pies. Joyce had eaten there a few times, learning one evening that if you didn't stop them beforehand, your order would arrive with viscous caramel-colored gravy cratered in the mashed potatoes and oozing over the roasted chicken. Still, it was a nice-enough place, a welcome change from the places where she usually went with friends.

"Breakfast or lunch, dearie?"

"Neither, thanks. You have something if you're hungry, Mr. Wachtel. I'm still on German time."

"Actually, I grabbed something earlier, at McDonald's." Joyce must have given him a funnier look than she realized because he added with a shrug, owl-eyed, "It's quick and not half bad."

"Is this an official visit?"

"Flo and I pick on each other a lot but we're old friends, and I'm doing my best to represent his son."

"What's going to happen at the trial?"

"Any lawyer who makes predictions should be disbarred." He smiled humorlessly, one of his standard jokes. "I'm just trying to give Brian every break we can."

"And you think I can tell you all about Jamie Pitt."

He eyed her for a moment. "I know everything I need to know about Jamie Pitt." He seemed a bit stiff, almost embarrassed. "I'd like you to stay away from Flo until the trial's over."

It annoyed her that he knew, that Florian had probably told him. Then she laughed.

"I'm sorry you think it's funny. If you had any idea what Brian's facing, you wouldn't—"

"I know what Brian's facing. What's funny is being told to stay away from someone I haven't seen in two months."

"I thought if you managed a whole summer apart, you could survive a week or so longer."

"I can't go back to Europe, you realize. I've got a job."

"Maybe, considering how busy Flo will be with the trial, and you with school, you just won't have time for each other. It might not matter, but you know how small-town gossip gets around."

Hoping to catch him off guard, she asked: "Have you spoken to my husband?"

He weighed this. "I'm not prying into your personal life, Mrs. Johnway. I just hoped you'd be willing to help Florian, Brian, all of us."

"If you and Florian are such good friends, why didn't you tell *him* to stay away from me?"

Wachtel blinked without any show of emotion, least of all humor. "Because he'd knock my head off. Thanks for seeing me. I'll appreciate anything you can do."

Because the man was so low-keyed, so middling and earnest in his talk, it wasn't until she got back to her motel room that Joyce realized how much she resented the intrusion. It simply wasn't fair to lay something like that on her. What did Wachtel think, that some Medway Kmart clerk would see her with Florian and form a lynch mob to go after Brian?

She'd been intending to call Florian to let him know she was back, and did so now, almost as a matter of principle. If Flo himself wanted her to stay away, she would, but she wasn't going to do it because of some lawyer.

She got Florian's father, Salvatore, and she told him she'd just got back and called to say hello, to see how everyone was.

"Oh, everyone is okay. We're doing all right. Even Lucille, you know, she may even be getting a little better, it's hard to tell."

"What do you mean? What's wrong with Lucille?"

He told her that she'd collapsed almost a month ago but was home now from the hospital. She couldn't move one side; she couldn't talk.

"I'm terribly sorry," she said, wondering why that fool Wachtel hadn't prepared her for this, wondering if she'd missed a letter from Florian. It sounded like a stroke, but Salvatore didn't use the term, and neither did she. "Is there anything I can do, any way to help?"

"No, no. Thank you. We manage okay. We get by. And Brian, he came back from California after it happened. He's a good boy, you know, he helps a lot."

"Maybe I could come over—sometime when it's convenient—to say hello, wish her my best."

"Oh, yeah," he said, but with more politeness than enthusiasm. "That'd be very nice. Florian, meanwhile, he's not here right now. Handball, you know. They wear gloves and hit a little black ball against the wall and afterward go to the midget frankfurter place for lunch."

"Midgets serving frankfurters?" she said before she could stop herself.

"You'll see," Salvatore assured her, not at all offended.

For Salvatore, life had become simple: he stayed with Lucille every minute, day and night. Since they'd brought her home from the hospital, Lucille slept nights in the downstairs guest room, in the hospital bed Florian had rented from the medical supply house in Medway. Salvatore slept on the couch next to it.

"I'll do it," he'd said, shaking off Florian's ideas about a cleaning woman, a cook, a nurse, a companion. "Don't worry. We're okay."

By Labor Day weekend it'd been three weeks since her collapse in the vegetable aisle of the Market Stop—checking through bunches of celery, the manager told them—on that hottest day of the summer, after walking the mile there dragging her little puller behind her. But the heat, the long walk had been incidental, the doctors said. She'd had a stroke, a major aneurysm of a blood vessel in the brain. It was quite serious and would have happened no matter what.

She'd come home after a week in the hospital, the doctors saying the family could give her the medicines and do the exercises. If she was destined to improve, she would. You couldn't tell this early.

When the visiting nurse came to instruct them, Florian and Brian had also gathered around Lucille's bed, but Salvatore stepped in front, blocking them off, so the nurse had to talk directly to him. He listened carefully and practiced the exercises for her approval, moving Lucille's right arm gently, slowly, up and down.

"When you give her something to drink, just put your left arm behind her head to support it like this. . . ."

Florian had never before dealt with real sickness. Lucille and Salvatore, Elly, the kids, had always been healthy. In the first days after his mother's collapse, Florian pumped the doctors for information and studied the book on stroke they recommended. Desperately he tried to learn everything he could. It was a way to keep from being overwhelmed, to stay on top of things.

Salvatore showed no interest in what the doctors said, what the medical books explained, and turned stony when Florian tried to pass information along. He'd gotten all the day-by-day information he needed from the nurse and beyond that asked no questions. What happened happened, so you dealt with it. All that counted was that Lucille lay in her special metal bed with the big metal crank and could not move the drooping right side of her face, the paralyzed right side of her body. She could eat and drink only if someone held the spoon or glass for her, could stand only if someone lifted and supported her, could go to the bathroom only if someone managed the bedpan or got her onto the toilet. Someone had to bathe and dry her, and if she was to go anywhere beyond the guest room someone had to raise her from the bed and strap her into the wheelchair and then push and steer it. She could not talk and did not seem to understand anything said to her.

Nothing else mattered. Lucille needed help and Salvatore would provide it. As for the name of her troubles—Salvatore never once uttered the word *stroke*—or its cause, its current state, its future prospects, what difference did any of that make compared with getting her through each day?

At any moment, Salvatore concentrated only on what Lucille needed at that moment. He prepared and fed her all her meals. Reluctantly he let Florian and Brian take care of their own breakfasts, since he was busy at that time getting Lucille up and dressed, but insisted on making lunch and dinner for everyone. He'd wheel Lucille into the kitchen twice a day so she could watch him fuss at the sink and stove and refrigerator. "She keeps an eye on me," he said. "Maybe if I do something real bad she'll yell at me, but so far she ain't complained."

When he vacuumed or mopped or dusted around the house, he'd wheel her from room to room with him, keeping an eye on her for the first sign of tiredness. She could give way in an instant, without warning, slumping down in the chair or flopping helplessly to one side, kept from tumbling out by the wide cloth strap Salvatore never forgot to fasten.

When he'd turn on the TV set, she'd watch the ball games, the quiz shows, the comedies, the same way she watched him cook and clean, her right arm lifeless in her lap, her right leg splayed, her face alop, her right eye unfocused.

On nice days Salvatore would wheel her outside, all bundled up, for fresh air, making sure her wide-brimmed hat kept the sun out of her eyes. Padgett would join them out there, either tagging along at Salvatore's heel or circling the wheelchair, trying to get Lucille's attention by barking up at her, "WHOUFF! WHOUFF!" Salvatore wouldn't shoo away the animal or try to quiet it. Who knows, maybe Lucille liked the movement, the sounds. After all, it was Lucille's dog, and maybe it had really done its best that night when the people broke the windows. The vet had fixed it up pretty good, although a big dark scar showed through the hair on the top of its head, but all in all, Salvatore said, it didn't seem as much of a pain in the ass as before.

Salvatore spoke to Lucille all the time, reversing his lifelong habit of listening. With lively expressions and exaggerated gestures, he rambled on about the weather, the TV shows, what he was doing, where he was wheeling her. "Okay, hang on," he'd call to her. "We're going out and don't want you blowing away in the breeze. Maybe we need a sweater, what do you think? Let's get one."

Before Lucille's collapse, Salvatore had never, either in the Bronx or in Trent, picked up a broom, washed a dish, ironed a shirt. Most amazing of all was his cooking. Confronting a stove and oven for the first time, he wasn't half bad, certainly nothing like those goofy TV husbands who couldn't drop bread into a toaster. Hoping to encourage him, Florian thought of presenting him with a couple of cookbooks but dropped the idea after discussing it with Brian. They were afraid he'd take it the wrong way. Lucille had never owned a cookbook.

Salvatore stopped going to the Polecat without saying anything to his pals up there. Why didn't he at least call, Florian asked, so they wouldn't be worried? They won't be worried, Salvatore assured him, and he was probably right, because none called. It was like the handball court: the place itself was part of the friendship, and what happened outside didn't count. If Salvatore's buddies bumped into him somewhere else, they'd feel funny and not have anything to say.

Salvatore insisted that Brian get out of the house regularly, see his friends, ride his bike, whatever, insisted that Florian keep up his handball. "Otherwise you just get grumpy, and Lucille already got one grump in me and don't need two."

As for himself, Salvatore didn't even drink beer at home now. He hadn't gone fishing or worked on the yellow Duster, whose overheating had been a problem the last time he'd taken it out, the day of Lucille's stroke. The gardening he kept up, although at first he had trouble wheeling Lucille over the bumpy ground to watch him work. He was afraid the chair might get caught in a rut and spill over, so he sent Brian to the lumberyard for sheets of plywood to make a path.

Salvatore joked a lot, not wanting them to think caring for Lucille was getting him down. "It's like Tony's pushcart," he said about the wheelchair after laying out the plywood. "His friends, you know, they ask Tony, *How does it go?* and Tony, he tells them, *It don't go, dummy, you gotta push it.*"

He worked in the garden late afternoons, with Lucille watching from the shade of the surrounding trees. Afterward he'd come in, steering the wheelchair ahead of him with one hand and pulling behind him Lucille's little market basket filled with green peppers and zucchini and fresh parsley and basil and crunchy heads of romaine.

"It's coming okay," he'd say about the garden. "Everything's coming good this year."

Back in street clothes after the game, Florian and Sam and Tom grabbed their gym bags and walked down the block to Mio's, where they took their usual back table away from the bar and TV. Maeve brought over a pitcher of Genesee Cream Ale. "Franks all around, right? Two pair mustard, one pair kraut."

Tom was in the middle of a long joke about why condoms came in packages of six, seven, and twelve, with Florian aimlessly taking in the room, when he went right past Joyce. It was as if the difference between what he saw and what he expected to see was too great. Slowly he turned back. Alone at a table across the room, Joyce seriously, relentlessly, met his gaze.

Florian waited, hoping for a clue from her expression. She always looked as if she wanted to *share* something with you, some kind of connection—a joke? A story? A secret pleasure? Some sadness or disappointment? At the moment she seemed unconcerned about how out of place she looked in her very simple but probably very expensive summer dress. Even though Mio's was a few steps above the Polecat, it got mostly a factory crowd, the only women coming from IE or Easy Breeze Curtains or the bottling plant, older women in hair nets and stretch pants and big billowing print blouses.

Florian dropped three singles to the table as he got up. "I have to see somebody," he said to Tom and Sam, moving away. He hurried over and put his hand on the back of the empty chair at Joyce's table. "Expecting someone?"

"You," she said, so quietly he could hardly hear her over the noise from the other tables, the TV at the bar. "Your father tipped me off."

Both could have been frozen, she in her chair, he still standing. He hadn't seen her all summer but somehow Mio's was the wrong place, too public by half, for the enthusiasm he felt. He compromised by bending over for what would look like a friendly kiss on the cheek, hoping to make up for it by whispering, "God, I've missed you. You can't imagine how good it feels to see you again."

She looked pleased, seemed to understand. "Did you have a good game? Salvatore said you'd be in a better mood if you won."

"We split."

"So-so then."

"Better right this minute than I've been along the way. You probably did the right thing, getting away. I've been lousy company. Was Europe good? Did you have a great time?"

"Oh, yes. It was fine. Of course, now that I'm back, you've got the trial and I'm going to have to make some decision about Benn." She reached across the table, bumping her almost empty coffee cup, and touched his hand. "I just heard about your mother. I'm terribly sorry."

"I didn't write or anything about it. I figured what the hell, you were on your vacation. Anyhow, that's how it goes. We're getting used to it. You wonder, though, what it's like for her, with the light switch in your head suddenly being turned off. The mistake, I guess, is looking for some kind of logic, thinking you got the right to some kind of explanation."

"Both your parents are such wonderful people. You've got a great kid too, in Brian."

"You think maybe I'm the black sheep?"

"I think you're absolutely terrible," she said.

Maeve snuck up with two glasses of Genesee and four of Mio's midget bun-wrapped franks on a paper plate. Florian glanced back at the other table: Sam nodded; Tom made a sweeping gesture.

"It looks like your friends are treating."

"These two are yours," Florian said. "I hope you like mustard." He yanked a napkin from the metal dispenser, cradled a frank in it, and handed it to Joyce. She seemed to be examining it, maybe two inches long, then laughed. Mio's theory was that both men and women got a kick out of them. "They're delicious," Florian said.

She took a bite and chewed thoughtfully. "Very tasty indeed," she said, putting the frank back on the paper plate. She looked past him, narrowing her eyes, and he turned to see Sam and Tom walking over. Both nodded, smiling at Joyce as Tom dropped Florian's gym bag to the floor with a clunk and kicked it under his chair. "You forgot this." He slapped Florian's back, hard enough to sting, eyeing Joyce. "We trust you're enjoying the local cuisine, Miss—ah—"

"It's exquisite," Joyce said. She glanced down at the two and a half franks left on the paper plate. "Unfortunately I didn't realize you were going to be so generous and had lunch before I came."

Florian considered leaving them standing there, gaping mindlessly, but relented. "This is Sam—Tom—a couple of aging handball players whose knees are shot." He gestured toward Joyce. "This is a friend who just arrived in town."

"The raving beauty you told us about?" Tom suggested.

"A special someone?" Sam put in.

"You got it," Florian said.

"Griselda the Fair," Joyce said, accepting Tom's offered hand, then Sam's.

"It's a shame they both have to run," Florian said.

Nodding, smiling, explaining how lovely it was meeting her, they edged away, shuffled along, left.

"Your lawyer warned me about seeing you," Joyce said.

"What?"

"He thought it could cloud the issue or whatever during the trial. He's probably right, but I thought just bumping into you here by accident would be okay. A couple of friends sharing a tiny frankfurter."

"Sometimes that guy's an absolute pain in the ass."

"I'll call—he didn't mention anyone tapping our phones. Oh, Flo— I hope so much it works out for Brian, and you too, all of you. I'm so *happy* to see you again."

It seemed a funny thing to say while starting to cry.

Monday morning Joyce went to school to pull things together, expecting to find the place deserted over the Labor Day holiday. She'd even wondered if she could get in, but there must have been a dozen cars in the faculty lot. The front door was wide open, teachers all over the place, getting supplies, organizing lesson plans, setting up homerooms.

The janitorial staff was so shorthanded you couldn't expect much more from them than an emptied wastebasket. She'd come prepared, though, wearing an old sweatshirt and her Eleanor Roosevelt jeans, and after borrowing a bucket and sponges from the storeroom, she scrubbed her windows, her blackboard, her desk, the kids' desks. Her predecessor had used this room seventeen years, Joyce twelve; during that time it'd been painted once. If this were a prison, you could probably get a court order condemning it. (Brownie had a plaque on his office wall: *Education is not the filling of a pail, but the lighting of a fire*, prompting Katarina to comment, "I don't know about suggesting the lighting of fires to anyone in this place.")

Every year the energy and hope and enthusiasm you'd thought had deserted you forever in June miraculously returned over the summer. By August you were jotting down ideas, clipping newspaper articles, under-lining passages in books you'd begun reading just for relaxation. What she found most frustrating was the curious contentment most Medway kids exhibited about their lives. Sure, they wanted their cars and TVs, jobs good enough to let them get by and marry and bring up kids they could send, one day, to Medway High. They were fiercely proud of their families, their school, their city, and would defend all that to the death against the mocking condescension they felt coming from Trent.

Only Trent kids could have dreamed up that idiotic MORP. And it was a Trent kid Joyce had seen driving a jacked-up pickup with a bumper sticker reading:

NO FREE RIDES
GAS GRASS OR ASS!

It was the Trent kids whose rock groups called themselves Religious Vomit and Metal Mucus and Death Eats a Cracker.

They'd grow up, all of them. They always did, in Medway as well as Trent, and except for a few lucky or unlucky exceptions, the vast majority would go the ways that kids from Medway and Trent always went.

She was working at her desk in her empty homeroom when Brownie himself came by. She was impressed: even the principal was boning up for tomorrow morning. Then he handed her a stapled packet of mimeo-graphed pages in an orange cover:

"Our Responsibilities in the Days Ahead"
Do NOT Show to Students

"I hope you can give this some of your time," he said, not wholly without sarcasm. "The rest of us went over every word during orienta-tion. We're going to have to deal with that trial every day, for as long as it lasts."

Going through the packet after Brownie left, she guessed it was the work of the same visiting grief counselors who had come by after the drownings.

She turned toward the sound at the open door: Jamie Pitt. Joyce had never expected him to set foot in the place again. And the tan sweater, the creased trousers and polished shoes, made him vastly more presentable than his usual jeans and ratty sneakers. He'd also gotten a shorter, neater haircut. Maybe he'd gone off, diploma in hand, and landed a dress-up job.

As always, he was smiling. "I didn't know if I'd even find you here, Mrs. Johnway. I hope it's not a bad time."

"It's a fine time. It's good to see you again." Joyce stood up, closing the packet and turning it over on her desk. He stared, not at it but at the small hand-painted glass bowl that she kept on her desk. A tenth-grade girl who'd gotten pregnant a few years back and couldn't talk to her parents because she was afraid they'd beat the living daylights out of her, couldn't talk to the boy because he'd left town, had painted the bowl and given it to her with a pink note inside saying *Thanks!*

"Where are you these days, Jamie? What are you doing with yourself?"

He seemed to turn shy, but wasn't that always how he played it, not quite shuffling and obsequious, but close? Then she realized he was simply confused. "Where am I? Jeez, Mrs. Johnway, I'm here. Right here. Going to school, starting tomorrow like everyone else. Where'd you think I was?"

"But you graduated."

"I guess you didn't hear—someone said you were away all summer. What happened, you see, was all the right credits didn't actually pan out the way they were supposed to."

"How could they not pan out? You must have failed something."

"Man and Woman in Lit," he said.

Sometimes Jamie absolutely infuriated her. That was just like him, flunking a gut course like that (C and C, the kids cheerfully called it, Cocks and Cunts) while passing hers, which was far more demanding. Again, she focused on the clothes, the haircut. "Are you working after school then—with only one credit to make up?"

"The boatyard. Remember?"

Of course: it was the trial he was dressing for, not any job. He'd be testifying, and some lawyer, the prosecutor, somebody, had groomed him for it.

"I won't take up all your time," he said, "but just wanted to ask if maybe you could pass something along. You know that kid's father, don't you? The Rubio kid?"

Joyce could feel her facial muscles going rigid, like a clay mask drying. Good God in heaven, first Wachtel and now Jamie Pitt. She sees Florian a few times and everybody seems to think it's the Duke and Duchess of Windsor. She took a slow breath, hoping Jamie would go on, but he seemed willing to wait. "His name's Brian," she said at last, sharply. "And yes, I've met his family. They're neighbors, a few houses down."

Those wide, polite eyes did not waver. "I read about them in the paper. The father, he started out real poor and worked his way right up. That's how it goes, right? The good old American way. Only I happened to hear around, you know, that the father's saying things like I'm out to get his kid and it's my fault for all kinds of things I never did. I mean, I don't think he'd try to do anything to me—"

"Of course he wouldn't."

"Still, he's bad-mouthing me all over the place. It'd just be nice if he at least understood—and you too, I'd really like you to understand this—that I'm only doing exactly what people tell me I gotta do, which is tell the truth."

"I have no idea what anybody's saying about you, Jamie, or what kind of truth you're telling. I do remember, though, that when you came to the house right after the drownings you never even mentioned the girl—Brian Rubio's girlfriend, his date that night, whatever. You know who I'm talking about."

"If it was up to me, Mrs. Johnway, I'd as soon the girl was willing to tell the truth too, just like me. You'd think, wouldn't you, if it was true that I did anything to her, she'd be anxious to say so. Anyhow, all I actually wanted to see you about was this special school requirement."

"You just said you wanted to see me about Brian's father."

"That too. But since I didn't graduate like I was supposed to, I'm back now on special probation for the extra credit and need a special adviser. So I wanted to ask if you'd, you know, be my special adviser."

"And that's it then? No more reasons why you came to see me?"

"Oh, no," he assured her. "Those are all the reasons right there."

When she finally pulled everything together and headed out to the parking area, she saw two janitors working to the right of the entrance. The man on the ground steadied an extension ladder against the front of the building while the other clung with one hand at the top, two stories up. She walked farther out and saw that the one high up was slicing through the rope at one corner of a big white sheet with flaming red letters:

RICH KIDS CANT
GET AWAY WITH MURDER!!!

All four of them—Florian, Elly, Brian, and Salvatore—agreed it would be best not to take Lucille to the courthouse. The question was whether

Salvatore would leave her behind every day—with a stranger, somebody who had never known the way she was before, the real Lucille. They discussed the possibility of her sister coming up from New York, but Salvatore had never liked Aunt Rosa. What, turn over his responsibilities to someone like that, a bossy loudmouth?

Salvatore was not prepared, for whatever reason, even his grandson's trial, to desert Lucille, yet couldn't bring himself to say so. Neither could Florian. It had to come from Brian.

"There's nothing to decide," Brian finally told him. "All you can do there is sit. At least here you can take care of Grandma."

On the first morning Salvatore got up early so that he had Lucille all dressed and in her wheelchair in time for him to make everybody breakfast. He then steered Lucille outside so he could say good-bye to them at the car. Salvatore almost crushed Brian in his hug before twisting away. Brian bent over the wheelchair and kissed Lucille on the cheek, holding her face in his hands, then quickly got into the Fairlane.

Outside the Hollisworth Inn, Elly waited beneath the awning. Brian helped her into the front seat and moved in back himself.

Elly didn't even try to smile. She'd gone easy on the makeup, the hairdo, the quiet suit and low heels. Florian himself wore a blue pinstripe, Brian brown trousers, nice brown tie, tan sport coat. Yesterday Salvatore had spent all afternoon ironing enough suits and shirts and ties to last them a week. Lucille had never allowed anyone to send clothes out; she washed and ironed everything herself, so now that was what Salvatore did.

"How are we all?" Elly asked. She didn't even try to hide the strain, her voice thin and a little harsh.

"Okay," Brian said from the back seat.

Although Elly had been prepared for it, seeing Lucille had disturbed her. She'd flown east steeling herself for one disaster and didn't seem to have anything left over for another. Elly had always liked Florian's parents; she and Lucille had been real friends.

"Well, everybody certainly looks very nice," Elly said, still coldly, turning to look back at Brian as Florian pulled away from the curb. "Did you have breakfast?"

He laughed. "Grandpa made enough for an army."

Elly probably hadn't gotten anything down beyond black coffee. Last night at dinner she'd eaten just enough to keep from offending Salvatore, who'd made a special lamb and beef stew for her. Earlier in the summer Elly had looked good with her California ruddiness. Now, especially without much makeup, she seemed pallid and taut. Her eye sockets had darkened, and she'd probably lost ten pounds since July.

Florian himself had stopped using the scale at the handball court after having dropped from 180 to 164. The guys said he was playing better than ever, quick as a cat.

"Have you heard any more from Wachtel this morning, any last-minute news, any new ideas?"

"No," Florian said. Over the years he'd forgotten how sharp Elly could sound when she really wasn't put out at all but just scared and worried. Although right now she was infuriated because *all this had happened* when anyone with half a brain could see how easily it could have been avoided. All right, maybe it wasn't exactly anyone's fault, but it happened, and shouldn't have, and it ate the hell out of her.

On the porch of the big white colonial on Quahog Lane, Wachtel waited with briefcase in hand. He'd wanted them to arrive at court together every day, which was okay with Florian, but when Wachtel offered to pick them up, Florian said no. He didn't want to depend on his goddamn lawyer for that too.

Wachtel hurried down the path and emerged from under the rose trellis in a three-button navy blue suit and glistening black shoes. He bent down at Elly's window and said hello, reaching in to take her hand briefly. Florian had never mentioned Elly's lack of enthusiasm for his services, or her preference for Harry Diggs, but Wachtel had pretty much figured that out. Still bent over, he glanced across to Florian, back at Brian. Maybe he was checking their outfits, chicken colonel at the white glove inspection. "Everybody all set?"

"All set," Florian said.

"I asked about the parents," Wachtel said. "They're not coming until we really get under way."

"Thanks," Florian said. He hadn't known how he would handle it if he had to face the parents, the grandparents, the brothers and sisters of those two dead kids. All along he'd tormented himself with idea of going to their homes to tell them how sorry he was. More than once, late at night, unable to sleep, he'd feel a sudden rush of emotion and swear, *I'll do it. I have to do it. I'll do it tomorrow.* But in the morning he could never bring himself to it.

Florian headed north toward Medway on Route 15, glancing up at the mirror a few times to see the big Buick a cautious distance behind, Wachtel's face ghostly behind his windshield. A few days ago Florian had said something to Wachtel about how nice the autumn leaves looked. "One good rainstorm and they'll all be down," Wachtel had responded, and it struck Florian as a perfectly lawyerly thought. Wachtel agreed. "All good lawyers," he said, "are drags."

The Friendly's down the street from the Mt. Early Hall of Justice served as the big hangout for the courtroom crowd, and Florian could see through the glass window the men and women drinking coffee, smoking cigarettes, hunching over tables. He'd met Wachtel there a couple of times. Everybody was always dressed for court, but the lawyers looked perfectly natural in their perfectly tailored suits. Their clients, all those unlicensed drivers and underage drinkers, those shifty thieves and foulmouthed barroom brawlers, those battered wives and garnisheed machinists, gave the impression of having dragged their outfits out of mothballs for the first time since Uncle Charlie's funeral.

As he pulled into the parking lot across from the hall, Florian saw the big gaudy Channel 6 van parked on the street, and in the lot, an even bigger one from Channel 22 in Springfield. Maybe thirty or forty people, a lot more than had shown up for the arraignment in July, clogged the broad white steps of the hall.

"Oh, my God," Elly groaned.

"I warned you," Florian said.

Wachtel parked alongside and got out, straightening his jacket, touching his tie. "Don't talk to anyone," he told them. "If they want your picture, which they will, let them take it. Don't look like some hood hiding behind your hat. You don't have to smile, though. A good straight, serious, confident look will do fine."

The people on the steps craned their necks, stretched onto their toes, jostled for position. The few cops looked steady and bored as two men moved forward shouldering black bulky cameras, each man with an eye pressed against a black rubber ring. A half-dozen men and women with pads or microphones also emerged, leaving maybe twenty straightforward gapers on the steps.

Wachtel raised a hand to salute the cameras, nodded, kept nodding, even smiled a bit, then said to the reporters, "No questions right now, fellas, ladies. Please. It's not nice to keep the judge waiting."

They shouted their questions anyhow as Wachtel kept shaking his head and moving. "Please. Please. Please." Florian and Elly and Brian stayed close behind. Two cops made way for them through the smear of faces, with the reporters and cameramen noisily pressing in on them, and then swung open the big glass door for them and positioned themselves in front of it to hold everyone else back for a minute. The closed door abruptly cut the shouts, and the marble-floored lobby seemed eerily quiet.

"Well," Wachtel said to Florian, to Elly, to Brian. "Here the hell we are."

Less than an hour later, after a few preliminaries were cleared away, Harry Diggs rose mountainously in his disheveled suit, white carnation glistening, and requested a separate trial for his clients. With no objection from Delehanty, Judge Ingersoll gaveled once, and amid some hubbub a lumbering Harry Diggs made his way up the aisle and out the door with the three grinning kids and their families in his wake. Florian was happy enough to see the last of Diggs, but the sight of Brian and Wachtel alone at the long table shook him. Brian was *it*, the whole shebang, the focus of all this fuss and attention. The kid had joked about it at breakfast: with the Trent Quartet broken up, what would the papers call him now—the Soloist?

BACK AND RARIN' TO GO! That's what the big white banner over the entrance proclaimed when they returned every September, and it did so this year, Joyce's twelfth, with as much bravado as ever. God knows it was more welcome than the unnerving sign the janitors had pulled down the day before.

Joyce had driven in, as always, in her VW Beetle which, when it rotted out from road salt last year, she had sanded down and repainted a chocolaty shade that Benn dubbed cockroach brown. Even the kids at school drove better vehicles, washing them down on weekends, under highway overpasses when the sun was hot, sudsing the tires, spraying vinyl cleaner over the dash. That's what they worked for after school, nights, summers: they lusted for their wheels, their rubber-ripping wheels, and would do anything to keep them spinning.

Bennett refused to believe she'd *want* to drive a heap. Could she at least hide it in the garage when she got home?

She was also careful with her school clothes. Everything came from Penney's or Bradley's or one of Medway's "Ladies Wear" shops featuring *Elegant modern fashions at prices everyone can afford*. Every year she'd assemble a school wardrobe of blouses and skirts and sweaters, even shoes, just like the ones the kids saw on their mothers and older, dowdier sisters. She wouldn't dare show up in anything that even suggested a Trent boutique, let alone the Saks or Bergdorf outfits that Benn had always wanted her to wear.

Once she got her class settled into their homeroom seats, she read announcements about assembly times, club meetings, the home football opener, ignored their groans and eye-rolling shrieks as she handed out their schedules. Every year the students groaned at the sight of their schedules. It had become a tradition, exemplifying their right to object to the very idea of going to school.

Sometimes she felt like part of a sinister cabal struggling to keep alive, despite the students' obvious lack of interest in any of it, the wisdom, the history, the stories and songs and folklore of a world that had died before theirs was born. Most of these kids had lived in Medway all their lives, yet knew practically nothing about the county's settlers, about the missionaries, the Indians, the hunters and trappers, about the workers in the early hat factories and paper mills, about the way the expanding IE plant had for fifty years helped their fathers and grandfathers eke out something resembling a livelihood. Now, of course, as department after department got shut down on orders from IE headquarters in Philadelphia, their own modest hopes for steady work close to home looked chancier with every passing year. But still you'd see them smiling and joking, as if they didn't have a worry in the world. Joyce sometimes wondered if all that carefree bounciness came from some arcane knowledge of their own that they (unlike their parents and teachers, who desperately wanted to pass along the sacred watchwords) refused to share with the oldsters all around them.

At first Brownie's crackling speech over the loudspeaker sounded as energetically upbeat as all his other *Back and Rarin' to Go!* talks. Then, abruptly, his tone changed:

> As I'm sure you all realize, the beginning of school this year is marked by a sobering awareness that we all share, both within our own halls and in the community at large.

From his stilted cadence Joyce could tell he was reading the statement—one more sign of his concern, his caution. Maybe this too had been ghostwritten by the grief people. At any rate, the kids stopped fooling around and actually listened, as somber as students ever got. Maybe it was her own fault, trying so hard all summer to put the drownings out of her mind, but she hadn't expected the two kids—dead now over two months, including a girl who'd never set foot inside Medway High—to be such a *presence*.

> Perhaps there's nothing that hasn't already been said about the tragedy of last June. But two lessons stand out.
>
> The first is that our lives continue, although the sadness remains, as will our eternal recollection of lost friends. Each of us can

dedicate ourselves in the year ahead, as students and citizens, to goals that will honor the memory of those no longer among us.

The silence of the classroom awed Joyce. Even the fiddlers, the pencil tappers, the shoe scrapers and rubber-faced grimacers, hardly blinked. A couple of girls sniffled.

> The second lesson pertains to one of our great democratic rituals. The state will provide a fair and equitable setting for a review of all pertinent facts. The carefully measured indictments will be examined and cross-examined in great detail. Most importantly, the rights of everyone involved will be meticulously protected.
> We must never look upon this sacred ritual as a public spectacle in which we, like the unruly mobs of ancient Rome, goad one combatant against another. Let us pledge our commitment to truth and justice, and agree to defend those ideals against all corruption.
> What we shall witness is the sad, yet ennobling, display of human strength and weakness, of human error and human hope. There will be no winners. There will be no losers. And no matter what the outcome, there certainly should be no cheers, no celebrations.
> In order that we may not only acknowledge the importance of this fundamental legal procedure but also understand its history and logic, your homeroom periods will be extended this morning to allow your teachers to conduct a special and I'm sure fruitful discussion of exactly how and why a trial takes place. . . .

It wasn't easy competing with the kids' view of the legal system via *L.A. Law* and *People's Court* and black-and-white *Perry Mason* reruns, but Joyce did her best to cover the points in Brownie's mimeographed handout.

"We have to look at a verdict the same way we look at a law," she told them. "We don't necessarily *like* all the laws of the country, but as citizens it's our duty to obey them." The looks she got were hardly encouraging, and when the kids opened up, she had to keep herself from saying, *No! That's all wrong! That's exactly what we're talking about.*

One boy said that as far as he was concerned, what counted was punishment. "I mean, what the hell, you do something wrong, you get the shaft. Why have a trial and everything if the guys that screwed up don't get what they deserve?"

Another boy raised his hand. "I think we're spending too much time talking about all this legal crap. What about Polly Dunn? He was my friend, and now he's dead. I was on the team with him and everybody feels the same. He's dead and gone because of what happened and there's no way to change that. All the teams this year are gonna wear black bows on their uniforms, on the right shoulder, in memory of Polly, and his number, fifty-five, is gonna be retired by the team and never used again by anybody, forever."

The rest of the class clapped.

At the first morning break, Joyce went to the office to get Jamie Pitt's homeroom, then learned from his teacher that he hadn't shown up. She wasn't surprised. She just wondered, given Jamie's knack for turning everything assbackwards, whether this time he'd screwed up by not showing, or hadn't shown for fear of screwing up.

Joyce always found the first day strenuous but this year's took the cake and she was exhausted when she got to the motel that night. She saw on the local news that the other three boys had walked out, free until their own trial began, if it ever did, and that the rest of the day had been spent trying to get a jury. She kept calling Florian but got only busy signals until, at nine-thirty, ready to give up and go to bed, she finally got through.

They were doing okay, Florian said. The court stuff was pretty dull. Salvatore was staying home with Lucille, so only Florian and Elly went to court with Brian every day.

"How's Elly taking it?"

"As well as any of us. She's inside right now—playing Scrabble with Brian."

"Of course," Joyce said, dropping the idea of asking Florian if he wanted to see her. She hadn't really thought about how—or where—the ex-wife would be spending her time. "I don't know if you're interested or not, but Jamie Pitt came to see me at school yesterday to complain about you bad-mouthing him around town. I'm not sure what he expected me to—"

"What?" Florian shouted incredulously, almost sputtering. "I mean, Jesus, what a real shame. Like who the hell am I to say anything against this guy descended straight from the goddamn kings of England?"

"Not kings, prime ministers—and he just happens to have the same name."

"Maybe that explains the poor slob's inferiority complex, a comedown like that. Let's just drop Jamie Pitt, all right?"

He wasn't only angry, he sounded bone-tired too, and she didn't even tell him that Jamie Pitt hadn't shown up for school today.

Until she mentioned it to Florian, Joyce hadn't realized how annoyed she herself was at Jamie Pitt for cutting classes exactly one day after she'd agreed to work with him getting his needed credits. She called him at home to find out what was going on. If he was so all fired up about her being his special adviser, then damn it all, she'd give him some special advice. She just hoped the father wouldn't come on howling and cursing, the drunk who sometimes wandered in and sometimes didn't. Would she take the coward's way out and just hang up? Maybe she'd get one of Jamie's sisters or brothers.

The mother answered, against a background of blaring one-liners, raucous canned laughter. Joyce shouted into the mouthpiece. "Could I speak to Jamie, please?"

"He's not here," the mother yelled over the TV.

"Do you know where I could get in touch with him?" Immediately she realized how pointless the question was. She wasn't about to stroll into some Dairy Queen, some bowling alley, some roadside bar not too fussy about IDs where the jukebox flashed and vibrated. That'd be wonderful, sashaying over to Jamie while his teenage friends whistled and gave the sarcastic eye to this weird overdressed old lady.

"Who is this?"

"Mrs. Johnway, one of his teachers. Jamie brought me to visit last semester—remember? In June. I'm sorry it's so late, but I—"

"What?"

Joyce took a breath. Was she supposed to repeat the whole thing?

"His *teacher?*" the woman said incredulously.

"One of his teachers. His adviser, actually. Could I call another time? Do you know when he's expected back?"

"Is he in trouble again?"

"No, nothing like that. I just—"

"He had to go somewhere. Out of town. I don't know where."

"Did he say when he'd be back?"

"He just said he was going. You want me to tell him? You want me to say you called?"

"Yes. Tell him to come around again if he gets the chance."

"Around where?"

"School," Joyce shouted. "He can find me in school, just like always."

When she was in bed, her thoughts flew everywhere at once. Then, saddened by how down Florian had sounded tonight, she remembered that first time they'd been alone together, when he'd brought her out to Greenhills, when he'd taken her arm as they strolled about and showed her the lovely freshet beyond the giant wild rhododendrons, told her about the trees and shrubs, the wildflowers, the birds, even the insects, with an energy and excitement that had in turn energized and excited her.

"How'd you *learn* all that in the Bronx?"

"I didn't. But if you want to get away from there, that's one way to do it."

"With trees and butterflies."

"All kinds of things."

Even though the world, with or without butterflies, hadn't been designed to encourage the Florian Rubios from the Bronx—or the kids of Medway—Florian had somehow learned to shape things to his own ends, confident that if you were smart enough and worked at it hard enough you could create for yourself a life beautifully suited not only to your ambitions but also to that part of you that you wanted to encourage, to treasure. And certainly one of the high points must have occurred last year when his youngest child, that prized and beautiful son he'd hardly known and had probably lost hope of ever knowing, had miraculously reappeared to become an intimate part of his life again.

And then it all turned to ashes. Well, as Florian would probably say, *You got no guarantees.* At any moment, no matter who you were or what you'd done, no matter how good you were at anything else, it could all go in a flash.

"Trials," Wachtel had warned Florian, "are public extravaganzas in which nothing happens, very slowly."

Between Tuesday and Friday the only real action had occurred the first morning, when Harry Diggs ceremoniously led the other kids and their families out. In the courtroom Florian could see only his son's back. At home Brian remained quiet, fairly composed, maybe a little edgier than before. He still spoke of the other three kids as his friends, still talked and joked with them on the phone. It wasn't their idea to pull out, he told Florian.

For Elly, the development was devastating. Couldn't Florian have seen this coming? Couldn't Wachtel, that brilliant lawyer of his? What on earth had they been *doing* while Diggs was taking care of his own kids and leaving Brian twisting in the wind?

As soon as Diggs and his entourage had departed first thing Tuesday morning, Judge Ingersoll gaveled the courtroom into silence and denied, one after another, a whole laundry list of motions from Wachtel—for a directed verdict, for dismissal of all counts, for change of venue, for sequestering the jury, on and on and on. Wachtel hadn't expected any success but said the attempt couldn't hurt and might even help if they ended up on appeal.

The publicity still bothered Florian. Three months had gone by since MORP night, and he'd hoped that people would have calmed down. Even in Mt. Early County, after all, accidents happened, people died, kids did dumb things. He'd been encouraged by the guys at the handball court, even by people he met around town, who seemed long past the shock of the first days. The trial, though, got the newspapers and TV going again. Florian still hung up, slammed the door, walked away. He couldn't believe that reporters *expected* him to talk to them.

The clerk had called three hundred potential jurors, the largest pool anyone could remember. A hundred marched in that first day, with Delehanty and his assistant at one long table, Wachtel and Brian at another. Florian and Elly sat in the first row behind them.

The judge read aloud the names of Brian and his family, the three friends who'd be tried separately, the two drowned kids and all their families and friends, the lawyers, and finally the potential witnesses (twenty-eight all told, including Brian and Jamie Pitt and Brian's three buddies, although Wachtel assured Florian there was no *commitment* to call any of them). A whole slew of potential jurors were dismissed when they raised their hands to indicate that they knew someone on the list. A series of whispered conferences brought the dismissal of thirteen more for financial or medical reasons, and four for their connection to Medway Junior High or either of the high schools: two teachers, a janitor, and the husband of an art supply coordinator.

The judge then interviewed each of the remaining panelists. Those who admitted to having made up their minds about the case, or of having read or talked about it, were dismissed. The judge also asked about their attitude toward the police, toward high school students, toward crime, toward prisons, toward a person's financial and social standing in the community. All recent graduates of Trent or Medway High were sent packing, along with parents of present students.

North County residents honest enough to admit not liking South County people were dismissed, and vice versa. One elderly farmer who otherwise seemed okay got rejected when he complained about Trent summer visitors stopping their cars to steal apples from his orchard.

After all this, Judge Ingersoll accepted twenty-three people on Tuesday, but by the time Wachtel and Delehanty used their challenges, only two survived. The first, a housewife in her sixties, assured the judge that she never read newspapers or watched TV news, "except for that Peter Jennings fellow, I kind of like the funny stories he ends up with sometimes." She recalled, but only vaguely, her husband mentioning the drownings. "Last year sometime, wasn't it? At one of the lakes?"

The second, a retired handyman, said he was willing to serve because he wasn't all that busy these days. He too seemed proud of a lifelong commitment to ignorance that expanded out from Mt. Early County to include all of the world at large.

Stalin! Florian wanted to shout. *Columbus, Marilyn Monroe, Mickey Mouse, Wrigley's Spearmint!* Who in Christ's name were they looking for? Some eunuch living with bats in a cave? A horse in a fancy hat?

"Will we ever get twelve?" Florian asked Wachtel on one break.

"Fourteen. You need alternates."

"Are there really fourteen complete idiots in Mt. Early County?"

"Sure. There are even a few I know personally."

On Wednesday and Thursday they seated five more. When the lawyers ran out of peremptory challenges Friday morning, they came up with their final seven.

To pass the time along the way, Florian made charts and graphs to assess the jury. He drew steady lines for neat columns.

The panel they got, which they'd have to live with, kowtow to, pray for, was composed of nine women and five men. Four were retired, two unemployed. The first housewife was joined by two more and the retired handyman. The others either worked at, or were looking for, or had retired from, jobs as dietary assistant at the IE lunchroom, telephone operator, sheet metal fabricator, beautician, secretary at IE, fund-raising trainee from the Split Rock Ballet (by far the youngest, and God knows the best-looking), dairy farmer, tractor mechanic, space salesman for the weekly *Dollar Saver.*

Two men were bald. Three women and two men were fat, two men and one woman skinny. Florian worked out tall versus short ratios, categorized neckties, plaid shirts, dresses, hairstyles and colors.

He'd always been good with numbers and worked out the computations by hand.

Eleven of the fourteen (78.57 percent) were married, widowed, or divorced. Nine claimed a grand total of 23 children, for an average of 2.5555 kids for each parent, or 1.6428 for all fourteen jurors. Two were black (a housewife and the unemployed sheet metal worker), thereby making up 14.2857 percent of the panel, a somewhat higher figure than for the county as a whole, which Florian remembered being around 5 or

6 percent. One of the housewives leaned heavily on a gnarled cane with a silver handle, and the retired handyman had a bad limp. All but four of the panelists wore eyeglasses, which seemed high for people who obviously hadn't spent long hours poring over *Time* and *Newsweek*.

"A great jury," Wachtel confided on their Friday morning break. He said it with real fervor and didn't notice Florian's astonished look.

Nine of them, including seven from Medway itself, came from North County. Five, including three from Trent, came from down South. Given the heavier population up North, it was as good a split as Wachtel had hoped for.

The one quality they all shared was *seriousness:* thin of mouth, stern of eye, lanternly of jaw. Florian had trouble imagining any of them smiling, telling a joke, singing at a party. He had no trouble, though, seeing them whipping sense into any of their 1.6428 kids who stepped out of line.

As for himself, Florian was careful to project the image of a straight, everyday, caring father who couldn't possibly have raised a criminal. He wouldn't even smile when someone gave the judge an answer so weird it cracked up everyone else.

Elly, sitting next to him, looked worried the whole time—*distraught* might be the better word, or terrified. (Christ knows, maybe he did too, despite all his efforts.) They spoke little in court, little on the breaks or at lunch, or during the evenings at the house.

At night Salvatore would shake his head and say, "I thought it would be over already. I thought people would just tell what happened and that would be the end of it."

Even though he wasn't there to see for himself, Salvatore seemed well aware of how much they all were in the power of the judge, the jury, the lawyers. How could you trust people like that, people you didn't even know, to do the right thing? Salvatore was ready to swear before Christ Jesus Himself that Brian was innocent, but all those strutting pigeons running this whole crazy business—how could they in a million years *understand* anything?

Still, he refused to lose hope and struggled mightily to cheer up everyone else. "He's a good boy," he said one night to Florian and Elly after Brian had gone upstairs and Salvatore was preparing to wheel Lucille inside to put her to bed. His voice was heavy with feeling. "They'll see how he's telling the truth. They'll do the right thing for him."

Florian stopped looking at newspapers, stopped watching TV. When the phone rang at night, though, the calls weren't always from reporters.

The relatives in New York said they couldn't find out anything down there about the trial. After talking to four or five of them, Florian decided he couldn't manage that every night. He phoned Aunt Rosa back —she'd been the first to call—and said he'd give her the news every night and she could pass it along to whoever was interested.

"Everyone's interested," Rosa said. "What do you think, they don't care?"

Joyce had called Tuesday night, saying she'd gotten a busy signal for hours.

"Out of town?" he said when she told him about Jamie Pitt. "It makes him sound like a traveling salesman."

She did her best to laugh. "Maybe he'd be good at it."

On a brief recess after the fourteenth juror was seated Friday morning, Florian and Elly headed down the block to Friendly's, where they sat at the counter and ordered coffees. The man on Elly's right surprised them by leaning forward to speak to both of them. "Hi—Barnaby Rollins, Channel Six. Hey, don't look like that. No questions, Scout's honor. Just thought I'd say hello, that's all."

During the week you saw him in front of burning buildings and twisted wrecks on the highway. Weekends he filled in for the regular anchor. Actually, Florian kind of liked him. He was older and jowlier than the type, less given to pretty-boy smiles and giggly jokes with the black sportscaster and woman coanchor.

Rollins flagged down another coffee and said, "One thing about a trial is you sit a lot, instead of running all over the county keeping the feeds coming at six o'clock, seven o'clock, eleven o'clock. And sure, everybody figures *There's old Barnaby with his face on the tube again, making his million.* Only I'll tell you. Sports, that's who's got the deal, them and weather. Most viewers don't know that."

Florian glanced at Elly, who seemed content enough listening. What else did they have to do?

Blowing on his coffee, Rollins raised an eye to speak directly to Elly. "What it is, you see, is that news side we got a code. Your typical viewer could care less, but we got it. It started back with the biggies, before Cronkite, back with Murrow and Kaltenborn and those guys, and it's still strong, because you can't have news side people selling cat food, right? Because you never know, one day a cat food story comes along and you gotta play it straight, like anything else. I mean you can't pull punches. So if somebody comes up and says, *Hey, how about a few quick bucks for putting on a funny jacket and playing with this cute-as-a-button kitten here*—you gotta say no. But the jocks, the weather people, they rake it in, flacking the big auto and furniture dealerships."

"I didn't realize," Elly said, sounding vaguely sympathetic.

"They got no code, that's why." Rollins watched the young waitress jiggle by on the other side of the counter, then turned and eased off his stool, shook Florian's hand, nodded to Elly. "Even though we have to report things, we got feelings too. We got kids. So hey—my very best."

"Thank you," Elly said.

They watched him leave, and then, as if unable to stop herself, Elly laughed, and Florian got a flash of that easy humor, that smile always about to break through, that he'd been taken with twenty-five years ago. But she couldn't completely hide the worry now, and he could see how much she'd welcome a friendlier hug, a little more warmth and closeness. He felt it too. You couldn't be married to someone for years without getting used to clinging together when things got rough. And they'd spent the last three days together, in court, at lunch, at dinner with everyone in the house, sitting by themselves after Brian headed upstairs and Salvatore wheeled Lucille into the guest room. It'd been strange, seeing Elly that much, feeling her hand on his arm, feeling her body against him when, usually around midnight, like a couple of kids coming home from a movie date, he'd drive her into town and walk her to the door of the Hollisworth and she'd kiss him on the cheek and clutch him for a moment.

When they returned to the courtroom, Florian was grimly pleased that the parents of the dead kids still hadn't shown and began to hope that maybe, for whatever reason, they would not come at all.

Delehanty then began his opening statement, promising to be brief, letting the facts speak for themselves in the course of the trial. A large, thick-chested man with squarish mustache and baritone voice, he spoke slowly and calmly, without theatrics, yet Florian, after three days of boredom in the courtroom, suddenly felt himself caught up: in fear, in an almost breathless concentration, in a tingling electric surge. Now everything counted. Now every word had to be paid attention to, analyzed, weighed, considered, recalled over and over in search of some ultimate revelation.

Not that he wasn't aware of the irony of paying such attention to a speaker as unexciting as Delehanty. Yet the guy was okay—as clear and controlled and to the point as Wachtel had predicted. He also gave every indication of believing everything he said, and that in itself was enough to scare the hell out of Florian, who realized now how much he'd been praying for a doddering, half-assed jerk.

A young boy and an even younger girl, Delehanty told the jury, facing them directly with his beefy arms crossed, not moving on the polished wood floor, died as a direct result of a violent confrontation brought on by the defendant. It was as simple as that. It was as incontrovertible as that. He would show, step by step, exactly how the activities of the defendant on the night in question amounted to an assault and battery upon the two victims and additionally, through the use of the Corvette, constituted a clear-cut instance of involuntary manslaughter.

The jury listened. Oh, but they listened.

When Delehanty finished, Judge Ingersoll nodded to Wachtel, who stood up and said his opening statement would be even briefer. God knows it was, and presented in a tone and manner even flatter than Delehanty's. (Were they competing against each other for the Dull Speakers of America award?)

"The prosecution hopes to show," Wachtel intoned with all the passion of those radio announcers who reported the stock exchange closings every afternoon, "a cause-and-effect relationship between the actions of Brian Rubio and the unfortunate, accidental death of those two tragically drowned individuals. I am convinced that they will not be able to do so and am further convinced that you, ladies and gentlemen, in the course of these proceedings and your deliberations, will also reject any such connection. That is all, Your Honor."

The judge raised one eyebrow in mild surprise and thanked him. A few of the jurors frowned as they watched Wachtel return to the table and take his seat next to Brian.

Not exactly thrilled with the performance himself, Florian nonetheless received a pretty unrelenting look from Elly. Last night he'd tried to prepare her for this by laying out Wachtel's reasoning. "Delehanty is the one, not us, who has to prove things," he'd pointed out, suspecting now that he'd taken more time then making the point with Elly than Wachtel just had with the jury. "We don't have to worry about anything like that. So by starting out with absolute confidence, without any pressure at all to prove anything, Wachtel figures it'll plant the idea with the jury that we're not worried, that all we have to do is sit back and watch the other guy turn himself inside out trying to prove something that they and everybody else will see *can't* be proved."

She'd been unimpressed then, and right now, with her glare, she seemed to be pointing out how completely she'd seen through both Wachtel's strategy and Florian's explanation of it.

In his stomach Florian felt a small gnarled tightness, pulsing deliberately. He smiled at Elly to reassure her, to show his confidence, his unrestrained pleasure at how well things were going.

For the rest of the morning and most of the afternoon Delehanty called up his preliminary witnesses.

A police officer said he got to the public boat ramp on Bottleneck Lake at 12:42 A.M. to find twenty or thirty youths of both sexes, many wearing MORP T-shirts, milling about in a state of considerable agitation. Upon learning that a passenger "ve-*hick*-le" had disappeared into the lake, he and his partner jumped into the water and dove repeatedly in an attempt to locate it. The water was deep and murky and thick with weeds. It wasn't until 1:26 A.M., after the scuba divers arrived, that the automobile was located, and it wasn't until 2:14 A.M. that it was hoisted out. It was a red 1974 Plymouth Valiant, and he had no idea how it got into the water. Wet and exhausted, he had been sent home while other officers questioned witnesses.

The doctor called to the scene said that when the youths, identified as Paul "Polly" Dunn and Willa Hufnagle, were extricated from the red 1974 Plymouth Valiant, he determined that they were both dead.

The director of the crime lab, a calm gray-haired man in a business suit, presented blowup photographs that Delehanty placed on an easel in front of the jury: the crowd on the boat ramp, the police cars, the fire engine, the ambulances, that same, now awesomely familiar picture of the car dangling and dripping from the chain, the car back on the ramp, its doors open, after the bodies had been removed, and finally a picture of Florian's Corvette. Thank God there were no grisly pictures of dead bodies. (Wasn't that what prosecutors were supposed to do, tug at the heartstrings, shock the jury with the horror of it all?)

The county surveyor placed an enlarged aerial photograph of Bottleneck Lake on the easel, with arrows indicating the public boat ramp, the beach, Hammond's Boatyard. He used a Game and Fisheries chart to show how quickly the water deepened, right off the ramp, to between twenty and twenty-five feet in the area where the car sank. That was why, he explained smugly, the county had decided to locate the ramp there.

The coroner said that Willa Hufnagle and Paul "Polly" Dunn had died from "freshwater drowning." Both had several bruises, which may have occurred before they got into the red 1974 Plymouth Valiant, or during its plunge into the water or their attempt to escape after it had gone under. The bruises did not contribute to their deaths.

Wachtel declined to cross-examine any of these witnesses.

Delehanty waited with his thick arms crossed, watching the coroner leave the courtroom, before addressing the judge. "The state wishes to call several witnesses, including Jamie Pitt, whose testimony will be somewhat lengthy, but given the lateness of the hour—"

"The court stands recessed until ten A.M. Monday," Judge Ingersoll announced.

9

When Brian returned from California after Lucille's stroke in August, neither he nor Florian had felt comfortable going off by themselves for a day, even though Salvatore took care of everything Lucille needed. But now with the trial under way and a whole weekend free, Salvatore practically threw them out on Saturday.

"Go," he commanded, shooing. "Have a good time. What do I need you for?" He even made them lunch, stuffing it all in Brian's backpack.

This was only days after Florian, amazed, finally heard from the California detective.

"I don't know exactly what kind of input you're looking for, Mr. Rubio," the guy said over the phone.

"I forgot all about you. It's been months."

"You know how it goes sometimes. Things on your desk slide under other stuff, and since you weren't bugging me, I guess I got tied up with guys who *were* bugging me."

"Sure," Florian said. "The Kremlin moles, Kennedy assassination, Lindbergh baby." Where on earth, he wanted to know, did Wally Brown dig up these guys?

"Hey, no one's mentioned the Lindbergh baby in years."

"I don't have any leads," Florian said. "But you'll be the first to hear."

The guy laughed appreciatively. "Like I say, I wasn't sure exactly what you expected from out here but—"

"I told you exactly what I expected. My ex-wife suddenly sent our sixteen-year-old kid to live with me, and I was curious why. Not all that complicated."

"But hard to pin down, what's going on in someone's mind like that. Anyhow, did she give you any sort of reason herself?"

"She said he was too rambunctious, running around with girls and everything, and she found it too much strain."

There was a considerable silence before the guy said, "Well, even ex-wives have been known to tell the truth sometimes."

"I just wanted you to check it, in case there were other reasons."

"Well, I looked around and talked—surreptitiously, of course—to neighbors and everything, and that was pretty much the story I came up with, that she and the boy just weren't getting along too good."

"It took you all summer to find that out?"

"You wanted her story checked out, and I figured you meant thoroughly. I even dug up things like medical records, you know, found out that she takes medicine prescribed for depression, and also has over the years seen various different types of shrinks, which naturally doesn't mean all that much, especially out here, where everybody, you know, figures a trip to the local head soother is like writing *Fill up Gas* on your shopping list."

"Okay."

"I don't usually even mention this, but I been going myself every week for years, and it makes a difference. It really helps."

"I'm glad," Florian said.

"I'd also like to say on your ex-wife's behalf that I never heard that she ever blamed, er—Brian, right?—Brian in any way for her occasional depression or anything else. I mean, she was what you would call a very devoted mother and—"

"Okay," Florian said.

"It's just that some cases we get, you know, they're really not very pleasant at all. I just want you to understand we're not talking abuse or anything like that here."

"I never figured we were."

"What it boils down to is I think Mrs. Rubio just felt increasingly frazzled taking care of kids by herself all these years and figured she could use a break while—you know, while she was still young enough to enjoy herself."

"Perfectly understandable," Florian said. "Thanks a lot."

"I'll send you the full written report."

"The bill too," Florian said.

"Oh, yeah. You'll get the bill."

Six A.M. Saturday he and Brian took off from Mannix Field, just south of Medway, in Ken Faulkner's old Comanche four-seater, the plane straining and gasping as it picked up speed before lurching aloft at the end of the grass runway. Summers Ken Faulkner gave half-hour aerial tours of Mt. Early County for fifty bucks, the soft green hills, the glistening expanse of Bottleneck Lake, even the streets and rooftops and IE structures of Medway, capping it off with a swing around Mt. Early itself.

The plane shuddered in downdrafts, rattled and vibrated as they gained altitude over Bottleneck Lake, the sky an icy blue bowl overhead, the morning sun flashing off the water, the roads, the houses.

"Wow!" Brian said up front, alongside Faulkner, who pointed out the sights for him over the engine clatter.

Florian sat behind with Brian's knapsack. Before long they reached the county's western expanse, where the Sargasso River zagged like a lightning bolt through the craggy, thickly treed hills. You saw no towns or villages amid all that greenery, those flumes of changing colors, only ponds and streams, a rare house, a few twisting narrow roads. Spotting the stand of birches in the Sargasso's sharpest turn, Florian touched Brian's shoulder. "There," he shouted into his ear. "It starts right there."

They swooped down to a hundred feet and flew back and forth over the Fitzwilliam property. Hunched over in the low cabin, Brian peered through his window, and Florian hoped he shared the same shiver of awe and wonder.

They returned to Mannix Field before eight, then drove back to the property in the Jeep, bouncing and rattling all over the place, the plastic and canvas doors flapping, the ride almost as loud and jostling as it'd been in the plane, and Brian looked like he was enjoying it as much. Tramping in along the riverbank, past the dramatic stand of birches and the rapids, the silky-smooth pools, they climbed through the pines and maples to the property's highest point, a flattened hill at its western boundary, 120 feet above the river. From there you could see the autumn colors blazing all the way back to the rapids, where the Sargasso sparkled as it rushed and swirled over the jutting rocks and fallen tree trunks.

They ate lunch there, Brian digging through the knapsack and spreading out the four meatball sandwiches, the plastic bowl of escarole salad, the sliced bulb of finocchio, the two cans of beer and three of orange soda, the Stella D'oro cookies. They finished everything.

Florian didn't ask Brian about the property. He wanted the boy to bring it up himself, and finally Brian said, "Are you really thinking of buying all this?"

"I already did, when you were in California. It was that or lose it." He squinted in sun. "I figured we could look at it anyway."

"It's great. The plane, everything."

"One time we were flying over a piece and got peppered with buckshot. A couple of aging hippies were squatting in the woods below us, growing pot."

"It's really beautiful."

"Now that I've got it, God knows what I can do with it."

"Do you really buy land without knowing what to do with it?"

"It's the only way I buy. If somebody's ready to turn it into a summer camp or a ski area or homes, whatever, it drives the price straight up. You have to buy before that and then wait, a year, two years, five years. I have pieces nothing may ever happen to, including a few that I hope nothing ever will, so I can leave them behind to you and Joe and Annamarie."

"No kidding?"

"I figured it'd be more fun than a batch of stocks in a bank vault."

"It sure would be. But don't you lose money if you can't sell stuff?"

"You really shouldn't, in the long run. We're not talking Hula Hoops."

"Hula Hoops?"

"Torn jeans, pet rocks, the latest fad that'll die six months after some Madison Avenue genius conjures it up. Land'll survive anything you throw at it—storms, lightning, forest fires, no rain and too much rain, no snow and too much snow. You have to be patient, though. But if you are, and own one free and clear stretch of acreage somewhere, no one can just write you off."

He couldn't imagine why Brian was smiling.

"Hey, that's okay, Dad. I just can't imagine anybody thinking he *could* write you off."

"When I was a kid, that's all people wanted to do. But out here the only real disaster would be an army of backhoes and bulldozers and logging trucks. In the Northwest, Canada, Brazil, they just strip thousands of miles of incredibly beautiful land for lumber, for mining. But Mt. Early's small beans, so the conglomerates leave us alone. There's nothing to mine and not enough lumber to bother hauling out."

"If you don't know what the land's good for, how do you know what to buy?"

"You buy what excites you. You talk to people and study the paperwork and keep telling yourself to play the wily businessman, but what you always end up buying is what you fell in love with the minute you saw it. A few lots somewhere, a couple of acres maybe, up to something like the Greenhills estate, which I got four years ago and sold this June."

"Did you do okay?"

"It'll get you through Harvard if the urge should ever seize you."

Florian said it lightly, and Brian took it with a shrug. "You didn't go anywhere, Dad. Mom hardly did. Annamarie didn't. And how long did Joe last—a semester? I can't remember."

Florian couldn't either.

"You people did okay."

"We're not talking about us. We're talking about you, and how you have to look beyond the trial. Soon it'll be over and forgotten and you can move on."

Brian seemed to be weighing this. "I feel bad about Grandma. No matter what happens at the trial, the last thing she'll ever know about me is I had something to do with two kids drowning."

"Your grandmother never for a second thought you were guilty of anything. None of us did. We know you, your mother knows you. We believe in you." Christ knows, that was true. Florian ached for the kid to be rid of all this. At the same time, even though he thought he hid it better—did he?—he was as angry as Elly. There must have been *some* way Brian could have managed things differently, saved himself and those other kids, saved everyone.

"According to Wachtel," Florian began, tentatively, watching Brian closely, "it's okay for me to hate Jamie Pitt, but it presents a real problem for you to. He worries about motives. If you were really out to get Jamie Pitt . . ."

Brian was toying with a small fallen branch from the sugar maple overhead, the glossy red leaves still attached. "Jamie dragged Nique into the woods. She was my date, I was responsible for her, and Jamie and his friends came along and grabbed her. Wouldn't you have gone after them?" He flung the branch away but then took a breath, a few breaths. "I really can't imagine what it must have been like for those kids. I mean, they're yelling and screaming, cursing at me, and then they're in the drink. And then they're dead."

"There's no way this is going to be easy," Florian said. "Start with that assumption. It's going to be rough, and it's not going to feel too good."

"It sure doesn't right now."

"All that matters is what you *meant* to do. And you didn't mean to kill anybody."

"Jesus, Dad, of course I didn't."

"The fact that you were angry with Jamie Pitt is something else entirely."

"Maybe I'm lucky he didn't drown too, or there'd be no question about my motives. Maybe him just still being alive is my big break."

"Depending," Florian said, "on what he tells the jury Monday."

"Yeah, we'll have to check that out before thanking him too much."

They were quiet on the hike out, until Brian said, while they were still walking, "I really feel bad about loading all this stuff on you people. Especially Mom, having to fly all the way out here and everything."

"Jesus," Florian said, pushing branches aside as they trudged along, "stop worrying about everybody else. No one's complaining. No one's blaming you. Your mother, everybody, we're rooting the hell out of things for you."

"I know," Brian said, and was silent again until they emerged into the clearing just beyond the birches. "That old estate you just sold," he said, walking alongside now.

"Greenhills. They're turning it into a resort—hotel and restaurant, condos, golf course, swimming, tennis. I saw the plans. Pretty nice."

"Hardly Mt. Early's most crying need—one more fancy resort."

"There are uglier things than a golf course, a swimming pool."

They reached the Jeep and paused, Brian gazing back. "What was it that struck you about this piece when you saw it?"

"Look at it. You could put Adam and Eve in there."

Brian let a slow smile develop, his face bronzed in the afternoon sun. "Isn't that what they say—every man spends his life trying to rediscover his own lost Eden?"

"Oh?" Florian said, amazed to hear this from Brian, wondering where it might have come from—the catechism? The Bible? One of the kid's secret notebooks? "Maybe you're right," Florian said. "That's what we're all going for. And if it isn't, it damn well ought to be."

"Along with making money on it, right?"

Florian kicked at an egg-size rock, not angrily, just to see what it would do, and watched it hop erratically toward the stand of birches. "Short of taking vows in the monastery, or going on welfare, or sleeping over the subway grates, you gotta spend your life doing something. But it helps to remember that it's only play money. It's not real. People are real. Your family's real. What you think of yourself is real. And as far as what I'm doing out here, well, I'm not required to salute anyone. I set my own hours. All I have to do tomorrow is look for even nicer pieces of land. Maybe it ain't Eden, but until someone comes up with a better line of work for a clunky guy from the Bronx, I guess I'll stick with what I got."

"Hell, Dad, I'd hire someone to kick your ass if you didn't."

* * *

She hadn't started the day intending to see Florian. Even if the lawyer was being overly cautious in trying to keep them apart, she had to agree: why take chances? But then, Saturday afternoon, with the first week of school behind her, she decided she really didn't want to spend the day in her motel room grading quizzes while peeking out at the parking lot and imagining what the changing leaves would look like in the sun.

There was no way it could hurt anybody if she dropped by on this lovely afternoon and paid her respects to Florian's mother. It wouldn't, after all, be a public occasion.

That's who she found there, Florian's mother, along with his father and ex-wife. The three of them must have been out for a ride, pulling into the parking area just in front of Joyce, with the ex-wife—Elly—at the wheel, Lucille in back, Salvatore already lifting the folded wheelchair from the trunk. Salvatore was slighter than Florian, wiry and compact but kind of hobbling as he walked. Yet he quickly leaned into the back of the car and emerged a moment later with his wife's head on his shoulder, her arms flopping as he held her around the waist, pulling her after him and then in a single smooth motion placing her gently into the wheelchair. He buckled the strap as Joyce and the ex-wife watched, as the huge dog barked at them in welcome.

Joyce hadn't been sure what, if anything, to say to someone who wasn't hearing you, who didn't understand what was going on. Yet you couldn't treat her like the nearest fence post.

Salvatore handled it easily enough. "Hey, it's time now we gotta work in the garden, right?" he said to Lucille as Joyce came over. Lucille's expression remained as blank as the moon. "You wanna eat, you gotta dig in the dirt, ain't that what they say?" he went on as he swung her chair around. "We see you later maybe," he called back over his shoulder and pushed her across the driveway, over some rattling plywood sheets to the fenced-in garden at the edge of the wooded area, the enthusiastic dog bounding after them. Joyce suspected Salvatore was running off because he didn't want strangers seeing his wife like that.

"Florian's with Brian," Elly said as the wheelchair bumped noisily over the plywood boards, with Salvatore still chattering away at his wife. "But it's after five, they should be back soon." Polite, reserved, not really interested, Elly had more important concerns than whatever woman happened to be involved with her ex-husband. Elly wore a full tweed skirt and a loose sweater—outdoorsy, very New England. Florian said she did artwork for an advertising agency: good eye, good taste, nice feeling for color.

"If you'd like to wait," Elly said, "I'm sure Florian would be glad to see you." She pulled open her car door. "We've been driving around for hours, just for something to do, and I'm absolutely worn out." She gestured toward the house, the patio. "Please, make yourself at home." With a noncommittal nod, she got in the car and drove off.

Joyce sat on the patio and watched Salvatore working in the garden, with Lucille nearby in the shade, the dog having settled down at Lucille's feet. Perhaps fifteen minutes later Florian and Brian drove up in the Jeep and came onto the patio looking ruddy, almost flushed, and in amazingly good spirits. She'd been afraid that this first long dull week at court would have taken a real toll on them. Maybe it had, but at the moment they looked like a couple of guys with the world on a string.

Still, Florian seemed flustered for a moment with his son standing there. Finally he laughed and reached forward to put his hands on her shoulders, holding her, looking at her in the afternoon sunlight, then, grinning, gave her a hug, then held up his hands to show how grimy he was and said, "Let me wash. Brian'll keep you company, okay?"

Brian told her about the land they'd hiked through that afternoon. "It was great. We flew over it first, practically scraping the treetops, just incredible." Despite the enthusiasm, the boy seemed relieved when his father returned and he could leave.

Florian had shaved, changed into fresh clothes, maybe showered too, and arrived bearing a tray with a wineglass and an iced bottle for her, a glass of scotch for himself. He looked better, more upbeat, than she could remember since those first easy and wonderful times together. Putting his arm around her waist, he led her to the railing, facing out over the lake, and toasted her. "The nicest surprise in a long time— finding you here."

He kissed her, held her tight, kissed her again.

"I was pretty unsure about coming," she said. "It's nice to see you both looking so happy. Good news?"

"A good day together, that's all. It's funny, he really loved it out there, but I'm not sure he *approves* of the whole thing—selling land for money, turning a profit."

Joyce sipped her wine. "As someone who hangs around high schools a lot, let me just say that there are only two types of teenagers, cynics and idealists, and both switch sides several times a day." She paused. "What were you like in high school?"

"Mainly I just wanted to do okay without becoming like the guys I saw doing okay. *What a bunch of jerks,* I thought. *What wipeouts.* Only I didn't want a little wooden stand somewhere either, shining shoes." He said it with surprising fervor, then shrugged it off. "Have you seen Bennett?" he asked. "Have you talked to him?"

"No," she said. "I keep putting it off." Slowly she moved up against him, letting him pull her closer. She felt as if she were melting into him.

"Will you stay?" he asked quietly.

She leaned back to offer him a tilted smile. "For another glass of wine? Dinner? The evening? The night?

"Whatever. It's an old Italian tradition, offering hospitality to unexpected guests."

"Including women?"

"Especially women. Whose virtue, of course, you're expected to protect with your life."

"I seem to remember some Italian-type guys in New York who—"

"Because they didn't pay attention. They lost the old ways. My father, my uncles and aunts, you know what they would say? *I spit on them.* Forget them. The night is young. The fish are jumping and the cotton is high. What do we want to do?"

"Oh, the lady has choices?"

"Damn few, actually. We really don't want people seeing us carousing at some local hot spot."

"Nor, I think, should I stay here overnight."

"Which leaves us?"

"A small but familiar motel room," she said, "and a pizza delivered to the door."

And so, for a couple of hours, Joyce found it awfully good again, as it had been at the beginning, just the two of them, nothing intruding, both of them happy and lively, interested in each other, comfortable with themselves. With the leftover pizza slices in the open cardboard box on the chest of drawers, reflected in the big mirror, they sat for a long time on the couch, sometimes talking, sometimes not, with quiet Saturday night jazz on the FM, neither anxious, neither wanting to change the light tone or spoil the moment. It was wonderful to see Florian relaxed again, as if whatever happened with his son today had given him new confidence, new hope that things would start breaking his way again before too long.

Just as it got dark outside, and in the room too, they made love, and she could see how excited he was, as if he simply could never get as much of her as he needed, could never give her as much as he wanted, finally coming with a rush so wild, her coming too, that both of them were left panting for breath.

While they were resting afterward, he touched her breast and said, "You have such nice nubbly, nobbly little nipples."

"Heavenly days, I've been laid by a poet. Only I'm not so sure about *little.*"

"An affectionate term, not a measurement."

"You're forgiven, for the moment."

After lying together for some time, the music still playing low, they made love again, more slowly this time, more quietly. She felt happy for herself and for him too, and he told her he hadn't felt so good in a long time, and she said he didn't have to tell her, she could see for herself and hoped it would last.

When Florian left late Sunday afternoon, he said he'd be tied up that evening with the lawyer; Elly had set up the meeting, and he had no idea what it was about. Maybe, he said, they'd be going over strategy for dealing with Jamie Pitt's testimony tomorrow.

Even the thought of this didn't darken his mood. Joyce also felt terrific. Last night had been their best time ever together, in every way, and they were both elated by what that suggested for the future, once they got out from under everything else.

She had dinner with Katarina at the Pewter Pot, and they enjoyed themselves catching up on each other's adventures the last two weeks of the summer, when Joyce had traveled alone through Italy.

Afterward she'd barely stepped inside her motel room when the phone rang. She flung herself across the bed to grab it, sure Florian was calling from home, maybe because the meeting had been called off, or to tell her again how nice it'd been, how much he already missed her. Only it was Bennett. She'd answered with such enthusiasm that she gasped when she heard his voice. They hadn't talked since her return, hadn't talked all summer.

"Are you all right?"

"Of course. I wasn't expecting a call—it startled me."

Bennett let out a sharp laugh. "I know how you feel. I'm sitting here catching a little bit of the game on TV when this guy shows up looking for you. He figured you still lived here, so I didn't argue. I said you'd be right back."

"Why'd you do that?"

"It's the kid from school that's all wrapped up in everything—Jamie what's-his-face. He's inside waiting. Unless you want me to give him directions to the motel."

"I'll be right there," she said, and put the phone down before Bennett could say anything more.

Florian tried not to think of having to meet with Elly and Wachtel to squabble over God knows what. Yesterday had been such a good day, first with Brian out at the Fitzwilliam property and then overnight with Joyce, that he wanted to enjoy the glow as long as possible.

But he couldn't stop himself from thinking ahead on the drive home, and then arrived to find Salvatore making dinner in the kitchen while chattering at Lucille in her wheelchair, to find Elly playing Scrabble with Brian. Sure, everyone else being the good Scout, oozing with responsible behavior while he's out doing the motel bit with his girlfriend. It'd only been a few lousy hours, he felt like pointing out. He had a life too, and as much right as anyone else to screw it up or save it, as the case may be, and right now he was perfectly ready to announce to everyone in sight that he felt better than he had in months.

But the euphoria was already fading, and Elly killed it entirely when she rose from the game board and announced that the meeting with Wachtel had been moved up and they'd have to leave right away.

"I was wondering whether you'd even make it back in time," she added.

Driving out of South Corner with Elly, they passed the police car cruising back and forth on Mark's Lane. When Brian had returned right after Lucille's stroke, they'd kept his presence pretty quiet and there didn't seem any need to patrol, but since the trial had started the cops had been out there day and night.

They got to Florian's office on Nailing Hill Road before Wachtel, and Elly, who'd not been there before, checked out the place, including the rooms that Florian barely used, then studied the geological survey maps on the office walls, then looked briefly at the cork bulletin board covered with all those haphazardly pinned photos of kids and parents and cousins and aunts and uncles. She shrugged and turned away, maybe figuring her own picture wouldn't be there—it wasn't—and that except for their three kids the pictures would all be of his family, not hers.

Wachtel, of course, had been to the office a number of times, and he'd always take off his hat as he stepped through the door and place it on the little table in the hallway. In the living room office he'd pause for a quick look around, maybe say, "Nice place," or "Warm out today," then move right to the bulletin board to bend forward with hands clasped behind in his best Sherlock Holmes stance to take a close look, moving from one to another. He'd never comment about them, and Florian wondered each time what had captured his attention. Was he looking for family resemblances? Making the point that he didn't consider Florian merely a well-paying client but appreciated him as a human being, a family man, the focal point of all those interlocking generations?

When Wachtel showed up this night, another car followed right behind, and Wachtel came to the door with Harry Diggs.

Florian gave Elly a hard look. "I love surprises."

But Elly had her eyes on Diggs, who was lumbering toward her. "Ah, greetings, greetings. Elly, how are you? Flo?" Harry gave Elly a peck on the cheek, shook Florian's hand.

"I appreciate your coming," Elly said to him.

Wachtel ignored the bulletin board and sat down on a hard wooden chair while Harry and Elly took more comfortable seats. Elly and Wachtel looked pretty grim, and even Diggs, trying for his usual flowery cheerfulness, fell considerably short.

Florian leaned back against the edge of his desk with his arms folded, his feet crossed. "Since I'm the only one without the foggiest idea what's going on, maybe someone'll fill me in. The last time Ira brought me any news from you," he said to Diggs, "I learned that Brian's three buddies were dumping him. What's the good news this time? If you keep the fun coming at this rate, I won't be able to stand it."

Diggs looked at Elly and waited. Wachtel did the same.

Elly seemed to take a breath. "I arranged this, Flo, because I've been very worried and giving matters a lot of thought and didn't want you saying I was doing things behind your back."

She was trying hard to sound reasonable, to placate him, but Florian shook her off. "The point's pretty clear, right? You want to drop Ira and take on Harry."

Elly nodded. "They're aware of that, and that it has nothing to do with Mr. Wachtel, either personally or professionally. I'm sure he's a very fine person and an excellent lawyer. I just want Harry in there for us. I want Harry in charge. I want Harry making decisions."

"Harry's still making decisions for those other kids. He's concerned with them, not Brian."

"They're not being tried at the moment. They probably never will be. Harry can take care of Brian and worry about the others later."

"The trial's already under way."

"We've discussed that. Look, it happens, people change lawyers.

You see it in the papers all the time. The judge won't be happy and'll probably declare a mistrial and lecture us about wasting everybody's time and tax money, but if we all go to him—you, me, Brian—and declare no confidence in Ira Wachtel, he'll have to give Harry time to make his case."

"The only problem with that," Florian said, "is that I have every confidence in the world in Ira Wachtel. He's a real hand-clapping first-rate ball-busting lawyer, as I've pointed out on several occasions." He looked at Wachtel, at Diggs, who'd been sitting like stuffed dummies with pasted, forbearing smiles while Elly carried the ball. "You guys, are you in on this? Is this what you want? Is it a done deal?"

Each looked more than ready to defer to the other. With a shrug Wachtel spoke. "No lawyer likes being kicked off a case. But if that's what you want, Flo, that's what you get. I wouldn't dream of trying to argue you out of it."

"As for me," Diggs said, "you must understand, as I'm sure Elly will confirm, that I've all along spoken against changing counsel and have strenuously voiced my high opinion of Ira and his professional abilities."

"But you're willing to go along."

"Ira and I both understand each other's position. It's the right of every defendant to have the representation he chooses."

"If he can afford it."

"We won't argue," Diggs said, "although we've both done our share of pro bono work over the years. My position, simply, is that if you and Elly both want me to take the case, as an attorney I would feel obligated to do so."

Florian turned angrily to Elly. "It's all your doing, right? Harry's not pushing, and neither is Wachtel. So what we're dealing with is cold feet, pure and simple."

Although, Christ knows, he'd had cold feet from day one, and would until the very end. Only what good could Harry Diggs do? They could get Moses with his Ten Commandments on stone slabs to defend Brian, and he'd still be scared to death.

"Look," he said to Elly, "we've been through this before. You want Harry and I want Ira. Did you bring us here to flip a coin?"

"It's not just us, Flo. Brian's the one with everything on the line."

"Have you talked to him about this?"

"No. But maybe we should."

"And then no matter what he does, he ends up pissing off one of us. Does the kid really need that right now? Look, I've talked to him about

Ira. He's been in on it from the beginning. I wasn't about to get some lawyer he didn't like. He thinks Ira's just fine. He hasn't mentioned one single word of complaint."

"He's got no basis for comparison," Elly said. "He doesn't even know Harry."

"Well, he knows Wachtel well enough to like him. He's perfectly satisfied. You keep saying that since the kid was living with me when this happened, I should've kept him out of trouble. All right, but you can't have it both ways. If you're blaming me because I had the responsibility, then damn it all, I have the responsibility, and I'm using it to get the guy I want representing him."

Jesus Christ, he hoped he was right. He'd cut his goddamn heart out if it'd give him a clue, tell him once for all what the hell he should do.

Elly patted her purse before standing up. All her old mannerisms, lost for so long in the dimness of memory, kept coming back to somehow throw him off balance.

"Will you drive me back to the Hollisworth, Harry, since you're going that way?"

"Of course, my dear," Diggs said, heaving to his feet.

"If this turns into a disaster," Elly said to Florian in her best ice pick voice, "at least now we'll know why."

Florian also remembered this knack of hers for laying out guidelines ahead of time—for buying a house, selling a car, picking a restaurant. "Sure," he said. "If we win, you shrug. If we lose, you say it's all my fault."

(What annoying thickheaded traits was she seeing in him again for the first time in a decade, things that drove her crazy enough to sweep up the kids and head off with this guy digging holes for new forsythias, who afterward actually sent Flo a bill, from California, for his work?)

"Brian can lose," Elly said, her voice catching, her eyes about to well up. "That's all I'm worried about, Brian losing, and I only hope you haven't just done something to make that happen."

"Come," Harry Diggs said, putting a heavy arm behind her, guiding her forward.

Florian and Wachtel watched them leave, with Harry Diggs, hugely rocking from side to side, holding her arm.

Eventually Wachtel said, with as much feeling as he'd ever shown in Florian's presence, "I appreciate the vote of confidence, Flo."

"I just hope to hell you deserve it. One other thing: if you ever again tell anybody they can or can't see me, I'll get rid of you so fast you'll think you've been flattened by a falling rock. I'll take fucking Mickey Mouse over you if that's the only choice I have."

Joyce drove steadily, focusing on the road. It was nine-thirty, near her bedtime on school nights, but she felt energized from having been with Florian, and from the call, the sharp September night air. She let herself into the house, willing enough to play along with Benn. It was hardly Jamie's business, after all, that she'd left her husband.

"There you are," Benn announced loudly, coming into the vestibule. "Someone dropped by, and I said you'd be right back."

How strange, though, not having seen your husband for two months, to be greeted with a charade aimed at fooling a teenage boy. In his suit and tie, Benn looked little changed, although his eyes seemed quizzical, less focused, his posture just slightly askew, as if he were rocking on the balls of his feet, testing his balance. On the vestibule table, where Benn must have put it when he answered the door for Jamie, lay *The New York Times* folded in quarters to the unfinished crossword, a ballpoint lying on top.

Benn led her into the kitchen, although she assumed he'd have brought Jamie into the living room, like anyone else. But there he was, seated at the breakfast table. And it wasn't that he'd shown up scroungy. Sitting primly over a glass of milk and a dessert plate with the crumbly remains of a cookie, Jamie Pitt looked as neat as he had the other day at school. Benn never wanted her keeping sweets around because he tended to put on weight, but maybe now, batching it, he enjoyed indulging himself. He did look a little heavier. (Or was she just flattering herself? Sure, she takes a summer holiday and Benn turns chubby while Florian, who seemed a good deal thinner, wastes away.)

Jamie stood up, smiling again, always smiling, doing his damnedest to come on like some lost and cuddly lamb, although he could never wholly disguise that glint of someone who'd love, just this once, to put everyone else in their place. "Sorry to bother you at home, Mrs. Johnway; only I missed you at school."

"I didn't think you were at school." Maintaining his smile, Jamie neither claimed that he'd been there nor admitted that he hadn't. Joyce turned to Benn. "Maybe Jamie and I can talk alone."

"I already told him I've been working to get the Trent kids off. All the Trent kids. We understand each other."

"Sure," Jamie quickly agreed, seeming to relish the idea of validating Benn's honesty. "We understand perfectly." After a hesitation Jamie sat again, his chair back from the table. He started to slouch and cross his legs, then seemed to think better of it and sat up straight with his knees pressed together, his hands clasped in his lap, like some altar boy with a sweet, composed expression. "My mother said you called about seeing me, so I figured I better come as soon as I got back."

Benn glared at her, obviously wondering what kind of scheme she'd worked up with this grinning kid from the wrong school, the wrong town, the wrong world.

"Whatever I want to see him about," she said without heat, "I can discuss with him alone."

"Sure. The Medway connection. That's who signs your paycheck."

Joyce felt no need to answer, to argue, to defend herself. A landmark, she realized, aware that she might well go through the rest of her life not caring what Bennett Johnway thought. During the months in Europe she'd sometimes have trouble sleeping, wondering in the lonely early-morning hours if she hadn't just made the biggest, stupidest mistake in her life. Everything still seemed tentative back then, as if something more *real* were happening elsewhere. Now for the first time she seemed perfectly comfortable with the idea of Bennett Johnway remaining forever a stranger. But maybe the headiest realization was that he'd always been a stranger.

Left momentarily off guard, she blinked when Jamie stood up. "We can talk anywhere you want, Mrs. Johnway." He didn't even look at Benn.

"How did you get here?"

Jamie shrugged.

Did that mean he hitched? Walked? Been dropped off by a friend? Would the prosecutor or some lawyer have driven him here? At least, given his dry clothes, he hadn't swum across. "I'll give you a lift home," she said.

"That'd be real nice."

Glancing at Benn, she decided to keep up the pretense, although she couldn't stomach anything as shameful as *I'll be back*. She settled instead on "This'll give you time to finish the puzzle."

As Benn escorted them to the door, he actually picked up the pen and folded newspaper from the vestibule table.

Not eager to deal at the same time with Jamie and the oncoming headlights along the hilly, tree-shrouded wanderings of Route 15, she ran through her choices. Her motel room was obviously out, Jamie was too young for a cocktail lounge, and the local burger joints were probably packed with his friends and her students. He solved the problem for her by saying, "I could show you something if you're interested. Just take a left at Bottleneck Road—if you want to, I mean."

"Where to?"

"Two places, actually. You ever been to Nanny Point?"

"Not really," she said with a little laugh. Nanny Point used to be a summer hangout for college kids, but the high school crowd had taken it over—a sign, maybe, of how fast kids got into the swing of things these days. A looping arm of land that reached out into Bottleneck Lake and curved back in until it almost touched land again, Nanny Point lay inside Fischel State Park, almost a mile from the nearest houses. More important, its tiny beach on the inside of the arm couldn't be seen from the camping and picnic areas, or from boats on the lake, making it the perfect spot for skinny-dipping. Park rangers occasionally wandered down to shoo the kids away, although Benn's theory was that the Smokies were just out for a little recreational viewing. Mostly the kids used the point after the park had closed for the day.

She could imagine Florian's reaction at her heading off to Nanny Point with Jamie Pitt in the middle of the night. But he was a high school kid, for heaven's sake, and she dealt regularly, calmly and confidently, with high school kids. "What are we supposed to see there?"

It took him a moment to answer. "You still think it was all my fault, don't you? I mean, you always been nice to me and I always appreciated that, but you're friends with Mr. Rubio and everything, so you're getting the story from him, who naturally gets it from his kid. So you figure —right?—me and my buddies jumped the Rubio kid and started everything, and then I—well, you know—I did whatever I was supposed to do to the girl that was supposed to be his date."

"Veronique Thrane."

Jamie let out a harsh puff that she took to be a laugh. "Yeah. Nique Thrane. Good old Nique Thrane."

"What does that mean?"

"It's funny, you know. Like, my mother, she figures it's all because of my father, the way I turned out. And the old man, he blames my mother. You'd think maybe I inherited leprosy or something and everybody says it's the other one's fault."

"I never said anything was your fault. And I really don't think your parents would—"

"The turn's coming."

She made the turn, wondering if even a boy with as much going for him as Brian Rubio felt the same frustration, the same inability to satisfy either, let alone both, of his parents.

"Take a right now, then a left."

"The boatyard?" She'd dropped off Jamie there last spring and had gone there often enough with Benn, but never at night. She turned in and stopped at the horizontal pipe blocking the dirt road. It'd keep cars out but not anyone on foot. She'd have thought, after those boats had been vandalized here on the Fourth, Hammond would have been more careful. Maybe he had a watchman now, a guard dog.

"The easy way to Nanny Point," Jamie said.

"Suppose someone's around?"

"I work here, remember? It's okay." He looked across the seat at her. "I'd just like, since you always been good to me in school, for you to have the right story about what happened. That way, when you hear about what I testify, you'll see that all I'm doing is telling the truth."

"Okay," she said. Whatever Jamie Pitt's problems and idiosyncrasies, at least he was not at the moment stoned, or drunk, or out of control in any way. Rather he seemed quite sober and intent. He ducked under the pipe, and after a hesitation she did too, ignoring the hand he offered. Did he really see her as that ancient, too creaky to straighten up?

She followed a few feet behind as he walked, pivoting slightly from side to side the way thickly muscled kids did, into the clearing of the boatyard. Only a weak porch light on the bait hut gave any illumination, Hammond's concession maybe, forty dim watts, to a security system. It was still too early for people to mothball their boats for winter, so the yard was fairly empty, just stacks of canoes near the water and some rental powerboats and rowboats and pontooned catamarans scattered around the grassy slope, everything somberly hunched under the hazy moonless sky. Had Jamie planned this outing beforehand or, as she suspected, dreamed it up on the spur of the moment? She kept expecting some grizzled deputy to emerge from behind the bait hut, sighting them down his gun barrel, turning their little expedition into one more example of Jamie's well-documented knack for screwing up anything he touched.

Jamie deftly slid a glistening silvery canoe off the nearest stack, bent under it, and lifted it overhead, perfectly balanced, then flipped it over into the lake. He pulled it back onto land and tossed in a couple of paddles. "Beats tromping a half mile through the woods."

At least she hadn't worn heels. When in doubt go with slacks and flats—and in September, in Mt. Early County, a cable-knit sweater. And thank God it was a cool night; at least they wouldn't surprise a couple of bare-assed bathers over there.

He held the canoe steady for her as she stepped in and moved forward with gratifying agility, then hopped in himself and shoved off. When she turned and picked up the other oar, he said, "You don't have to."

"It's all right."

"Okay."

Skimming over the inky, ripe-smelling lake, she made out the hazy outline of Mt. Early. Down toward the left, past the black expanse of Fischel State Park, the lights of the South Corner houses glowed fuzzily in the mist—including, of course, the house where even now Benn might be finishing his puzzle while, a few houses closer, Florian and his parents and Brian and the ex-wife were maybe watching TV together and talking about the trial, or not talking about the trial.

They covered the mile or so across the lake quickly as Jamie stroked powerfully behind her. He steered them through the water lilies, closed up at night, into the narrow passage between Nanny Point and the mainland and nosed the boat onto the dully phosphorescent beach, the keel slushing as it knifed through the damp sand.

They stepped onto the beach, which was perhaps a hundred feet long, ten or fifteen deep. With his back to the water, Jamie gestured toward the woods that rose into Fischel Park. "Now, if you knew your way in from the road, you'd climb over this real steep hill here." He looked at her, as if making sure she was following.

"Okay."

"But you don't want to take a wrong turn on top, or you won't hit the beach at all but end up down near the picnic tables. You know the spot?"

"Alongside the road, yes."

"Well, if you ended up there, the best thing would be to walk back along the shore until you got here."

"Okay."

"The question is, if someone ended up in the wrong place, which would it be, some guy from Medway or some guy from Trent?"

"I haven't the slightest idea."

"Because you don't really know Nanny Point."

"I've heard of it, that's all." She tried to envision the little beach on a hot summer night. Did kids on dates just sneak here for a few intimate moments together, all secret and sensual, or would you find entangled couples sprawled all over the beach, thrashing in the water? Maybe it was like those European beaches, where everyone lounged around radios, eating lunch and reading newspapers amid all those bared breasts and penises and pudenda, the scene as refined and abstemious as croquet on a lawn. Unlikely, given the voltage of high school libidos. (Out of nowhere, she remembered the girls at college, getting their bras out of dormitory bureaus only on their way home to visit parents.)

"The first thing about Nanny Point," Jamie said, "is that if you're from Trent, you can come anytime you want. If you're from Medway, you better stay away."

He'd taken on an almost teacherly tone, and she wondered if he was at all aware of the irony. "I never heard that," she said.

"That's why I'm telling you. Even the rangers, they find anyone from Trent here, they figure, well, kids will be kids."

"And from Medway?"

"Now you're catching on. So if someone ends up down by the picnic tables, it's gotta be someone from Medway, because this ain't familiar territory."

"And that someone is you, on MORP night—with a few unfortunate friends, two of whom ended up drowned."

"Yeah, whom. That's the ticket. Whom." And then after a moment: "I guess you could say I was the lucky one. I could've drowned too, but didn't. And I could've made other people get drowned, but didn't do that either, so I'm just lucky all around."

"What were you doing here in the first place?"

"That will all come out at the trial. I just wanted tonight to tell you some things that—"

"If you're going to tell me what happened, tell me what happened. Don't drag me out here and then say you can't—"

"I didn't mean to get you mad."

"Maybe you think attendance at school is voluntary these days, but I have to be there every morning at seven-thirty and right now would just as soon be home getting some sleep."

"Well, I guess me too, as far as sleep is concerned, because I'll probably end up testifying tomorrow. But I just wanted you to understand, so when the rest of the story comes out you'll have a better idea how it all fits in. Like, a guy coming here along the shore, he couldn't see anything until he got right on top of those little dunes there."

"So you didn't know who was on the beach until you got here—is that what you're saying?"

"That's exactly what I'm saying, Mrs. Johnway, because why would I ever come here that night to make trouble if I didn't even know who was here? I just wanted you to understand that. Maybe now we can head back, so I won't keep you up too late."

The haze had thickened over the lake but Jamie steered straight to the boatyard with barely a swerve. At least he could paddle a canoe, could find his way across the black water. (As always, she wasn't entirely ready to believe Jamie, but how absolutely Jamie-like it would be if that horrible night *had* started with something as ludicrous as Jamie Pitt getting lost in the woods.)

"I said I'd give you a ride home," Joyce told him after he'd nimbly replaced the dripping canoe on top of the stack.

"One more thing—if you're still interested."

"I've had enough running around for one night."

"It's right here," he said, and she followed him around the bait hut. He took out a key and unlocked a big shed and pulled open its warped door to reveal a crammed, dank-smelling jumble of tools and paddles, a lawn mower, small anchors and ropes and seat cushions, along with an upright metal locker, like the ones in the halls at school. God knows, he might have stolen it from school.

"This is for my personal stuff," he said, picking up a flashlight and opening the combination lock. He brought out a small white envelope. "If you'd just hold this, I'll show you."

Reluctantly she took the flashlight as he slid out a small flat silver medallion, a couple of inches across, with *The Spenser Academy* scripted around the edge, encircling the robed and heroic female figure.

"Actually, it's a locket," Jamie said, prying it open with his thumbnail.

In the flashlight's cone, Joyce stared at a photo of two heads, close, cheek to cheek, Jamie beaming, the girl beaming too. She closed her eyes briefly. "Is that Veronique Thrane?"

"You got it. Good old Nique Thrane."

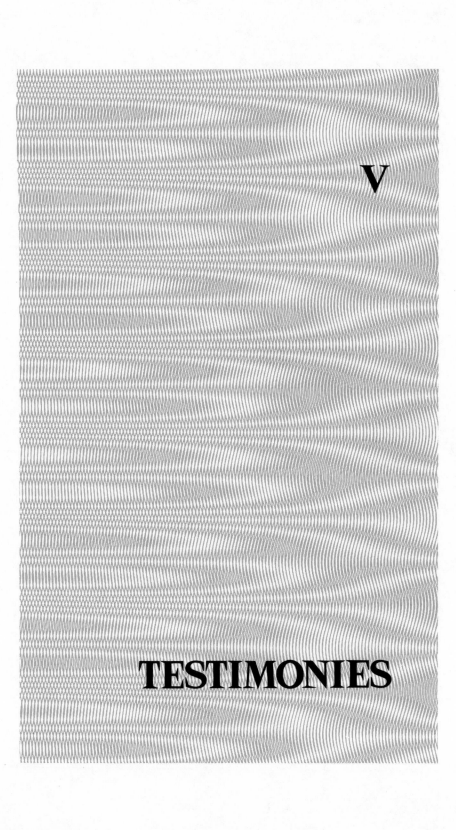

V

TESTIMONIES

10

Once again wearing their long, public faces, the fourteen men and women seated behind the wood paneling watched the first witness of the day take his place in the large raised chair inside the witness stand. Florian couldn't fault their commitment. They focused intently on every word, every gesture and expression, every shift of tone. But not even the most dedicated juror could match his own concentration. What did any of this mean to all those secretaries and housewives and retired repairmen—a civic duty? a few days of excruciating boredom? or a sudden heady realization that the sword of righteousness had been thrust into their hands?

Thank God, the parents of the two dead kids had still not come. Florian could understand. What solace would they have found here? What solace, indeed, was there here for anyone?

Thankfully Delehanty seemed eager to focus on essentials and move along. Perhaps he was looking forward to the arrival of Jamie Pitt and merely wanted to nail down a few details first.

During the course of the morning Delehanty called three Trent seniors and a college guy. A girl who'd been at Tiny Arkins's party admitted that people were drinking and that when someone came in yelling about cars being wrecked out front, there was a lot of cursing and screaming, a lot of guys swearing to get back at whoever had messed up their cars.

Calmly, pleasantly, in no great rush, Wachtel got up for a little friendly cross-examining.

Yes, she knew Brian Rubio. She saw him at the party but had not seen him drink anything. At no time did he appear to be intoxicated.

Wachtel thanked her and sat down.

Leaning forward with his eyes narrowed on Wachtel, Florian felt a little inward wince at the way the man, hardly imposing under any circumstances, seemed even less so in the broad open area of the courtroom, as the focal point of the judge high on his left, the witness in front of him, the jury on his right. At least Delehanty, although no great orator either, had a certain size and weight going for him, a bass voice that bounced off walls, a mustache thick enough to be spotted a block away. Wachtel's problem wasn't that he gave a bad impression but that he gave practically no impression at all. He seemed awfully insignificant as the center, even for a moment, of everybody's attention.

Delehanty called two Trent seniors who testified they'd been parked on the ramp with their MORP dates at the time Brian Rubio and a bunch of other Trent kids showed up around midnight. When a Plymouth Valiant pulled in and parked at the other end and five guys got out and walked off toward Hammond's Boatyard, Tiny Arkins used the Corvette to pin the Valiant against the edge of the ramp.

That's right, Tiny Arkins, not Brian Rubio. No, Brian Rubio didn't protest. Brian Rubio didn't say, *Stop, that's my car, my father's car, you can't do that!* No, Brian Rubio didn't complain or get angry at Tiny Arkins. No, Brian Rubio didn't try to move the Corvette away.

After Delehanty finished with each boy, Wachtel got up, again calmly, in no great rush, for a less than sparkling cross-examination in the form of a single question.

No, they were not on the ramp when the Valiant went into the lake. They left when a car pulled in, lighting up the whole area.

Delehanty's next witness *was* on the ramp at the crucial moment.

Twenty-one, he said, a junior at Cornell, forestry major, home for the summer last June, living with his parents in Westfield, out here that Friday night on a date with a girl also from Westfield. They were parked on the ramp when they heard some kind of ruckus at the other end of the ramp.

They started to leave but slowed down, then finally stopped, to watch what was going on from the safety of his own car, maybe twenty feet from the action: these two cars bumper to bumper and maybe a dozen kids screaming and yelling and jumping onto hoods and kicking at windshields, swinging and punching and wrestling. It was a miracle someone didn't fall into the lake, the way they were going at one another right at the edge. Even with his windows closed he could hear the yelling and cursing. And then these two cars started banging back and forth at each other and suddenly the one car just zoomed right off the ramp into the water. Yes, he could see who was in the Corvette. He pointed to Brian.

No, he said when Wachtel got up to cross-examine, he couldn't see what the driver of the other car was doing, because that car was farther away, and the angle was bad. No, he didn't see that driver pull the gearshift down. He didn't see him do anything with the gearshift. He couldn't even tell who was in that car.

"But you did see the two cars banging back and forth against each other, correct?"

"Yes. It all went very quick, and of course there wasn't much light, but that was very definitely what seemed to be happening."

"When that car zoomed, as you put it, into the lake, did the Corvette lunge forward, as it might if it had just rammed forward into the other car?"

"No, sir. I didn't see it do that."

"It did not lunge forward?"

"I did not see it lunge forward."

"Did it bounce backward, as it might in recoiling from a push?"

"No, sir. I did not see it do that."

"Were you watching closely? If it *had* lunged forward or bounced back even a little bit, would you have seen it?"

"I think I would have, yes."

Thanking him, Wachtel sat down. Delehanty reminded Judge Ingersoll that he expected that the testimony of his next witness, Jamie Pitt, to be lengthy, and the judge declared a lunch recess until two o'clock.

As always, the first thing Florian did when they returned was check for the Hufnagles, the Dunns, but not even the appearance of Jamie Pitt had been enough to draw them out.

From the unmoving back of his son's head, Florian couldn't even guess at Brian's feelings toward this rough kid on the stand, who was not exactly as Florian had imagined. For one, he hadn't expected Jamie to talk that well. Granted, Jamie Pitt slurred words and dropped *g*'s while trying to cover his nasal street corner twang with oozing politeness. "Honey or bile," Lucille used to say, "you can get by on one or the other," but Jamie seemed to be offering a disarming combination of both, switching back and forth at will. He was quick, though, and sharp, and somehow always came up with the word he wanted. Surely he'd been rehearsed by Delehanty. Still, Joyce and his other teachers had nothing to be ashamed of—and that jolted Florian. First Delehanty and now Jamie Pitt, both a lot more impressive than he'd bargained for. Jesus, was everybody on the other side going to wow the jury while Wachtel, the silent wonder of the legal world, twiddled his thumbs and shambled over occasionally to ask a few harmless questions?

Jamie Pitt was also remarkably, insistently, cheerful. He smiled all the time, at everything, like those mindless TV anchors who read the most gruesome horrors off their TelePrompTers with the happiest of expressions. Jamie's smile seemed as automatic as a bank clock, a tic, the arching of a cat's back.

He was much shorter than Brian but thicker through the chest and shoulders, with an abrupt, jumpy way of gesturing. His features were blunt, although Florian could see high school girls going for his rough guy looks: a large nose, broad lips, eyes flat and quick beneath dense black brows and black curly hair. Once or twice Florian gradually closed his eyes to slits, until Jamie's face hazed over except for the black mass of hair, black slashes of eyebrows.

Pitt—not kings or prime ministers by a long shot, the father from coal miners in Wales, according to Wachtel, the mother part Irish and Hungarian or Romanian or Slovenian or whatever. It was hard to tell what Jamie had inherited from all those strains or which, if any, meant anything to him. How could you not think of yourself as *something*? What the kid looked like, though, was one of those flashy Bronx wops Florian had grown up with, oily hard-assed guys who slipped combs into their back pockets and wore tight polo shirts with cigarette packs folded into their sleeves, who made sure their bare arms rippled when they ran the combs through their slick, glistening hair. (Except those guys made a point of *not* smiling.)

A swimmer, Brian had told him, quickly adding that they didn't compete in the same events, as if that explained something. The Trent kids made fun of Jamie, even though he won his share of races, calling him the Corkscrew because his form was so lousy, all flinging and flailing and twisting. But Brian blamed that on Medway's lousy coach, a science teacher in need of a few extra bucks who did nothing at practice—at the Y, since the school didn't have a pool—but hope no one got hurt.

From the witness stand Jamie Pitt tried earnestly to project an absolute and unshakable confidence. Couldn't anybody besides Florian see that this was exactly the unblinking performance you'd expect from a tout, a huckster, a con artist?

Jesus, Florian would have given anything to be running on grass somewhere, loosening up in the sunshine, throwing a ball around with Brian. He remembered when Brian was maybe four or five, showing him how to hold a bat, endlessly feeding him underhand pitches, big and fat and soft.

Jamie Pitt testified that he'd been seventeen and a half on that day last June, a senior at Medway High, when he learned that he wouldn't graduate with his class. After finishing his afternoon job at Hammond's

Boatyard, he ate dinner at home with his mother and sisters and brothers and called a couple of buddies, including one who owned a car, to see what they were doing. It was a Friday, after all.

That's right, a '74 Valiant, red, which had a few miles on it and needed muffler work. You could hear it coming and going. Also, both doors on the driver's side had been dented pretty bad so you had to get in from the other side and slide across. Oh, no, these weren't the kids that drowned. They came later. These were different friends.

It was a nice night and they figured on driving around, maybe a movie, although they weren't sure what was at the multiplex. Yes, they knew it was MORP night but that had nothing to do with anything. They were from Medway. They didn't care what the Trent kids were doing.

So they drove around and eventually the driver, who was the only one old enough, picked up a six-pack. Later he picked up another, but they didn't finish that one. Maybe two, three cans each the whole night. No, nobody got drunk. Never for even one second was anyone ever drunk.

(Was any of this the truth? Was it even believable? Florian couldn't help remembering the old saying about a little truth helping the lie go down, yet he could envision the scene: cruising around in your friend's rattletrap on a lovely June night, when in Mt. Early County the azaleas still had flowers and the blooming white and red rhododendrons loomed up in your headlights like dense clouds, when the spring air reeked of loam and heat and sex, and there you were, three guys with nothing to do, nowhere to go, no one to see. As a kid, Florian had never cruised like that because no one had a car. When they had nothing to do, nowhere to go, no girls left in the world, they spent their nights walking up to Fordham Road under the El tracks, or to Crotona Park, or hanging around the pool hall, the bowling alley, over hamburgers in the White Castle on Tremont Avenue. He couldn't even, back then, recognize an azalea or a rhododendron.)

Jamie's two buddies weren't graduating either. The driver had fallen short a couple of courses, while the other friend was still a junior. So yeah, all three were back in school right now. And yes, Jamie was working real hard to make up his missing credits, glad to get a second chance under the strict supervision of a special adviser.

No, they weren't sore back then about not graduating, or about the Trent kids and their MORP. No one had bad feelings about anything, no plans for trouble, no reason to do anything but smile, smile, smile the summer night away.

Let's backtrack, Delehanty said, standing motionless with his hands clasped behind his back, a steady, impartial stance, this hulking questioner, orchestrating Jamie's performance with a relaxed congeniality. Did anything unusual happen that day at Hammond's Boatyard?

Late in the afternoon, while Mr. Hammond was in town and Jamie was alone at the yard, caulking canoes, this guy showed up out of nowhere and said: That was you in that boat just now, wasn't it? What boat? Jamie wanted to know. The boat that roared around the swimming ropes at the beach where he was lifeguard, which Jamie had already figured out from the patch on his shirt. He saw it head back to Hammond's, the guy said, and gave Jamie a poke, a shove, a push, something like that, and then the guy seemed to lose interest or give up and left, saying he had to get back to his lifeguarding.

Yes, Jamie said, he was sitting right over there. Brian Rubio.

(Maybe if Jamie and Brian had just settled things on their own, then and there, it all would have added up to nothing more than a couple of bloody noses.)

At the break Florian stood in the hall with Brian and Elly, no one saying much because you couldn't talk with all the other people around. Wachtel was outside, probably staring into the eye of the Channel 6 videocam. Florian tried to get some sense of Brian's reaction to the testimony but couldn't. Not that the kid seemed full of fun. But you wouldn't have guessed he was on trial for manslaughter. He might have had an algebra test coming. He looked sober, preoccupied, maybe a little tired.

Time became important. When did that happen? Are you sure? Were you wearing a watch? Did you check it regularly?

Around seven, after picking up chips and pretzels and that first six-pack, they headed to Fischel while the sun was still out. No, they didn't know alcohol was against the law in state parks. People did it all the time, didn't they? That was the last thing on their mind, breaking the law.

Around seven-thirty, no later, they talked about a swim at the public beach across the lake since it was one of the first warm nights of the year. The problem, though, was no one had their suit, and if they all went home to get them the sun would be down. So they headed for Nanny Point, where everybody knew you could take a quick dip without suits. Only when they climbed up over the hill they got lost at the top and ended up at the picnic tables maybe a quarter mile from the Point.

Yes, there were people at the tables, but no, he didn't remember anything written on their shirts or any bumper stickers on their cars.

They left their shoes and socks in the car to wade along the shoreline to Nanny Point. That meant all three of them were barefoot, which made a difference later on.

(Jamie Pitt related all this with such determined innocence that Florian half expected him to swear that he and his friends, solid citizens all, had carefully deposited their empty beer cans and pretzel bags in the receptacles provided by the Parks Department. Still, everything he'd so far admitted to had been harmless enough. You couldn't even find a reason up to now for Jamie Pitt to lie. A little bare-assed Tom Sawyer plunge? A lousy couple of cans of beer?)

They'd waded maybe halfway to Nanny Point when they realized someone was following them, not through the water but on shore, two guys in T-shirts with different crazy sayings. No, he couldn't remember the sayings. They looked like code. Anyway, the two guys told them in no uncertain terms to stay away from Nanny Point, but Jamie and his friends said it was a free country and kept going, with the two guys still following along the shore until they suddenly ran ahead onto dunes over the beach, like they planned to stop them right there.

No, he didn't recognize either one. No, Brian Rubio wasn't one of them. But he figured them for Trent guys because of their MORP shirts and expensive fancy sneakers.

Jamie and his friends came out of the water to climb the dunes, not about to let just two guys scare them off, only then from nowhere ten or fifteen guys in T-shirts and cutoffs were suddenly up there howling and screaming and then charging down the dunes and punching and kicking them and knocking them down.

It was the no shoes. Otherwise they could have just taken off. But you couldn't run that fast barefoot or defend yourself that good. Every time Jamie tried to fight off somebody he'd step on a sharp rock or stub his toe. Eventually they escaped back into the woods, and luckily the Trent guys didn't come after them.

Around eight o'clock and almost night, especially in the woods. Sure, they were angry, getting beat up like that. But what could they do? The main thing, the driver said, was to make sure his car was okay.

So they sore-footed it back through the brambly woods to the parking lot, where the Valiant was fine, and barreled out of the park, glad they were still in one piece.

Was the Rubio boy, Delehanty asked, motionless, arms across his broad chest, among those who beat them up at the dunes?

No, Jamie said, he didn't think so.

Through all this Elly only occasionally glanced at Florian. She fixed her gaze on Delehanty for the questions, on this earnest, shaggy kid for the answers. She seemed unflinching, but her face had no color, no life. When Jamie said Brian hadn't been on the dunes, Elly seemed to seize on this as a positive sign. Florian himself tried not to react, tried to look serious, businesslike, confident. Jesus, he hoped he looked confident. The hinges of his jaw ached with a fierce nervy pain.

Meanwhile, Wachtel, their all-knowing lawyer and slick mouthpiece, their pinstriped savior, sat alongside Brian with a big yellow pad and several sharpened pencils in front of him and seemed, more or less, to be paying attention. He didn't yawn, or doze, or rubberneck around the room. But he hardly gave the impression of someone riveted to the proceedings. He never wrote on his pad. Only once did he lean over and whisper into Brian's ear—while Jamie was making a big deal about the Trent kids in their hundred-dollar Reeboks—and Florian thought maybe Wachtel had seized upon some slip that could blow Jamie's whole story. But when Wachtel caught the judge's eye, Ingersoll announced a five-minute recess. Wachtel and Brian, the only ones ready to move, beat everyone else to the men's room.

It wasn't until they left the park that Jamie and his friends realized how teed-off they were, how much they wanted to get back. Maybe it wasn't right to feel that way, but they did. He just wanted to be honest.

(Jamie's honesty aside—was even one word of this the truth?— Florian could see it. You were a goddamn high school kid, in no mood to take any shit. They kick your ass, you kick theirs. What else would anyone expect?)

The perfect solution—that was Jamie's word: *solution*—was to go back to Nanny Point and get the Trent guys where they'd been gotten themselves. Maybe those same ten or fifteen would still be there in their fancy sneakers. Maybe even more. That was okay. Because this time they wouldn't come over the hill or wading over the sharp rocks along the shore. And this time they'd have the edge: not just sneakers but a speed-boat.

Judge Ingersoll ended the trial for the day at four o'clock. After a whispered conference with the lawyers, though, he said tomorrow's session would not begin until after lunch: one of the principals had a previous commitment for the morning. In the middle of the crowd moving slowly out of the courtroom, Florian angled over to Wachtel and gave him a look, raising his brows. *How are we doing? Better than you figured? Worse? Is that goddamn kid killing us?*

Okay, Wachtel's look said. *We're doing okay.*

* * *

If it was his own trial, Florian really couldn't see himself letting some lawyer call the shots. All his life he'd believed you never got anywhere, on anything, with someone else telling you what to do. That included accountants and office managers and investment counselors and any other flacks you might in a weak moment think were smarter than you. You paid them for what they had to offer and then made your move. It went for priests and politicians and stock market gurus and doctors and teachers and garage mechanics. And God knows it went for lawyers. You couldn't let them take over.

Only how could you take the chance when it was your son's life? All you could do was pray that this one time this one expert knew exactly what he was doing.

Florian grabbed Wachtel's arm in the parking lot as they were about to split for their cars. "I'll be right with you," he told Brian and Elly, guiding Wachtel between parked cars until they were far enough away to talk. "All right, the son of a bitch did okay. But why should anybody believe a single goddamn word of it?"

Wachtel looked at him steadily. He seemed on the verge of one more rerun of his *Let's not get all excited* speech, but instead just shrugged.

"Sure," Florian said, giving his favorite lawyer a smile, a friendly pat on the shoulder. "Another day, another dollar."

It was hard to tell how Jamie's testimony affected Elly, but she seemed weary beyond words and barely nodded when Florian dropped her off at the Hollisworth. He headed for South Corner, and Brian, up front now, said, "I guess Jamie did better than I expected."

"Is that the story, what Jamie gave us today?"

"It's Jamie's story, that's for sure. Of course, I wasn't even around for most of the stuff he talked about today."

"Still, do you think he was lying?"

"He certainly left things out, I'll bet."

"Don't let it get you down," Florian said as he swung the Fairlane onto Mark's Lane, past where the empty guard booth had stood all those years before being torched. "It's not over by a long shot."

"Mr. Wachtel says you can't pop up and down like a roller coaster every time something happens. It's the final outcome that counts."

"Absolutely," Florian said. "He's a hundred percent right. Listen to him."

"I'm going biking," Brian said after they pulled into the parking area. "I'm stiff as a board from sitting." He took off on his ten-speed, his long legs pumping easily, with Padgett, hairy ears flopping, hairy feet flopping, loping after him for twenty yards or so before giving up and circling back.

Down at the water Salvatore was throwing bread to the ducks. A flock of maybe twenty lived on the lake from early spring to late fall, and Salvatore had for years fed them every evening at dusk. Now he always wheeled Lucille down with him so he could chatter away at her as the gabbling, clucking ducks darted for the stale chunks. When Salvatore couldn't make it, the ducks would swerve and circle, honking expectantly, before finally giving up and moving on.

Florian bent over the wheelchair and gave Lucille a kiss. "How's it going, Mom? Pop not boring you too much?"

Salvatore turned the brown paper bag over and rattled out the last crumbs. At this the ducks turned in unison and paddled away, as poised as royalty, only their invisible feet moving. "The other boy, he testified today? Good? Bad?"

"Who knows? I'll tell you all about it so you can tell Aunt Rosa."

Salvatore lowered himself into a lawn chair at the water's edge. His feet were probably bothering him from the standing he'd done for the ducks. He motioned his head toward Lucille. "The boss, she wouldn't sleep this afternoon. You think she knows something's up?"

"We oughta let Rosa come, give you a hand. You could get away for an hour, have a beer."

"This guy, he's crazy, right?" Salvatore said to Lucille. "He wants your sister up here, scaring the birds out of the trees."

"Rosa's okay," Florian said. "She's lively, she keeps you awake."

"Lively? Hey, you must be kidding. She keeps the birds awake, the rocks. You know Rosa."

And Florian of course did, but Salvatore was referring more specifically to his own touchstone, his profound, head-nodding capsule of memory that, for him at least, added up to *Rosa:* she had a set of dinnerware that she so cherished she never used a single piece from it, either alone or with company, to make sure it'd always be available.

Spurred on maybe by the day he'd spent alone, talking to Lucille, telling her jokes, Salvatore went on, in his own way, about the family in New York. "Sure," he said. "And Stella."

Florian nodded. Watching the news on TV, old Aunt Stella would shake her head when some foreign dignitary spoke in his own language. How come these big shots couldn't learn English, when she, a poor peasant from the Neapolitan hills, had managed it? Could it be so hard?

"Jake," Salvatore said, making a face. "Right?" he said to Lucille. "Jake."

Thankfully, they rarely saw Jake, an in-law, married to a cousin, a morose, heavy-lidded man well into his seventies who had but one comment on his life and times, recited weightily whenever you saw him, whether you gave him an opening or not: *We buy Fords, you know. We always buy Fords. Henry Ford started making them, what, fifty, sixty years ago, and we been buying them ever since. It ain't that we got anything against the others, although I'll tell you, we wouldn't touch those foreign jobs. You got more real metal in one fender of a Ford than a whole Jap tin can put together. And it ain't that you don't get problems with a Ford. Front end, exhaust, rings, you know. You get that with any car. It's just, I guess, we're like a Ford family, so we buy Fords.*

"Dave," Florian said, giving Salvatore a shot at it.

"Dave!" Salvatore responded with a puff, a laugh for Lucille. Dave, a distant cousin from across the river in Jersey, was seen even less than Jake at family gatherings, and Salvatore was remembering his own remark, not meant to be funny, said a little wistfully after he and Lucille and Florian had returned to Trent from Dave's funeral: *We spend more time driving back and forth to bury Dave than we ever spend talking to him.*

There were others, a whole familyful of them: Henry, who wrapped all the Christmas presents himself because his wife used too much Scotch tape; Sal, who would pat his stomach, eminently satisfied, and say *I was a fat kid, I'm fat now, and if everything goes right, I'm gonna be a fat old man;* Beth, who died young, barely fifty, saying, *At least I went through my whole life with my own teeth;* Donna, who told her teenage son when he got a little too full of himself running after girls, *Hey, that wrinkled little chicken neck you got there, who's gonna care about that?;* Grandpa Sevvy, who as he was about to die in his nineties said, *So soon?;* Paulette and Jerry, who owned a florist shop on Gun Hill Road and expected their daughter Ginny to still help out on weekends and holidays, so that at forty, with a full-time job of her own, Ginny was still unmarried, having lost a whole string of boyfriends who got tired of never getting to see her; Uncle Mario, who'd written in his Christmas card one year, *Hope you have a good Xmas and a Happy New Year,* which, Aunt Cecille said, Mario had agonized over for hours, wanting to get it just right for his rich nephew up there in the country.

Of course, Florian had a few cameos of his own, not to be shared with Salvatore, of Lucille reminding him every time he took a bath as a kid, *Take the soap out now; it's money melting away in the water;* of how young and proud and beautiful, incredibly beautiful, Lucille looked in her wedding picture; of the time she'd come home after visiting her sister Irene, hospitalized for cancer treatments, and said that Irene's hair had fallen out and the poor woman had to wear a scarf to cover her baldness, adding, *It's a pretty scarf, she looks very nice in it.*

Of Salvatore, too, who'd never had a truly decent job in his life but had done his best at every one and couldn't understand people who didn't care about their work. Back during the Depression Salvatore spent a while cleaning windows for the trolley company. Florian, only a little kid then, remembered him explaining over dinner:

You want clean windows, you gotta hose first, then squeegee. But the company, they don't care, they just wanna save money, so we hose but can't squeegee, and what you get is streaks. After a snowstorm, rain, hail, all the cars and trucks kick up the slush and everything and the windows get just black. You can't even see through them, so everybody knows you can't just hose but have to squeegee too. But the bosses, they don't care, so what're you gonna do?

What Florian most remembered was the way his father, without education, without sophistication, without any pretense of worldly knowledge, could make sense of things. Last winter he heard Salvatore explaining to Brian, *In good weather, always get the firewood from the far end of the pile. Then, when you have to come out in a storm, there's stuff nearby.*

"The guys, they came down today," Salvatore said.

"What guys?"

"From the Polecat."

"They did? Did you call them?"

"Why would I call them? They see the news in the paper, on TV. So six of them, they all have a few beers and pile in this car and come down to say hello. Polcari himself, he can't come because he has to keep open. But he sent word—to you too. He said hello. Everybody said hello. That's why they came, to say hello and wish us good luck."

"That was real nice."

"Only, you know, they felt funny. They never been here, didn't know what it looked like or anything." He gestured toward the house, the patio, the view of the lake, maybe even the birdfeeder. "At first, when they saw it, they thought it was the wrong place. Anyhow, they didn't stay too long."

"You made them feel at home, didn't you?"

"Sure we did, didn't we?" he said to Lucille, then shrugged. "They just felt funny. Still, it was nice. Lucille, I bet she liked all these men around for a change saying how nice she looked and flirting with her. Ain't that right, boss? Fun, eh?" Salvatore held his smile a long time, before turning to Florian. "Tell me now what happened today," Salvatore said. "I'm ready."

11

So far, nothing in Jamie's testimony struck Joyce as a revelation: a bunch of high school kids on a Friday night prowl. It all sounded, if anything, rather mild, no one even soused enough to take a leak beyond the glare of the headlights (unless, of course, Jamie was too delicate to mention it). No pot, no speed, no shooting up. No knives, bats or cinder blocks. No screaming breakneck chases, no drag racing over speed bumps, nothing more notable than a minor brawl or two, a few bumps and bruises—and the mention of their determination to get back at the Trent kids, and to use a speedboat to help them do it. The earlier testimony by the other kids on the ramp seemed more damaging than anything Jamie had said.

Channel 6 showed Jamie entering the courthouse, squat and broad-shouldered in his natty sport coat, and the *Express* gave his testimony the full treatment, column after column of small-print capitalized Qs and As.

Part of his apparent credibility surely resulted from his admission of wanting to get back at the Trent kids, of him and his friends going through a few six-packs. *Look,* he seemed to be saying, *I'm holding nothing back, not even things that make me look bad.* His refusal—so far, at least—to single out Brian as the main culprit helped too, showing how much he was bending over to be fair. Would Jamie have been shrewd and cool enough to design all this on his own, if it had been designed at all? Maybe it was just a more public version of the tour he'd given her of Nanny Point, his lovey-dovey photo with Veronique Thrane. Had he hoped to convince Joyce he'd be truthful on the stand, or soften her up for all those carefully wrought lies? And why, for heaven's sake, did he care what she thought in the first place? Whether Jamie realized it or not, the kid always seemed fated to explain away how—through no fault of his own, through just the sheerest coincidence, or bad luck, or inexplicable circumstance—he'd once again plunged smack into the middle of some royal freewheeling mess.

But kids could fool you, and Joyce had learned to be wary of her own prejudices. Growing up middle-class Long Island Jewish wasn't the worst fate in the world, but there were things you still—three decades later—had to keep fighting off, bits of cultural wisdom handed down along with the crystal and good silver. You were expected to see yourself as different from, and superior to, not only those on the bottom (lazy, loud, crude, breeding and stabbing in their steamy tenements) but those on top too (selfish and arrogant, spoiled rotten by their servants). Only your own kind, spitting images of yourself with their perfect accents, contentedly settling into the very middle of some middling suburb, could be trusted.

She'd nonetheless grown close to a lot of Medway girls, girls without mothers or in trouble with their mothers or about to become mothers, girls who'd show up with puffy faces and black eyes and purplish bruises, sometimes from boyfriends, sometimes from fathers and mothers, girls who remembered getting beaten up or molested as babies, girls who'd been kicked out of their homes for real or imagined transgressions. She'd also, thank God, gotten to know a lot of just regular everyday high school girls with everyday high school problems. (Once in the teachers' room someone said the kids you really liked were just substitutes for the sons and daughters you never had. Katarina had cheerfully disagreed: "Or substitutes for the kids you *did* have, giving you another shot at getting it right.")

All in all, Joyce had gotten a bigger dose of Jamie Pitt the last two days than she'd ever bargained for, from any student. Maybe it all simply served to remind her once again how alien she'd always seem to someone like Jamie—or Willa Hufnagle, or Polly Dunn, even Brian Rubio, even maybe those girls she'd gotten to know and love. She was Mrs. Johnway, the starched and distant history teacher, listening and nodding and trying as hard as she could to get with it, but lost and uncertain, light-years away, without a hope of ever truly understanding the first thing about what they did and why they did it.

Having decided not to bother Florian, Joyce spent the evening catching up on last month's *Atlantic* and *Harper's* with one eye on the chained-down motel TV. She dearly wished for the trial to end, for the ex-wife to go back to California, for Florian to emerge from under all those lawyers and worries to perhaps again discover a free hour for a friend. Only what if they convicted Brian? What if they sent him to prison? What would that do to Brian—and to Florian?

Too tired to watch the eleven o'clock news with its inevitable rehash of Jamie and the trial, she turned off the set and was heading into the bathroom when she heard the knock. She frowned, motionless, then moved quietly to the door and viewed Benn's almost comically distorted head and shoulders through the magnifying peephole. At this time of night? She shrugged and opened the door with hardly any emotion at all, thinking again of the women she'd known whose separations had brought all sorts of frantic upheavals and self-doubts, paranoid fears, nightmarish visions of hopelessness and suicide. Except for a few sessions of doubt in Europe, she'd been spared most of that. Maybe she'd waited so long before making her move that all the torment had been used up. As undramatic as it might seem, she didn't even feel any great antagonism toward Benn. She was simply pleased, finally, to have reclaimed her own life.

"Sorry to bust in so late," said Benn in his elastic-banded slacks, his green alligator shirt, a slight bulge thickening his middle. He didn't kiss her, didn't touch her at all. He laughed, that harsh ironic puff she'd grown used to over the years. Benn rarely laughed at things other people found funny. His sense of humor came edged, a commentary on man's (and woman's) folly or stupidity or inability to understand nuances, complexities, delicate balances. "Something's come up with the trial," he said when she made no move to invite him in.

"I was just about to go to bed."

"Sorry about that. We were wondering how you'd feel about helping out."

The request was so unexpected she blinked. "Helping who?"

"Good question. Look, I know how you feel about those hardworking kids up there at Medway, but—"

"You don't know how I feel."

"Tell me then. How do you feel?"

"Why don't you tell me why you're here?"

"Okay, but Christ only knows where this whole el weirdo enterprise is heading, least of all me. If we were talking profit, you wouldn't catch me within miles of something like this."

"What are we talking?"

"That we'll have to see. Meanwhile, the Queen of Sheba is sitting outside in the royal sedan chair, kind of young and jumpy but otherwise not half bad if you want this old man's opinion. She was too shy to pop in on you uninvited but could really use some soft female understanding, if you get my drift."

"Veronique."

"Herself. Nique Thrane, ex-heartthrob of just about everybody, Mt. Early's volunteer bed and breakfast establishment. Be that as it may, her parents are already beating the bushes for her, so the obvious places won't do, and we figured having her stay with me wouldn't hit the right note either."

"You keep saying *we.*"

"I thought you understood. Me and Wachtel and, in the overall picture, Harry Diggs."

"Not Florian?"

"The guy's too bugged sweating out his worries to think straight."

"Did you bring her down from Maine?"

"In all truth, your eminent scholar James J. Pitt did the honors, although I'm not sure how. Maybe they thumbed back together, like in the old Clark Gable movie. He hides behind a bush and she shows a little leg. Anyhow, they made it, although I hear it didn't go as smooth as silk."

"What do you mean?"

"I don't know details, I just heard they ran into problems. Anyhow, you game for some graduate-level baby-sitting?"

Dubiously Joyce glanced back into the room. "It'll be cramped."

"Not here. We got a place."

"Isn't this kidnapping?"

"Diggs is a fucking lawyer and oughta know what kidnapping is. It's all the girl's idea anyhow."

"I wish I knew who this was supposed to help."

"Well, if Diggs and me and that doodlebug Wachtel are busting our horns over it, it's gotta be to help the Trent kids, including, and maybe even especially, the Rubio kid. Only right now I got a skittery sixteen-year-old who's about to pee on the floor mat if somebody doesn't take over. You were the one person we could think of."

"We again. I've got school tomorrow, Benn. I need time to pack and organize and pull together five classes."

Clearly the thought hadn't occurred to him. He recovered. "You got six thousand sick days coming. Take one, for Christ's sake."

"What are you people expecting me to do?"

"Make it easier for her, that's all. She's had a tough day. Long ride. Heavy emotion. It'll probably just for tonight, okay? The kid's really bushed." He gave the motel room the once-over. "I promise, the accommodations will be an improvement. We'll wait out front."

She washed her face, combed her hair, grabbed her briefcase, threw things in a bag for school tomorrow. (Why was she doing this? Maybe, in her perverse gossipy curiosity, she wouldn't mind getting a look at Veronique Thrane.)

Outside, Benn waited leaning against his black Continental with his arms crossed, the motel lights flashing off the grille. Joyce expected Veronique, in the passenger seat, to get out and say hello, toss a wave, something, but she remained inside, staring off into the distance, her face wan behind the glass.

"Where are we going?"

"I'll show you."

"Tell me."

"Abby Allen's gone back to New York but the Saddle House hasn't been shuttered yet. We didn't think anyone would look there."

Patiently waiting in the car, Veronique still seemed lost in God knows what teenage daydream.

"We just wanted someone with her. You know, the strain and everything."

"I'll follow you."

"Right," he said after figuring it out. "You'll want your car there. We'll get her settled and then work out the details."

The Trent Theater Festival closed every year after Labor Day, so the visiting stars (Alan Alda and Geraldine Page this year, along with some famous bleached ingenue Joyce never heard of from some famous TV sitcom she never watched) had all, along with Abby Allen Oliver herself, departed for New York or Hollywood or wherever, along with all those young, lithe, pigtailed, incredibly charged apprentices and curtain pullers.

Joyce loved researching the old estates, those storied places as unreal to her kids as the craters of the moon. Some old-hat factory magnate's last heir, Alston Brainard, had chosen an actress of vague accomplishment as his third wife, and when she died, he dedicated his estate to "the progress of serious dramatic arts and performance." Perhaps he blamed the lack of local theatrical opportunity for his wife's so-so career, and the local feeling at the time, supported by levelheaded editorials in the *Express*, was that this sleepy little town in the hills of Mt. Early County could no more support serious drama than it could the next world's fair.

The first years were tough but eventually, to everyone's surprise, the festival became a success, and led to the Shell concerts, the Music Barn, the Split Rock Ballet, the Pro Musica Society, along with all those galleries and shoppes and restaurants and inns and summer homes and lakeside condos for which Mt. Early County was now famous—and, of course, to the soaring prices of all those lovely properties Florian bought and sold. "Sure, the guy's smart," Benn said one time, "but he was lucky too, coming in just when everything took off, so he could ride the boom all these years."

The Saddle House on the old Brainard property served as the summer home for the festival's artistic director, and Benn unlocked the door and threw it open for them like a real estate salesman showing a hot listing, although Joyce, of course, had been there for festival fund-raisers. Nique went in first, somewhat cautiously, and Joyce followed. They faced the wide carpeted stairway to the second floor, with the living room through an arch to the right, the spacious dining room on the left. Abby Allen hadn't been charmed by the original rusticity and had turned the interior cool and spare and modern, with white couches and white walls, molded Lucite chairs and end tables, white bookcases, huge zebra-striped throw pillows, minimalist paintings: a New England barn wrapped around a Central Park West apartment, deposited in the middle of forty landscaped acres.

Nique looked it over, moving only her head. Was she reacting to the décor or simply numbed by one more surprise after everything else that had happened this long and wearying day? Maybe, given the way her parents lived, she was deciding that the décor was a bit theatrical.

Benn plodded in after them, toting Nique's mauve suitcase, a size that'd get you to India and back on a tramp steamer. Joyce envisioned the Maine runaway scene as a cartoon strip, Nique tossing the suitcase from her upstairs bedroom window and climbing down a ladder steadied at bottom by Jamie Pitt.

The girl wore stone-rubbed jeans with Diane von Furstenberg's autograph across her very tight, very trim right butt. She was braless under a thin peach sweater with short sleeves. Tanned face, tanned arms, as firm and lovely as young flesh gets, gleaming black hair past her shoulder blades, pure porcelain features.

Since Nique hadn't spoken or even changed expression yet, Joyce wasn't sure how much brainpower, if any, lurked behind those limpid aqua eyes. She was maybe six inches taller than Joyce (no big deal for high school girls nowadays) and looked incredibly fit. She had shoulders too, by God, and shapely legs straining against those tight jeans, and a body fit for an idealized sketch—all airbrush and soft pastels—of some statuesque Olympic high diver.

"The bedrooms are upstairs," Benn said. "I'll drop the bag up there and let you girls work out the arrangements."

"You can leave it here," Nique said. "We'll manage."

Her first words: maybe she was just tired, but she certainly sounded jaded—although high school girls were always ripe for romantic ennui, for some lost generation or other. If not so much at Medway, more so at Trent, more again a few miles away at Spenser Academy.

"I'm glad to meet you," Joyce said, tempted, comically, to add, *After everything I've heard.*

Nique turned to Joyce. "It's nice of you to come like this." She sounded exhausted, bone-weary. After all, it was almost midnight.

"Anyhow," Benn said to Joyce, "Wachtel's holding a big powwow tonight, so nothing's really definite yet, but they'll probably want to use her tomorrow or the next day. Somebody'll be in touch, probably tonight, so she should stay available and give some real thought to how she's—"

"What are you telling her for?" Nique said sharply. "You're talking about me."

"Okay," Benn said, eying her and letting out a breath, as if facing some bratty child making impossible demands. "So that's where we are. Strategy, tactics, who knows? Once you testify, of course, you'll be free and clear to do whatever you want."

"Hey, it's not me we're worried about being free and clear."

"We all understand that," Benn said, "but if you just want to head back to Maine after you're finished, we could arrange something. We feel somewhat responsible, after all." Benn sounded sincere enough but also drearily resigned to whatever was coming next—for her? For himself? "And one way or another," he added, "you really oughta get in touch with your parents."

"I'll call them right now," Nique said, hoisting the suitcase easily and heading upstairs, "so they won't worry."

Benn said he wanted to say something and nodded toward the screened-in porch, the only part of the Saddle House whose woodsy aura Abby Allen had left intact. It was lovely there, the soft night air stirring the mildest of breezes among the trees of the estate, a nice change after the view of the Log Cabins parking lot.

"How are you doing?" Benn asked with a little nod in Joyce's direction—nothing specific, just a sort of *Well, here we are, knocking down a few cool ones together* gesture. Only there weren't any cool ones. Benn had checked and found the refrigerator unplugged, the liquor cabinet bone dry. She was just as glad; she could smell the bourbon, could tell from his movements and hesitations that he'd already had more than enough this evening.

"I'm doing all right," Joyce said. "Is the girl going to testify, is that what's going on?"

Benn leaned back against the screening, looking her over with his hands in the rear pockets of his elasticized slacks. "I guess that's up to the lawyers."

"You mean you people dragged her all the way down from Maine without even knowing whether she'd be testifying?"

He pulled out his wallet and tossed some bills onto the split-log table. "Stock up for a few days, okay? Only she shouldn't hit the stores with you. Half the cops in the county are probably looking for her by now."

"I wish I knew what was going on, Benn. Are you trying to say that the Trent lawyers and Jamie Pitt are working together now?"

"Oh, no. Jamie Pitt got the girl down here, but then she called the lawyers on her own. How Jamie feels about all this I have no idea. I'm only involved because earlier I promised to do anything I could and they called in my chit." He seemed to be trying to stare her down, then said, "You probably see me behind the whole thing, pulling strings. You give me more credit than I deserve. You always have, as if I've got a stranglehold on everything. Maybe that's where your resentment comes from, why you're over at that half-assed motel, to say nothing of the European culture tour."

"Benn—you asked me to stay with the girl. Let's not drag in everything else."

"Every time I mention anything, you say it's the wrong time. It's not something that happened twenty years ago, Joyce. It's still a live topic."

"And the minute it comes up you yell at me or toss my stuff in the lake or pin me against the wall. How can anyone talk under those circumstances?"

"Maybe we can treat each other with a little honesty, okay. I know all about you and the Italian stallion back then, and believe me, it ain't exactly fun and games at the old corral. But we can deal with that. Meanwhile, why don't you start by saying, *Benn, I'm in the middle of a lot of heavy stuff with Florian and it's sort of complicating my feelings about you and everything else, including the goddamn kid on trial.*"

She'd again and again imagined Benn saying something like this, without ever being able to conjure up the self-assured response that would settle everything as simply as snapping a purse shut. "Yes," she said. "I've seen Florian a few times. There's not much else to say."

"I didn't ask you to say anything. I only wanted you to acknowledge it."

"I just did."

"It wasn't so hard, was it? Step one. Step two is maybe my turn to be honest, so let me say that your pulling out seems unfortunately timed. There's no way you can suddenly disappear just when things turn sour for me without my seeing a connection."

"How could there be a connection? I don't know what your business troubles are. I never have."

"That's hard to believe, and you have to admit it sure looks funny, running out on me the exact night I fly back from California to try to keep from losing my shirt."

It was her turn to glare at him. "You said you came back to help the Trent kids."

"Because I was still trying to pull things together, to save the investment, and thought I still had a chance and didn't want you worrying unnecessarily. The problem is I was thinking of you and the girls and wanted something good and solid and long-range in case anything happened to me. But it didn't work out the way I thought and I got somewhat overextended."

He didn't seem to want to go on about it, so she said, "I'm sorry it came up this way, Benn—about Florian."

"What other ways are there?" He gestured back through the door into the Saddle House itself, gave her a funny smile. "That Abby Allen, I bet she'd really be a nice little piece, wouldn't you say? Florian, for one, ought to know. I understand he spent one whole summer screwing her."

"Who were you screwing that summer, Benn? And where? How often?"

"Right now, Joyce, I don't need one more person coming at me, okay? Especially you. Meanwhile, all I'm doing is wondering if this thing with Florian . . . was that what did it? Is that the answer to everything?"

She didn't want to answer and wasn't even sure she could, except maybe by quoting him that line from Yeats (a first, using poetry on Benn): *How can we know the dancer from the dance?*

She started back toward the living room, but Benn grabbed her arm and yanked her to a stop next to the log table. He thrust up against her, breathing right into her face. "Believe me, I've tried to understand this, Joyce. I truly have. I've been extremely patient and have given you every benefit of the doubt." He took a breath: "I—just—do—not—know—how—this—happened."

Everything told her to be wary: his hard breathing, the strain in his voice, the cutting pressure of his fingers on her arm. Everything warned her: be careful, be smart, don't play games. She was shocked by the pain in his face, the looseness of his mouth; she'd never seen him this wounded, this broken.

"I'm not sure I can explain anything," she said quietly. "Maybe the big things, the big surprises, are the hardest to make sense of. People change. Situations change. Things fester."

"What the fuck does that mean—fester?" His breath rasped. "I'll tell you what gets me about Florian. It happens all the time. The fake-a-roony with nothing to lose puts on a big show and bowls over the women every time. The guy that really cares and plays it straight ends up with shit."

"Really, Benn—how can you talk about playing it straight?"

"If my wife hadn't died, we'd still be together. I'm not the one whose wife dumped him to run off to California."

He pulled back, both of them startled by the voice from inside:

"Hey, the stinking phone's dead." Nique stopped at the open door to the porch, her eyes widening. "Ooops, sorry. I didn't—" She swung about and disappeared, and they could hear her running up the stairs. Maybe she'd seen and heard enough arguments at home to recognize the looks she must have caught on their faces.

The interruption seemed to defuse Benn. "Damn, I wanted to call and let them know you people were all set here. Maybe next time they'll use carrier pigeons." He shook off any further discussion, clambered past her and through the house. Motionless on the porch, drained, Joyce heard his engine start, heard his car roar off.

Upstairs she found Nique waiting in the big bedroom. "Why don't you just keep this one?" Joyce suggested cheerfully, not wanting the girl to feel bad about busting in on them. It was Abby Allen Oliver's own room and took up half the second floor, the picture windows opening onto great vistas of the natural amphitheater and stone-walled formal garden with the purple hues of the moonlit Mt. Early off in the distance. "The one down the hall's fine for me. I won't be staying long."

"Me either," Nique said. "You know, I bet they killed the phones on purpose. They sure trust us, don't they?"

"It can't be that. They probably disconnected everything when they closed up last week."

"The lights work. The water's running."

Joyce gave up. How was she supposed to know what they did or didn't turn off?

"I really wanted to call my parents. I didn't realize I was supposed to be in prison."

Here we are, Joyce thought, *ten minutes gone and already I'm the jail matron, fat and fascistic.* She hadn't been prepared for any kind of confrontation with Benn before, and certainly hadn't expected him to leave then without another word. He could have at least explained what her sworn duties were supposed to be, beyond hiding Nique from her parents and the cops. To keep her from escaping? From talking to anyone? From feeling lonesome and blue? And if Nique did decide to run off, where would she go? For what imaginable purpose?

"It's too bad about the phones," Joyce said. "Benn never mentioned them."

Nique waved it off and surprised Joyce by saying, quite pleasantly, "Mr. Johnway's your husband, isn't he?"

"Yes, he is." When Nique didn't pursue the point, Joyce added, "I'm at the motel because we're not living together right now."

"Sure, all the strain is right out front; anybody could see that. Only you know, he still thinks an awful lot of you. He couldn't say enough nice things about you before. Anyhow, my parents aren't exactly a hot item either. Mainly they spend their time *faaarrr* apart. I mean, they never announce it to anyone, let alone me, but everybody understands. He's in one place and she's in another. Who knows? Maybe it's as good as most other solutions."

Joyce wasn't sure whether she welcomed the gratuitous information. Some kids at school would regale you with the most intimate family details. It could be taken as a compliment, some troubled teenager opening up, trusting you. With others, though, it was just a tap turned on full flush for anyone willing to listen.

"I don't really know your parents."

"No one around here does. Mr. Johnway was telling me about this place, how hard it is raising money all the time to put on the plays every summer. I think he was talking about my parents because they never give to local stuff. They support tons of things but mostly in New York, or like the Kennedy Center in Washington."

Joyce waited in the silence. "Are you back in Trent for school?"

"Spenser doesn't start till next week. You know, I really don't want my parents thinking I've been kidnapped or anything."

"C'mon," Joyce said. "You'll need food and stuff for tomorrow anyhow."

"Mr. Johnway wasn't keen on me going anywhere."

"They should have left the phones on then. Tie a scarf around your head and stay low in the seat."

In the VW, Nique checked it over with undisguised interest, front and back, maybe something she'd never seen from the inside before, and said, "You think I could call while you're getting the food?"

Joyce parked in front of the convenience store on Route 15, its windows plastered with signs for Slurpees and cigarettes and doughnuts and Wonder bread, hoping no one there would recognize the girl (one of the maids from Sargasso River Highlands, out on the town?). A few other cars filled slots in the floodlit area, and some kids lounged near the door.

"Would you mind picking up some Diet Sprite? I go through it like water. Oh, yeah, I'm sorry, but I don't have any change."

Joyce dug a couple of dimes out of her purse, remembering the stories of JFK, worth more millions than he could count but never carrying cash, sponging off Secret Service men.

The guys in front of the store studied Nique's tight jeans as she pigeon-toed to the outdoor plastic shield with its dangling dog-eared phone book. They also checked out Joyce going into the store, obviously disappointed. Her *mother?*

Nique was waiting in the car when Joyce returned. She handed back one of the dimes. "Thanks."

"How are your parents?"

"Okay. Not thrilled, I mean, but they'll survive."

"That's what parents are supposed to do. It's in the contract."

As they swung past the big ice machine, one of the front-door loungers took off his peaked orange cap and swept it in a flourishing, grinning Cyrano bow. Nique, already scrunched down and hooded in a big scarf, either didn't notice or didn't care to. Joyce had visions of the cops barricading Route 15, stopping every car to shine a flashlight at the faces. *Okay, Sarge, we got 'em right here, the good-looking kid and the schoolmarm. Should we run 'em both in?*

"If your parents are so worried, how did Benn, or Jamie, or whoever, manage to snatch you away?"

"After the water got too cold for swimming I took long walks every day, so had a few hours' leeway before they'd think anything was up. I just thought it'd be nice now to tell them not to worry."

Thankfully, no cops with twirling nightsticks awaited them at the Saddle House. Nique helped Joyce put away the stuff and then twisted a Sprite from the plastic six-pack cover. "I'll just take this up with me and hit the sack, okay? I'm really bushed from all this. Maybe tomorrow, you know, we could talk or something."

"I'll probably be leaving early for school."

"That's okay. I'll be up early too. And you know—thanks again."

In her own, much smaller bedroom, her head still full of Benn, Joyce considered the fact that she had no plans for the girl, no questions, nothing to say. She still doubted whether the whole escapade could possibly be in anyone's best interest, and wasn't at all sure how she felt about Nique, whose every look and gesture seemed to proclaim British nannies and designer kiddie clothes, whose perfect teeth no doubt resulted from invisible braces designed by the world's most exclusive orthodontist. Nor could you help noticing her softly modulated voice, her shrugging-off, turning-aside way of speaking, as if nothing was really worth getting terribly excited about. (Spenserian classes in elocution, in drawing room reticence?) Yet, in her own way, the kid seemed kind of sweet.

This late, on this night, Joyce wasn't up to thinking very deeply about Nique or anything else, and she was already in bed and drifting off while Nique was still running water in her own bathroom.

12

Leaving the house with Brian after lunch on Tuesday, picking up Elly at the Hollisworth, waiting for Wachtel to emerge with his briefcase through his white picket fence and trellis, Florian, who had slept badly and spent a draggy, listless morning, felt as if the trial had already become interminable. He was ready, right now, immediately, for it to end. Those cases that went on for weeks, months, years: it must be like living inside a bubble at the bottom of the sea. No: he shook off the image.

Wachtel looked okay, clean-shaven, fresh, in a nice crisp suit and striped shirt, blue silk tie. What the hell, he did this for a living. Florian too had showered and shaved and put on a fresh shirt—but he felt burnt out, his reserves gone, his patience shredded. Elly had hardly spoken on the way to Wachtel's, and every few minutes, looking out the window, she'd take a long breath and sigh.

Even Brian was beginning to look like he could use a couple of weeks on a beach somewhere, a lot of sun, plenty of fooling around.

"I think they'll wrap it up with Jamie today," Wachtel said when he leaned down to say hello through Elly's window. "Maybe tomorrow, Thursday it'll be all over. Everybody okay, meanwhile? Everybody up to snuff?"

All he got in response were a few halfhearted grunts.

On the stand Jamie Pitt resumed with that same smiling earnestness, as if tirelessly determined to counteract the rough, almost pugnacious expression that seemed, when he let his guard down, to come to him naturally. On and on he went, regaling them with time and place, with character and event, in such a seamless self-confident flow that he seemed willing, if that's what people wanted, of going on forever.

That's right, they'd decided to get themselves a speedboat, only to get to Hammond's on the other side of the lake they had to drive around the Neck in Medway, where the houses were small and mostly ramshackle, crowded together a block or so from the water. Even the ones right on the shore weren't much because the Neck was so narrow the houses looked across the little bit of water practically into each other's living rooms. These places were also right near Hammond's, which meant they got the noise and oil slicks from the boats coming in and out. You found the expensive houses, the big and fancy farther-apart ones, down in Trent, in South Corner, where the lake was a lot wider.

(Why the hell didn't Wachtel object? Who was this kid—some expert in land use management? Did they teach that at Medway High? Maybe it was one of the rare courses he passed.)

As they were driving through this section they happened to see a couple of guys from school who lived there, standing in front of the mini food blaster.

What? Judge Ingersoll asked. It was his first interruption. The 7-Eleven, Jamie said. Oh, the judge said, and settled back.

So they pulled into the parking lot and these other guys said since they didn't have any wheels on this nice Friday night, could they just pile in with Jamie and the others?

Naturally they said okay. Only first they told them what had already happened, and what they were planning over at Nanny Point. Well, the two new guys said, sure, if there was room in the car, room in the boat, they'd go along and help out. So all five squeezed in and headed for the boatyard, passing around cheese twists and the beers left from the six-pack.

Yeah, these two guys were seniors at Medway. Yeah, they'd passed everything and were set to graduate.

Their names?

One was Mickey Connors, Jamie responded with a little shrug, as if saying this name wasn't the important one, and then, loud and clear, announced that the other one was Paul Dunn, who everybody called Polly. Whom, he corrected. Whom everybody called Polly.

Except maybe for the jurors, blessed in their ignorance, everyone knew Polly Dunn's name. They'd seen his picture, read his obituary, and knew all along that at some point he'd come forth to play his part in Jamie's story. Yet the recitation of the name brought a shimmering silence to the courtroom. Some looked around for his parents. For just an instant Jamie had somehow, magically, brought the boy back to life, in an image everyone had seen a thousand times—bored teenagers slouching against the ice machine in front of a 7-Eleven, tossing cheese twists into their mouths from a tinfoil sack, waiting for the excitement to begin. It was as if Polly Dunn suddenly had a chance again, the tantalizing possibility that things might yet turn out all right for him in the hours ahead.

And Willa Hufnagle? Florian was sure he wasn't the only one in the courtroom now wondering at what point she would make her entrance, with Jamie somehow creating for her too the illusion that she still could do things differently, still had a chance to come out of all this alive.

But everyone knew that those two doomed kids—and Brian, too— would have to act out the same final moments again, no matter how desperately they all cried out in their hearts, *Stop! Stop!* Once more the story would have to end the only way it could, with the same dripping Valiant dangling above the black lake at the end of a chain.

No, Jamie said, it wasn't a yacht or anything like that, just a speed-boat, like for towing water-skiers, but plenty big enough for five. Yes, he realized just taking it like that wasn't exactly legal but they were too angry to think about that. Besides, they never thought that they were stealing it, but just borrowing it for an hour or so.

Probably near nine, barely light enough to see, with all the other boats probably in.

So off they went, four guys sprawled around on the padded swivel seats and Jamie at the wheel. He slowed down as they got near Nanny Point, then cut the engine altogether and let the boat drift around the arm to the beach. They still didn't have a real plan. Mainly they figured on just razzing anyone they found there, especially if they were swimming without clothes.

Well, all they found was one canoe beached on the sand and one guy and one girl in the water up to their knees. Yes, it was light enough to recognize them. The guy was Brian Rubio, but did he have to give the girl's name? She wasn't involved in anything and he didn't want to drag her in if he didn't have to.

Delehanty and Wachtel huddled with the judge. Wachtel flared one hand—seemingly saying, *Fine, fine, all right with me.* He went back to his seat next to Brian, and Delehanty told Jamie that at least for the time being he could proceed without naming the young lady.

Brian Rubio, naked, still holding the naked girl's hand, yanked her around and ran with her onto the little beach, where they grabbed their clothes and bolted into the woods.

Jamie and his buddies jumped onto the beach after them. This time they had the advantage of not being barefoot, so they caught up pretty quick. What Jamie did then, since he didn't want the girl being any more embarrassed, was take her away from the others so she could put her clothes back on, cutoffs and one of those T-shirts with code words. He warned her about the bad blood going on between some Trent and Medway kids and offered to take her back in the speedboat so she could go home and stay clear of the whole thing. She said no, she just wanted to find Brian Rubio.

But Jamie's friends came back then and said Brian Rubio got away. The girl didn't believe them, and Jamie wondered too how this barefoot naked guy could get away from four guys with sneakers, but the girl really went wild, yelling they must have left him bleeding and dying somewhere, and tore into the woods to look for him.

No, no one tried to stop her. In fact, Jamie almost went with her, to help, but figured Brian Rubio might get the wrong idea, and so instead talked his four friends into taking the speedboat back to Hammond's. Actually he was beginning to worry more about something happening to the boat than about Brian Rubio, who his friends kept saying really did escape and was perfectly all right, although they still had his clothes.

By now it was real nighttime even outside the woods, even on the open lake, so his friends put Brian Rubio's cutoffs and MORP shirt and skivvies and sneakers into the canoe and towed it out and cut it loose in the middle of the lake. Jamie himself still wanted to just head back, but his friends talked him into taking a swing around the lake. He went pretty slow, one, because he didn't want to put any lights on and maybe have somebody wondering what was going on and, two, to keep the noise down. On the way back, though, just as they were passing the drifting canoe, they saw a small whitecap in the water, moving very slowly toward the canoe. It was Brian Rubio swimming, you could spot his blond hair. The other guys wanted to buzz him with the speedboat and then tow the canoe way down to South Corner, to give him a few more miles to swim. This time Jamie really put his foot down. He said no. He wouldn't do it. The guy could get drowned. Even a good swimmer could get a cramp or something.

So they left him swimming for the canoe and about nine-thirty moored the speedboat at Hammond's and squeezed into the Valiant and took off for some more beer and stuff to eat.

Was this the second six-pack?

Actually they bought a couple this time, because now there were five of them, and went to the drive-in for the nine-thirty show, figuring they'd just forget about the guys from Trent. Then after the movie someone said, *Hey, let's go out in the boat again.* Jamie of course was absolutely against it. Just because they lucked out before didn't mean something bad wouldn't happen this time. But everybody really wanted to go sailing, which was what they called it. Why not? they wanted to know. What was the big deal? It was just for fun.

No, he couldn't just say no. What'd stop them from going out on their own and wrecking it, or stalling out in the middle of the lake until Hammond discovered it missing in the morning? They could easy enough take the key to the bait hut from Jamie and get the ignition key from the pegboard, just like they'd seen him do when they borrowed the boat earlier. Maybe, looking back, he could've figured a better way of handling it, but you can't always think of everything ahead of time at exactly the right minute. He was sorry now he'd ever gone near the boat in the first place. Still, he figured he'd be better off going with them, steering, than having them take it out on their own.

Florian could see it, even smell it: Jamie and his friends jammed into the Valiant with their six-packs, the floor littered with crushed cans and crumpled crinkly bags, the odor of malty foam and cheese and popcorn and chili dogs everywhere, even though they'd cranked open all the windows and the warm night air rushed in as they sped toward Hammond's Boatyard. Feeling pretty good about themselves. They had, after all, gotten in their final licks against the guys from Trent. They'd cut the canoe (Florian's!) adrift and left Brian chunking his way through the water in hopes of rescuing his clothes. They'd probably enjoyed the movie at the drive-in too, joking around in the car while ogling the girls strolling to the refreshment stand in their shorts and halters—maybe even thinking back to that brief twilight view of the tall, lovely, naked Nique Thrane knee-deep in the water. And they had more fun still coming, joyriding around the lake in somebody's thirty-thousand-dollar boat.

Not bad for kids who didn't otherwise have a hell of a lot going for them—although they weren't really that bad off. One, at least, could afford a car. Jamie had a job at Hammond's, and the others were solvent enough to keep themselves in beer and skittles. Two of them—Mickey Connors and Polly Dunn—were set to graduate, while the others still had a shot at it. All things considered, they were in a hell of a lot better shape than anyone Florian grew up with.

No, Jamie said, they weren't drunk. They were enjoying themselves, that's all, except for himself, who was too worried about the boat to enjoy anything and, besides, had a funny feeling, almost like what you'd call a premonition. What if someone spotted them and called the cops? The first time they'd just left the Valiant on the dirt road outside the pipe gate to Hammond's. Now Jamie realized how dumb this was, how easy it would tip off people that something fishy was going on.

So they left the car on the public boat ramp, a few hundred yards down Bottleneck Road, sort of halfway between the boatyard on the north and the public beach to the south. The ramp had a paved area about twenty feet wide that slanted down into the water, for launching boats from their trailers, and about ten parking slots on each side, where at night kids sometimes parked, because of the view across the lake.

So they weren't surprised to see a couple, three cars at the south end when they left the Valiant at the north end, closest to Hammond's. They couldn't help but notice one car, though, a practically white Corvette, glowing in the moonlight, although they didn't really think about it. They walked along Bottleneck Road and ducked under the pipe gate to Hammond's, then froze. The bait shed was lit up like a Christmas tree, with Hammond's pickup right in front.

Someone must have seen or heard them earlier and tipped off Hammond. So they backed off real quick and broke into a run on Bottleneck Road with only one thought in mind: to get the Valiant and themselves as far away from there as possible. So all five of them came racing full tilt onto the ramp and got an even worse jolt. Jamie and Mickey Connors, leading the way, pulled up so short the others practically ran up their backs. The Valiant was right where they'd left it, but jammed up behind it, blocking it bumper to bumper, was the white Corvette. Jamie absolutely couldn't believe it. For the life of him he couldn't imagine what was going on.

Then they noticed four guys around the two cars, Trent guys. Earlier, if Jamie had realized the Corvette was being driven by kids, not grown-ups, he'd have realized they had to be Trent kids. And of course even more guys could be hiding behind the cars. But when the owner of the Valiant said, *We gotta get the car back,* no one could argue. They owed him.

No, they didn't think of calling the cops. It was the last thing in the world they'd ever think of.

So they moved forward real slow and easy, not looking like anybody spoiling for a fight. Because they weren't. All they wanted was their car back. Then suddenly another half dozen or so guys popped up from behind the cars, and Jamie and his friends tried to keep things cool by just asking politely if they could please get their Valiant out of there.

The Trent guys, whooping, swarmed all over Jamie and his four friends. It didn't last long, but the whole time all Jamie could do was try to protect himself from two or three guys coming at him at once. It was hard to tell if they were the same Trent guys who'd beaten them up on the dunes. You couldn't see much that time of night, and things really got wild. The only one Jamie definitely knew was Brian Rubio, who was back in his clothes now.

And what was Brian Rubio doing?

The same as the other Trent guys, tearing into the Medway guys, you know, really trying to hurt them, and also to keep them from getting into the Valiant.

Was Brian Rubio doing anything *different* from the others?

Well, he was yelling and screaming more and telling the others what to do, like, *Get that one! Don't let him get away! Get 'im! Get 'im!*

Did he seem to be out after anyone in particular?

"Me. He kept coming after me, chasing me around the Valiant, yanking me out of it one time, by the arm, punching me while someone else was holding me, coming up from behind one time and slugging me on the head with something, I don't know what, but it knocked me down to my knees, and then kicking me while I was down."

Delehanty must have figured this a good time for a break, with this image hanging in the air, so he turned from the witness stand to glance quizzically at the bench, and Judge Ingersoll, checking his watch, gaveled a brief recess.

Actually, Jamie said when they returned, everything happened so fast it was hard keeping track, but right after Brian knocked him down and started kicking him, some car pulled onto the ramp from out of nowhere and its headlights lit up the whole place real glary and ghostly, and a bunch of guys, figuring it was the cops, started running in all directions, only the car pulled out then, leaving everything darker than ever. It must've been some couple wanting to park who took one look at the ruckus and changed their mind.

Then Jamie realized it was Trent guys that'd run off, with only four of them still there, whereas the five Medway guys, including Jamie, had stayed behind, still wanting to get their car back and get out of there in one piece.

Did he know at the time who was driving the Corvette that evening?

No, he didn't. He had no idea.

Did he know the Trent boys who remained on the ramp?

Still just Brian Rubio. But he got a good look at the others and picked them out afterward for the police. Darrell Sampson, Joe Caid, Jr., and Tiny Arkins. Anyhow, he'd been banged up pretty good and was just thinking about getting out of there in one piece. But the driver of the Valiant was even worse off, with one eye completely closed and the other bleeding, and was in no shape to drive, so Jamie took the keys and jumped in, having to slide across from the passenger side because of the jammed door, and right away he felt this really incredible jolt from behind and heard this motor roaring behind him, so he automatically slammed his foot on the brake and turned around and saw through the rear window that it was Brian Rubio in the Corvette, ramming forward against him, trying to push the Valiant right into the lake.

What made him think that was what Brian was trying to do?

Well, like the Valiant was facing the lake, right at the edge, with only this little pavement bump there to keep a car from just sliding off, and Brian Rubio in the Corvette behind him was revving it up full steam and ramming forward into the Valiant, so what else could he be doing? Anyhow, the other Medway guys, seeing this, tried to drag Brian Rubio from the Corvette, so Jamie got out and ran back to help them, and they all managed to drag Brian Rubio out and kind of throw him to the ground. When Polly Dunn saw this, he must have figured this was the time to try to get the Valiant out again, so he ran to it and jumped in from the passenger side, and the other Medway kids came running right after him, including Jamie, leaving Brian Rubio down on the pavement. That's when he saw Willa Hufnagle.

Everybody had been paying pretty close attention as Jamie's voice grew raspier, more hushed, but the mention of Willa Hufnagle brought on, somehow, a deeper stillness.

He knew Willa Hufnagle? He recognized her?

That's right. He knew her. He recognized her.

Where did she come from?

He didn't have the slightest idea. Maybe she'd been just hanging around. Maybe she'd been on the ramp the whole time and he never noticed. Anyhow, when Polly Dunn jumped into the Valiant, Willa Hufnagle jumped in after him, all this happening right in front of Jamie, and the others too, all wanting to get into the Valiant, and in fact Willa slid to the middle of the seat to make room for Jamie, who was right behind her. But she'd already slammed the door shut and must have locked it too, maybe because she was worried about some Trent guys, particularly Tiny Arkins, coming after her, and so when Jamie tried to open—

Why would Tiny Arkins be coming after her?

Well—she was his date.

Tiny Arkins's date? For the MORP?

That's right.

"But if she was with Tiny Arkins, why would she follow Polly Dunn into the Valiant?"

"I don't know why she got in the Valiant. I have no idea. All I can say is she just did."

"You said you tried to open the door. To get in yourself?"

"That's right. Only it was locked, like I say. And before Willa could even reach over and pull up the button, while I was standing right there, only like inches away from the door, I hear this great big roar and bang and suddenly the car just flies forward. I couldn't believe my eyes. It zooms right over the little bump there and off the ramp, right into the lake."

"Did you see what made it do this?"

"Yes I did. I was really kind of stunned but when I looked back what I saw was Brian Rubio behind the wheel of the Corvette."

"But did you *see* the Corvette ram the Valiant into the lake?"

"Well, I was standing there, inches away from the side of the car, and suddenly I hear this bang, I hear this motor revving way the hell up, and the Valiant goes shooting forward right before my eyes, and I look back and there's the Corvette, braking like fury, screeching, to keep itself from going forward anymore and going right in after the Valiant."

"And then?"

"Then it made this really tremendous splash, the water going way up in the air and soaking us standing there, and with everybody watching, really stunned, it settled into the water, gurgling, and then, right in front of everybody, it just sank right out of sight into this great big swirl in the black water."

After noting Wachtel's request that the witness return in the morning for possible cross-examination, Judge Ingersoll adjourned for the day.

Outside, as they were approaching their two cars, Wachtel waved off the reporters and TV people and then whispered something to Brian, who went ahead and got into the Fairlane, sitting alone in back. To keep him away from the reporters, who were still buzzing around?

Wachtel then said to Florian and Elly, "We've got to do some talking, some deciding, and we've got to do it tonight. Brian could use a break so there's no need dragging him along. The problem is, it's four now and I'm tied up with another client for a couple of hours."

"Maybe we can get together right now and—"

"Sorry, Flo. The fellow's in jail and mightily annoyed that I didn't come by hours ago. I'll call the minute I'm free and then you can call Elly."

"Where are we meeting?" Elly asked.

"Whatever's convenient."

"If we use my hotel room, I won't have to come out again."

"Done."

Elly said she was too tired for dinner, and as Florian walked her to the door of the inn, with Brian waiting in the car, he said, "I sure wasn't taken with any of that crap we've heard the last two days."

She stopped on the path and looked up at him. "Suppose it's the truth?"

"You really think a guy like Jamie Pitt went in there to tell the truth?"

"Whatever, he certainly lit into Brian. Call me when Wachtel calls, okay? I don't have anything to drink, but there's room service."

Back in the car, Brian said, "I pretty much expected him to come on like that. Still, he was pretty tough."

"We're seeing Wachtel after."

"He mentioned. He said I didn't have to come."

"Is there anything Jamie said that we could tear into? We could mention it to Ira and see if—"

"Mr. Wachtel knows the whole story, Dad. He has from the beginning."

"Good. I'm glad someone does." When Brian didn't respond, Florian added, "Are you worried, kid? Is it getting you down?"

"A little, I guess. I mean, you wonder what's to keep anyone from believing every word he's saying? It doesn't even have to be every word. Sure, the guy's slanting things to make himself look good. Who wouldn't? But if they just buy into the main stuff, I'm in enough trouble right there."

"I think Wachtel's definitely got something in mind, that he knows exactly how he wants to handle this."

"He probably does," Brian said.

"I'm sure he does," Florian said.

"What's your guy in for that took you so long, high treason?" Florian said when Wachtel called at seven o'clock.

"Stealing his six-year-old back from his ex-wife. This is ex-wife night. See you at Elly's in twenty minutes."

Florian found Wachtel waiting for him in the Hollisworth lobby, all thick rugs and chandeliers and fat soft chairs, pleasantly active now, in September, but not mobbed, and they rode up together. "You've had a long day," Florian said.

"I'll go to any lengths," Wachtel said, his voice a little raspy, "to uphold the integrity of the legal system."

"Well, yeah. Who the hell wouldn't?"

Wachtel was lugging an old briefcase with a ratty handle, bits of leather peeling off everywhere. It was a lot bigger than the flat hard Madison Avenue job he took to court, and it was bulging. In the other hand he clutched a big white McDonald's bag. "I never got any dinner," he explained. "I didn't get anything for you guys because I figured you'd already eaten."

Wrapped up in a long reddish terry-cloth robe, Elly let them in with a nod. "You people want something from room service?"

"Not for me," Wachtel said, holding up the bag and giving her the same explanation. "Maybe Flo wants a drink."

"Let's see how far we get," Florian said. Although he was familiar with the restaurant and lounge downstairs and the brick courtyard with sun umbrellas over the tables, this was the first time he'd been inside a Hollisworth room. He wasn't sure whether Elly's was standard or top-of-the-line, but it was pretty impressive either way. The furniture looked like something you'd actually find in a nice home, the curtains almost as thick as the rugs, the walls decorated with watercolors of Mt. Early scenes by a local artist type whose work did not come cheap. Besides the classy appointments, the room was about three times the size of Joyce's at the Log Cabins. Maybe Elly had assumed Florian would be covering the tab.

They all sat, Wachtel settling the briefcase on his lap, leaving the white bag on the floor next to his chair. "I'm sorry I ran so late, but let's get to it. I said we had some decisions to make, which we couldn't do before tonight because we had to see what Jamie came up with. And we can't wait any longer because we have to make our move tomorrow morning. You know what," he said to Elly, "on second thought maybe I'll go with room service. A little before-dinner cocktail."

Since Florian was closest to the phone, he ordered a couple of double scotches.

"We've been preparing all along for various contingencies, and I'll give you whatever benefit you want, maybe more than you want, of my thinking on these matters. But we're not talking technical legal questions here, so I wanted you people in on it. Brian too, of course, but I've thrashed this out with him enough to know his thinking. Besides, I didn't want to make him sit through what you're going to sit through."

"You certainly make it sound like fun," Elly said.

"Let's look at things in the order we'll have to face them. Tomorrow morning we have to decide, first of all, whether we want to go after Jamie." He held up his hand to stop Florian before he could get started. "Hang on, all right? Our hope, of course, was that Delehanty's case would fall apart of its own accord. If we don't think that's happened, we have to decide whether we still wish to stand mum or get on our white horse and charge. But right now let's just lay things out. Later we can go over things in as much detail as you want."

"I think your hamburger's getting cold," Elly said.

"It'll wait. What we could call Question One-A is whether, if we do cross Jamie, we should stick to relatively straightforward questions of fact, or try to utterly destroy the kid."

Neither Florian nor Elly had any great ideas to offer.

"Question two is whether we want to put Veronique Thrane on the stand. There are a couple of other potential witnesses if we decide to make a case but they don't present problems, so let's skip right to number three, the real lollapalooza."

"Brian," Florian said.

"Brian. I want you to understand that the prosecution can't put him up there. Only we can. But once we do, the prosecution can cross-examine the hell out of him." He undid the old-fashioned straps and buckles of his briefcase and brought forth a clutch of manila folders, maybe three inches' worth. "You play the hand you're dealt. According to Jamie's testimony, Brian had every reason in the world to be sore and was taking it out by attacking Jamie on the ramp and urging on the others to all sorts of mayhem, culminating in the moment when Jamie says he saw Brian ram the Valiant into the drink. That's what we've been dealt."

"I've had better hands," Florian said.

Wachtel tapped the folders. "Harry Diggs has been good enough to let me take a look at the statements of his three clients, Brian's buddies, giving us—"

"Why the hell would he do that?"

"It'd help, Flo, if you could understand that Diggs's interests are not opposed to ours. Let's face it, Brian's in potentially a lot more trouble than any of the other kids."

"Including Tiny Arkins? For Christ's sake, he's the idiot that moved the Corvette behind the other car in the first place. He brought along the thirteen-year-old that got drowned. And where the hell's he? Why is Brian the one hanging by a goddamn thread?"

"C'mon, Flo. Tiny Arkins is neither your son nor my client, so let's not waste time over him. Anyhow, given the situation, Harry did the right thing for his clients by getting separate trials, and he's doing the right thing for them by helping us as much as he can. I was even going to ask him to join us tonight but figured you'd have a fit, so I didn't. So don't have a fit. But the easier Brian gets off, the easier it'll be for Harry's kids, so he's more than ready to do whatever he can for us."

"If Flo wants to stew," Elly said, "let him. Go on."

They fell silent at the knock. An elderly, stooped man shuffled in wearing a red jacket with the Hollisworth crest over the breast pocket. He placed the tray on the walnut coffee table and straightened up to see who'd grab the check. Florian did, frowned at the $24.17 total, and dropped thirty bucks onto the little plate. You could lay in a week's supply of Chivas for that.

After a sip, Wachtel put down his glass. "These folders contain the statements the other Trent kids gave Harry. They're valuable to us because they indicate what kind of testimony the kids would give if Delehanty chose to call them. Only I don't believe he will—unless we take out our hatchets on Jamie Pitt, in which case he might be tempted. In general, Brian's buddies essentially agree with Jamie's version of the events on the ramp. That would not help us at all, Brian's pals corroborating Jamie Pitt. And since Delehanty might well call on them to do so if we challenge Jamie, we want to consider that option very carefully."

"You don't realize," Elly said, "how hard it is listening to some despicable kid doing his best to send your son to prison. You want to fight back."

"I do understand how difficult it is. And we are fighting back—in the best way we can. There's something else to consider. You two see Jamie as the guy who started the fight with your son, his natural enemy, his rival for the beautiful girl cavorting around in the buff. But most people, including the jury, connect Jamie sympathetically with the two Medway kids who drowned. They're the victims, and Jamie Pitt has managed under Delehanty's expert tutelage to drape the mantle of their martyrdom over his own shoulders. It's tough blaming victims, especially if they're poor and deprived and dead."

Elly said: "They do it all the time in rape cases."

"And if I thought it'd work for us, I'd be doing it too, in spades. But that's why we're here, to see what'll work best." Wachtel lifted the folders, gesturing with them. "Transcripts are made from the taped statements of a client." He dumped the folders to the floor and removed a small cassette player from the briefcase. "Brian."

The scotch, Florian's first of the evening, could have been his fourth. He felt light-headed, abstracted, tight between the temples. Why drag out these tapes now, after all this time? To make Wachtel look good? To show how hopeless Brian's case had been from the beginning?

If Wachtel wanted them to know Brian's story, why'd he stop the kid from simply letting his parents in on it from the beginning? Right now Florian wasn't even sure he wanted to listen. Short of Brian proving that he wasn't within miles of the ramp when the kids drowned, what could he say that'd make anyone feel any better?

Elly wet her lips and turned to Wachtel, still holding the cassette in one hand while helping himself to a sip of scotch with the other. "Should we?" she asked. The edge was gone from her voice. She sounded, and looked, awed, almost scared.

"If we're going to make decisions, we'd better have something to base them on."

"Lawyers are a lot better asking questions than answering them," Florian said, all patience and reasonableness, simply making a point. "Why'd you wait till now even to let us know this stuff existed?"

"First of all, there wasn't any *need* before now to put you through this. Besides, Brian was absolutely against it. He's since changed his mind—as long as he doesn't have to listen with you."

Neither Florian nor Elly said anything.

"The whole thing runs for hours, with a fair amount of backing and forthing, but I know where the key parts are, so we can cut and skip. What say? You guys game?"

"Yes," Elly said.

"Yes," Florian said.

Wachtel leaned over to punch the cassette buttons with a surprisingly long and slightly curved finger, then settled back in his chair, trying to open the McDonald's bag as quietly as possible.

Nique had kept her promise of getting up Tuesday morning before Joyce left, but only by a few minutes, coming down the stairs wearing a half-buttoned man's dress shirt as a cover-up. She'd looked scrubbed and fresh and alert, looked even taller as she descended the crimson and wheat abstract runner at a steady, unhurried pace, her head high, as if she were somehow used to making entrances down broad stairways. (How strange, talking of *entrances* by a sixteen-year-old.)

"Oh, don't worry about me," Nique had assured her. "I could use a day of hanging out. I've got the kitchen radio and my tape deck, I can walk around the grounds, I got stuff to read. Hey, I can even take a nap. What else is there to do without a phone or a car or a TV? Daniel Boonesville."

"I'll pick up something for supper on the way back."

"You like pizza? Or Chinese if you'd rather. The best pizza's at Big

Joe's, okay, over on Walnut, the thin crust. And I wouldn't mind a Greek salad on the side, they really make a good one. And a pack of Diet Sprite, okay?"

After school Brownie held a faculty meeting during which he did a little more public worrying about the trial. He also thanked the teachers for how well they'd done keeping the kids calm, focused, under control. "So far you people have been magnificent. Let's just pray it doesn't go on too much longer."

In her own classes the kids had been handling it coolly. It was almost a game for them, a real kick, their own buddy Jamie Pitt becoming famous in the papers and on TV. They were in the stands cheering for the home team, with Jamie scoring the big touchdown.

Returning to the Saddle House with the pizza and salads, Joyce found Nique in stone-washed jeans and white cashmere sweater, her shiny black hair plaited into a long ponytail. She was starved, the girl announced enthusiastically, but otherwise felt great because she'd just gotten up from a terrific nap. They ate at the kitchen table and listened to the seven o'clock local news on the radio. The whole program only lasted five minutes, including commercials, and the trial got maybe one minute at the opening, after the winning lottery numbers.

Nique put down her steaming slice to pay close attention. Twice she made a face and said, "Huh!"—once at the mention of Brian Rubio and his unnamed girlfriend being surprised at the nude beach, which they shamelessly used to headline the story, once when the announcer said Jamie Pitt had definitely identified Brian Rubio as the Trent student who pushed the other car into the lake. The real surprise for Joyce—that Willa Hufnagle had been the MORP date of one of the Trent kids—Nique didn't react to at all. Had Florian and Wachtel known this all along? Did it make any difference?

They turned off the radio and, while cleaning the dishes, Nique said, "Mr. Johnway mentioned last night that you had Jamie in your class. What do you think of him?"

Joyce couldn't help laughing. "It's become my claim to fame. Anyhow, I had five classes last semester, with thirty-five students each, so I never got to know him that well."

"I got to know him, all right. Brian too. It really is weird, you know, both of them right in the middle of the trial like that."

"But Brian's the one in trouble."

"I know. That's scary."

Joyce brought a cup of tea and a tin of macaroons into the living room, and Nique joined her with a fresh Sprite after a quick trip to the upstairs bathroom. "I really should go easy on these," Nique said after popping a macaroon into her mouth.

Wasn't it always thus? Some willowy kid wearing a size 4. Or maybe Nique, whose skin was as *sweet and clear as moonlight through the pines*— what song was that?—was worried about acne. Meanwhile, the girl had ensconced herself on one of Abby Allen's mod chairs, her long legs pretzeled beneath her in a way only a teenager would risk, let alone find comfortable. With a smile of mock naughtiness she helped herself, daintily this time, to another macaroon.

The mind-boggling gyrations of girls that age—one minute pigtails and Mary Janes and the next, as if someone had abruptly dimmed the lights, all sultry eye shadow and plunging necklines. It made you wonder why you could never recall yourself at the same age being either that coltish or that sexy, that worldly-wise.

"You must be pleased," Joyce said, not sure just how far Nique wanted to go in discussing things, "that Jamie didn't mention your name."

"Daddy arranged that with the prosecutor and everybody, because I wasn't really involved."

"Why'd your parents take you off to Maine then?"

"They're like that. Daddy especially. He's a very retentive type and doesn't like taking chances."

"Were your parents," Joyce began, still willing to shut up on request, "hiding you from your boyfriends or from the lawyers?"

"That's what they've done all my life—hide me from people. I mean, are all parents like that? Do you have kids?"

"I inherited two daughters from a previous marriage. They were older than my own would have been."

"You must have understood then what they were going through. I mean, you didn't fight all the time, did you?"

"Oh, no, no fights," Joyce said. Benn's younger daughter Linda had been plain, serious, hardworking, kind of lonely. Now on the verge of graduating from law school, she'd never, as far as Joyce or Benn knew, gotten seriously involved with a man. Maybe there'd been hundreds, and she'd simply never mentioned them. "Your parents didn't like you going out with Jamie, was that it?"

"They don't like me going with anybody. If I showed up with Prince Charles, they'd say his ears were too big."

Two kids dead and Brian Rubio on trial for manslaughter, and what was it but some goddamn *puppy love* at the heart of everything. Although when in your sophisticated maturity were you ever again so *overwhelm-*

ingly in love? Still, what matter that Nique had maybe whirled through a little boatyard escapade with Jamie, then skinny-dipped on the beach with Brian, in each case sending the other guy into some postpubescent explosion of jealousy? Or was it first with Brian and then Jamie and the smiling photo in the locket and *then* back to Brian? Plus whatever high school hunks, if any, were lucky enough to score in between. Who gave a bloody flying fling? The least important thing in the world, your heart-throb at sixteen, the kid you kissed behind the billboard or struggled to get your blouse off for in the front seat of his jalopy. Nothing for a nice young boy and girl to have to die over.

Yet there was Jamie, roaring across the lake in a speedboat to over-take Veronique Thrane, she of the Spenser School locket, romping with Brian Rubio at Nanny Point. She must have been a real eyeful, this nude slender Venus on the half shell. Towering over Jamie: Joyce had never thought of that, and wondered what kind of turn-on, or ache, this pro-duced for Jamie, stretching to look up into Nique's eyes. And what, if anything, had transpired between Jamie and Veronique in the woods? Had he really just taken her away from the others to let her put her clothes back on?

Maybe Joyce was dismissing the girl's feelings too glibly, too un-fairly, by only paying attention to her lovely face, her professionally preshrunk, prefaded jeans. "I'm sorry about your parents being like that, but I hear the same thing all the time from girls at school—how their mothers and fathers keep shutting them down."

Nique gave her a quick look, as if not sure about the Medway com-parison. "What gets me is how parents are always worrying about stuff that kids, you know, never give a second thought to."

"What gets me," Joyce said, laughing, "is how the same young lady can get involved with two boys as different as Jamie Pitt and Brian Ru-bio."

Nique thought this over, then made another of those jumps that seemed so natural for her. "The real burner for Daddy was the skinny-dipping. It wasn't just Brian; it was Jamie and all his friends finding us there. He really sweated blood to keep that out of the trial but they said no way, so we had to settle just for not mentioning my name. Daddy absolutely shit a brick thinking of the headlines. NUDE THRANE GIRL AT BEACH ORGY BEFORE DROWNINGS. What it is, you see," she went on in a clear, pleasant tone, as if the transition were perfectly natural, "is that Mother *worries*, but Daddy becomes a total asshole. You can't believe the things he calls me. So Mother and I just decided not to tell him about being pregnant or anything until it was all over with, but Mother in a weak moment—"

"What?"

Nique took a breath, as if organizing the sequence. "We figured since it was only a few weeks along it wasn't like a real operation or anything, so we just wouldn't mention it to Daddy. Only Mother let it slip, and he went through the roof. Daddy's what you could call a racist, you know, or a bigot, which covers even more territory, and what he kept saying—along with a *lot* of other shit—was how it was just like some Harlem twinkie dropping little black pickaninnies every spring, pushing a carriage and knocked up again for all the world to see. But cripes, even at Spenser, which is really a teeny school and as *white* as you can get except for all the millionaire Arabs and stuff, there were four girls last year that everyone *knew* got pregnant, which means a whole lot more, counting the ones like me that never told anyone."

"Who was the father?" Joyce inquired evenly. She had no right to ask, of course, but Nique answered as brightly as ever.

"Well, it *had* to be either Jamie or Brian. Otherwise the timing would be all wrong." After a moment, seemingly thinking this over— counting months?—she added, "I mean, if you have any brains at all, you try to avoid one-night stands."

Try to avoid? What Joyce said was, "I'm sure it's all for the better, what you did." Nique wasn't the first high school girl to hear that from her, and she hoped it sounded individual enough to do some good, because thank God, thank God, this pretty child was not about to bring forth her own pretty child, no matter who produced the fortuitous spurt of sperm.

(Katarina's method after years of teaching family studies was to make her freshman girls carry around a five-pound bag of flour for a whole week, never letting it out of their sight for a minute, to give them a sense of the joys of motherhood.)

And if Brian had been the lucky sire, it would be Florian's grand-child!

"That's what Mother said, how it was really for the best. And sure, that's what parents want, what's best, only we can't always be perfect exactly the way they want us to. I mean, they keep telling us we're not grown-ups, we're kids, so how can they expect us to act like we're sixty-four years old? Not that it's such a great deal, the way grown-ups go around screwing up all over the place. Daddy keeps saying grown-ups have all been kids but no kids have ever been grown-ups. So what, right? We still have to learn for ourselves, like they did."

Joyce couldn't help smiling at Nique's vehemence. Outsiders always thought the worst torments for kids came from each other, and they sure could get into some messes that way, as the young lady nibbling on a macaroon could certainly testify. But day after day, year after year, the kids agonized most over, complained most about, suffered most from, and caused the greatest grief to, their ever-loving parents. God knows your heart went out to anyone, son or daughter, mother or father, struggling to make the best of that most delicate and difficult and permanent of all relationships.

Just momentarily, Joyce was caught up in the thought of what a daughter of her own might be like if she ever had one. Like Nique? Benn's daughters? Willa Hufnagle? It was an amazing concept, the number of permutations and combinations that could come up when they drew the straw for you.

"I was surprised," Joyce said, "that the junior high girl who died wasn't with the other Medway kids that night, but the date of a Trent student."

"Tiny Arkins," Nique said, reacting with a huff of impatience. She changed position on the chair, kicking one leg out. "And it certainly wasn't my idea, I can tell you that much."

"I assume it was the idea of the boy who asked her."

"Tiny Arkins," Nique repeated. "Anyhow, I wouldn't know about any of that—although if you really want to know what I think, I think any senior in high school who gets turned on by some little lumpy-dumpy thirteen-year-old, well, I really have to wonder. It's not as if you had some real Lolita with boobies out to here. I mean, she was pudgy, that's what she was. It was baby fat, for God's sake." Nique breathed deeply. "Don't you really feel sad about someone like Marilyn Monroe? I mean, she was dead before I was even born, but it really gets me. Here you are, you want to be this great actress, and all anybody ever thinks about is your titties. No wonder she went crazy."

Nique paused again, more thoughtfully this time. "Should that be *is* your titties, or *are* your titties? When I first started at Spenser, you know, we had this English teacher that actually made us parse sentences."

"You and Willa were in the same group that night, weren't you?" All along Joyce had been unable to envision them together, even for a few hours.

"Right, all at Tiny Arkins's for the big party. But Willa and I really didn't spend a whole lot of time engaged in fascinating conversation. I mean, this kid was in *eighth grade.*" Nique took an angry swig of her soda. "Although, Jesus, she's dead. The goddamn kid gets invited to the big Trent fling-a-ding, this pudgy little kid from who knows what kind of hole in Medway, and she ends up fucking dead."

Nique was crying, quietly, softly, her head down. She rubbed the sleeve of her sweater across her eyes, tried to smile, made a vague, hopeless gesture with one hand. She swallowed. "What can you do, right? What the hell can you do?"

It was hardly the first time Florian had been cooped up at night with someone or other in a hotel room, but no one this night was even saying a word as they passed the time gazing at the ceiling or picking at their fingernails or staring dopily at the hand-size cassette or the crumpled white bag next to it on the coffee table, listening to this achingly familiar voice that the microphone or the tape or the tiny speaker made sound brittle and metallic and slightly off. Most of all, what got Florian was how *distant* everything seemed. It wasn't just that Brian had spoken into this machine months ago. All of it—the disembodied voices, the clicking counter, the softly whirring reels, his three-thousand-mile-away ex-wife looking desperate and practically holding his hand alongside him in this weird séance—seemed so artificial and improbable that, hard as he tried, he was afraid there was no way he could ever *connect* with what he was hearing.

Barring a few rough spots, Brian sounded composed, thoughtful, quick to follow Wachtel's guidance. Prompting him, occasionally asking a direct question, Wachtel seemed tenser, the machine giving his voice, hardly profundo to begin with, a slightly higher pitch.

When did you first get to know Veronique Thrane?

On March thirtieth.

You remember exactly?

We had a dual meet with Spenser Academy. They're private, but we compete in swimming. Nique took the butterfly and placed in the hundred free.

You began seeing each other?

For six weeks, until she broke it off May nineteenth, the day of the regionals.

At the instigation of her parents?

No, although they wanted her to stick more—well, to Spenser types. I never really spoke to them.

Never *really*?

Her father called once to tell me to stop seeing her.

Because you weren't good enough for her?

He said she ran around with everyone and I'd be crazy to think I was anything special.

This is her father talking? About his daughter?

They had it in their heads she was some kind of tramp.

I take it you didn't believe these accusations.

For a while she went with me; for a while she went with Jamie. That doesn't make you a tramp. I think they just didn't like the lower-class types she went with. Like me and Jamie.

And when she broke up with you at the regionals, she introduced you to Jamie Pitt?

I knew who he was from a dual meet earlier, when he came in second in the fifty free. His form was really weird, all whirling and flailing, like his life depended on it. Kids called him the Corkscrew, although not just because of his form. He had a reputation with girls. You know, for screwing them.

Kind of a male version of a tramp?

Not just version. Prototype.

So he became Nique's new boyfriend?

Actually they'd gone out before I knew Nique.

And then a month later she agreed to go to the MORP with you?

She'd stopped seeing Jamie.

How'd he take that?

He kept calling her—which made her parents even worse. He also laid in wait for her the day before the MORP. Her parents wouldn't let her have a car, so she always biked to school. Jamie and a friend with a car grabbed her off the bike after school and drove around while Jamie tried to talk her into going back with him.

Was she assaulted? Injured? Threatened?

She sure took it as a threat—being grabbed like that. And you never know how far Jamie'll go.

Did she realize it constituted kidnapping? Did she mention it to her parents? The police?

Her parents weren't crazy about her biking to school anyway; they wanted the chauffeur to drive her every day. She knew they'd crack down if they heard what happened.

And your reaction?

I was lifeguarding and knew Jamie worked at Hammond's up the road. The next day, the afternoon of the MORP, he started jazzing around the safety ropes with a speedboat. I was positive it was him because I sighted him with the binocs. On my break I walked up to the boatyard to tell him to cut the crap with the boat and leave Nique alone.

And got in a fight with him?

That's what I told my father because I didn't want him worrying, and now everybody assumes that's what happened. But Jamie obviously knew that Hammond wasn't around, in town or somewhere, and pulled that stuff with the boat knowing it'd tick me off, giving me the finger as he went zooming by, just to get me to come after him, because he had his buddies over there, laying in wait with clubs and sticks and everything.

How'd you manage to get away?

Jamie is just such a jerk sometimes. Most times. I'm coming along the dirt road there leading into Hammond's, just past the pipe gate, and I hear voices. I hear guys talking. That didn't seem so strange, but when I hear someone go SSSSHHH!, I get very suspicious. So when I get to the end of the trees along the dirt road, at the open area, I sort of peek around to look over things and see Jamie all alone there, working on a canoe and whistling away in this jerky, phony manner like one of the Seven Dwarfs, so I bolt, just take off, and these guys charge out with these clubs or thick branches or whatever, but I had a good head start and besides could probably outrun them anyhow, and got back to the public beach and all the people, so naturally they didn't even show their faces.

So they didn't hurt you at all?

Actually, I hurt myself. I kind of scratched up my face against a branch getting out of there.

When'd you next see Jamie?

That night, MORP night. Nique and I took the canoe out and fooled around with some friends on the lake. When the others headed over to Tiny Arkins, we checked out Nanny Point and saw nobody there, so went for a swim. The sun was pretty much down when Jamie and his gang plowed up onto the beach in the same speedboat he'd used that afternoon to buzz the swimmers.

He seems to have developed something resembling a proprietary interest in that boat.

That's Jamie. He figures since he doesn't have much, if he sees something he wants, he can just take it.

Did he know you were at Nanny Point or just find you by accident?

They must have seen us canoeing over. Anyhow, Jamie grabbed Nique and hauled her into the woods.

Did you see them together?

Only him dragging her off.

Did you hear anything?

I heard her screaming. The four guys were pushing me around in the woods, shoving me from one to another, daring me to try anything. They might have been the same guys from Hammond's that afternoon, although I couldn't tell because I never got a good look at them earlier. Maybe they were different guys, because they didn't have clubs or anything. But when they heard Nique screaming, I think it scared them, because they probably figured they could get in trouble too if Jamie did anything to Nique, so they knocked me down and told me to stay there and took my clothes and disappeared.

And then?

I tried to find Nique but couldn't hear her screaming anymore, couldn't hear anything, and it was awful hard to see more than a few feet away under all those trees. Then I heard someone crying and found Nique sitting up against a tree, crying, with her clothes in a little pile next to her.

So you didn't see Jamie do anything?"

Except drag her off.

Did she say he did anything?

No, but I could tell by how she looked that he must have done something. I knew Jamie. We both knew him. He didn't have her naked in the woods without doing *something*.

What?

I think he made her go down on him. She was spitting and coughing, practically choking, when I got to her.

But she didn't *tell* you he did that?

I kept asking her to tell me but she wouldn't.

Why not?

She knew how I felt about Jamie and I guess didn't want to get me any more worked up.

Then?

The canoe was gone but it was still light enough to spot it out on the lake, so I swam out to get it. Nique could have made it too, of course, but she was still pretty shook up over whatever happened with Jamie, so I went alone. It was just as well because Jamie and his friends were cruising around in the powerboat, and when they saw me they started playing games, roaring straight at me at full speed. I'd watch them bearing down, hoping to hell Jamie could see me well enough to miss me if that's what he wanted, because he'd wait until the last possible second, until they were right on top of me, before cutting away. I got swamped every time but the worst was how scared I was. I've never been so scared in my life, out there in the dark with these maniacs coming at me in this boat, which from down in the water looked like a runaway ocean liner. All I hoped was that they were just having fun, that Jamie wouldn't, on the last pass, plow right into me. I was so scared I couldn't breathe. I was shivering in the water. I mean, who'd ever be able to prove anything? Would they even be able to dredge up my body from the bottom of the lake? The first time they came at me, when I was absolutely sure Jamie was trying to kill me, I just, well, lost my bowels, right there in the water.

Wachtel was on his feet, moving toward the tape deck, but he found the stop button a second too late, and they heard Brian's voice break, heard the kid cry out: *"I mean, first he fucked my—"*

"What are you doing?" Florian said.

"Giving a kid a break in front of his parents."

"What's he saying that you don't want us to hear?" Elly demanded.

"He doesn't say anything the next few minutes that he doesn't say before or after. Just a little primal screaming. A little cursing and yelling. Some sobbing. I kept taping at the time in case he *did* say something. We took a break, went out for cheeseburgers. I'll advance this a bit if you want to hear the rest."

"Yes," Florian said.

"Yes," Elly said.

—finally left you alone?

After they towed off the canoe, way down to the south end of the lake so I'd have a couple more miles to swim.

When you got back to Nique, did either of you consider going to the police?

No. We canoed back to my house. My father was out, so we waved to my grandparents and took off in the Corvette. I thought Nique might want to go home and skip the rest of the night, but she said no, she wasn't up to dealing with her parents, so we joined the party at Tiny's, not planning on saying anything about what happened. But the guys there told us about that earlier stuff, Jamie's gang crashing Nanny Point.

Had your friends at the party been drinking?

Well, sure, but they were a lot more pissed than drunk.

And you?

I'm no drinker.

What else was going on there?

Well, it was a party, graduation, people out for a good time. But none of that had anything to do with anything. Someone rushed in and said he saw a gang of Medway kids out front banging up our cars and letting the air out of tires.

So you checked your father's Corvette?

Boy, did I. Thank God it was okay. Luckily, since we'd gotten there late because of all that other crap, we had to park around back, where the Medway guys probably never saw it. Anyhow, that was the final straw, flat tires and cut cables and everything, so everybody started talking about going after them. By this time Nique wasn't feeling good at all so I zipped her over to her girlfriend's house, where she was supposed to be staying anyhow, and when I got back to Tiny's a bunch of eight or nine guys were just about to take off after the Medway kids.

With their dates?

The dates stayed. Except for Willa, Tiny's date, who wanted to go.

Why?

I don't really know. I'm not sure just—

The tape ended with a loud clack, and Wachtel got up in the silence to flip it over. He fast-forwarded it, watching the counter. "We chit-chatted a bit before getting back to things. Here."

—any of the eight or nine of you, excepting yourself, of course, sloshed?

Some, maybe a little.

And you went in three cars, including your father's Corvette. How come, if you were so worried about it?

It was one of the few still movable. Besides, it was my date Jamie roughed up, so I couldn't just bag out. We figured Jamie and his friends would still be around the lake somewhere because that's where they'd been all night. We checked the roads and hangouts but didn't find them and after a while pulled onto the boat ramp to stretch our legs and decide what next. Some wanted to head back to Tiny's and their dates, some wanted to keep looking.

And you?

I was ready to go back.

Despite how sore you were at Jamie Pitt?

I wasn't anxious for some drunken gang fight. I could deal with Jamie on my own.

What did you all intend to do if you found the Medway kids?

We never discussed it.

You weren't tearing all over Mt. Early County to trade baseball cards. And if you happened to meet them on the boat ramp?

We never figured on meeting anyone there. We only pulled in to talk things over.

I merely mention possibilities, given everyone's state of mind.

Anything's possible, right? All kinds of things happen that no one ever figured were going to, or thought possible.

The tape went silent. Maybe Wachtel was contemplating Brian's statement—its philosophical implications? Its usefulness to a defense lawyer? Maybe Brian was now munching on his cheeseburger or someone was hitting the john, and Wachtel, ever frugal, was saving tape.

Florian didn't look at Wachtel, didn't look at Elly. He was within a moment's impulse of stopping the whole thing. How nice to know nothing. Friday in court he'd roamed the night streets, haunted the neon glare of the mini food blasters with Jamie Pitt in a jam-packed Valiant with a couple of crushed doors. Today he was scouring the unlighted country roads with Brian, his own car reeking of booze and marijuana. Still, with a couple of breaks here and there the whole thing could have ended up as nothing more than your basic madcap teenage roistering, full of pratfalls and hilarity, something to laugh over the next day—like the MORP itself was designed to be. But you knew now that those breaks would not come, those laughs would not take place, and that your son was destined forever to go careening off into the night with every chance in the world of ruining his life.

Let's forget possibility and probability. After you saw Jamie and his friends arrive and leave their car there, Tiny Arkins moved the Corvette behind it. With your permission?

No, on his own. It was my fault, though. I left the keys in the ignition when we got out.

Where were the other cars and the rest of your friends?

Those were the ones that wanted to get back to the party, so they'd left.

Before the Valiant arrived?

Minutes before.

I thought you also wanted to go back.

I did, but the guys who wanted to keep looking wanted to borrow my car. I figured, great: *Sorry, Dad, but I lent the 'Vette to a bunch of drunks and they totaled it.*

Who are we talking about now?

Tiny Arkins, Darrell Sampson, and Joe Caid. Joe Caid, Junior.

There were reports of more Trent boys on the ramp.

Some other Trent kids were parked there when we arrived—you

know, with their dates. When they realized something was up, they came over to check it out, only they had their girls to worry about, so when they saw what was happening they just took off.

What was happening?

Well, when Jamie and his buddies came back and saw their car jammed in like that, they really went wild. So did we. It was a real madhouse for a while.

Were you trying to push the Valiant into the lake?

Again there was a long pause on the tape, and Wachtel, with both Florian and Joyce eyeing him for an explanation, held up one finger: *Wait.*

I really want to tell you the truth, Mr. Wachtel.

Tell me the truth. I'm your lawyer. My job is to help you as much as I can, no matter what. But you have to tell me the truth. I have to know what happened. You can't wait until we're hanging by our fingernails before you level with me.

The truth is, I saw Jamie get in the Valiant. Just Jamie, no one else. There wasn't enough light to really recognize anybody in the other car from where I was, but outside you could recognize people, and I saw Jamie get in the Valiant and slide over and saw and heard and smelled the exhaust when he started it up. It sounded like a cement mixer. I figured that he was ready to call it quits, at least for the time being, that all he wanted was to free up the car and let his friends hop in and get out of there.

And how did that idea strike you?

It struck me just fine. I liked that idea. I thought it was a great idea.

This is the truth now, right?

This is the truth.

But if he wanted to go, and you wanted him to go, why on God's green earth didn't you simply *let* him go?

I tried to. I looked around to see if anyone was standing behind me, but before I could back off I felt this incredible crash that sent me into a kind of reverse whiplash, my whole body snapping forward, my head banging on the steering wheel. And then it happened again, and again. Jamie was smashing back into me as hard as he could, and I realized that he wasn't just trying to get free but was trying to wreck the goddamn Corvette. By then he'd probably figured out that it was mine and so, *Great, this way I'll really put it to Brian, I'll bang the shit out of his nice fancy car.*

You don't *know* that's what he was thinking.

But I knew what he was doing. He was banging the shit out of me. And then suddenly Jamie stops plowing back into me and these Medway guys come over and pull me out and throw me on the ground. I thought they were doing this so I wouldn't be able to brake or anything and Jamie could just batter the hell out of the Corvette and maybe even—the thought actually occurred to me—push *it* into the water. All this, you have to remember, happened very fast and was more confusing and crazy than you can imagine. When they throw me on the ground, I figure this is it, but Tiny and the others chase off the Medway guys and I jump back up and into the Corvette. What I'm thinking is this must be my really lucky night because these guys have been trying to cream me the whole time and somehow I'm still all in one piece.

So you were feeling pretty good. Not angry anymore.

It's very hard to explain exactly how I felt. Yeah, I felt good because everything seemed to be lucking out. But I also had about fifteen good reasons for being pissed at Jamie Pitt, the last being a real try at wrecking my father's car. So when I got back in the Corvette and saw the Valiant just sitting there, I figured, *Well, here's my chance.* I couldn't tell if Jamie was still in the Valiant, but if you want the truth, I hoped the hell he was. If he wasn't, I assumed it would just be empty, but I really hoped he was still in there. I never in my life felt so much like I really wanted to hurt someone as I did right then. It was like an electric wire going haywire inside me.

And then?

Without even realizing I was doing it, almost part of the thought itself, I hit the gas.

To push it into the lake?

To—push—it—into—the—lake.

Were you trying to kill Jamie?

God, no. I never thought of killing anybody. What was going through my mind was, *I'll fix that son of a bitch. I'll show him something. I'll dump their fucking car into the lake and let Jamie—who'd made me swim a few miles that afternoon to get my clothes back and practically sliced me in half with a speedboat along the way—see what it's like swimming around a bit himself.*

You never thought anyone would drown?

Anyone? I was never thinking of anyone. We're talking split seconds here. I never saw Jamie Pitt get out of the Valiant. I never saw Polly Dunn and Willa get in. What I was thinking was putting the shaft to Jamie, whether he was in the car or not. And if he was, he was this terrific swimmer, this fucking Corkscrew. He'd just push open the goddamn door and float up and swim back to the ramp.

Only?

Only the Valiant lurched ahead so hard the tires squealed. I swear it left rubber. It leaped straight off the edge and nosed into the water with this really incredible splash. That was it. Somehow you'd think a car would float first. Maybe it did. Maybe we all just went numb, and it actually took longer than it seemed. But nobody moved or yelled or anything. That gigantic geyser sprayed up into the air and came down, and we all just stared, watching the water turn black again and settle over the car, and suddenly I was just praying, over and over again, that Jamie Pitt wasn't still in there.

And of course he wasn't. The wrong people died.

I didn't want anyone to die.

What did you do when you found out it was Willa and Polly?

I can't even tell you. I could say my mind went blank, but it didn't go blank. It just blew itself to smithereens like some gigantic neon light exploding. The next thing I remember, I was kneeling at the edge of the ramp, puking into the water.

13

"Nine-twenty," Wachtel announced, checking his watch as he slipped the cassette into his briefcase.

Florian got up, hands shoved into his trouser pockets, and walked to the window. Three flights down, Elderberry Street was already dark and dead, Rob's Mobil closed, everything closed, a few store windows grayly lit by night lights, no traffic. Pleasant town, Trent. Busy all summer but real quiet off-season. Nice place to live if you had a few bucks.

"I'm not sure we want to decide everything tonight," Wachtel said, "but we have to deal with Jamie. I can't walk in cold tomorrow. As it is, I've got a few hours' prepping still ahead of me."

"I thought you were prepared for contingencies," Elly said.

"There's always some last-minute fine-tuning, depending on what the witness says. Jamie had a lot to say."

Florian had been listening to them behind him. He went back to his seat, pulled an ankle up to rest on his other knee, cracked his knuckles. "What do you think of what he had to say?"

"My feeling is Delehanty hasn't made his case, but we might have to emphasize that a bit for the jury. Sure, Jamie's testimony is damaging, but does it prove *manslaughter*? Does it rely on statements that we can challenge?"

"Jamie raped Nique and almost killed Brian with the boat," Florian said. "Tiny Arkins put somebody else's car in a stupid, dangerous position. Jamie started the ramming. Tiny brought along the underage girl that drowned. Doesn't *any* of that count for anything?"

Wachtel paused without seeming to consider these points. "We're in a court of law, Flo, dealing with a certain charge against a certain fine young man named Brian Rubio. That's all we're dealing with. It's a self-contained box that bears maybe a passing resemblance to the life that goes on—or that went on last June—outside it."

"I'd sure like to think that what happened last June has something to do with it."

"It does. Delehanty's used it to extract his most useful version, and we're doing the same. The point, though, is that the jury can deliberate only on what has been presented to them. What some little birdie told you on the street corner—or what you happened to hear on the tape tonight—isn't part of that box that we and Delehanty are both working so hard to fill with all the right kinds of goodies. Now, at some point in the more leisurely future, I'll be glad to discuss the philosophical implications of all this, at my usual rates. Meanwhile, we have about eight hours before reconvening. Do we want to cross Jamie, and if so, do we want to take the gloves off?"

"You really should have invited Harry," Elly said. "It would give us another experienced voice, another point of view."

Wachtel made a little gesturing bow toward the telephone.

"Christ knows how many pink ladies or whatever he's sleeping off right now," Florian said, and Elly gave him a sharp look. She didn't argue, though. "Give us the pros and cons," Florian said. "Make it simple and straightforward and very, very clear."

"Jamie's testimony is not without holes, and we could catch him on some, maybe use a couple of witnesses to help out. That's the easy part, disputing fact and consistency. How much good it will do is hard to say because most of it's before the ramp and Brian's on trial for what happened *on* the ramp."

"You talked about demolishing Jamie," Florian said.

"Ah, yes, Flo, something dear to your heart. And I believe, frankly, that we could do it."

"Why don't we?"

"The pro side is obvious: anything we do to undermine Jamie's veracity, his impartiality, his general all-round sweetness and upstanding character, will plant doubts in the jurors' minds as to how much they should believe him, about *anything*. That's the big plus, not to be sneezed at."

"The minus?"

"We've mentioned this before. The more we show how much Jamie deserved to have someone hunting him down, the more clearly Brian emerges as the macho get-even guy whose attempts at revenge somehow resulted in two kids from the enemy camp getting drowned. Remember, Jamie ain't mentioned anywhere in the charges. What does it profit us to make him look bad unless it helps Brian look good? Good enough, indeed, to get out from under a manslaughter charge?"

"Oh, God," Elly said, absolutely fed up, infuriated. She eyed the phone, again on the verge of rousting Harry Diggs out of whatever alcoholic haze he might be in, but again she thought better of it. What she said was "You make everything sound so *dismal*."

"Sorry, but I want to make sure all the cards are on the table. After all, if everything was coming up roses for Brian, you wouldn't *need* a lawyer. We do, however, have some things going for us. Delehanty has to absolutely convince the jury that whatever Brian did, it very specifically violates the manslaughter statutes, or at least constitutes assault and battery. I'm not sure he can do that, and meanwhile we'll be doing everything we can to make his job even harder. Manslaughter isn't all that simple; there are shadings and ambiguities that could very easily confuse an earnest layman sitting in a jury box. That's one of the few valuable things you learn in law school: if your client's accused of breaking some law, kick the shit out of that law. But that's not what we're discussing. Let's put aside the Jamie question for a minute and take care of Nique Thrane, which is a lot more clear-cut. If you want advice on this, I got advice."

"Which is?"

"We don't want Nique Thrane within ten miles of the witness stand."

"I talked to her," Florian said. "In Maine. Even talked to her father."

"She told me."

"You talked to her too?"

"Of course," Wachtel said. "What do you think I do to earn all that money you're always complaining about paying me? Nice girl. Very sweet. Even wants to be a lawyer, which immediately convinced me of her intelligence and high moral standards. It's conceivable she could help us, and she really wants to, but she wasn't even on the ramp where everything happened. Beyond that, the essential drawback with Nique Thrane is Willa Hufnagle—poor and not very smart, with not many chances in life, nothing going for her, plain of face and unattractive of body, from the lower depths of Medway and certainly the only date at the MORP who hand-stitched her own gown, now dead and gone at thirteen."

"Why the hell did Tiny Arkins get involved with her in the first place?"

"Who cares? What we're talking about is whether we think we can save this kid from Trent accused of killing Willa by bringing to the stand this smashing millionaire dish not only from Trent but from Sargasso River Highlands and the snootiest girls' school north of the Mason-Dixon line. I'll do it if you really want. I'll put her up there in her hundred-dollar loafers and thousand-dollar designer-coordinated outfit, this raven-haired six-foot beauty with her perfect Spenserian accent, but if you—"

"No," Florian said.

Wachtel nodded, pleased. "Elly?"

"I don't see what her looks and height have to do with anything." She lowered her eyes to avoid their dubious stares. "Okay," she said. "Let's not take any chances."

"Farewell to Nique. I'll get word to her, thank her for being—"

"You know where she is?" Florian said.

"Yes. Now, while we're discussing potential witnesses, I've no idea whether Delehanty will call Tiny Arkins and Brian's other friends."

"We could also call them, couldn't we?" Elly said.

Wachtel gave her an incredulous look. "I think I would prefer not to."

"We seem to be running away from an awful lot of witnesses."

"Sometimes less is more."

"What if Delehanty calls them?"

"I for one will be holding my breath."

"If they scare you so much, why wouldn't Delehanty call them?"

"Because what they say might surprise him. The jury's reaction might surprise him. It could look like overkill, Brian's buddies ganging up on him. So maybe, taking everything into account, Delehanty may be content to sink or swim with Jamie. The question is, how do *we* handle Jamie?"

"I say crucify him," Florian said. "If I was on a jury and the DA's whole case rested on some guy you can show to be a jerk, a liar, a slob, I wouldn't convict Jack the Ripper."

"*Crucify* is an unfortunate term. Jamie the Medway Martyr is scarcely what we have in mind."

"What about him raping the Thrane girl? Could you get him on that?"

Wachtel took a patient breath. "It never fails to amaze me, Flo, how concern for a loved one can turn even the best of brains to cornmeal. The only person who could accuse him of rape is Nique Thrane, who we've just very wisely dropped from our list. And as I think I've pointed out previously, we're not in the business of bringing forth any more reasons Brian might have had for revenging himself upon the Medway kids. Elly—how do you feel about me going after Jamie tomorrow?"

"When you say *demolish him,* what do you mean?"

"Florian's got the idea. Get the jury to see him as a jerk, a liar, a slob, a mean, spiteful, dangerous kid wholly concerned with making himself look good."

"Can you?"

"A lot depends on how Jamie reacts. He did well under Delehanty's gentle touch. Who knows how he'll handle less friendly questioning. There's always the chance I'll end up the bully, this fancy pants lawyer picking on a poor disadvantaged kid from the slums."

"You came from the slums," Florian said. "So did I." Immediately he realized how stupid that sounded. Who gave a shit? He felt his certainty weakening. "What are the odds if you go after Jamie?"

"I got a shot at it." He made a gesture toward Elly. "Maybe other attorneys more skilled in the forensic arts could give you an absolute one hundred percent guarantee. . . ."

"I say go after him," Florian said. "Tear him to shreds. I don't know the exact definition of manslaughter but right now I think we're down a couple of touchdowns and can't afford to play it safe anymore."

Elly bristled. "What on earth does football have to do with anything?"

Wachtel gave her a moment to calm down before asking, "What do you think, Elly?"

"I don't see that we have any choice. We've been backed into a corner and are going to have to fight our way out."

Florian exchanged a glance with Wachtel, as if wondering together whether her metaphor was really all that much better than his, and Florian could feel a kind of bizarre lightness coming over him, sort of oozing out between seams of tension. But when he spoke, his voice felt as tight as it had all along. "What about you, Ira? Forget pros and cons. If it was your kid, what would you do?"

"I'd try to chop Jamie into mincemeat." Maybe Wachtel was beginning to turn weird, too, because he allowed himself a small smile, which pretty much seemed to baffle Elly, and said, "Just because you're between a rock and a hard place, you don't have to throw in the towel and let the other guy use you for a doormat." He took a moment to appreciate his verbal flourishes, then continued briskly: "We can let the Brian decision wait, now that we've gotten this far. I'm pretty tired and would like to grab a few hours' sleep before pulling everything together. Jamie'll probably be on the stand most of the day, along with maybe a couple of others, and then we'll decide whether we want Brian up there. At least now we get to make the choices. Jamie's ours for the taking, but Delehanty can't get at Brian unless we let him."

Florian rose, more than ready to go.

"I don't mean this at all personally," Elly said, "but being a lawyer must in some ways be a very unpleasant job. You're always dealing with people in trouble who want you to save them in the next fifteen minutes, half of whom hate you for not doing it even sooner."

"Three quarters," Wachtel said. "Four fifths."

They were all, Florian realized, turning a little giddy. It wasn't that late, not even ten, but could have been three in the morning, this over-size, overdecorated hotel room some weird space module, the oxygen regulated, the temperature and humidity regulated, the hazily glowing blue orb of Earth growing smaller and smaller through the hermetically sealed window.

"Keep your hopes up, Elly," Wachtel said. "We'll leave now so I can do my prepping and we can all get a night's sleep. You'll be able to spot me in the morning because I'll be the one on the white horse."

As they walked down the carpeted hallway, Florian said, "I got a lawyer joke."

"I got a million," Wachtel said.

"These two lawyers chatting on a street corner watch this real knockout walk by, and one says, *Boy, I'd like to screw her,* and the other says, *Out of what?*"

Wachtel smiled obligingly as they reached the broad staircase lead-ing down two flights to the lobby. "How, Flo, can you tell the difference between a rat and a lawyer when they're both squashed on the highway? There are skid marks in front of the rat. Do you know the difference between a lawyer and a Mississippi River catfish? One is a bug-eyed scum-sucking scavenger and the other is just a fish. What did St. Peter say when this lawyer arrived at—"

"You heard 'em all," Florian said.

"I heard 'em all. Be encouraged by the fact that the lawyers in the jokes are real mean bastards who'll cut someone's balls off to win a case."

"I'm impressed you know where the Thrane girl is," Florian said.

They were about to step out through the lobby's grand entrance, the door held open for them by an elderly man in a toy soldier outfit, when Wachtel stopped, giving Florian the once-over before saying, "I even know who she's with, in case you're interested."

Tailor-sitting on the chair now, knees pointed out, Nique slugged away at her soda. "I guess the main thing was when I realized I was knocked up. My first time ever. The big bang theory, they call it at Spenser— boom! everything happens at the speed of light. Of course this was back in May, the worst possible time in terms of who, you know, might have been the one.

"And there was no point saying anything to Jamie, since we weren't seeing each other, only then I was biking home from Spenser—three-point-seven miles from our gate on the old bike-o-meter, usually a real nice and uneventful ride through all that countryside and everything. Most of the kids I know go away to schools, of course, but Mother and Daddy said there was this real good private school practically down the road, which translated from parentese meant they wanted me nearby to keep an eye on me.

"Anyhow, on the day right before el Morpo this old wreck of a station wagon with fake wood side panels cuts in and pins me against the side of the road, and who jumps out but Jamie. And I'll tell you, when Jamie's pissed, he's pissed. The whole world could just use a telegram saying, *Stay out of his way unless you got beans for brains.*

"Another kid was driving, keeping his eyes on the road. He never said a word or looked around, like he was being paid not to see or hear anything. He could've been set for life as a chauffeur. All he needed was the black jacket and cap."

She paused, frowning in thought. "Did you ever notice how Meryl Streep and Larry Bird, like, they have the same mouth?"

"What?"

"The one look I got, the kid had a real small mouth. What it is with Jamie is you never know what's next. The way he grew up and everything, you learn pretty quick that if you want something, you take it, unless someone can stop you. Once when he was a kid he watched these two bigger kids get in a fight and before he could blink they had knives out and one was dead and the other covered with blood. I mean, how could you not *notice* something like that?

"Of course by the time I met Jamie not many kids would try to stop him from anything he wanted. Not that he was some bonehead bully. Jamie's no bonehead. He just didn't fool around. If he liked you, you knew it, and that was a real hoot, if you know what I mean.

"Only we'd been apart a real long time, weeks and weeks, almost a month, when Jamie and that car cut me off on the bike, and during all that time he'd been hassling me on the phone until he had Daddy kicking furniture and Mother getting chest pains. The first thing he did was toss the bike down the ditch and shove me into the back seat and belly-whop right on top of me as his friend zoomed off for all those back roads that Mt. Early's got tons of.

"Right away Jamie starts giving me a lot of heat in the back seat, and staying right on top of me, partly, I guess, so any other cars couldn't see anything except this one kid behind the wheel, tooling around the county on a nice June afternoon.

"Jamie got really worked up, you know, pawing and grabbing and pumping on me and clawing my clothes half off and, believe me, I know what Jamie's like when he figures it's play time. I just made up my mind there was no way I'd let him put it to me like that, in the back seat of a car with some crazy friend up front playing chauffeur.

"So I told him to go blast it out his blowhole and just tell Tonto up front to take me back to my bicycle. I mean, what did he think he was doing? Where were his fucking brains?

"The truth was, I was really scared of what Jamie might do if he got any more pissed, so when I told him to stop and he pulled up off me a little, both of us all grimy and sweaty, to say, *Why? Why should I stop now?*, about nine hundred sixty-nine things flashed through my mind— that he was hurting me, that I was appealing to his honor, his sympathy, that I'd tell my parents, the cops, Brian? The way he'd been coming on, I couldn't see any of that cutting much ice. What popped into my mind as the only thing I could possibly say was, *The reason you better let me alone is I'm three fucking months along and the doctor says it's very iffy and not to do anything that could hurt it.*

"The true part was I was pregnant, all right, but less than one month, not three, and hadn't been anywhere near a doctor.

"But Jamie's face turned real weird and his eyes narrowed and I could see he was counting back, and right then he went, you know, soft, and it almost struck me like the joke about the guy who couldn't walk and chew gum at the same time. Anyway, three months made it right in the middle of when I was going with him and not seeing Brian. He was really stunned, but I think feeling kind of good too, even proud, along with being scared and confused and not knowing what was going to happen, either to the baby or to him. He actually looked down at my stomach, like he expected me to *show* already. But the main thing was his whole mood changed, and he said we'd have to talk everything over, and I said, not now, with this crazy schizoid way you're behaving, just take me back to the bike. Then he said I shouldn't be biking in my condition and they'd drive me home instead.

"Which was exactly what I needed, being dumped out of some beat-up old station wagon by a couple of drooling guys, looking like I'd been in a mud-wrestling match. But Jamie insisted, so I straightened myself up the best I could and prayed the whole way that no one would see us arrive. Only it was really my day. We pull up to the gate and there's the fucking gimpy gardener on the other side, gaping like a shot deer, and my mother too, all flounced up in her big floppy gardening hat and flowery gloves, showing the gardener this little rosebush with burlap-wrapped roots, both of them smudged and dirty in their smudged and dirty outfits, staring through the gate as if we were delivering some bubonic plague virus on a plate. Thank God I had the brains to say I'd fallen off my bike and these guys had given me a lift home; I think maybe Mother even believed me when she drove me back to the spot and we found the banged-up bike still in the ditch."

Nique jiggled her can of soda. "No one knows how glad I'm gonna be when this is all over."

Her testimony? The trial? Her on-again off-again flings with Jamie and Brian? The escape from her parents?

Joyce turned at the sound of the car pulling up outside. She could feel her face tightening: it had to be Benn, playing messenger again for the lawyers.

Nique must have thought the same thing, giving Joyce an anxious look.

Joyce shook her head: the sound was wrong for Benn's car. She left Nique in the living room and hurried to the front door, then waited there, not touching the handle, for the knock. "Who is it?"

"Me."

Startled, she flicked on the outside light and yanked the door open, almost laughing with delight until she saw Florian's expression. He looked like he hadn't slept in a month, and the smile he was working on just wasn't materializing.

"Oh, Florian." She sighed, hugging him. At first he seemed unable to respond, but then he slowly moved his arms up and put them around her and clung to her. She wriggled her face free and stretched up and kissed him hard on the lips, holding it until they were both struggling for breath. "Are you all right?" she whispered. "Has something bad happened?"

"Not really."

"What have you been doing?"

"Talking to the lawyer mainly, listening to stuff he had on tape."

"You look pretty grim. Was it discouraging?"

"A few surprises here and there. I was about to head out to your motel looking for you when Wachtel mentioned you were here."

"Did he think it was all right of you to come?"

"I forgot to ask. Besides," Florian added with a wave that included the Saddle House, the other vacant buildings, the surrounding woods of the old estate, "it's just you and the girl, right?"

"Do you want to say hello?"

"I've got news for her."

"She's incredibly . . . well, articulate. We've been talking for hours, about everything. C'mon, I'll introduce you."

Florian said nothing to this, but when he followed her into the living room, Nique jumped up from the couch.

"Mr. Rubio!"

"You've met," Joyce said.

Both acknowledged this with something like a shrug.

"How's your wandering lawn mower dog these days, Mr. Rubio?"

"As frisky as ever," Florian said.

"Mrs. Johnway's been real nice," Nique said with a nod toward Joyce.

"I'm not at all surprised," Florian said, finally managing a smile. He sobered almost immediately. "I tried to call ahead, but your phone's out of whack."

"You're telling us," Nique said.

Her vehemence caused Florian to lift an eyebrow, but he didn't pursue it. "I wanted to tell you in person how much we appreciate your coming down to help out. I know Brian appreciates it too. We understand how much pressure you're—"

"But," Nique said. "Get to the but."

"The truth is, I don't myself really understand the kind of logic lawyers use in things like this, but—"

"Now we're getting somewhere. But what?"

"He's decided on a strategy that won't require you to testify."

This silenced Nique briefly. "So okay, they don't want me. Is that definite? Is it official?"

"Looks like it. Again, we really appreciate—"

Nique spun away and moved quickly to the big window, gazing out at the woods with her arms folded.

Florian stared at her back, trying to figure it out—unless, of course, he was merely admiring her fetching black ponytail against her white sweater, giving her stone-washed jeans the same friendly once-over she'd gotten from the guys at the minimart. After only a moment, though, he looked to Joyce for help.

Joyce smiled in sympathy but had little to offer. As readily as Nique had discussed her intimate tribulations, the girl could hide things too, and right now Joyce couldn't even guess if Nique was angry, or disappointed, or relieved. Maybe the girl just needed to escape from their inquisitive stares to decide for herself which it was.

Nique turned from the window, no rush now, quite composed, and glanced at Florian, then at Joyce. "If you two want to talk, I'll just freshen up a bit."

Florian waited until they heard Nique's door upstairs, then took Joyce's hand and led her outside. The sky was clear, and even away from the lights of the house the grounds were surprisingly bright from the moon. They walked down the gentle incline of the lawn, the dry autumn leaves swishing under their steps. Florian stopped under a large oak and swung her around, held her, kissed her.

"You really shouldn't stay," Joyce said, not wanting him to feel pressured. There had to be apple trees nearby, for she could smell the winy sweetness. "Brian and the others will want you with them."

He didn't argue. "Besides, it's against my principles to make out with the baby-sitter."

She pressed against him, her head turned on his chest. "I didn't realize you were so fastidious. I've been getting a real earful from her, by the way—if you've got a few hours. Of course, she never got near the boat ramp, so I'm not sure it means that much."

"Do you think we made the right move in not calling her?"

"I really don't know," Joyce said, pulling back to look up at him. "Maybe if I was a lawyer—"

"It has nothing to do with being a lawyer. Wachtel's other big decision tonight is that he's going to try to break down Jamie's story tomorrow."

"Can he?"

"We sure hope so."

He paused for her reaction, maybe even wondering whose side she'd be on. "Oh, Flo," she said. "I'm absolutely praying for Brian, you know that. I want all of you free of all this."

He shifted his feet, noisily stirring the leaves, reminding her how silent the woods were around them. "How do you think Jamie will hold up?"

"Well—he seems to have done all right so far, hasn't he? He's not a dope."

"We're betting Wachtel isn't either." He let out a short hard laugh. "We're betting he's the smartest damn lawyer in the world." He turned apologetic then. "I left Brian and the others at home hours ago."

"Go back to them. They need you. But you can kiss the baby-sitter first."

"I intended to."

"I'm glad you came."

"So am I."

"Hold me."

He did, for a long time.

She'd barely stepped back inside when Nique came down the stairs, at first appearing relieved at being spared the ordeal of a prying, embarrassing public testimony—surely she'd have been identified as the naked girl at Nanny Point—but before she was halfway down her outrage burst through. "Those assholes, treating me like a goddamn pawn in their fucking chess game." She let out a snorting breath, although by the time she reached the living room floor she'd shifted back into a more analytical mode. "Maybe," she said, searching Joyce's face for support, "they just figure Brian's in real good shape and doesn't need my help."

"Let's hope so," Joyce said, and then, when this didn't seem to do the job, she added, "I'm sure that's it."

"You know," Nique said, "you really don't have to stay all night, especially if I'm not going to be involved or anything."

"Hey, we're all set, let's make a night of it. Believe me, it's a lot nicer than the motel." She'd checked her watch on the way in, a quarter after eleven, well past her weeknight bedtime, but when she saw how sweetly Nique was smiling at her, like one girl to another at their all-night 'jama party, Joyce relented. "Maybe I'll put up another cup of tea."

"And I'll pop another Sprite on my way to the johnny," Nique said. "It's a real symbiotic relationship we got, each going through the other like water."

"The one thing I really don't understand," Joyce said when they'd resettled themselves in the living room, Nique all flexible limbs and angles on the couch, Joyce with her legs crossed in the armchair, "is why Jamie would bring you down from Maine in order to help Brian's lawyers? I mean, Jamie's been saying some awfully damaging things about Brian at the trial."

Taking a swallow of soda, Nique seemed to be giving her answer some thought. "Originally I wanted the lawyer to bring me down, or maybe even Mr. Rubio, who in case you're wondering I met when he came all the way up to Isle de Pierre early in the summer in a funny little baseball cap to try to talk me into helping Brian. He's kind of a nice guy, I think, but you know how it is, him being Brian's father and everything, I just never felt really comfortable saying anything to him. He volunteered, though, to help me get down if I wanted, but when I got in touch with Mr. Wachtel he told me absolutely not to even mention it to Brian's father, so I just dropped that idea. Of course Jamie wasn't in on any of that; he was just trying, you know, to get together again, to spend some time with me, and I figured, okay, if being with Jamie for a while is going to be what it costs, I'll pay, because if I got down here maybe I could get Mr. Wachtel to change his mind. I didn't care about my reputation or anything, as long as I could help Brian. So Jamie, who'd been in touch—I had my own numbered box at the PO that only Brian and Jamie knew about—came up and got me in that same bomber of a station wagon, only he was alone and driving it himself this time. This was Sunday night, and believe me, it was a real three-ring circus, with Jamie actually going to the wrong house up there, number seventy-one instead of seventeen, and actually getting into such a row with the people that they were threatening to call the cops on him and have him arrested. Wouldn't that really have been something? Why he finally came to seventeen, he never said. Do you think he's dyslexic and figured it out? Anyhow, it was okay after that; my parents were doing other things and thinking I was going on a walk when I managed to sneak out with the suitcase. Anyhow, on the way down I naturally had to be kind of nice to Jamie, for driving all the way up there for me. What was funny, though, was that Jamie was actually hoping I'd take the stand too."

"Why?"

"He must've figured it'd somehow make him look better, or maybe make Brian look worse. I don't know; it's no picnic figuring out what's going on in that mind of his. Right now, anyhow, I'm really scared for Brian. Do you have any idea what's going to happen to him?"

"I couldn't even guess, although Jamie's testimony certainly didn't help him." Joyce waited a moment, then asked, "If they use you, what will you say?"

"The main thing would be that a lot of it was really my fault. I mean, first I tell Jamie it's his kid, and then, because I was afraid he'd brag about it, I quick tell Brian before Jamie could, but don't say it was three months but only one, and therefore his. I know—real retard. But once you get into something like that, it just gets worse and worse. The only thing you could say for me was I started all the confusion just to keep Jamie from raping me in the back of a station wagon with his goony friend bopping along in the front seat. It's weird in a way, you know, but at the time, even though Jamie was the one trying to put it to me, for some reason the guy I was most furious with was this other kid, for being such a jerk to be even part of it, especially since Jamie, you know, was saying all these filthy things in the back seat, what he wanted to do to me and everything, and I think the kid up front was just getting his jollies from listening and maybe sneaking a peek in the mirror." She paused. "Anyhow, when I told him about the kid, Jamie became really protective and everything. When I told Brian and said it was *his*, he completely threw me for a loop by becoming totally pissed, like it was all my fault, and telling me how he really didn't want any way, shape, or form of a baby dropped on his doorstep. Not that I figured he'd be doing jumping jacks or anything. I just didn't expect it to go down like that."

"Is that what you were planning to testify?" Joyce asked after a silence.

"Not so much that. Mainly the fight in the boatyard the afternoon of the MORP. What really happened was Jamie came over to the beach where Brian was lifeguarding and started, you know, saying things to him, about me being knocked up and everything, and how it was his, not Brian's. I mean, can you believe that, like it was some two and a half gainer he'd done at the Olympics that he wanted a ten for? Of course that was all Brian needed to hear, so he went to the boatyard and really got into it with Jamie. That's what I guess I should testify, that it wasn't their fault but mine, because of all the retard things I said to both of them. Only what else could I've said?

"And then, even though I knew it wouldn't exactly make me look good, I was willing to testify about the real reason Jamie came after us at Nanny Point." She stopped abruptly, maybe assuming that it was all too obvious to need spelling out.

"Why *did* Jamie Pitt come after you at Nanny Point?"

"Well, he just decided, since it was his baby, that he wasn't going to have me running around with someone else, especially from Trent, especially Brian Rubio, and especially for something as crazy as el Morpo, which was what he always called it, because he thought it was such an asshole idea. So he hung around the Rubios' house, figuring Brian wouldn't pick me up at my place because of my parents, which was true. I biked there, after setting everything up very carefully with my parents about staying overnight at a girlfriend's, although of course if they paid any attention to what was going on in Trent or even looked at the *Express* once in a while, they'd have known the MORP was on that night, but all they ever read is *The New York Times* and *The Wall Street* fucking *Journal*."

"Is that what you were going to testify?"

"Not so much that. But once Jamie saw Brian and me out in the canoe, heading toward Nanny Point, he and his friends in the car zoomed up to Hammond's and took off after us in somebody's speed-boat."

"I thought they first tried to get to Nanny Point along the shore, when all these Trent kids—"

"Well, I don't know about that. I can't swear to every single thing for every single minute. Also, what Brian and me and the other couples heading for the MORP did first was have this goofy canoe battle out on the lake with balloons filled with colored water, so maybe that accounts for it being later and all. I wasn't crazy about that anyhow, not being much taken with war games and stuff, but the others seemed to like it, and Willa Hufnagle, of course, she was laughing and squealing all over the place, like getting splashed with red ink was the height of sophistication or something. After it was over, I told Brian I didn't want to stay with them, who were going back to skinny-dip in Tiny Arkins's pool before the other kids arrived for the party, which is how Brian and I ended up alone at Nanny Point."

"I can't believe that through all this Jamie Pitt would be so certain that you two would end up alone at Nanny Point."

"Maybe what really happened was that Jamie was out in the speed-boat, keeping an eye on us, and then saw us canoeing over to Nanny Point."

"Did he rape you in the woods?"

"Who?"

Who? Who? Am I losing my mind? "Jamie," Joyce said patiently. "Wasn't it Jamie who dragged you into the woods?"

"I don't know about *dragged*. The real problem, you know, was how agitated he was about not hurting the kid. He really thought if Brian and I *did* anything, it'd be bad for it."

Joyce worked for a measured tone. "What did Jamie do to you in the woods?"

"Well, he didn't *do* much of anything. I mean, what was to do? He was just mainly totally agitated about me going around with someone else with his kid inside me. So the first thing he did was insist I put my clothes back on, because he didn't like the idea at all of me and Brian bare-assed together, let alone all his goopy friends checking me out from top to bottom. I did put my clothes on, but beyond that, even though I was scared of Jamie, I always am, I wasn't about to let him chase after me like that telling me what to do. I get all I need of that from Daddy. So I told him to leave me the fuck alone and forget about the kid because I was going to have it taken care of and that would be the end of it. Well, that really threw him, and he started shaking me, real hard, and slapping me around, which I guess was kind of contradictory, wouldn't you say, from this guy so worried about anything hurting the kid? Anyhow, his friends came back then and got him to stop, and Jamie said okay but wanted me to go back with him in the boat, and I told him absolutely no way and ran off. Thank God his friends stopped him from coming after me because Brian and me finally found each other in the woods." She took a long breath. "That's what I thought I'd testify."

Joyce struggled to sort it out, still not sure exactly who Nique thought she'd be helping. And she hadn't even mentioned the drownings yet. "What happened after Nanny Point?"

"We went to Tiny Arkins's party but left early. Brian was driving me to the girlfriend's house where my parents figured I was anyhow, because I felt so shitty from everything that I didn't think I could last the night, let alone be any fun to be with. Sure enough, I even got the heaves and Brian pulled over so I could at least do it out the window and not mess up the inside of his father's classy machine. Some splattered, though, down the outside of the door, so we turned around and headed to the all-night automatic car wash up in Medway and hosed it down and started again for my girlfriend's.

"We were just driving along, not fast or weaving or anything, when we get the flashing lights in the mirror and *Oh, shit, it's the cops!* Really weird too, because they come up behind us after Brian slows all the way down and we hear this weird ghostly robotlike voice over their loudspeaker saying, really polite, you know, but scary too, *Please move to the right and stop. Thank you. Please do not exit the vehicle.* The cops, of course, knew it was MORP night, and seeing these kids in this jazzy white car naturally got them suspicious. Even at Spenser, no one drives anything like a classic Corvette, although most do have their own cars, unlike me, because my parents don't trust me even to get my permit, like that's some magic way of keeping me out of trouble. Brian doesn't have a car either, but at least has a license, so that part was cool with the cops, and he had the ownership paper right there in the glove compartment, and was straight ahead sober.

"So they let us go, and we thought, gee, at last a lucky break. Only of course after everything else happened we realized it wasn't lucky at all. Because if the cops had taken us in, or just spent more time checking the registration or making Brian walk a straight line, anything, it would have been the best thing that ever happened to Brian, because after he left me at my girlfriend's, he got back to the party at almost exactly the second a bunch of kids were taking off after some Medway kids who messed up their cars. If he'd just been a couple of minutes later they'd have gone without him."

"How come Willa Hufnagle ended up with them on the ramp? Did all the dates except you go with the guys?"

"No, just Willa."

"Why?"

"Maybe she thought it'd be a lot of fun, being the only girl with a bunch of half-drunk guys. Maybe she just didn't want to be left behind with all those Trent girls who, let's face it, weren't exactly crazy about her being there in the first place." Nique looked at her watch, shook her empty Sprite can. "Gee, almost midnight. I didn't think it was this late." She popped another macaroon.

Joyce couldn't keep down a little laugh: Nique might have looked exhausted when she'd started, but she'd gotten peppier as she went on—oh, youth! oh, vitality!—and now looked ready to scale mountains, her eyes shining.

"Maybe I'll just grab another soda and hit the sack. I didn't mean to bend your ear."

"I'm glad we talked."

Nique stood up and seemed to take a steadying breath. "Do you think it was all my fault—because of what I said and all the dumb-shit things I did?"

"Of course not. It wasn't all anybody's fault. It was tragic and horribly unlucky for everyone. What else can you say about something like that?"

"What it is, you see, is I really don't have great gobs of what you could call self-confidence. It's always like no matter what I do, it probably isn't right. So I'm always just ready to take whatever I can get, figuring it's probably better than I deserve anyhow. I don't have the touch, you know, that some people have, that everything always goes right for."

"There's no one everything always goes right for."

"Maybe if I'd just been a teeny bit more careful, I wouldn't have got knocked up in the first place."

"You're not the first woman who ever said that. Stop blaming yourself, really. At least you were trying to help people, not hurt them. At least you weren't out to beat anybody up." Joyce paused. "You've got so much going for you, Nique—anyone can see that. Don't let people put you down. Don't put yourself down."

"Thanks a lot, Mrs. Johnway. Really—thanks." The girl gave her a quick hug, her face turned away, grabbed a soda from the fridge and ran upstairs.

Watching her, frowning, sniffing, Joyce waited until she heard the door close upstairs before going into the kitchen. She picked a couple of empty soda cans from the trash can and sniffed them, shook her head and tossed them back in.

After finishing in the hall bathroom, Joyce sat up in her flannel nightgown with a pillow propped behind her in the big fluffy bed. As late as it was, as tired as she was, sleep seemed impossible. She tried to concentrate on her paperback and not think of Florian or Benn, not think of Nique and Brian and Jamie Pitt chasing each other all over Mt. Early County on that night back in June, not think of Willa Hufnagle and Polly Dunn trapped in that sinking, waterlogged automobile.

What haunted her, though, was a medieval painting she'd seen this summer in the Museu Calouste Gulbenkian in Lisbon, a portrait of a strikingly beautiful young woman, hardly more than a girl. Over the centuries the canvas had cracked and mottled, overlaying that pure youthful skin with the wrinkles of age, with an inevitable weight of mortal years that those shining eyes could not even contemplate.

She'd finally tossed the book aside and turned off the bed lamp and was almost asleep when she heard what sounded like creaking and then, distantly, faintly, the squeak of a door. From the window she saw Nique and Brian—it had to be Brian, tall, his blond hair luminous in the moonlight—running hand in hand away from the house and into the thick and shadowy wood.

Flo—you could have stayed!

Florian got home just before midnight, the house dark and silent. He tiptoed into the kitchen to fix a drink, without ice, tiptoed upstairs. It didn't put him off, so he went down for another.

Even so, he lay awake in bed hearing Brian say once more, admitting again and again, that he *wanted* to put Jamie and that car into the lake. All right, not to kill him, not to kill anyone. But how much did you have to want to hurt someone for it to be manslaughter when someone else ended up dead?

When sleep finally came, it was fitful and nightmarish. The image that kept recurring was not one he would have expected, not Jamie Pitt mesmerizing the jury from the witness stand, not Brian lost in the catacombs of some medieval prison, but rather that dangling car spotlighted above the midnight blackness of Bottleneck Lake, water cascading from some jagged rupture, bulbous weeds clinging, Florian trapped inside with those doomed kids, clutching them, unable to scream as the water filled his mouth, his nose, his lungs. . . .

Around four A.M., dozing groggily, he was startled by a noise. A door? A window? Steps? He lay absolutely still, hardly breathing, trying to decipher the sounds, decide where they were coming from. Christ, had he really lost it? For the first time in ten years he wondered if he'd be better off with Elly lying alongside him, but the idea was a bad one, he could see that right away. They'd spent years trying, and it hadn't worked. Joyce was who he wanted beside him, talking to him, holding him—maybe even reassuring him that she too did, or didn't, hear some unnerving sound in the night. Was he imagining monsters hiding in the closets? He thought of the windows smashed on the Fourth, of dopey Padgett whacked on the head with a brick. Was somebody now, in the middle of the trial, ready to pull something even worse?

He got up and moved, barefoot, down the stairs, not making a sound except for the small creak of one step. Did it always make that noise? He looked out every window. Nothing anywhere. Not a sound, a movement, a light. Not even a leaf trembling.

Still, the flutter in his chest wouldn't quit. Inch by inch, almost rigid with caution, he'd eased Brian's door open wide enough to peer around it, incredibly relieved to find him stretched out on the bed that was clearly too short for him (something Florian had never thought of before), sleeping like a baby.

14

Setting off for court Wednesday morning, picking up Elly and heading out to join Wachtel for their daily two-car caravan to the Hall of Justice, Florian noticed how drained and puffy-eyed Brian looked. Maybe the strain had finally caught up with the kid. Maybe he was worried about Jamie Pitt smiling effortlessly through Wachtel's questioning and emerging with the wings of an angel.

Elly, who never missed much, said, "Are you all right, Brian? You don't look good."

"Me?" Brian said, his voice rising. "Hey, I look as good as anybody else around here."

Wachtel was waiting in front of the white picket fence with his flat hard courtroom briefcase. He strolled over, as always, to say hello at Elly's window, not looking at all like a guy who'd been up all night cramming for his big test. Florian wanted to take that for a positive omen: his low-keyed, confident lawyer feeling no pressure, at the top of his game.

"Maybe," Wachtel said, "you people ought to have some idea what's coming up."

"Wow—a first," Florian said.

"Because this is the first time we're controlling things in there," Wachtel pointed out. "Anyhow, Jamie's picnic is over, but I don't want you people expecting a shoot-out at the OK Corral. We just want to very carefully take him apart like a watch, to expose all the wheels and cogs, and then later, in our summation, point out how those pieces are bound to tell lousy time."

"Sounds great," Florian said, hoping to buck him up. "Terrific."

Wachtel accepted this modestly. He'd no doubt worked hard on the explanation and expected a more enthusiastic reaction. "Everybody okay, meanwhile? Everybody up to snuff?"

In response, he got two halfhearted grunts and Elly's sigh.

* * *

Benn was right: she had about three thousand sick days coming and decided to take one. Still, she woke at six as usual, while Nique, of course, was still sleeping away in Abby Allen's big second-floor bedroom after Joyce had heard her tiptoe back in around three A.M. Sure, the kids in the thick of the trouble have plenty of time and energy for a midnight romp in the woods, whereas the dutiful old folks like herself and Florian spend the night fretting in their cloistered cells.

The girl might well sleep through the day, and Joyce wondered if she shouldn't just leave a note and head in to work after all, but she'd just poured her second cup of coffee when Nique descended the curved stairway in a white bathrobe, this girl who'd had three hours' sleep after an evening of nonstop talk over vodka and Sprite and a postmidnight tryst with the tall blond boyfriend she hadn't seen for months. She looked great. She looked wonderful. You could have put her glowing face and sparkling eyes on the cover of a health and fitness magazine.

"I don't usually booze it up like that," Nique said before she even reached the bottom step. "I hope I didn't say all kinds of jerky things that'll make you think I'm a real batbrain."

"Everything you said was perfectly intelligent." But then Joyce added, hoping she sounded more sympathetic than naggy—teacher to the bloody core, guardian angel of teenage miscreants—"Although you probably *shouldn't* drink that much."

"It's the tension and everything about the trial, to say nothing of facing Daddy afterward."

Nique checked out the fridge and settled on a frosted apple turnover from the convenience store, surely 97 percent sugar.

"We can heat it in the oven."

"I like them cold, Mrs. Johnway."

"Please—call me Joyce."

Nique giggled. "I'd feel real funny doing that."

Joyce decided not to dwell on this, maybe even take it for a compliment. "Obviously the one place we're not going today is the Hall of Justice. Beyond that, what are your plans?"

"Gee, I don't know. I came down here figuring on testifying and everything. Poor Brian, I really hope this ends for him soon."

"When you saw him last night, how was he holding up?"

Nique seemed to be thinking over her options, coming down on the side of casual honesty. "Actually I thought he was really okay. I mean, not down in the mouth or anything."

"He must have been glad to see you after all this time."

"Yeah, I guess so." Nique laughed. "At least I *hope* so." Angling her head to one side to take in the last piece of flaky turnover, she chewed and said, "Do you think maybe we oughta deal with my parents?"

"You didn't really call them the other night, did you?"

"Not actually. But I left them a really long note back in Maine so they wouldn't be worried or anything. They're probably down here scouring haylofts and looking under flat rocks for their long-lost daughter."

"Getting in touch sounds like a good idea."

"If you'd be nice enough to give me a ride out there . . ."

"Should we call ahead?"

"Oh, no. They'll be glad enough to see us, no matter what. But not right this minute, okay? Maybe we could just take a walk or something first. You know, kill a couple of years before we have to leave."

Delehanty had no doubt prepped Jamie for his appearance, and Florian detected no loss of confidence in the boy, who showed up in the same sport coat and slacks but a different tie—a conscious decision on someone's part? Too poor to own two jackets but too proud to be seen in the same tie? Jamie took the witness stand exuding the identical choirboy earnestness he'd shown all along, the ready, almost loose smile.

But instead of the lumbering, sympathetic Patrick Delehanty, he faced this humdrum guy with a reedy voice whose most impressive feature was probably the size and thickness of his eyeglasses.

Wachtel began quietly but abruptly, positioning himself directly in front of Jamie, close and head-on. "Mr. Pitt, you have testified that, at a crucial moment on the ramp, you had no idea why Willa Hufnagle got in the Valiant with Polly Dunn. Is that not what you said?"

Gazing off into the distance, Jamie considered this. "Yeah, something like that."

"Something like that? Did you know why Willa Hufnagle got in the car, or did you not?"

"Well, I didn't. I saw her do it, that's all. I didn't talk to her about it or anything. I was just standing there and saw her get in."

"Without any idea why?"

"That's right."

"You and Polly Dunn were good friends, weren't you?"

The question caught Jamie's attention. He looked right at Wachtel and answered firmly, as if denying some accusation. "Yeah, we were. Real good friends."

"And you'd spent hours that night in the Valiant with him, plus joyriding around Bottleneck Lake in that speedboat you borrowed from where you worked at Hammond's Boatyard?"

Wachtel came down very lightly on *borrowed,* barely suggesting sarcasm.

"Yes."

"Would you tell the court whether, at any time during that evening, Polly Dunn mentioned Willa Hufnagle?"

It was a while before Jamie answered. "Yeah, I guess he did."

"No guesses, please. Did he or didn't he?"

"He did."

"More than once?"

"I guess—I mean, yes. More than once."

"In his several mentions of Willa Hufnagle, did Polly Dunn show any displeasure over anything she'd done, or was doing?"

"I guess he was pretty angry at—"

"Please do not guess."

Delehanty rose angrily to object. "Your Honor, the witness is simply expressing himself in a natural and acceptable locution, and for counsel to suggest—"

"Objection overruled," Judge Ingersoll said. "The witness has earlier been given considerable time and leeway to testify in his own manner and language. He can now be expected to respond in a factual and declarative manner."

Wachtel remained motionless during this exchange, only moving his head to look up at the judge. Throughout, he'd moved a lot less than Delehanty. Occasionally, though, he'd raise one hand to touch the middle, fastened, button of his jacket, as if to reassure himself that it hadn't come open. Once he raised the same hand to touch his glasses.

He again addressed Jamie. "I repeat: Did Polly Dunn voice any displeasure that night about anything Willa Hufnagle had done, or was doing?"

Whether he realized it or not, Jamie himself showed considerable displeasure at the question, and he answered resentfully. "He was sore because she went to the MORP with this guy from Trent that I mentioned before, Tiny Arkins."

"I see. And why would this bother Polly Dunn?"

Florian could actually feel a cold, spidery tingling in his bowels. This was exactly what Wachtel had all along said he was determined to avoid —attacking the two dead kids. Was this some shrewd ploy, or pure and simple desperation?

"Because Polly used to go with Willa," Jamie said, talking into his necktie. "Actually, they went out together until Willa told him she was going to the MORP with Tiny Arkins."

Again Wachtel touched his glasses, but not, it seemed, for any kind of effect. Wachtel didn't possess effects, let alone a bag of tricks. "How come, Mr. Pitt, you failed to mention this fact in your earlier testimony?"

"No one asked about it."

"But you testified that you had no idea why Willa followed Polly Dunn into the Valiant. Doesn't it seem likely she got in the car because of her prior relationship with Polly Dunn?"

"Objection," Delehanty said without anger, almost bored. "After previously complaining about the witness's speculation, counsel is now *asking* him to speculate."

"Sustained. Counsel will confine himself to questions of fact."

"Did you witness anything with your own two eyes," Wachtel went on, his voice as thin and dry as ever, "that indicated a reason for Willa's presence in that vehicle?"

Jamie lowered those two eyes, as if trying to encourage them to replay for him what they had seen. "Yes."

"And what was it you saw?"

"I saw Polly Dunn pull Willa into the car after him."

"Oh? And where were you when you saw this?"

"Like I said yesterday, I was right there, waiting to get in myself, only Willa pushed down the lock and I couldn't—"

"Willa pushed down the lock? But if she was dragged in by Polly, why would she want to lock herself in?"

"Objection," Delehanty said wearily.

"Sustained. Counsel will please desist from asking the witness to make conjectures."

"Your Honor," Wachtel said, "a scrutiny of the witness's prior testimony will, I believe, show a great many similar conjectures as to reasons and motivations clearly beyond his direct observation."

"The court was very lenient," Ingersoll said, "in allowing the witness to recount events in his own language. The court, and the jury, are of course capable of distinguishing between the informal assumptions of such a narrative summary and the more stringent parameters of specific cross-examination. Please confine yourself to questions of fact."

Wachtel took a step closer to Jamie, and Florian realized that he had not yet so much as glanced at the jury. "Now, Mr. Pitt, you've made one rather important correction of your previous testimony, admitting that you saw, with your own two eyes, Polly Dunn *pull* Willa Hufnagle into the Valiant. Let's turn now to the undressed young woman that you and your friends discovered with Brian Rubio at Nanny Point. You've asked permission of the court to refrain from naming this undressed young woman, have you not?"

Jamie seemed to have been expecting a different question entirely, and he took a moment to respond. "Yeah, because she wasn't involved with anything that happened after, the drownings or anything."

"Let's see if in this instance, as with Willa and Polly, you have any corrections to make concerning your earlier testimony. You recognized this woman, did you not?"

Jamie answered with some reluctance. "Yes, sir, I did."

Florian noticed the *sir*, a departure. The kid didn't seem all that shaken, his voice still loud and steady, but along the way he'd given up on the smile. He'd become more wary, more focused.

"Had you and this young woman any prior relationship?"

"Well . . . we went out a few times."

"You did not previously make us aware of that fact, did you? Over what period of time did you go out with this young woman?"

"A few weeks."

"During this period, would you characterize your relationship as serious?"

"I guess so."

"Please—"

"Yes."

"Intimate?"

"Objection!" Delehanty said, rising noisily to his feet.

"Your Honor," Wachtel said, "this bears directly on the actions and motivations of the individuals on the boat ramp."

"The witness may answer."

"Yes," Jamie said after Wachtel returned his gaze to him.

"Physically intimate?"

"Yes."

"So far, then, we have established that Polly Dunn and Wilma Hufnagle on the one hand, and you and the unnamed, unclothed woman with Brian Rubio on the other, had prior relationships of a more than casual nature. Is that an accurate summary of your testimony this morning?"

"Yes."

"Even though yesterday you did *not* testify to these facts?"

"Like I said—no one asked."

(God, it was hard to imagine Nique going out with this guy! All these kids—was it some kind of rampaging epidemic among them, Polly Dunn infuriated with Willa for going with Tiny Arkins, Jamie vowing revenge because Nique Thrane, his rich, taller-than-thou beauty, had switched to Brian? All over which high school kid was taking which other high school kid to the goddamn MORP? Didn't their lives give them anything else to get passionate about?)

"Earlier, Mr. Pitt, you testified that you were behind the wheel of the Valiant when you say the accused began to smash or bang or ram his vehicle into the back of your vehicle. What gear did you have the Valiant in while this was happening?"

"What?"

Wachtel gave him the benefit of a respectful pause. "You understand the function of automobile gears, do you not? There you were, sitting in the Valiant, allegedly being bumped from behind. Did you believe at the time that the bumping was violent enough to push your car into the lake?"

"Oh, yeah. That definitely occurred to me."

"But with all that force being unleashed upon your vehicle—enough, you say, to push you into the lake—you still were not injured in any way. There is, after all, no record of your receiving any medical treatment that night or the next day. The police, who interviewed you only hours later, did not mention any bruises or lacerations."

"I was holding the wheel real tight."

"Had you turned on the ignition? Was the engine running?"

"Yes, it was."

"Since it was an automatic, you had no clutch to deal with. In order to start the engine, you simply had to put the gear in either park or neutral, correct?"

"I really don't remember. Like I said yesterday, it was very wild, with everybody yelling and screaming and running all over the place."

"But you were right on the edge, facing the water. You would not have put it in forward, would you?"

Jamie thought this over. "No."

"When you got out to join your compatriots in forcibly dragging Brian Rubio from his car, did you leave the gear in park or neutral? Or had you put it in reverse in order to push back against Brian's car?"

"I really don't remember. I was only in the car for seconds, maybe a minute, and it was all very mixed and confusing."

"During that brief, mixed, and confusing time, what kept the Valiant from being rammed into the lake?"

"I must've had my foot on the brake."

"That would be almost a reflex action, wouldn't it? Slamming on the brake as hard as you could?"

"I guess so. Sure."

"And then, when the ramming stopped, you got out to help your friends—I quote from your testimony—*drag Brian Rubio from the Corvette*. What did you and your friends do with Brian Rubio after pulling him out of his car?"

"We didn't do nothing. We just left him there because all we wanted was to get our car away from there."

"Left him where? Standing? Lying on the ground? Thrown to the ground? Draped over his car? Where?"

"Sort of on the ground."

"Prone?"

"Prone?"

"Did you leave him *lying* on the ground? Stretched out? Facedown?"

"I really couldn't tell."

"Can you tell us how he got on the ground? Had he been beaten and thrown there by you and your friends?"

"I don't know. There were a lot of guys involved, Trent guys, Medway guys. I keep saying, it was all very confusing."

"Let's return to an earlier time, when you came upon the defendant and your former intimate girlfriend at Nanny Point. You testified that you followed the naked young woman into the woods in order to spare her further embarrassment by giving her the opportunity to put her clothes on. Did you think she'd be unable to dress herself *without* your assistance?"

The edgy laughter caused a frowning Judge Ingersoll to reach for, but not use, his gavel. Wachtel, arms folded as he stared at Jamie, did nothing to indicate any responsibility for the reaction.

"I just said I helped her get away from the others," Jamie said. "I didn't say I helped her get dressed. Actually I turned and looked the other way when she was getting dressed."

"Of course you did," Wachtel said, bringing on a few more laughs, which he again ignored. "You then said that you offered her, in the same spirit of commiseration for her plight, a ride back in your *borrowed* speedboat, but that she instead ran off to find Brian Rubio wherever your friends had left him in the woods. Then you testified that at your friends' insistence, and over your own objections, you set Brian's canoe, containing his clothes, adrift in the middle of the lake, and then cruised around in your *borrowed* speedboat until, when you saw Brian swimming out to reclaim his canoe, you said you persuaded your friends *not* to buzz him but to let him reclaim his canoe and clothes without any further harassment from you. Is that a fair summary of your testimony?"

"Yes, sir."

Wachtel surprised Florian, and maybe everyone else, by rotating slowly from Jamie to face the jury, scanning the panel from one end to the other. Florian couldn't see Wachtel's expression, but he seemed to be just checking them out, making sure they were all present and accounted for.

"Why, Mr. Pitt," he asked with a friendly, inquisitive smile, "were you so nice, so thoughtful, so protective, toward this young woman who had broken off an intimate relationship with you to accompany Brian Rubio to the MORP celebration? Why, indeed, were you so nice and thoughtful and protective toward Brian Rubio, the handsome young man who'd stolen her away from you, by convincing your friends not to harass him with the speedboat while he was swimming in the lake?"

"I just was. I didn't want to hurt anybody."

"You didn't want to hurt anybody?"

"That's right."

Wachtel swung away from Jamie and took a curious little circular stroll, maybe a fifteen-foot diameter, around the polished wood floor before returning to the precise position he maintained all along, directly in front of Jamie. He had a funny little hitch in his step that Florian hadn't noticed before. Did he always walk like that, or only in court? An old Columbia football injury? A human failing designed to endear him to jurors?

"Tell us, if you would, Mr. Pitt, what emotions you felt when you discovered your former intimate girlfriend romping naked in the moonlit waters of Nanny Point Beach with a tall and handsome—and equally naked—rival from Trent High School?"

"Objection!"

"The question, Your Honor, goes to the heart of the witness's motivation for his actions later that evening."

"The witness may answer."

Jamie squirmed. "Well, sure. I mean, I wasn't, you know, crazy about that."

Wachtel waited a long time, not moving, studying Jamie's face, before continuing. "Earlier in the day, that afternoon, when you testified that Brian Rubio came to Hammond's Boatyard to complain about a speedboat endangering swimmers at the public beach—even then, you had no desire to hurt anybody?"

"No, sir, I didn't." The slightest waver had crept into Jamie's voice.

"Not at any time?"

"No. Not at any time."

"Now, on the day before the MORP, did you see or have any contact with the unnamed young woman you'd formerly been intimate with?"

"No, sir."

Wachtel pulled his head back, as if truly surprised by this answer. "Are you sure? This is a vital point, and we want to be certain we're hearing you right. You're saying you did *not* see the young woman the day before the MORP?"

Wachtel's pressure turned Jamie defiant. "No, sir, I did not."

Wachtel spun about quickly. "No further cross-examination," he said to the judge and headed back, a faint mustache of perspiration glistening over his lip, to join Brian at the table.

It was almost eleven, and Judge Ingersoll inquired of Delehanty whether the state intended to call any more witnesses. This was when they'd learn whether the prosecution would call Tiny Arkins, but Wachtel didn't even seem to be listening as he sorted through a sheaf of papers at the table, with Brian, appearing equally unconcerned, leaning close to watch.

Delehanty answered with a decisive "No," and Wachtel didn't skip a beat in his fussing with his papers.

The surge of relief Florian felt lasted only seconds. Maybe Delehanty was so encouraged by the way Jamie Pitt had handled the cross-examination that he felt no need of other help.

Wachtel stood to announce that the defense intended to call several witnesses but would be brief enough with all of them to finish by noon.

The ride out to Sargasso River Highlands was pleasant enough. The morning was sunny, the September air cool, and Nique, for an AWOL kid about to rematerialize for her frantic parents in the hands of a stranger, seemed remarkably poised. Her huge mauve valise took up most of the back seat of Joyce's VW.

"How do you feel about school starting again?" Joyce asked. Partly she wanted to keep Nique light, at ease, but she was also interested; what was it really like at Spenser Academy? Growing up, Joyce had known kids who went to both local and distant private schools, although she, and her parents, had been too entrenched in their middle-class split-levels for her ever to become friendly with the preppies. And teaching at Medway for twelve years, you lost touch with the top end of the economic scale.

"Huh?" Nique said, rousing from some reverie or other, some past, present, or future dream of Brian Rubio or Jamie Pitt or her parents, that Joyce would never in a million years be able to guess. Once more she couldn't help wondering what the girl, if given the chance, would have testified, and what difference it would have made for that tall blond kid sitting in there facing a manslaughter charge.

"I was wondering how you felt going back to school."

"Oh. Well, I feel okay. It doesn't start until next week, but you know, it's school."

"Are you doing well?"

"Oh, sure. I mean, it's no big deal, but if I keep at it this year, I have a real shot at valedictorian."

"That'd be wonderful," Joyce said. Again it struck her what an incredible *revolt* it must have been, for a daughter whose parents considered Brian Rubio beneath contempt, to get involved with someone like Jamie Pitt. What was the message she was sending to her parents, herself, the world at large?

"My only real competition, you know, is Ling, this girl from Taiwan. I mean, all she does is *study*. Talk about pounding it, wow. It's not that she's not nice or anything, but give me a break. What is it about these Chinese and everything anyway? Are they all supposed to be geniuses?"

"Studies show that the longer they're here, the more they become like American kids."

"You mean dumb?"

"Closer to average."

"Well, kids at Spenser'll be glad to hear that. I mean, some teachers grade on the curve, so when you walk in and spot this little clump of bubbling bright-eyed Orientals smiling away at the blackboard, right off you figure, *Holy shit, there goes my GPA.*"

"Clearly that hasn't been true for you."

"Not yet, I guess. My father and mother are both really smart, so I must've picked up some of it."

The road through the Highlands was nice enough, but no prettier than the rest of Mt. Early County. The mansions were what made the area spectacular, and you couldn't see any of them from the road. Possibly Benn had been inside some of them, but Joyce hadn't. She didn't think she'd even met any member of the Five Families before Nique.

Her first year at Medway, Joyce had worked up a local history unit on the Highlands and those five nineteenth-century entrepreneurs who'd chosen that area for their twenty- and thirty- and fifty-acre estates, for their twenty- and thirty- and fifty-room houses. Before the turn of the century, the families would congregate at the Sargasso River High-lands gymkhana for lawn tennis matches, for (actually!) duck and piglet racing, for the Mt. Early Horse Show, where they displayed, under the reins of liveried servants, their gleaming equipages and pedigreed horses. Every spring, for the Trent Hunt, the members rode to hounds, English style.

The study unit was such a flop with the kids that she replaced it next time around with a segment on Medway's early hat factories and the seething sulfurous match companies. The students listened, awed, to all that grimy tragedy and deprivation, those stories of men and women working seventy-hour weeks, dying of asbestosis, blacklisted for even mentioning the word *union*. Those people were their grandmothers and grandfathers, their great-grandmothers and great-grandfathers. Medway kids couldn't care less about the dainty ladies of the Five Families at their croquet parties, the men in plus fours on their private golf links.

"That's the gate coming up now, right between those pillars." Star-ing straight ahead, silent and motionless, Nique looked exactly as she had when Benn had brought her to the Log Cabins in his Lincoln. It was eerie, almost as if the girl felt as unsure about facing her parents now as she had about meeting Joyce for the first time.

Joyce nosed the VW up to the pillars and stopped. "What are the little plaques?"

"They're supposed to be our family's fucking crest, and believe me, if I get this place when Mommy and Daddy die, the first thing I'm doing is coming out to chisel them down with my own two hands."

Wide-eyed at her anger—and at the idea of Nique inheriting God knows how many million dollars' worth of property, to say nothing of everything else the Thranes owned—Joyce sat for a moment before ask-ing, "How does one get *through* these pillars?"

"I've got a gizmo." Nique scrounged around in her shoulder strap purse and brought out a tiny metallic pad, which she pointed at the left pillar. Slowly the huge gate swung open.

"How convenient," Joyce said.

"I'd really like you to come in and say hello."

An elderly gardener looked up from a wheelbarrow to frown at the cockroach brown VW chugging along the road, then doffed his crum-pled hat when he recognized Nique, who smiled and greeted him with a little offhand wave. "You can swing around and park by the garages in back," she said as they approached the house after the long drive in from the gate. The building was situated at the top of a broad rise, high enough over the trees to provide what Joyce could already tell were magnificent views in every direction. Lawns surrounded the house, leading down on one side to a private lake big enough for the half dozen rowboats and canoes lined up along its shore.

Twenty rooms, she guessed, huge by South Corner standards but modest (indeed, they were called cottages at the turn of the century) in comparison with the Great Estates like Greenhills and the old Brainard property. But all those Estates had become too costly to keep up, and all, at one time or another, had fallen into disuse before being resurrected as schools, hotels, resorts, as the Trent Theater Festival. Sargasso River Highlands had survived because, although you needed servants, you probably could get by with a mere three or four. The Thrane house itself, once you accepted its size and isolation, was not spectacular: an arched marble drive-through protecting the entrance, stone turrets at the corners, handsome brickwork, large windows, broad second-floor balconies with stone balustrades.

The gray masonry structure in back housed five garages with five leaded glass doors. She parked alongside, not blocking anything.

"I told you they'd be here," Nique said, apparently having recognized one of cars behind a glass door. "Well, here goes nothing," she said, almost under her breath, and got out. Flipping her seat forward, she managed to wrestle her huge mauve valise from the back before Joyce got there to help. She started lugging it toward the house when a back door opened and a woman rushed out. Surely Nique's mother: a handsome woman in her forties, not nearly as tall as her daughter but with the same dramatic black hair.

"Veronique!" she cried in what sounded like heartfelt relief as she hurried to them, pushing the valise down with one hand. "Leave it for Thomas, silly." She glanced quizzically at Joyce, then the VW.

"This is Mrs. Johnway," Nique said. "She's a teacher from Medway who's been wonderful, really terrific, and I thought it'd be nice if you met her."

"Oh?" the mother said, taking Joyce's hand. "From Medway?"

"We got together sort of by accident," Nique said.

"Well, we needn't go into everything right this moment." The mother waited, apparently unsure whether Joyce was a guest, her daughter's accomplice, or merely a convenient driver who could now be thanked and dismissed.

No longer sure herself, Joyce was about to make at least a perfunctory gesture toward leaving when from the same back door a man emerged, large and balding, older than the mother.

He stomped to Nique. "So?" he demanded. "Now what?" When Nique, eyes down, remained silent, the man glared at Joyce. "Who's this? Someone from the hospital?"

"She's a teacher from Medway," the mother said.

He turned impatiently back to Nique.

The girl raised her eyes and offered a little girlish shrug. "I really don't want to have a great big discussion right now, okay? Maybe we could just—"

He slapped her across the face, incredibly hard, a blow, and Joyce let out a cry. Nique wavered, hands to her face, and sank to her knees at her father's feet.

"Get up, God damn it," he said, and when Nique didn't, he grabbed her arm with the same beefy hand and yanked her up. She collapsed against him, turning away from Joyce.

"You can't hit her like that," Joyce blurted. "You've hurt her. You could have really injured her."

He shoved Nique toward the house, and she kept moving, tripping and stumbling, as he kept prodding her, staying on her heels all the way with her arm still in his grasp.

The mother had not moved, not cried out or uttered a word. "I'm sorry about that," she said. "But really, you have to understand . . ."

"He ought to be reported, for God's sake."

"Please—don't. It'd be really unfortunate."

"That's abuse. That's battering. What's he doing to her inside now?"

"It's been so hard on him. I don't know what Veronique's told you . . . do you even know how many *times* she's run off like this? Do you know how many *times* we've had to put her in treatment?"

"If this is the way she's welcomed home, it's no wonder."

The woman stiffened. "Believe me, her father knows and cares for her a lot more than some stranger. Thank you for bringing her here. Is there anything else I can do for you?"

"Is he beating her up in there? Is that what he's doing?"

"You're being terribly unfair—taking a momentary lapse like that, from someone who's suffered far more than you can imagine, and assuming he's some monster."

Joyce turned on her heel and got into the VW. The road swung around the house, and there, running out from under the covered marble archway of the front entrance, waving frantically, came Nique. Joyce hit the brake and reached across the front seat to unlock that door, so the girl could jump right in.

But Nique merely bent down at Joyce's window. The left side of her face glowed hotly, but she made a gallant try at good cheer. "To get out, you have to push the button on the little building there."

"You mean that's what you came running out to tell me?"

"Well, you have to get out, don't you? But yeah, I wanted to thank you, very much, for everything. Really, you were just great."

"Are you all right? Why did he hit you like that?"

"He just gets really impatient sometimes. You know how it is."

"He ought to be reported."

"Oh, my God, don't ever do that."

"Does he always treat you that way?"

"Oh, no. Really. But if you say anything I'll never hear the end of it. Please, I'm just fine, you don't have to worry about me at all." She tried that same little smile, that same girlish shrug. "After all, I'm back home, right? Everything'll be just fine."

15

During the short recess Florian saw Jamie Pitt heading for the streets with a bunch of reporters in pursuit. Was that it, his last glimpse of the kid? Suppose he ran after him, grabbed him by the collar and pushed him up against a wall—what then? Exactly what points did he have to make? What, in turn, did he expect to hear from the guy? In all his life Florian couldn't remember anyone he thought about so much and had so little to say to.

Wachtel motioned Elly and Florian aside in the stairwell and said he planned to call the driver of the Valiant and the other Medway kid who'd spent MORP night cruising around with Jamie. Obviously they were Jamie's friends and wouldn't undercut the basic thrust of his testimony, but he was hoping they resented the way Jamie had blamed them for all the evil thoughts on MORP night. "I'm just hoping they'll defend themselves enough to nibble away at Jamie's credibility."

Florian, who hoped they'd do more than nibble, nodded. "I thought you did okay with Jamie. I thought you had him squirming."

At the same time he couldn't help wondering if all lawyers, no matter what side they represented, Delehanty and Wachtel and Harry Diggs and maybe, for whatever he knew, the judge, weren't part of the same Tuesday evening poker club, tipping each other off to their every courtroom move with their marked cards, all engaged in this complicated game that only they knew the rules of, and that only they, in their polished black shoes and hard-assed briefcases, could never lose at.

Back inside, Wachtel first called the Medway kid who'd owned the Valiant and had driven Jamie and the others around on MORP night. He looked awfully uncomfortable and mumbled his answers with his eyes down. Wachtel, on the other hand, seemed livelier, more incisive and energetic, than he had with Jamie, more *warmed up* maybe.

No, the boy said, he didn't remember Jamie telling the others, after they'd left Nanny Point in the speedboat, not to buzz Brian Rubio in the water. What he remembered was everybody, including Jamie, saying what a great idea that was, and all of them shouting and laughing when they did it, with Jamie steering the speedboat the whole time, cutting close enough to Brian Rubio in the water to make a real sport out of it.

"But no," he said. "No one wanted to hit him. It was just, you know, having fun."

The other Medway friend said that Jamie seemed to be having an argument with Brian's date when they surprised her without her clothes at Nanny Point, and that when she ran off it wasn't Jamie that stopped the others from chasing her, but the others that stopped Jamie, because they were afraid he'd do something to get them all in trouble.

"On the afternoon of the MORP, did you spend any time at Hammond's Boatyard?"

"Yes."

"Was Mr. Hammond there?"

"No. Jamie said he'd be gone for a few hours."

"So who was there besides Jamie?"

"Me and some of his other friends."

"How many?"

"Maybe five altogether."

"What brought you there?"

"Jamie asked us. He said this lifeguard at the beach—Brian Rubio—had been bugging him and wanted us to catch him by surprise and scare him off."

"That's all? Just scare him off."

"Right."

"You needed five or six kids for that?"

"I don't know. When the guy showed up, we just chased him back to the beach."

"You didn't catch him?"

"He had a big head start."

"What would you have done if you did catch him?"

"Nothing, I guess. Like I said, it was just to make him stop hassling Jamie."

"None of you, not even Jamie, had any intention of inflicting harm on Brian Rubio?"

"I know I didn't."

"Again we can only commend all of you for your impressive restraint and self-control. Thank you," Wachtel said before Delehanty could leap up to object.

Unfortunately, under Delehanty's cross-examination, both boys solidly backed Jamie's version of what happened on the ramp.

The Valiant owner said that he'd been beaten badly around the eyes, which was why he hadn't jumped into the car himself, and therefore why, he guessed, he was alive today. Then, in answer to Delehanty's question, he said, "The other car, the Corvette, pushed it in."

"Is that what you saw?"

"Yes, sir. I saw the Corvette with Brian Rubio behind the wheel bump my car from behind and send it into the lake."

His friend readily agreed. "It was pushed, sir."

"By whom? By what?"

"By Brian Rubio, in the Corvette jammed up behind it."

When this kid left the stand, Elly gave Florian a troubled, questioning look. He shrugged and turned away, unable to offer much encouragement.

Wachtel called a third friend of Jamie's, this one the owner of a station wagon who said he'd been asked by Jamie on the day before the MORP to drive him to pick up a friend.

"We don't need the name of this friend. Just tell us whether or not you recognized her."

"I did. I recognized her."

"In what connection?"

"She was this girl Jamie used to . . . you know, go with."

"Now, on this day before the MORP, how did you two manage to meet up with this young woman?"

"She was biking home from school along this road, and we kind of pulled over and Jamie asked her to get in, in back with him."

"How forcefully did Jamie make this request?"

The kid on the stand looked glum. "I don't know exactly how to put it. I mean, he told her he wanted her to get in, and she did."

"Did she appear to do it voluntarily?"

"I really couldn't say exactly. I was behind the wheel and didn't watch or hear everything they said."

"Would you say this young woman appeared to expect Jamie to invite her into your car, or would you say she appeared surprised?"

"I think I'd say surprised."

Wachtel let this hang in the air a minute. "And what happened after she got in?"

"I drove around a bit while Jamie and her talked in back."

"Did you by chance overhear their conversation?"

"Some things but not others. I wasn't trying to listen in or anything, and besides, you know, it's a real old Chevy that makes a lot of noise."

"You say you recognized the young woman as Jamie's former girl-friend. Did you know, or did you learn from what they said in back, anything else about her? Not her name—anything else?"

The kid hardly seemed eager to answer. "Well, I could tell from what Jamie said that this other guy was taking her to that prom thing the Trent kids had on. You know, the MORP."

"Was this other person Brian Rubio?"

"That's right."

"And this was the day before the MORP, correct?"

"That's right."

"Thank you."

Delehanty cross-examined sharply: Was he with Jamie or anyone else on MORP night? Was he on the ramp when the Valiant went into the lake? Did he have any direct knowledge of what happened on the ramp the night of the MORP?

No. No. No. He'd graduated the year before and worked nights as a janitor at IE Plastics, so wasn't anywhere near anything that night.

After a whispered conversation at the bench among Wachtel, Dele-hanty, and Judge Ingersoll, Wachtel produced a sergeant from the police lab.

"Your official report has, of course, already been entered into evidence," Wachtel began, seeming fairly relaxed now and less intense than he'd been with the Medway kids, standing with one arm loose by his side, the other in his trouser pocket, leaning slightly to that side as he faced the uniformed policeman. "But I'd like you to be good enough to state in person certain of your findings. First of all, was there any damage to the front bumper of the Corvette?"

"As the report states, sir, there was no discernible damage to any area of the Corvette."

"If it had rammed another car with enough force to propel the other vehicle off the ramp, would it not have sustained damage to the front bumper?"

"I couldn't speculate, sir. We did not, in our tests, find discernible damage."

"In your investigations of other cars involved in ramming accidents, Sergeant, did those cars sustain bumper damage?"

"Every instance is unique, sir. You can't take findings from one instance and apply them to another."

"Was the Valiant damaged in any way?"

"The '74 Plymouth Valiant, sir, was found to have many areas of damage. Which in particular are you asking about?"

"The rear bumper."

"As the report states, sir, the rear bumper of the Plymouth Valiant exhibited numerous scratches and dents. In addition, the right end or tip of it was twisted upward at an angle of forty-eight degrees for a length of five-point-seven inches."

"In general, are your tests able to determine *when* certain damages occurred?"

"Not precisely, sir, such as the day or hour. But on the basis of rust and accumulated grime and other elements, we can often determine if the damage is relatively recent or not."

"Was any of the damage to the Valiant's rear bumper relatively recent?"

"Not as far as we could tell, sir. Everything appeared to be long-standing."

"Can we therefore conclude, on the basis of your scientific and technical investigations, that you found no evidence of damage to either car that might indicate any kind of ramming going on between them?"

"As our report states, sir, we could not find conclusive evidence that such a ramming did, or did not, take place."

"And the transmission of the Valiant—was it damaged in any way?"

"No, sir, it was not."

"You found it in good operating condition?"

"Yes, sir."

"You've been very helpful, Sergeant, and I thank you for your clear and forthright answers. One final question. In what position did you find the gearshift lever when the car was pulled out of the lake?"

"I have no knowledge, sir, of its position when the vehicle was dredged from the lake. The '74 Plymouth Valiant was removed from the lake at two-fourteen A.M. My initial inspection of the vehicle commenced at three-seventeen A.M."

"Where did this observation take place?"

"At the boat ramp, sir. I was called from home to take photographs and make an initial on-site observation before the vehicle was moved to the impound yard for further tests."

"So you first checked the car several hours after it went into the lake, and more than an hour after it was removed. Did you note the position of the shift lever at that time?"

"I did, sir. It was in neutral."

"Do you know who placed it in that position?"

"I beg your pardon?"

"It's a simple enough question. Do you know who put the shift in neutral?"

"Of course not, sir."

"Were the two doors on the driver's side jammed shut when you conducted your observations?"

"They were."

"Thank you for your very helpful testimony." With an offhanded gesture toward Judge Ingersoll, Wachtel said, "The defense is now prepared to take advantage of the lunch recess so generously offered by the court, with the much-appreciated agreement of the prosecution."

"We will reconvene at two P.M.," Ingersoll said, "at which time, if the defense does not call additional witnesses, we will begin the summations. With a degree of luck, we may be able to guarantee everyone a timely dinner."

"Okay," Wachtel said, sitting next to Brian, across from Florian and Elly, in a padded leather booth at the Friendly's down the block, lunch already ordered. "Now we decide. Do we want Brian up there? We've heard the prosecution's case, had our shot at Jamie, and maybe lucked out when Delehanty decided not to chance bringing in Tiny Arkins. We even did better than I expected with Jamie's buddies." He took a drink of his water. "Now what?"

"Am I supposed to still have ideas?" Florian said. "Maybe you have some. Maybe Elly has. God knows I don't anymore."

The waitress loomed over them with a huge tray, checking her pad, blowing up from one side of her mouth at the hair sticking to her sweaty forehead: who had the double cheeseburger, who wanted the New England chowder, how many coffees, who gets the Coke? They buttered their rolls, passed the pepper, slapped the catsup jar. Brian dug right into his double cheeseburger, which must have been four inches thick.

Wachtel went for his coffee first, sipped, put down the cup. "Do we want him up there or not?"

"It'd put incredible pressure on him," Elly said. "Worrying about a slipup, some stupid contradiction, anything." She was dipping and turning her spoon to cool her chowder. "What's the point of letting Delehanty throw daggers at him?"

Wachtel, dissecting the veal cutlet, said, "There's no question we'd be taking a chance."

"It really frightens me," Elly said. "Look at how you went after Jamie. What's to stop Delehanty from doing even worse? He's probably been a lawyer longer than Brian's been alive."

"Could I get another order of fries?" Brian asked.

Florian signaled the waitress. He took a breath, drained his coffee, looked at Wachtel. "I don't think they've got a case," he said. "They've haven't proved a thing, and as far as I can see, you pretty much totally discredited Jamie."

"A rare compliment, Flo. Thank you."

"But will it do the job? Last night you asked us about Nique and cross-examining Jamie, and in both cases we just ended up doing exactly what you wanted. We probably will again, but at least give us the possibilities. What do we gain? What do we stand to lose? What are the odds?"

"We'd gain, obviously, through the appearance of a very nice, well-spoken, very reasonable young man who nobody in his right mind would ever think of as a criminal. We stand to lose by letting Delehanty repeat and reemphasize and underline all the reasons this nice reasonable young man had for getting back at those Medway kids."

"I'm not sure we want him doing that," Florian said.

"Of course we don't," Elly said.

"Let's step back a minute," Wachtel said. "What we're dealing with —the *only* thing we're dealing with—is the sworn testimony presented in that courtroom. Nothing else counts a soggy fig, including what actually *happened,* as much as that concept might offend our sense of logic and decency."

"Somehow," Florian said, "I'd think what actually happened *would* count."

"It doesn't," Wachtel said. "This is a trial. Guilty means the evidence convicted you. Innocent means it didn't. At this point, what people actually did isn't worth thinking about. We're concerned with testimony, with evidence, with the relevant criminal statutes—along with one real wild card: the mood and expectation and response and pure zany weirdness of the jurors. Everything else you can prepare for. With juries you flip a coin. With juries you clasp your hands in prayer. With juries you dig out the Ouija board."

Florian's impatience was about to explode. "So where are we? What do you want us to do?"

"First of all, I guess we should—"

"No guesses," Florian said.

With a little nod, Wachtel scored one for Florian. "We've got to consider the fact that although we've gone a long way to destroy Jamie's credibility, it's been almost entirely concerned with what happened *before* the ramp. The one exception is his changed story about Willa getting into the Valiant, but even this tells us nothing about how the car got into the lake. Let's face it, who cares why those kids got into the car? They're dead. That's what counts. We also ended up with a trade-off by bringing on Jamie's two cohorts that night. Sure, they cast some real doubts about Jamie's overall truthfulness, but both backed Jamie's version of how the Valiant went in, which of course those earlier witnesses who were on the ramp, especially the college kid, weren't all that positive about. So that's the testimony, the evidence, that we have to deal with."

"Can they convict him on that?" Elly asked.

"Got that Ouija board handy?"

"Please," Elly said. "This may be a lot of fun for you, but it's not for us."

"It's not fun," Wachtel said. "It's a challenge, and I'm trying to live up to it."

"Suppose," Ellen said, "Brian went in and denied Jamie's version. Suppose he brought up the whole thing about seeing Polly yank on the gearshift and—"

"I didn't," Brian said, looking up from his diminishing pile of fries.

"Didn't what?" Elly asked.

"See him do anything with the gearshift."

"You told me you did," Florian said. "That night, right after it happened."

"I figured it was something to say right then. I was scared, Dad. I had a million things going through my head."

Florian stared but said nothing. What could he say beyond wishing his own kid would at least have told him the fucking truth?

"I didn't want you thinking," Brian said quietly, "that I was stupid enough to take your car for the night and end up in the middle of a mess like that. Christ, Dad, there were two kids dead. I figured the cops would be coming after me any minute and didn't know what the hell I should say, to you or anybody else."

"Look," Wachtel said calmly, calmly, "none of that matters right now. You've both heard Brian on the tape. He was so sore he *wanted* to dump Jamie into the lake. Of course, it wasn't Jamie, it was Polly and Willa, but that's beside the point. Whoever was in the car, Brian at that moment, maybe with all the justification in the world, wanted to get back at those Medway kids who'd been hounding him and his girlfriend all night."

"Who wouldn't?" Florian said.

"Sure, but that's not the point. The point is that no such statement of Brian's intentions at the moment the car went into the lake exists in the trial record." Wachtel paused to impale a small square piece of veal on his fork, then looked up. "Nor can it exist unless Brian himself volunteers it."

Brian kept eating, eyes down, picking up an individual fry with his fingers, swiping it through the catsup on his plate. He seemed to be more or less listening.

Florian, who'd left most of his meal on the plate, crumpled his paper napkin and dropped it to the table. "Brian?"

Brian looked up, waiting.

"If you go up there, are you going to tell them the same thing you told me about the gearshift?"

"No."

"Why not?"

"Because I was going out of my skull when you came in from the boat that night and didn't know what the hell I was saying."

"What would you tell them?"

"The truth."

"C'mon."

"Jesus, Dad, I'm no good at lying. I don't like it and it shows. Maybe I fooled you that night but this is months later and I don't think I could fool anyone else."

"Actually we may yet get some use out of the gearshift," Wachtel said, "but I'll deal with that in the summation."

Florian still had his eyes on Brian. "So you'd just coolly walk in there and say you wanted to push that car in because you thought Jamie was inside?"

"I guess I would if he asked me—although I don't know how coolly. What would you want me to do, Dad—lie?"

"Yes."

"Would you?"

"For you? Sure I would. I'd do more than lie."

With a little shrug Brian said, "Well, I'd do the same for you."

"This is insane," Elly said. "He can't go up there. That's it. The discussion's over. There's nothing more to say."

Wachtel offered no argument. He merely looked at Florian.

Florian felt as if he'd undergone a sudden loss of air and bone and muscle. Only by a determined act of will could he keep his body from collapsing. "Okay," he said thickly, "it's unanimous."

"Good," Wachtel said. "We leave Brian right where he is, looking as sweet and innocent as the morning dew." And then, in a rare, strange, unnerving move that almost sent Florian reeling, Wachtel reached across the table and gave him a light punch on the shoulder. Christ, Elly was sitting there, too. Brian was sitting there. Why the hell was he the one that had to be consoled?

"Let's just see," Wachtel said, "if we can't talk real sense to the jury."

"That jury?" Florian said, trying to bring out a laugh, to show everyone how quickly he'd recovered from whatever they thought was happening to him.

"Hey, that's why we picked them, Flo. Delehanty too. We figured it'd come down to something like this and wanted people with enough brains to handle it."

Florian shook his head in disbelief, actually managing a laugh this time, and slapped Brian's knee. "How's it going, kid? How we doing?"

"We're doing okay," Brian said. "Nobody ain't hung us yet."

Florian at last saw them, recognizing them from the photos, the TV appearances: the parents of Willa Hufnagle, parents of Polly Dunn. Other relatives had come too, including the thirteen-year-old girl who'd been played up in the paper and on TV as the only person closely connected to both drowned kids. He couldn't remember her first name, but there she was, looking painfully young and distressed, the kid sister of the late Polly Dunn, the best friend of the late Willa Hufnagle.

The group numbered maybe ten all told, sitting together behind the prosecutor's table, and they all turned in their seats when Wachtel and Brian, Elly and Florian entered through the rear door. They watched Wachtel and Brian move down the aisle and seat themselves at the defense table, then stared at Florian and Elly. Florian looked away.

A podium of polished wood had been placed about ten feet from the jury, alongside the easel used earlier in the trial. Delehanty began his summation leaning forward with his large blunt hands clasping the edges of the slanted surface.

Again, he promised to be brief. The case was neither complicated nor hard to follow. He realized, of course, the terrible toll the drownings had taken on the family and friends of the dead boy and girl, and also on the defendant and his family and friends, on those who even in the most minor way had been involved in the events of last June 20, and ultimately on all the good and decent young men and women, indeed on every citizen, of Mt. Early County.

"My role," he said, "is not to convict but to see justice done." He studied the jury intently, seemingly examining each face. "And your role is not to let your sympathies, for anyone, cloud your judgment of the facts. All our hearts ache. Yet two of our children died because of the commission of a criminal act, and despite your dismay and distress I beseech you to carry out your sworn duty and find the defendant Brian Rubio guilty, first of assault and battery upon the two victims, and then, more fatefully, guilty too of causing their deaths by means of involuntary manslaughter."

In a steady, almost plodding manner, he summarized the events of the evening. Rightly or wrongly, Brian Rubio and his friends had sworn to avenge themselves upon Jamie Pitt and his friends for the fracas on the dunes, for surprising and embarrassing and threatening Brian and his girlfriend on the beach at Nanny Point, and finally for vandalizing their automobiles at Tiny Arkins's house. Even maybe for that occurrence much earlier, when Jamie and his friends chased Brian Rubio from Hammond's Boatyard.

"I'm not contending that the Medway boys were right, or defensible, or well behaved at all times. But no deaths occurred during these incidents, not even any serious injuries, just a scattering of cuts and scratches, bumps and bruises—all apparently shared fairly equally by youths from both towns.

"The real issue is not which boys, or which group of boys, may or may not have been at some point rowdy or foolish or overly rambunctious. This trial is not dealing with those issues. This trial is not dealing with any boys from Medway, or any other boys from Trent. The only person on trial here is Brian Rubio, and he is on trial because he has been charged with assault and battery, and with causing the deaths of a young boy and a young girl by means of involuntary manslaughter.

"Now, the events relating to these two charges took place at a certain clearly established time on the public boat ramp. What happened *before* certain individuals arrived at the ramp is of no matter. Whatever preliminary encounters occurred between various individuals and groups is of no matter. Whoever may or may not have tried to make his own actions look more defensible is of no matter. Whoever does or does not recall every single particular fact with absolute clarity is of no matter. None of that, not one bit, concerns us here, because none of it sheds even one flickering candle's worth of light upon the weighty matters before us.

"Let us clearly restate, and consider, the significant events that occurred on the ramp and led directly to the drowning of Polly Dunn and Willa Hufnagle.

"First of all, after their arrival in the Corvette and two other cars, a number of Trent boys decide to give up their unsuccessful pursuit of the Medway boys and return to their dates at the party.

"Brian Rubio does not—and thus we have decision number one.

"He could have left. By now his initial anger, whatever the cause, should have abated. By now cooler heads among his friends urge him to call off his vindictive search. But he doesn't. He continues to seek revenge, even though he surely realizes how fraught it is with danger and uncertainty, how terrible might be the unforeseen consequences.

"And then, after the Medway boys walk away from their Valiant at the other end, a Trent boy jumps into the Corvette entrusted to Brian Rubio by his father and drives it the length of the ramp to block the Valiant. Does Brian Rubio attempt to stop him? He does not. Why? We can only assume, my friends, that his overwhelming desire to get back at the Medway boys blotted out whatever good sense and judgment he was capable of at the moment.

"And so he leaves the Corvette blocking the Valiant: decision number two.

"And then, after five or ten minutes, the Medway boys return, and it's obvious to one and all that the blocking of their car is a provocative act, sure to cause a confrontation between the two groups. But there remains a simple, easy way to avoid the dangers of such a confrontation, which is for Brian Rubio to *get his car out of the way.*

"But he does not do so: decision number three. Once again Brian Rubio places his indelible personal stamp, through action or inaction, on the course of events.

"And then Brian Rubio does what he's been itching to do all along: he and his cohorts attack the Medway boys. That, ladies and gentlemen, is assault and battery. There is no way in the world that can be denied. Here we see not merely a passive failure to do the *right* thing. We see an active and conscious undertaking of the *wrong* thing. What Brian Rubio does at this moment, after depriving the Medway boys of their only means of escape, is to physically, aggressively, brutally assault them.

"Decision number four by Brian Rubio. Action number four by Brian Rubio."

At each number Delehanty raised high above the lectern his right hand, unbending one more blunt finger, like a goddamn headwaiter.

Florian glanced at Elly, pale as tap water, then tried to make something of Wachtel's expression at the defense table. Wachtel had turned slightly in his chair to watch Delehanty, giving Florian a view of one side of his face. Was he nervous about his own speech coming up? Confident? Still trying to decide on the exact phrase, the perfect tone, the right length? There he was, soberly exhibiting nothing but his bland court-room face. Good old Wachtel, their one lousy hope in hell, calmly taking it all in as Delehanty ticked off one crushing point after another on his beefy hand.

"We come to number five. At some point during this melee Willa Hufnagle and Polly Dunn decide they've had enough. Their reasons don't concern us. Perhaps fear. Perhaps pain from the assaults already inflicted upon them. Perhaps cowardice. Perhaps Willa has decided that she no longer wishes to stay with her date from Trent but instead wants to make up with her former boyfriend, Polly Dunn. Nor is it beyond possibility that they felt a sudden rush of common sense, of reason, of prudence, of an intelligence befitting two bright young persons about to graduate from high school and junior high school with commendable records in scholarship, in athletics, in school service. *It matters not why those two poor children were in that car.* All we need consider is that the choice they made, to get in the car and get away, was intended for one purpose and one only: they wanted to *end* the fight, the fracas, the assault, the riot, the confrontation, without further damage to anyone or anything. They merely wanted, achingly, desperately, to *escape.*

"Can any of us, in any manner or fashion, fault that wish on the part of this decent young boy and girl?

"Yet what, at that instant, was Brian Rubio's decision? Now, we don't have to dot every *i* and cross every *t* to arrive at a just and reasonable verdict. The basic facts are not in dispute. What Brian Rubio did when Polly Dunn and Willa Hufnagle got in the Valiant was to climb back into his Corvette, start the engine, and *continue and extend the assault and battery already under way* by using that powerful, expensive automobile to physically prevent a couple of Medway children in a dilapidated Valiant from leaving the scene of their own violent beatings and injuries.

"That awesome and regrettable action, ladies and gentlemen, constitutes fateful decision number five."

Slowly his hand went up, the thumb now extended with all four fingers. He held it up, solemnly, for a long time before, just as slowly, bringing it back down.

"As usual in matters of evidentiary testimony, not all witnesses agree on every detail, or remember events with exactly the same precision. Did Brian Rubio actually use the Corvette to push the Valiant into the lake? Of course he did—although I truly believe he had no intention at all of killing anyone. He pushed the car in to get back at his Medway enemies, with whom he'd already had several unfortunate and embarrassing run-ins that day. He wanted to damage their automobile and cause the individuals in that car a considerable amount of pain and embarrassment and fear. But that, ladies and gentlemen, is assault and battery. And since in the course of committing the crime of assault and battery, Brian Rubio brought about the unintended deaths of Polly Dunn and Willa Hufnagle, he is guilty of involuntary manslaughter. Not homicide. I have never for a moment thought Brian Rubio *wanted* to cause the deaths of those two unfortunate youngsters. But he did cause them, and he did so while engaged in committing the crime of assault and battery, and therefore, even though those deaths were unintentional, the law must hold Brian Rubio guilty of the crime of involuntary manslaughter.

"By preventing Polly and Willa from leaving the scene of the assault and battery upon them, Brian Rubio sealed their fates. In whatever manner the car was propelled into the lake, by being pushed, by accident, by some weird confusion with the gearshift, whatever, the crucial point is that if Brian Rubio had *not* gotten into the Corvette—in his fifth, final, fatal, decision—and had *not* used it to ram against the other car, or block it off, or whatever, we would none of us be in this courtroom today.

"At all five decisive points along the way, Brian Rubio had options, had choices, had decisions to make, actions to take. I suggest, ladies and gentlemen, that if, at any *one* of those five vital junctures, Brian Rubio had made a different choice, Polly Dunn would be alive today. Willa Hufnagle would be alive today. Any *one* of those five crucial decisions! But what is clear and undeniable from everything we have heard in this courtroom is that in each and every instance, on all five of those occasions, Brian Rubio instead made the choice that kept the clock ticking away on the last earthly moments of those lost children, until that final horrible instant when the car plunged into the dark and murky waters, and Willa Hufnagle, and Polly Dunn, breathed no more.

"I ask only for the obvious, the undeniable, the inevitable. As surely as those two unfortunate children were attacked and battered by the ramming of the defendant's automobile: guilty as charged on both counts of assault and battery. As surely as those two children are dead and gone: guilty as charged on both counts of involuntary manslaughter.

"Thank you for your attention, your dedication, your seriousness of purpose. I have every faith that you will arrive at the only verdict consistent with justice and truth."

Florian had to stand guard outside the men's room so Brian could use it without the swarming reporters and photographers crowding around him at the urinal. When he came out and Elly emerged from the ladies' room, the three of them left Wachtel to deal with the press and returned to the courtroom, where at least the bailiffs protected them. The benches were practically empty. Then Florian noticed the Hufnagle parents and family, the Dunn parents and family, again staring at them from the front row on the other side of the room. They too had probably decided to avoid the shoving and yelling outside, the endless questions. Maybe now, Florian thought, with no one around, would be the time to walk over, extend his hand, say how sorry he was.

He couldn't do it. God, this would be the worst time of all, after Delehanty had just ticked off the six million ways Brian had killed their kids.

"I think Wachtel's really well prepared," Florian said, hunching with Elly and Brian on the spectator side of the railing, hardly knowing what he was saying or, given the way he probably looked, who he was trying to convince. "He's been waiting for this all along. He's really ready to fly." *Shut up,* he told himself. *You sound like a jerk.*

"I'm sure he is," Brian said. "He'll do fine."

Elly's mouth was thin and hard. "It's just so infuriating, the way Delehanty can get away with the things he said. Half of that stuff wasn't even proved. He was assuming away all over the place."

"He can say anything he wants in the summation," Florian said. "It's okay. So can Wachtel."

Wachtel returned along with the crowd and joined their huddle. "I won't be any longer than Delehanty," he told them, "so Ingersoll's planning to instruct the jury as soon as I finish. We're moving right along."

"Are you all set?" Florian asked. "You raring to go?"

Wachtel looked at him. "C'mon, everybody. Let's relax."

"We're relaxed," Florian said. "You're the one with the job to do."

Wachtel and Brian went through the little gate and took their seats at the defense table. The jury settled in. The judge entered through the door beneath his bench, took his seat, settled his robe, gaveled them all into their seats.

Wachtel put a reassuring hand on Brian's shoulder as he stood up. Looking as relaxed as you could possibly hope for, like someone sidling up to the Polecat bar, he leaned forward over the lectern, rested his arms on it, clasped his hands lightly. He even offered the jurors a nice, genial, easygoing smile, although none smiled back. They were as sober and intent—as serious, serious, serious—as they'd been from the first minute.

"The job of the prosecutor is very simple," Wachtel began, confiding. "It's to eliminate all reasonable doubt. The prosecutor has to prove beyond a reasonable doubt that the sum and weight of clear-cut facts show that the defendant committed each crime as charged."

Gradually his expression had turned thoughtful, and he straightened up and stepped to one side of the lectern, arms at his side. "I won't imitate my respected colleague by giving you some kind of laundry list of what may or may not have occurred, because the issue before you is very precise: what happened between those two automobiles on that ramp at the exact moment the Valiant plunged into the lake?

"Let's look at that moment, and see whether the prosecution has indeed eliminated any and all reasonable doubt. Let's look for facts, for direct and specific testimony. Let's not be distracted by flimsy assumptions and unproved speculations.

"Of the several witnesses who observed that crucial moment, some say the Valiant seemed to leap forward under its own power. Others say they *think,* or *assume,* that the Corvette pushed it—although not a single person claims to have seen the Corvette lurch forward, or bounce or rock backward, as it surely must have if it provided the force that propelled the other car. And the oldest and only *neutral* witness at the scene, the college student from out of the county, stated categorically that the Corvette did *not* lurch forward or bounce backward.

"We must, ladies and gentlemen, give that impartial, objective, and factual testimony the weight it deserves.

"This college student was close by, and watching intently. Unlike the other witnesses on the ramp, he was not involved in any fight or melee at the time. He was not hectic and confused. He was not bruised or injured or breathless. He was not angry at anyone. Therefore, when he says that the Corvette did not rock back or forth—as it surely would have if it had rammed the other car into the lake—we must pay heed to that testimony.

"And if we pay that heed, ladies and gentlemen, we are already faced with a huge, unresolved *lulu* of a doubt, serious enough to throw the prosecution's whole case right out the window."

Wachtel's voice seemed to Florian to have deepened. He sounded more confident, more decisive, as if, damn it all, he not only expected people to listen but to accept the absolute, unquestioned, obvious truth of every word he spoke. (Unless, of course, Florian was wishing it so.) Beyond that, he saw little change. Wachtel had hardly grown in stature, did not gesture or move about. He stood, leaning slightly to the left in his unremarkable courtroom suit at approximately the same distance from the middle of the jury box as he had earlier positioned himself from the witness stand.

"But we have more doubts. We have, in fact, a *series* of doubts, brought on by a *slew* of conflicting and contradictory testimony, leaving us with a whole *jungle* of confusion and uncertainty.

"Do we really know what happened after midnight on that ill-lit boat ramp, amid all that commotion and chaos? I say we do not.

"Are we full of reasonable doubt? I say we are.

"Can we possibly convict on this basis? My God, how can we? How dare we?

"Let us carefully consider the testimony of the scientist from the police laboratory who inspected the Valiant, who found the gearshift in neutral. Now, would someone desperately trying to keep his car from being pushed over the edge put it in neutral? Of course he wouldn't. What he'd do, besides slamming his foot on the brake, would be to put it in reverse. Indeed, that same impartial uninvolved college student from Cornell testified that the cars were *banging back and forth against each other,* in which case the Valiant's gear would *have* to be in reverse, and nothing short of a bulldozer could have overcome the resistance of the brake plus the reverse gearing to propel it forward.

"The prosecution wants us to believe that the Valiant was pushed into the lake—*without* significant damage to either car. Let us recall that no damage was found to either bumper. Let us recall that no damage was discovered to the transmission of the Valiant.

"On the basis of all this, not only is it not proven that the car was pushed into the lake, but it seems impossible that it *could* have been. Of course, we can't prove it wasn't pushed, any more than the prosecutor can prove it was. But it is his responsibility to establish proof beyond reasonable doubt, and certainly, given these facts, we must conclude that he simply has not done so.

"How could the Valiant had gone into the lake then? Let's look at one possible explanation, which I believe you will find more convincing by far than the flimsy, indeed incredible, scenario the prosecution wants you to believe.

"Remember, Jamie Pitt was in the car first. He then got out to join his friends in forcibly dragging Brian Rubio from his car, but conveniently does not remember, he claims, what gear the car was in. At this point Polly Dunn got into the car and then, according to Jamie Pitt, pulled Willa Hufnagle in after him. All witnesses agree these events occurred within a very brief period of time, amidst a wild melee of yelling and screaming and fighting. Would Polly, behind the wheel of a strange car and with his now-reclaimed girlfriend beside him, in the midst of all the chaos going on around them, be composed enough to dutifully check the placement of the gearshift? Perhaps it's conceivable. Perhaps it's even possible. But likely? Proven beyond any doubt?"

With a surprising snort, Wachtel headed briskly, again with that funny hitch, to the defense table to pick up a large white poster board. He placed it on the easel next to the lectern.

"I can't see it," the judge said, and Wachtel held it up for him. After a few moments, Ingersoll said, "You're not introducing this as evidence, I take it?"

"Illustrative only, Your Honor."

"Proceed."

Wachtel placed it back on the easel, so that it could be seen by the jury and most of the spectators, including Florian:

P R N D L LL

"Most of us, I think, recognize the standard automatic gearing configuration. Let us for the moment assume that Jamie Pitt had left the shift in reverse, by far the most likely possibility."

With a black crayon he lightly sketched a line from the bottom center of the chart to the *R*. "Suppose now, in the confusion of the moment, Polly Dunn assumed that the car had been left in park. But he would, of course, want it in reverse, either to bang against the Corvette, or to back away and leave if the Corvette got out of his way. In that case, he would have yanked on the stick to move it one setting, from park to reverse, and he probably would have yanked it hard, since it is designed not to go easily into reverse. But if the car was *already* in reverse, and you yanked on it hard, it would slide first, very easily, into neutral. Now maybe that's what happened, and it remained there, in neutral, until discovered hours and hours later by the laboratory scientist.

"But if it were yanked on hard, would it not very possibly have slid into . . . drive?"

With a red crayon, Wachtel drew a much heavier line to the *D*, noisily scratching back and forth to thicken the line.

"Unlikely? Not at all, my friends. Not in the least as unlikely as the speculations offered by the prosecution. And this is the *only* explanation consistent with the convincing, impartial testimony of the student from Cornell, who unequivocally stated that the Corvette did not lunge forward or bounce backward when the other car when off the ramp.

"And immediately after moving the shift lever, what would a rushed, fevered, angered, perhaps confused Polly Dunn do next? Surely he would have *hit the gas*. How else could that car, which Polly intended to go backward, away from the edge, have leapt forward instead and zoomed off the ramp—as our various witnesses have testified—with such acceleration that its front wheels *jumped* off the pavement?"

Wachtel turned from the jury and gazed at the wall above the empty witness box, as if contemplating his own question. He turned back to them with his hands spread, as if to share his own earnest puzzlement.

"But how, we may wonder, do we then account for the gearshift being found in neutral? Let's remember, first of all, that it was discovered in this position long after the Valiant had struck the water surface with considerable force, long after it had plunged beneath and hit bottom, long after after the vehicle had been raised out of the water on a crane and deposited back on the ramp, long after the police and medical technicians and whoever else had entered through the passenger door, the driver's side doors being jammed shut, and removed both bodies back through the same door by dragging them across the front seat.

"Only *after* all this does the police investigator find the gear in neutral. How could it have gotten into that position? Good heavens, ladies and gentlemen, just count all the potential times and ways in which the shift could have been moved, or bumped, or knocked, or jostled, or kicked, or whatever. And regardless of which gear it might have *been* in, we should remember that the easiest gear for a shift to be *put* in is neutral.

"All in all, therefore, we must conclude that although it is highly unlikely the shift had been in neutral when the car went in, and almost impossible that it could have been in reverse, it is more likely than anything else that it was in drive—and thus the car itself may very well have provided the force, the forward momentum, to cause it to zoom off the ramp and into the water.

"We must now consider one more aspect of this crucial split second. The prosecution would have us assume that whatever Polly Dunn did in the Valiant with the gearshift and gas pedal was all in the interest of escaping from the threat of the Trent students. Can we indeed assume that? Up to that point the Medway boys, we must remember, willfully engaged the Trent boys in battle on several occasions, including the present occasion, when they returned to the ramp to discover the Trent students waiting for them. True, the Valiant had been blocked off. But did the Medway students not have the option to run away, to hide, to call the police, to come back at some later time to reclaim their car?

"Instead, the Medway boys stayed to fight. They were willing to take their chances. They wanted to have it out, as they'd wanted to all evening. They were itching for a real teenage knock-down drag-out street fight. Would the Medway boys have so decided if they had known it would result in two deaths? Of course not. Would the Trent boys? Of course not.

"You have been asked by the prosecution to blame Brian Rubio— and only Brian Rubio—for all the actions that took place between these two groups of boys. Is that something a reasonable, thoughtful person can honestly do? I ask you, while deliberating over the testimony of this trial, to acknowledge the obvious fact that Brian Rubio was not the only boy to make decisions, to take actions, during the course of events on the ramp, nor were his earlier actions the sole reason both groups of boys found themselves on the ramp that night. After all, the Medway boys had spent a good part of the afternoon and evening accosting, threatening, beating up, and chasing Brian Rubio, with or without his date present.

"Yet the prosecution implores us to believe that the motivations of the Medway boys and the other Trent boys on the ramp, and indeed throughout the whole afternoon and evening, were absolutely pure and peaceful and nonthreatening, that throughout the whole day and evening only Brian Rubio behaved in a manner that was aggressive and threatening and, indeed, criminal.

"Would not reasonable and intelligent men and women reject this as preposterous, making the prosecution's case so biased and lopsided as to defy belief?"

The big poster illustrating the gearshift positions still stood on the easel, and Wachtel paused at this point to walk over to it, study it briefly, return it to the defense table, walk back to the same spot next to the lectern to face the jurors, all of whom seemed intently caught up in his every move.

"I have discussed the many statements and claims and assumptions made in the summation by the prosecution. Now I wish to call to your attention two vital words that are nowhere to be found in the prosecution's summation: Jamie Pitt.

"Is it not strange that the chief witness called by the prosecution, the witness who spent by far the longest time on the stand, the witness whose testimony goes to the heart and soul of the prosecution's case— that this person is not even *mentioned* in the summation, nor, for that matter, is his testimony?

"I would say it is very strange, but perhaps the prosecution has its reasons for now trying to hide Jamie Pitt and his testimony under a barrel.

"Jamie Pitt, ladies and gentlemen, came in here and lied to you. You heard these lies with your own ears, and in the transcript we have these lies in black and white. In some cases, the lies were shown up by other witnesses. In some cases, they were shown by Jamie Pitt himself.

"Jamie Pitt said on one day that he did not know how Willa Hufnagle got into the Valiant. On the next day he said she was pulled in by Polly Dunn.

"Jamie Pitt said he had no intention at any point of harming Brian Rubio, yet his own friends testified that he arranged an ambush at the boatyard with the intention of ganging up on Brian Rubio.

"Jamie Pitt said he stopped his friends from chasing after the naked girl at Nanny Point, yet his own friends testified that they stopped *him*, because they were afraid of what he might do to her.

"Jamie Pitt said he talked his friends out of using the speedboat to buzz Brian Rubio as he swam out to rescue his canoe and his clothes, yet his friends testified that he was at the wheel of this boat that he had so casually *borrowed* from his workplace and therefore not only joined in the fun but was actually in charge of it.

"Perhaps most important of all, in light of subsequent events, Jamie Pitt clearly and loudly sat before you and denied having seen a certain young woman on the day before the MORP, yet his friend testified that he drove Jamie to a rendezvous with her, that Jamie got the young lady into the car against her wishes and drove around with her for a considerable length of time, and that this young woman was to be the MORP date on the following evening of Brian Rubio.

"Of course, we don't know Jamie's full and exact purpose in surprising his ex-girlfriend as she rode along on her bike, because he denied that this meeting ever took place, but common sense surely tells us he did not seek her out and pull her into that car to congratulate her on her choice of an escort for the following evening.

"I would suggest that from that moment on, through the attempted ambush the next afternoon at the boatyard, through the attack upon the Trent cars at Tiny Arkins's house, through the encounter with Brian Rubio and his date at Nanny Point, through the confrontation between the two groups of boys on the ramp, that throughout all these events, Jamie Pitt was driven by anger and rage and jealousy to hurt Brian Rubio in any way he could.

"And then to come in here and lie about it.

"Hardly an objective witness under any circumstances, Jamie Pitt had the best reason in the world to withhold information, to distort information, to twist and mold and shape his testimony. He wanted to convince you that he was the victim, the peacemaker, the one person in all of Mt. Early County filled with goodwill and decent intentions on that fateful day and night.

"Can anyone actually believe that?

"Dare we convict Brian Rubio on the basis of the testimony of this rejected suitor, this fellow infuriated at Brian Rubio for having, to his way of thinking, stolen away his girlfriend? Can we possibly take anything Jamie Pitt says as honest and objective and unbiased? Jamie Pitt *hated* Brian Rubio, as shown again and again during the whole of that day and evening by his unrelenting attempts to harm him. And that unreasoning hatred explains every spiteful and misleading and deceitful word of Jamie Pitt's testimony.

"Now, the prosecution has asserted that it is not out to convict Brian Rubio, that it merely wishes to see justice done. Ladies and gentlemen, let us all agree that our goal is to see justice done. Let us not convict a good and decent and innocent youngster caught up in some stupid teenage rumble that got wildly out of hand.

"I must address a delicate point. We all feel a deep and abiding pain over the tragic deaths of Willa Hufnagle and Polly Dunn. How anxious we all are to sympathize with them, to give them every benefit of the doubt. But we must deal first and ultimately with truth, ladies and gentlemen, because only the truth can lead us to our sworn goal of justice and fairness. We mourn deeply their untimely deaths. There is not a man or woman within a hundred miles of here who does not wish them back alive. But we must not take out our anger and frustration on Brian Rubio. It was not Brian Rubio's fault that those two youngsters are dead and he is alive. Because he survived does not make him guilty. Because the prosecutor claims that his motives and actions were criminal does not make them so. The prosecutor had the absolute necessity of *proving* his assertions, and he has not done so.

"We know that certain Trent and certain Medway students had one or more encounters during the evening. Some were drinking; some— including Brian Rubio—were not. Some were cruising about; some were attending graduation festivities. Many engaged in harassment, in fisticuffs, in provocations of various sorts. Many, from both schools, seemed at various times to be *looking* for trouble.

"Do I defend the Trent students? I do not. Do I defend the Medway students? I do not. Do I view any of this as *typical* behavior by our fine young students of Trent and Medway High? Of course I do not."

A numbness had settled over Florian. You sat and you listened. You felt eerily disembodied. By what rule of God or man did your son's life spiral down to some stranger spouting words at a roomful of other strangers, to be silently, effortlessly, tapped into a little machine by a court stenographer?

"The prosecution, in a farfetched attempt to interconnect everything, has labored mightily to have you believe that the drownings would not have occurred if Brian Rubio, alone of all the Trent and Medway boys and girls, had not done *everything* he is said to have done on the ramp that night.

"Only Brian Rubio? Particularly Brian Rubio? Even the most casual review of the testimony will indicate beyond a doubt that Brian Rubio was far more the *victim* of assault and battery throughout the afternoon and evening than he ever was, on the ramp or anywhere else, the perpetrator of it.

"And where, ladies and gentlemen, if we accept this concept of the seamless web of interrelationships, do we stop in our Keystone Kops chase after interlocking actions? Why confine ourselves just to the actions on the ramp, or just to that one evening and the participants thereof? Why not keep going back and back, keep spreading the net wider and wider? Why don't we say it was all caused when Brian Rubio's parents decided to allow him to attend his graduation party, or to do so in his father's Corvette? Or, before that, to enroll him in Trent High School? Or, ultimately, to have conceived and given him birth?

"Why not blame the county commissioners because the four-and-a-half-inch bump was a woefully insufficient and unsafe barrier—as they have admitted by having since replaced it with a metal fence? Why not blame the Fischel State Park authorities for knowingly allowing Nanny Point to be used after closing time for provocative and questionable activities? Why not blame the owner of the boatyard for not taking proper precautions to keep a part-time employee of high school age from so easily *borrowing* a speedboat whenever he felt like cruising around the lake looking for trouble?

"There is no end, ladies and gentlemen, to this wild-goose chase of connection, connection, connection. Do we dare go back to the Pilgrims, the Founding Fathers, to Adam and Eve?

"Ladies and gentlemen, Brian Rubio did not *cause* the tragic deaths of those two youngsters.

"To say that he did flies in the face of logic and common sense. It flies in the face of justice and morality. And it certainly flies in the face of the testimony that we have received during this trial.

"Not only did Brian Rubio not *cause* those deaths, but as the prosecutor generously admits, and I thank him for that admission, he never at any time *intended* to cause those deaths. In his conduct throughout that evening, Brian Rubio showed no more or less judgment, no more or less common sense, no more or less moral culpability, than any of a dozen other young men of his age and experience.

"I believe the law is fair, and just, and noble. Above all, I believe the law is moral. Therefore I am confident that if the law be served, if justice be served, Brian Rubio will not be convicted of any crime because he did not commit any crime.

"The drownings were tragic, they were terrible, and everyone in any way involved, including all of us here, will bear the scars of that moment for the rest of our lives. But those drownings were not a crime. Those drownings defy all our attempts to believe that life is rational and fair and good. Those drownings tear at our hearts and souls.

"But those drownings, ladies and gentlement, were an accident, and Brian Rubio is innocent. To find otherwise would be a corruption of law, of common sense, of decency and justice, of our deepest moral beliefs.

"Innocent, ladies and gentlemen. Innocent, innocent, innocent.

"I thank you for your time and attention."

Judge Ingersoll read from notes in front of him, every so often raising his eyes to the jury. His voice was dry, his pronunciation fussily precise, and he proceeded very deliberately. After explaining that it was the jury's responsibility to determine fact, his to explain the law, he read:

"There are four charges before you, each to be considered separately, two of simple assault and battery, two of involuntary manslaughter. You may find the defendant guilty or innocent on any one of these indictments, or any combination thereof.

"I charge you that assault and battery is a not a felony but a misdemeanor. Under the statutes there are two classes of crimes, felonies and misdemeanors, differing as to the severity of the penalties that may be imposed. A misdemeanor is the less serious crime, and therefore liable to a less serious penalty.

"Simple assault is any attempt to use violence with the intent and the ability to do bodily harm to another person. Battery pertains to the violent act being consummated. For example, if a person swings a fist in attempting to injure someone, that is simple assault. If the punch lands, thus realizing the threat, that is battery.

"The more serious charge you must decide is involuntary manslaughter, which is a felony and thereby punishable by a more serious penalty. For involuntary manslaughter to occur, there must, first of all, be the *un*intentional killing of a person. In addition, either of the following circumstances must apply. One, the killing occurred while the defendant was committing an unlawful act that was not a felony, that in other words was a misdemeanor. (If the unlawful act *were* a felony, the charge would be felony murder, which does not apply here and therefore is of no consequence.) Or, two, the killing occurred while the defendant was committing a *lawful* act, but in such a reckless and wanton manner as to make the death probable.

"When we speak of committing a lawful act in a reckless or wanton way, we mean that the act is committed with unjustifiable disregard of the probable harmful consequences of that act.

"Thus you must decide whether the defendant's actions, either through the commission of a misdemeanor, or of a lawful act in a reckless or wanton manner, were the *proximate cause* of the death of Willa Hufnagle and/or Polly Dunn.

"Now, with a charge of involuntary manslaughter, it does not have to be established that the actions of the defendant were the *direct and immediate* cause of death, or the sole cause of death. They need only be the *proximate* cause. Intervening acts or other causes do not exclude the responsibility of one who is the proximate cause. Proximate cause is the efficient cause, the cause which in a natural and continuous sequence produces the event without which the death would not have occurred.

"In another way, proximate cause can be defined as the cause that necessarily sets in operation the factors which caused the death or deaths in question.

"You must also distinguish between an act or several acts on the part of the defendant that are purely accidental, and an act or acts that signify intentional conduct on his part. A purely accidental act that results in the death of a person would not be manslaughter. But an intentional act, either a misdemeanor or a lawful act of a wanton or reckless nature, that sets in motion a continuous chain of events resulting in an accidental death, would be manslaughter."

My God, Florian thought, *all he's done is give them nineteen different ways of finding Brian guilty.*

The judge directed the jurors to be sequestered overnight but said he did not expect them to begin their deliberations until the morning.

16

The judge disappeared, the jury filed out, and everybody else stood up, milled, chatted in undertones. Wachtel straightened some papers and slid them into his briefcase, then came over with Brian to the railing, nodding to Flo, to Elly. Elly was pretty close to tears. Florian put his arm around her shoulders, hoping the gesture wouldn't be the final straw, the sign of how truly desperate everything was. But she held up okay, sort of leaning against him. He was hoping he'd hold up, too. At least Brian looked all right. In fact, when you considered what he'd been going through, Brian looked absolutely great. Maybe he was just feeling blessed at having been spared the ordeal of testifying. Still, the last thing the kid needed just then was both his parents crumbling in front of him.

"I sure hope you're right about that jury," Florian said. "I sure hope they're a bunch of certified Einsteins."

"Did you have trouble following the judge's instructions?"

"What, a guy with my brains? I'm just worried about them."

"They'll have all night to mull everything over. And so, of course, will we."

"We're gonna grab some dinner," Florian said. "Want to join us?"

"Love to, but I got things to tie up here first. We'll see you in the morning, okay?" He was looking at Florian. "Well," he said finally, "how'd I do?"

"You did okay," Florian said. "Better than okay."

"Yeah," Brian added. "I thought you were terrific."

Wachtel nodded. "I thought Delehanty was too."

"So did I," Florian said.

"I guess we'll find out eventually how terrific everybody was," Elly said.

The Roost wasn't fancy but featured a decent barbecue that Brian liked. Besides, the owner was a friend who'd promised, when Florian called earlier, to set them up where no one'd bother them. It wasn't exactly a private room, but an area with a table closed off by a low wall and sliding dividers.

Elly hardly touched anything. Brian ate his way through the Big Farmer Spread, half a barbecued chicken with a slab of ham and salad and potatoes and peas and biscuits and coleslaw and pickles and desert and a bottomless Coke from the help-yourself dispenser. Florian went with the standard barbecue chicken and did his best to look interested. He didn't want Brian thinking he was too worried to eat. He also had a couple of beers. Elly said she was surprised at how big the glass of white wine was, but she finished it.

"What do you think Wachtel's doing back there?" she asked.

"Maybe conferring with his worthy opponent," Florian said, "or the judge, or Harry Diggs, or getting some client off the hook for purse snatching. Christ knows what lawyers do. Maybe he's taking advantage of happy hour to belly up to a bar somewhere for a few quick snoots."

"I just hope the jury stayed awake through all that today. I hope they could at least follow what Wachtel was trying to say."

"Wachtel says you can never tell," Brian offered, after a big gulp of his soda. "He says there's no way of predicting."

Elly shook her head in exasperation. "Why doesn't he ever say anything specific and helpful? Why is he always so vague?"

Brian looked up from the barbecue-slathered drumstick in his hand. "How would you people vote?"

Neither responded.

"You sat through it all," Brian went on. "You heard Delehanty and Wachtel. You heard the judge."

"I had trouble with the judge," Florian said.

"You didn't really," Brian said. "It wasn't that complicated. Anyhow, just forget I'm your son or anything. If you were some secretary or mechanic on the jury, how would you see it?"

"How are we supposed to forget you're our son?" Florian said.

Brian still spoke evenly. "Just try to be impartial. What do you think? How'd it hit you?" He picked up a biscuit and twisted off a piece. "Would you send me away?"

Elly broke then.

"I'm sorry," Brian said, reaching across the table to his mother.

It took her a bit to stop choking. "It's not what you think, really," she said. "It's just somehow thinking of having to come tomorrow and sit around like a bunch of ninnies while all those people decide what they want to do with your life."

Brian lowered his eyes, slowly drawing a breath, and Florian could tell he was still waiting for an answer to his question.

"If I'm some mechanic on the jury," Florian said, "all I can go on is what I heard in there. You're asking us to forget everything we heard from you on that tape, everything we've talked about with Wachtel."

"Try," Brian said.

"If I'm sitting in there dealing with the evidence—innocent. No question in the world."

"You really think so?"

"Of course I do. Wachtel undercut their whole case by destroying Jamie—all those lies under oath."

"He also did a good job on the gearshift," Elly said. She clearly had little heart for the game but didn't want Brian thinking she couldn't find *anything* encouraging to say. "Why on earth would it be in neutral, for God's sake?"

"So—innocent," Florian said. "I couldn't tell *proximate cause* from a rat's ass, but Wachtel was absolutely right: you were the *victim* of assault and battery, starting that afternoon at the boatyard and going right through the whole night. Hell, if Delehanty wants to keep going back connecting everything to everything else, then *they* were involved in a crime when those kids died, because Jamie Pitt started the whole thing and kept it going and did more assaulting and battering than anyone, right up to the minute they died. And if you want to know who I think the next most responsible person is, it's that goddamn Tiny Arkins."

Florian had gotten pretty worked up, although he kept his voice low because he didn't want to be booming out past the dividers. What he sounded like, he figured, was intense. Brian, though, listened to it all placidly, interested certainly, but at the same time weighing it all—for what?—with a kind of evenhanded look. He nodded then, although he didn't seem to be agreeing with them so much as acknowledging or maybe even thanking them for their views. He put his knife and fork on his plate next to the chicken bones. "You know what Wachtel says: never count on anything."

"I'm *sure* that's what he said," Elly said.

"You done?" Florian asked, motioning toward Brian's plate. "How about dessert?"

"Sure. The chocolate cake's great here."

In the morning, in front of his white picket fence, Wachtel said that since he had no idea how long the jury would deliberate—surely a statement to delight Elly—he would arrange to get them a room in the courthouse where they wouldn't be bothered by anyone. He told them about a different entrance they could use to avoid the press people out front. "I'm still working on some things," he said, "but I'll join you as soon as I can. Or even sooner," he added, "if we get a verdict along the way."

"As early as this morning?" Elly said.

"You never know," Wachtel told her.

At ten o'clock they got in through the back door, with Florian waving away the one reporter in sight. Maybe the fellow had been tipped off, or was just trying his luck. A secretary in the bailiff's office showed them into a small anteroom. The room had shelves with lawbooks, law journals, bound copies of court proceedings, a square wood table that, along with the half dozen chairs squeezed around it, took up most of the space. A black telephone sat on the radiator in front of the one big window.

Brian got himself a Pepsi from the machine in the hall, and the secretary brought in two Styrofoam cups of coffee, pointing out the magazines on a bottom shelf. "A little out of date but feel free."

After she left, Florian dumped the magazines onto the table and the three of them sorted through the pile and picked out some, flipping pages, tossing them aside. Brian had suggested bringing along the Scrabble set, though, and they played a couple of three-handed games, with no one having much to say, until the secretary popped in at noon to say that Wachtel had called. The jury was taking its lunch break and wouldn't resume until one. He was still tied up but said they should go have something at Friendly's, on him.

"Just tell the cashier there to put it on his bill," the secretary explained.

Lunch didn't bring any great bursts of conversation either. The cashier said, "Oh, yes, Mr. Wachtel called. That'll be fine." Twenty bucks, big deal.

They returned to the room a little after one o'clock and played until Wachtel showed up an hour later.

"Sorry. How was lunch?"

They all nodded, smiled, thanked him.

"I ordered the most expensive item on the menu," Florian said, "which I think was the grilled cheese. What's happening in there?"

"You know the joke about the two-hundred-pound house cat that sits wherever it wants. Juries are eighteen-hundred-pound, twenty-four-legged beasts that sit for however long their twelve hearts desire." Wachtel checked the Scrabble board. "Hey, who got *zealot?*"

"Mom did," Brian said. "Triple on the *z.*"

"I'm impressed," Wachtel said, taking a chair directly across from Brian, with Florian to his left by the window, Elly to his right. Each had one side of the table. Wachtel clasped his hands, looking about as focused as when he'd addressed the jury. (Was it an act then, or now, or both times? Maybe everything a lawyer did was an act, part of the job.) "Something's come up," he said.

They waited for him to go on.

"Let's make sure first we've all got everything straight. Maximum for A and B is two and a half years in a house of correction, meaning the county jail over on Baxter Street. Involuntary manslaughter can get up to twenty in the state prison out at Parsons." He waited, but they waited longer. "I've been talking to people, other lawyers, friends, and finally, very delicately, with Delehanty."

"What'd you say to Delehanty?"

"Not much. You know how it goes: he floats a red balloon, I float a blue one. A little sparring, each testing the other guy out. He didn't commit himself, and I sure didn't. But after a lot of this I came away with the distinct impression Delehanty would listen to a guilty plea on A and B." He checked their expressions. "Do all of you understand what I'm saying?"

"Two and a half in the county jail," Florian said.

"Maximum two and a half. It could be less. But it eliminates any chance of twenty, of any time at all in the state pen. Now Baxter Street ain't great. It's crummy. It's crowded and dirty and no fun at all. But it's a lot easier than Parsons. You could also say, and I don't mean this as a joke, I'm serious, that the jail attracts a better crowd. Younger, less hardened. It figures, right? They're in for less serious crimes. The really bad guys are out at Parsons."

"You want us to take this deal, don't you?" Elly said flatly.

"I want you to understand the options and possibilities and consequences. I haven't asked anybody to say yes or no, and I won't. Believe me, this is your baby. I'm just doing everything I can to make sure you people understand everything you have to understand."

"Keep going then," Florian said.

"The judge would naturally have to agree. But I think he would."

"You've talked to him?"

"Let's not worry who I did or didn't talk to. Remember, no one's made any promises. No contracts have been signed. I'm just giving you my best sense of how things might go if we pursued this option."

"The only reason for Delehanty to go along," Florian said, "would be that he doesn't think he can get manslaughter."

"I wouldn't put it that strongly. But sure, no one makes deals if they're supremely confident of getting exactly what they want, and with all due modesty, I think we put a few dents in his armor along the way. Maybe he now feels he's only got a fifty-fifty shot at manslaughter. Maybe he's a half-a-loaf guy who'd rather take a sure thing on A and B."

"What about you?" Florian continued. "The only reason you'd go along is you're afraid he *will* get manslaughter."

"Again you overstate. I don't know what the chances are on manslaughter, but there *is* a chance. The judge didn't throw it out, did he? I turned myself inside out trying to knock holes in that proximate cause crap, but who knows, maybe the jury'll buy it."

"Anything else you'd like to pass on?"

"What I'd like to do now is leave, so you can talk this out yourselves. Last point: the minute the jury sends word that they've got a verdict, the deal's off. So that's your deadline."

"Only we don't know when that'll happen."

"Right. Can I leave now?"

"You must have *some* idea how scared Delehanty is, how anxious he is to make a deal."

"Look, it's always wise to assume that your worthy opponent is at least as smart as you are. I was very careful not to tip my hand, and so, with equal skill, was Delehanty. That's why everything took so long. It's a delicate process. No sledgehammers."

"You've got to have a better sense of our chances than you're letting on. Maybe with us you could take out the sledgehammer. Where do you think we stand with that goddamn jury?"

"Jesus, Flo, what you're asking me is how well *I* think *I* did. Well, sure, I'd like to believe I punched Delehanty silly, I'd like to believe I knocked him out in five. But it ain't my call. Besides, it ain't my kid. Furthermore, believe it or not, lawyers sometimes grow fond of their clients, and it's been known to cloud their judgment. Hell, if you guys don't want Brian for a son anymore, I'd take him on any day."

"We still want him," Florian said.

"I always told you you had a smart old man," Wachtel said to Brian.

"I'm calling Harry Diggs," Elly said, going to her eyes with her handkerchief.

"God, yes," Wachtel said. "Call anybody you want. Do anything you want. Ask me or anybody else anything you want. Believe me, Elly, I know what kind of hot seat I'm putting you on. But once the possibility arose, I had to present it to you, right? I couldn't take it on myself to dismiss it out of hand." He stood and gestured toward the phone on the radiator. "If Harry's not in his office, try the Mountaineer. I'll be down the hall. Let me know the absolute second you make up your minds, okay? I'd hate to have that jury come out and cut you down in mid-flight."

As the door closed behind him, Elly took out her light blue address book. "I only have his office number."

"The secretary will know where he is."

"He might even *be* there, you know. I mean, he makes a living at it."

"Diggs ain't exactly impartial either," Florian said. "If we take A and B, there's a damn good chance he can get Tiny Arkins and the others off with a slap on the wrist."

"I'll bear that in mind," Elly said, moving for the phone.

Florian stood too, causing her to glare across the table at him. "I'm listening in," he said.

"Oh, great. Goddamn fucking great. You hate Harry Diggs's guts. You haven't forgiven him for helping me out ten years ago and have never in your life said a single lousy word without knocking him, without making fun of him, and now you want to hear what he has to say. I mean, really—listening to a big fat sloppy pansy like that? Do you really think Harry Diggs could ever possibly have anything to say worth listening to?"

Florian took a breath. "Okay, you're right. You're one hundred percent right. But I'm listening. If you were calling the town idiot, I'd want to listen."

Elly twisted away and dialed, facing out the window. "This is Elly Rubio. Is Mr. Diggs available? Thank you very much." She gave Florian a kiss-off look and stretched the coiled phone line as she leaned back against the edge of the table. Florian stood next to her, bending down a little to get his ear close to the phone. Making another face, she relented by angling it slightly toward him.

"Elly, dear! How are you doing up there? I can just imagine the strain."

"Flo's listening in," she said. "Wachtel says we can cop a plea if we're willing to take assault and battery."

"I know. We discussed it."

"Sure," Florian said. "Everybody's in cahoots with everybody."

"What?"

"Florian's muttering. It's his favorite method of communication. We have to decide before the jury sends word out. Wachtel keeps saying it's up to us but I think he wants us to take it. What do you think, Harry? I mean, how on earth are we supposed to know what to do?"

Harry was a long time answering. "You want my advice, is that it?"

"Of course I want your advice. What do you think I'm calling for? You've followed the trial. You know what's going on."

"I haven't heard today's summations. I haven't heard the judge's charge."

"Look, Harry, the summations were terrific. I mean, really entertaining and full of all kinds of snappy one-liners. The judge's charge was marvelous. What in Christ's name do you think we should do?"

"I can't possibly make this decision for you."

"You can give us some goddamn advice. When Wachtel talked this over with you, what advice did you give him?"

"We only discussed what transpired between him and the prosecutor. We agreed that Delehanty was serious, that the deal was on if you wanted it."

"C'mon, Harry—should we take it or not?"

"Look into your boy's eyes, Elly. Look into your own heart. See if you can't once more, in this very special situation, reach out to Florian."

"You're not helping."

"Believe me, dear, I'm doing my very best. The boy himself—what does he say?"

Elly frowned, then glanced back over her shoulder. "Actually, none of us have said anything yet. We're trying to think it through."

"Speak to Brian, my dear. Do it now. It's his life, right? God bless you all."

Still sitting over the Scrabble board, Brian looked up, somewhat quizzically, when they turned to him. "Well, what did he say?"

"He said it's up to us," Elly said. "Especially you."

"What do you think?" Florian asked him.

Brian had taken one of his Scrabble tiles—a *K*, worth five points— and was moving it in a little circle on the table with his index finger. "You both want me to take the deal, don't you?"

"I'm not sure," Florian said. "But state prison scares me to death. Twenty years scares me to death."

"It *would* be less risky," Elly said. "And even if the judge gave you the whole two and a half years, what with good behavior and parole and everything you'd be out a lot sooner than that. And it'd be all over then. It'd be behind you. You could get on with your life."

"Both of you said you'd have voted innocent."

"We're not talking about how we'd vote," Florian said. "We're talking about that brilliant jury in there."

"So you want me to play it safe—right, Dad?"

Florian couldn't speak at first. Then he said, "Brian, I'm scared. I've never been so scared in my whole life."

"If it was you, you wouldn't play it safe."

"It's not me."

"What we never got to last night was how you'd vote based on what you know about what really happened? The tape and all. Everything else."

"Jesus," Elly said. "No more games, please."

"Even you don't know what really happened," Florian said. "Do you know what gear the car was in? Do you know what Jamie really did in the woods to Nique? Do you even know why Polly dragged Willa into the goddamn car after him?"

Brian wrinkled his eyes. "I thought Mr. Wachtel played you the tape."

"The key parts, I guess. He said the whole thing went on for hours. Look, the jury could be coming out any minute."

"I know why Polly dragged Willa into that car."

"All right, I guess we do too. He used to go with her, she was his ex-girlfriend, whatever. Christ, the same thing as Jamie and Nique. All these goddamn—"

"Polly never went with Willa. He knew her, though, because they lived right near each other and his little sister and Willa were best friends, so he saw her around a lot, like he was her big brother or whatever. In fact, it was the sister who told Polly why Tiny asked her to the MORP."

Florian realized that if he felt any colder, he'd be shivering. His skin could have iced over. He was also aware of how exhausted he was, and spoke with a kind of awful resignation. "Okay, tell us—why did Tiny Arkins ask a thirteen-year-old girl from Medway to the goddamn MORP?"

"I thought Wachtel played this for you on the tape. I wish he had. Anyhow, Tiny invited her because even though he wasn't really ugly or anything, he somehow never has had much luck with girls. The guys kid him about it all the time, and when he had trouble getting a date for the MORP, the guys said he probably couldn't even get Willa Hufnagle to go with him."

"Why her? How did they even know who she was? She was thirteen years old."

"I mean, what am I supposed to say? She's dead. But she had a reputation of being, you know, very easy. God knows how many guys said—" He shrugged. "Sure, maybe some were just bragging, but that was what you heard about her. Even if Tiny could get her to go, everybody said, they'd be willing to bet he couldn't score, even with her, and so that was the deal. He had to get the date first; then he had to get her in the bedroom at his house, during the party, and prove it by letting everybody come in and see."

"Oh, my God," Elly said.

"I really didn't go along on all that, but I didn't exactly try to stop it either, so what difference does it make? I went along on the rest. Anyhow, Willa said yes when Tiny asked her, but what the jerk does then is worry that if the guys come barging in when he's with her, she'll have a fit or make a stink or something, so he tells her he'd really like to make it with her at the party, but with all these other people around maybe someone'll come barging in by accident. She says that wouldn't bother her at all. According to Tiny, she actually got a kick out of the idea."

"And told her best girlfriend," Florian said, "who happened to be Polly's sister, who then told Polly, who ended up pulling her into the Valiant to get her away from Tiny."

"From everybody. From all of us."

"Jesus," Florian said.

"I've never heard anything so callous in my life," Elly said.

"Mom, I don't have a single solitary argument in the world against that. Anyhow, you wanted me to say how I feel about going along on the plea. Well, I'm not going along. From the beginning, what I wanted to do was just go in and testify and tell them everything and let them do what they wanted with me. Mr. Wachtel talked me out of that, and I'm still not sure I should have let him. But I did. Maybe I was just being a coward. But he also said how rough it would be on Willa's family, on Tiny's family—and on you guys too, so I said all right. Only now I'm not going to say all right. I wouldn't take any kind of deal now, for anything, because no one can say I could hurt anyone else by what I did. The only one I could possibly hurt would be me. You know how it goes—Dad, Mom. I'm not asking anybody for favors."

"It wouldn't be a favor," Florian said. "It'd be a deal, a mutual agreement."

"No more deals, Dad. I was hoping you'd both understand. I was hoping it'd be obvious."

"Can't you see that what the jury comes up with has nothing to do with guilt or innocence? You're putting your life in the hands of some insane bureaucratic process. The judge might just as well be sitting up there in a powdered wig for all any of it has to do with the real world. And those jurors—are those the people you want deciding anything? Suppose they nodded off, or just weren't listening? Suppose they feel sorry for the kids that died? Suppose they hate you and everybody else from Trent?"

"It's such a terrible risk," Elly said.

Brian frowned, looking at one, then the other. "You said before that if I took the deal, at least it'd be all over. Only it wouldn't. It'd never be over. Whatever I did that night, I did, and the only way I'll get out from under it is by letting the jury decide what I deserve to have done to me because of what I did. If they say I'm clear, I'm clear. If they say it was my fault, then okay, the judge will decide exactly how much I have to pay for being at fault. And I'll do it, I'll pay, and *then* it'll be over. I'll be even up—except, I guess, for all the things the judge and jury don't even know about."

Florian gave it one more shot. "I just want to make sure that you really understand the chance you're taking."

"It's not that complicated, Dad. Maybe you should tell Mr. Wachtel now, so he's not just fretting and stewing."

"Let's all go tell him," Florian said.

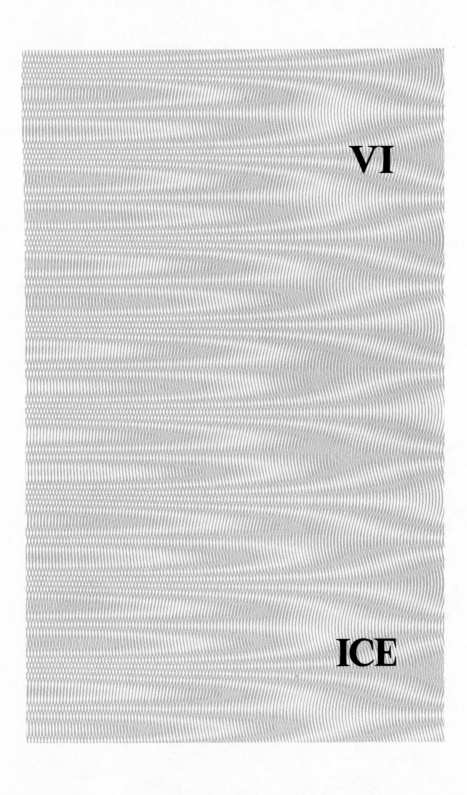

VI

ICE

17

When Lucille died from a second stroke early in December, the keeper gave Brian a pass to attend the services. He was just a few weeks shy of being eligible for weekend passes anyhow, and the keeper's main concern was that it be handled quietly. "Hey," he said to Florian over the phone, "we don't need any more riots anywhere."

Everyone from New York came. It was like the Fourth of July but more complicated, winter clothes and boots everywhere, the house more crowded with kids unable to sleep on the lawn or deck, apportioned through all the rooms with their blankets and pillows and sleeping bags. Most of the family hadn't seen Brian since he was a little kid back in New York. How tall, they kept saying. What a good-looking boy. How nice. How polite and well behaved. They let him out, without stripes or anything? Without handcuffs or a policeman to watch, to stand guard?

But Christ knows they were decent toward him. Uncle Gennario hugged him. Aunt Rosa said, "Hey, you get out soon, what're you gonna do?"

"Maybe college," Brian said.

"Hey," Gennario said to Florian, "you never went to college."

"He's smarter than me."

"Pray to God," Aunt Rosa said, "that our children, they're smarter than us."

"Is that a proverb?" Florian asked.

"What proverb?" Rosa said. "What are you talking, proverb?"

"I think my problem maybe," Gennario said, "is that if you don't go to school, you never really get ridden of your Italian accent." He turned to Joyce nearby, who he'd talked with earlier, impressed that she was a schoolteacher. "Ain't that right? Ain't that what kids learn in school?"

Joyce seemed unsure how to respond, so Florian told her, "Whenever they ask if something's right, say yes."

"Yes," Joyce said.

"See," Gennario said, poking Rosa. "I told you."

Florian knew that Joyce had been a little uneasy at meeting all these strange relatives from New York, wondering how they would take to this woman who had moved in with him, sharing his house and bedroom although she was still married, but even the old folks seemed to take it in stride.

The little kids, wide-eyed, awestruck, trailed after Brian. *What do you do all day?* they wanted to know. *Could you listen to the radio? Did you have earphones? Could you watch TV?* All the kids in school back in the Bronx and Long Island and New Jersey, all their friends, were dying to hear. *If you try to escape, would they shoot you?*

Elly flew in from California. She'd loved Lucille; it was like losing her own mother, she said, but still not as bad as the trial. She was pleased to see how good Brian looked. Elly herself seemed okay too, things back on track for her.

Brian was managing pretty well, Florian assured her. Three times a week, all you were allowed, Florian and Salvatore—who'd finally allowed Florian to hire a nurse to stay with Lucille on these occasions—drove up to Baxter Street and visited Brian. On the other days, Florian played handball, ferociously, told jokes in the little room off the showers, laughed at everybody else's jokes—*All right, how do you know if your wife's cheating on you? Why do condoms come in packs of six, seven, and twelve? What did the girl say the first time she saw her husband with his pants off?*—shared some midget franks and a pitcher with the guys at Mio's.

The jury had taken three days to decide. Assault and battery, they said. Not manslaughter. Brian, standing, his face composed, hadn't reacted at all. Florian felt a vast unnerving quiver in his gut, some gigantic bird taking wing. Elly wept. Afterward she said she would have wept no matter what.

The reporters got to the jury. WHY? WHAT WAS THEIR THINKING? DID THEY BELIEVE JAMIE PITT? DID THEY THINK BRIAN RUBIO SHOULD HAVE TESTIFIED? HOW DID THE VALIANT GET INTO THE LAKE? WHAT ABOUT THE GEARSHIFT, THE PARTYING, THE NAKED GIRL AT NANNY POINT?

The chairwoman, the sixtyish housewife who, except for her confessed fondness for Peter Jennings, didn't much keep up with things, said the main problem was they were suspicious of what the Medway boys in the Valiant were trying to do. If they thought the Medway boys really wanted to get away, they would have voted for manslaughter. What they figured, though, was the Medway boys were just trying to mess up the rich kid's fancy sports car. So the boy and girl drowned, God rest their souls, and all the other Medway boys were just as much involved in troublemaking as anyone else, so you couldn't blame it all on the boy from Trent, even though he was the only one being tried.

The Jamie Pitt boy, the woman said, didn't impress them at all. If he'd been put on trial, she was sure the jury would have convicted him of something. As far as they were concerned, he stirred up things more than anyone else, including the Rubio boy, who just happened to be in the wrong place at the wrong time.

But that boy and girl did end up drowned, so they felt someone should pay for it. After all, who was there to feel sorry for them? What kind of a sentence would bring them back? After a couple of votes they all agreed to settle on assault and battery, or else they would have been there for weeks. It was just a matter, she said, of coming up with some kind of compromise that seemed reasonable, rather than the exact definition of different kinds of crimes the judge had talked about.

At the sentencing Ingersoll said he'd concluded, from the reports of probation officers and various other materials that had come to hand, that Brian Rubio was a decent young man with no record of trouble in school or with the law or in any other manner. Although like everyone else in Mt. Early County, he regretted the awful circumstances of the evening of June 20, and wished that all the young men involved had behaved more circumspectly, he did not believe an extended incarceration of Brian Rubio would serve any purpose.

Two years, but with all except six months probationary. Six months, as the newspapers pointed out, meant three and a half months. By January he'd be out.

The other three Trent boys got suspended sentences for something like mischievous behavior. Florian passed Zack Arkins on Berry Street one time, as sallow as ever, but turned away. Thinking about it afterward, he wondered how much Zack knew about his son, and Willa, and everything else. What the hell, if Tiny was Florian's kid, he'd probably feel just as good as Zack did that his son got off.

Not long after the trial, Florian and Wachtel had a drink together on the glassed-in veranda of the Hollisworth Inn, which, the season having ended weeks before, was quiet and pleasant.

"The problem was never Harry Diggs," Wachtel said. "Harry and I are friends, and I wouldn't say anything against him, but I never made one move I didn't want to make, that I hadn't planned ahead of time to make."

"Including when Harry walked out on us with his three kids?"

"Absolutely. We were much better off with Brian looking like he'd been deserted, like he was being set up to take the rap for everyone else. If somehow all four of them had been tied into the proximate cause business, the jury might have gone for manslaughter, figuring at least everybody was taking their punishment together, not just one fall guy. And sure, I kept in close touch with Harry throughout. After all, I didn't want him thinking there was any percentage in screwing us, which of course there wasn't. Anyhow, with Harry working his tail off to help Brian, what you got, Flo, was two great lawyers for the price of one."

"What was the problem then, if it wasn't Diggs?"

"The problem, Flo, was that Brian was in your car when their car went in."

"There were parts of the tape you didn't play for us."

"What tape? You mean the one that went up in fire not long after the trial ended?" Wachtel finished his drink and actually ordered a second, the first time Florian had ever seen him do that.

"It's funny," Florian said. "Joyce and I were going to get together afterward and trade versions—you know, what Nique said to her, what I heard on Brian's tape—but we never did."

"Never got together? I thought—"

"Never traded versions. I think we both felt like Brian: once the jury said its piece, that was it. Over with. Time to move on."

"What *I* don't understand, Flo, is why you've kept me on as your lawyer all these years, and why, for Christ's sake, you kept me on for Brian."

"Maybe because you're good at telling me I'm full of shit when I'm full of shit."

"I'm good at it because you give me so much practice."

"It's better than telling me what a genius I am for walking into telephone poles. Do you think if we copped that plea, Ingersoll would have given Brian less of a sentence?"

"That's not the point, is it? Brian did what he wanted to do, and now, when he's ready to start feeling good about himself again, he can. That's more important than shaving a few weeks off his sentence. It even ought to let you feel good about him."

"I do."

"I think he knows that, Flo."

After the funeral everybody came back to the house for food and drinks, to stand around and talk, to remember the old days, to recall things that Lucille had said, had done, the way she looked as a girl back in the twenties, the first time Salvatore's family had met her. "Hey," Uncle Joe said, "when we first look at Lucille, we say, *Salvatore, what's his secret? Somebody like him without even a good haircut from Mama bringing home this beautiful girl like Lucille."*

While Brian was across the room, talking to the little kids crowding around him, Salvatore, in his suit and tie, his hair neatly combed, put his arm around Joyce, bringing her close in something of a hug, and then, nodding to Brian, said, "Next month, he's out. Only I always think, what if. I always think how bad it could have been." Salvatore shrugged then, gave Joyce one of his smiles. "For Lucille, though, it wasn't so lucky. Sometimes, you know, God, He wants a bribe. He says, *You ask for something, I give it to you, but you can't have everything. You gotta pay somehow, to even things up.*"

"It's strange with Mom gone now," Florian said. "After all those years, sometimes I still feel I never knew her."

Salvatore laughed, for Joyce. "He knew her," he said. "What else we got to do all our lives, but get to know each other?"

They worked like dogs in school those first few days after the verdict was announced, with workshops every day, with earnest talk from Brownie and one of the local judges, from Red Penneman, from the Medway coaches, everybody trying to keep the kids calm, to stop anyone from starting another crazy sequence of kids chasing other kids, itching for a fight. Joyce wasn't sure whether it was the result of their efforts or not, but the Medway kids seemed to take the verdict pretty calmly. Sure, the kids wanted manslaughter; they wanted Brian in the state prison out in Parsons, serving more years than assault and battery could bring. But maybe everything in the papers and on TV, the endless coverage of the trial itself, had served some purpose. Listening to them in the class discussions the day after the sentence was announced, Joyce couldn't help feeling they'd played out their emotions, gone as far in that direction as their energies would carry them.

Meanwhile, the students at Trent, saying they'd waited until the trial was over so it wouldn't look like they were trying to influence anyone, started a collection for two scholarships at Medway High and Medway Junior High, named for Polly and Willa, and pledged to raise ten thousand dollars every year.

When the sentence was announced a couple of weeks after the trial, the Medway kids still seemed fine—until they saw on TV the riots taking place out at Parsons. The whole prison just seemed to blow up. The convicts staged sit-ins, marched in the prison yard, hung sheets from their windows, set fire to the laundry room, set fire to mattresses. If *they* had to spend however many long years in the pen for whatever they were supposed to have done, how come this rich kid, who'd killed two young poor kids, kids like themselves, that came from places like Medway, how come he got off with a few lousy months at some soft-go local jail?

Somehow, that did it. As the riot continued at Parsons, swarms of Medway kids—and grown-ups too, some pouring out of bars, men leaving wives and kids in their apartments to join crowds they could already hear, walking off their nighttime jobs, whatever—turned into mobs on the midnight streets of Medway, smashing windows at the banks and setting off incredible shrieks of alarms, smashing display windows at Lagerfield's to set off yet more alarms as they scampered off with clothes stripped from the dummies, breaking into hardware stores to steal power saws and tool kits, stealing tires from Goodyear's, running through the streets with stereos and speakers and TV sets on their shoulders, smashing car windshields on the display lot at Howland Ford.

All in Medway. Nothing in Trent. Not a rock, a shout, an echoing footfall. If anyone thought of going down to Trent, no one did. They did what rioters and looters always seemed to do in this country: they tried their best to wreck their own city, their own neighborhoods, their own blocks, all those stores and banks and shops and bars that paid taxes to their own city hall.

What shook Joyce most was the mob's descent on Medway High, smashing windows, axing blackboards, tossing chairs out of windows, torching wastebaskets and storage rooms, with the fire department luckily arriving before the place went up in smoke. Attacking a school, a public school, her own or any other, struck Joyce as unforgivable. But if they were going to burn down a school, why in the world would they pick on their own? What did that say about all the things she'd spent a good part of her life doing in that building?

A few days later the local IE bigwig deplored the riot, saying it would only encourage those who had already given up on Medway's future and discourage the very influx of businesses and industries that the city desperately needed.

A few days after the trial, before the sentence, before what the Boston papers headlined as THE MEDWAY RIOTS, Jamie Pitt showed up when she was alone in her homeroom at the end of the day's classes. He wore neat trousers, a nice sweater, a clean shirt, polished shoes. Had his moment in the spotlight left him determined to show the world a new and more sophisticated Jamie Pitt? Perhaps the clothes were simply still fresh from the trial, and before too long would come to resemble the items he usually wore.

She'd thought he'd come to talk about his testimony, or the trial in general, or even to report to his special adviser on his progress in making up the class he'd failed.

He began as if letting her in on a secret he was sure she'd be delighted to hear: "I guess it won't be that big of a surprise, but I got the boot at Hammond's."

"It's not a surprise, but I'm sorry to hear it."

"It ain't gonna be easy around here. I don't mean just right now. Everybody in the whole county knows about me taking that boat, and even though it was just that one time, it's something bosses really don't like, messing with stuff that belongs to the business. So I think I'll just let the credits go and move on somewhere."

"It'd be so much better if you finished, Jamie. No matter where you go, a high school dipl—"

"Yeah, I know. I mean, sure, you're absolutely right. Only I figure, well, with just one course I could take care of it easy enough anywhere. You know what gets me, though? I mean, Brian Rubio's gonna serve a couple of months, and everyone's gonna say, *That's it, he paid his penalty and we can all just forget the whole thing.* But he's gonna be out in January, home free, and I'll tell you, it's gonna be a whole lot of Januarys before I could even get a job sweeping floors around here."

She got so angry, so suddenly, that she realized how much she must have been holding in. "My God, Jamie—don't come whining at me. I didn't steal that boat. I didn't go after Brian and his date. I didn't spend a whole afternoon and night trying to start some crazy gang war."

He took it with surprising calm. "Anyhow, I'm leaving, Mrs. Johnway. I just wanted to say good-bye." He hesitated. "It's too bad I guess that everybody's sore at me over what happened. Only you gotta remember—I just went in and told my side of the story, whereas the other guy was afraid to tell his, so it ain't exactly all my fault that he ends up in trouble. The lawyer even got some of my own friends, you know, to come in and testify against me, but still it was the other guy, not me, that ended up in jail."

She forced herself to calm down. She wasn't even sure what it was about Jamie after all this time that so infuriated her. Maybe it was frustration, pure and simple: what on earth could you make of this kid? If you could get past all that smiling and posturing, all those glib and ingenious explanations for all the messes he'd gotten himself into and out of, what would you *find*?

"What are you going to do with yourself now?" she asked quietly, in her best teacherly tone and manner. "Where is it that you think you want to go?"

He seemed to take this as a sign that he'd won her back over, and offered her his last, his farewell smile, full of the sort of sweet confidence you'd expect from someone heading into a world filled with nothing but success and good cheer. "I'll find something. First, though, I been saving my money from Hammond's to get myself some wheels, and then, you know, I can just go wherever I want."

The four of them met for the first time in October, in Harry Diggs's office in his shambly old Victorian house. They met for the second and last time in November, in Ira Wachtel's office in downtown Medway, alongside the bank. It wasn't that she and Benn were into shouting matches. They were both, beneath an admittedly shaky surface, trying to be reasonable. Joyce simply didn't want to sit alone in a room with Benn and step by step dismantle their marriage.

A good decision, Wachtel said. He didn't do divorces but made an exception for her, partly as a favor to Florian, partly because he expected an amicable settlement, although, as he pointed out, amicable couples rarely parted.

Harry Diggs, of course, was a real pro at divorces. Joyce wasn't concerned; she wasn't asking alimony, and Benn was ready to split everything down the middle after putting aside a modest amount for his daughters. The complications arose from the Blackberry Hollow receivership, which had tied up all of Benn's money and even threatened the house and, as he said, the Sierra Sunbridge. He'd also made the mistake early on, at the first signs of trouble, of trying to bail out the project by getting yet more people to invest. Old friends were suing. State agencies were investigating. Both Diggs and Wachtel saw the whole mess, and the divorce settlement along with it, tied up in court for years.

"And, as we all know," Diggs said, "the legal process makes up for what it lacks in decisiveness by what it offers in procrastination."

"Old lawyer joke," Wachtel pointed out, and Diggs responded with a pleased nod of acknowledgment.

Benn was taking it hard—not losing her, she suspected, but losing the deal—giving Joyce another reason for not wanting to keep seeing him. She couldn't bear the hurt in his face, couldn't take that lost, hopeless voice. Even watching all that money vanish before his eyes wouldn't have been so bad for Benn if he hadn't dragged others down with him, none of whom seemed eager to forgive him. It was all over the papers, and the gossip in town was even worse, especially among those whose admiration had always been so comforting to Benn, and so easy to earn.

Benn still consulted, still traveled around to the clothing manufacturers, and Joyce was glad for that, although she really didn't know how well it was going. Would bad news travel that far and hurt him in Chicago, in California, in New York and Atlanta? She hoped not.

They'd last met a few weeks ago in the middle of Elderberry Street, by accident, when she'd gone with Florian to pick up his new car. A week or so earlier, Florian's friend the police chief showed up at the door with the Corvette, tossing the keys. "Have a nice ride."

"I don't even want to look at it," Florian told him, tossing them back. "Look, I owe you a couple of favors. Just keep it. It's yours."

"Not on a bet," Penneman said.

"Then drop it off at Rob's Mobil for me, okay? Tell him to ship it to Peru or Saudi Arabia and find me something else."

And so, in early December, Joyce accompanied Florian into downtown Trent to turn in the car Florian had been driving since the drownings. She'd always felt it was nice and roomy, but he'd never liked it. "Rob found me a great old Thunderbird," he said. "Not exactly a Corvette but no Fairlane either."

"As long as you like it," she said, feeling pretty vague about the differences.

That's when they met Benn, as they were about to walk into Rob's. He was alone—walking to Harry Diggs's office? to another session with an outraged creditor? to the bank to see Bob Crawford, who was much involved in helping Benn survive because the bank was much involved in Benn's difficulties?—and she was on Florian's arm. Snow was falling, and that gave the scene a strange, Dickensian quality, the three of them on the sidewalk, no one quite ready to say, *Let's all get inside somewhere for a cup of hot chocolate,* their winter coats and hats turning gray, then white, Joyce holding tight to Florian and everyone trying at least to be polite on that almost deserted street.

"I hear from Harry you people are heading off for a week or so," Benn said.

"Our winter break's in February," Joyce said, "and we're looking for sun."

"St. Martin's," Florian said. "Brian's due out next week, so it'll be our delayed celebration. I'm not sure yet what he's doing for his."

"I'm glad he got through okay," Benn said. "I wish him all the luck in the world."

"I'll tell him."

The two men waited for Joyce to say something, as if somehow it was her place to end this so they could proceed on their separate ways as gracefully as possible.

"Good luck to you too," Joyce said, then realized this was exactly the sort of thing Benn once would have jumped all over: *Of course you wish me good luck. Every buck I salvage means another fifty cents in your pocket.*

But if anything, he seemed touched, maybe even, although she certainly hadn't intended this, a little ashamed at receiving, at being grateful for, sympathy. He shook his head brusquely, at God knows what, and hurried down the street in the soft snowfall. She gave Florian's arm a squeeze, and they headed down to Rob's to pick up his great new, or old, car, and drive off in it.

Right after the first of the year Florian decided it was now or never. All along he'd been stalling, coming up with reasons why it was a bad idea, convincing himself how much better it'd be if he just let a little more time elapse. But on January 10 Brian would be out and that, Florian felt, was the deadline.

He called the Hufnagle number and got the father. "I'd really like to come by and see you. I know how long it's been, but if it's at all possible, if it wouldn't be too much of a strain . . ."

Desperately, during the long silence that followed, Florian hoped the man would say, *Stay away, it'd be too unpleasant, too painful, goodbye.* But what he heard was, "Are you seeing the Dunns too?"

"Oh, yes. Of course. I just haven't called them yet."

Again a silence, as if the man was weighing every word—which he probably was. God knows Florian was.

"Well, we're neighbors, you know, good friends. Maybe we could have them over, and you could see us all together. Our families have always been close. You know, the kids and all were friends."

"Well, sure, if that's okay. That'd be fine."

"I'm not sure we can manage a dinner or anything. The place is really pretty small."

"Oh, no," Florian said quickly, frantically. "No dinner, nothing like that. And any day, any time of day, would be fine. You name it and I'll be there."

The following Tuesday Florian knocked at the first-floor apartment in the old three-decker, about a mile from the IE plants, at exactly five-thirty—before dinner but giving both Hufnagles and Mr. Dunn, all of whom worked, time to get home and get ready. Get dressed: the women wore jewelry and what must have been their classiest outfits. They looked like they'd gotten their hair done too. The apartment was spotless. The men wore suits and ties. A small stack of fancy paper napkins sat on the glass coffee table.

He couldn't believe it—they were trying to impress him. There weren't even any kids around to make noise or mess things up or get in the way.

The parents seemed sad, quiet, even mournful, but not angry. They offered him a glass of sherry, Mrs. Hufnagle using a silver tray to bring out five tiny stemmed glasses with etched designs. Florian didn't think they were sherry glasses, but what the hell did he know about sherry glasses? She put out tiny tea cakes and gave everyone a napkin. Everyone sipped and ate politely, delicately, sitting on the faded furniture in a living room lit now, in the darkening evening, by a peeling brass chandelier.

They listened stiffly as he told them how much, all along, he'd been meaning to come and pay his respects, how bad he felt, how sorry he was. Only another parent could understand their loss. He felt sick in his heart for them, and always would.

They listened in silence. He waited for the anger, the explosion. He waited for them to absolve him by letting everything out, by cursing and screaming. It was as decorous as a garden party.

"I know there's no way I can make this any better for you," he said, "but at least their memory—" He faltered. Patiently they waited for him to steady himself. "I've pledged to help the scholarship fund every year, to make sure it reaches its goal. It's not much, I know, but at least their memories will stay with their friends, with the ones who come after them."

They nodded. That was very nice. They appreciated it.

Mrs. Dunn asked how Brian was doing in jail.

"Pretty well," Florian said, surprised, wondering if it was some sort of trap. "He works tutoring some of the other prisoners, helping them with their English, their math."

"A lot of them there, they can't even speak English," Mr. Hufnagle said. "That's the way it is these days."

Florian thanked them for having him. "You've been really generous," he said. "Really kind. I couldn't blame you for being angry. I couldn't blame you for hating me. I don't know if I could've been this nice."

They'd all gotten up when he had, and the four of them exchanged glances, looks that could have been passwords, secret codes, setting them and their shared memories, their shared anguish, apart from anyone as lucky as Florian Rubio. That's what suddenly hit him, how lucky he was, and Brian, too.

"It's all right," Mrs. Hufnagle said. "There's nothing anyone can do now."

"We don't have any cause to be angry with you," Mr. Dunn said. "I mean, at the trial, the jury listened to everybody and made up their minds. No offense or anything, but we never thought it'd even get that far. We figured someone like yourself—well, you'd just take care of everything and get your boy off long before it ever got to a trial."

Every year the *Express* ran at least one story and photo on the big husky guy living just outside Trent, an outfielder for the Montreal Expos. By February the fellow had to be ready for spring training in Florida, so he had a batting cage with a mechanical pitcher in his backyard, a padded canvas draped over the batting area to hold in the warmth from the kerosene heater. Every sunny day he'd be out there in ski pants and a long john shirt, taking his cuts. People driving by would pull over to watch, and he'd wave to them, tip his bat in their direction. The newspaper and TV photos always went for the snowdrifts surrounding him, the icicles on the wire fence, his breath steaming in the frigid air, and a few times the stories even got picked up nationally. The Mt. Early people got a real kick out of it: baseball in January. It reminded you that April existed.

In mid-January, though, Bottleneck Lake was frozen solid, the ice a few feet thick from shore to shore. The wind coming across those square miles of ice could crust your eyelashes, crack your lips. On the coldest days, the thermometer outside the kitchen window would hit twenty below.

"The fish don't care," Salvatore said. He'd taken up the sport years back, after first making fun of guys sitting inside their tents or portable wooden sheds, or even out in the open. Some lugged wood and lighter fluid to start a fire in a metal can, or right on the ice. "When it melts through," Salvatore said, "you know it's time to go home."

After Salvatore started ice fishing himself, Lucille had made fun of him. "Crazy," she'd say. "If you don't freeze to death, you fall through the little hole and swim around with all the crazy fishes."

"The fishes ain't crazy. Where else they got to go in the winter?"

"Hey, but you—you got somewhere else. That makes you crazy, no?"

Most people drilled their holes fairly close to shore, but some preferred it way out in the middle. They'd drive over the ice in their pickups and sit inside the cabs with poles angling out the windows. First, of course, you had to plow the snow off the ice, or do some serious hand shoveling.

Salvatore didn't use a shed, or a fire, and didn't go out that far, but he fished almost every day. He'd put a bare hand in the water sometimes, pulling out a catch, and then rub it dry on his trousers before putting his glove back on. He kept a narrow path shoveled out, clearing it after every storm, just wide enough for him and Padgett, and he'd trudge out with his wide flat aluminum shovel, his rod and reel and bait box and net, his folding lawn chair, the eight-inch auger he used to drill his hole, turning the ice into swirling foam.

On the tenth of January, Florian assumed Salvatore would come with him and Joyce to pick up Brian.

"No," Salvatore said. "Why make such a big thing?"

"It is a big thing."

Salvatore waved him off. "When you all get back, look for me on the ice. They coop him up so long, maybe he'll come out and sit for a while. Maybe, who knows, we'll catch something."

Salvatore hobbled out along the path he'd shoveled, the snow up to his waist on either side, with his chair, his auger, his fishing gear, with Padgett loping behind and ahead, while farther out, the guys in their snowmobiles roared over the frozen lake, and across the way kids in their hot rods zoomed onto the ice at full speed and then slammed on their brakes, loving the looping skids, the whirling unpredictable spins.

GEORGE CUOMO grew up in the Bronx and was educated at Tufts and Indiana universities. He has taught at a variety of universities in the United States and Canada. *Trial by Water* is his eighth book of fiction, previous ones including *Family Honor* and *Among Thieves,* a Literary Guild Selection.

His stories, poems, and articles have appeared in both commercial and literary magazines, and he has received a Guggenheim Fellowship and a fiction award from the National Endowment for the Arts.

He is currently completing for Random House a book of nonfiction entitled *A Couple of Cops.*